PRAISE F

"Scot Sothern is the real thing. This is damn good writing."
—Dan Fante

"The job of the novelist is to conjure a whole world, and Scot Sothern has done that in spades here. Lush, large-hearted, antic, and fiercely feminist, BigCity is unlike anything else I've ever read."
—Ron Currie

"Deliciously strange and compelling, delightfully lurid and fun, Scot Sothern's debut novel reads like a feral mashup of Cormac McCarthy and William Gibson amped on cornjuice and spiderbite."
—Mark Haskell Smith

"Scot Sothern shows that he's not just a linguistic power-hitter, but a dynamic storyteller, too. There's enough imagination on every page of BigCity for an entire novel."
—D. Harlan Wilson

"An explosion of language and characters, a fast-and-loose yet potent and authentic way with our American history, rude and gross and gorgeous and hilarious and heart-rending, BigCity is everything you want in a novel, bold and challenging and surprising. I love it!"
—Julie Powell

"A masterful memoir, full of truth-telling, ugliness, beauty, tragedy, and humor. Curb Service is brave, funny, and heartwarming in ways you can't see coming."
—Bill Fitzhugh, author of Pest Control on Curb Service

"An absolutely amazing and essential book."
—Jerry Stahl, on Streetwalkers

"Scot Sothern has bravely and empathetically entered a hidden world of humanity. A place where the human condition bares itself on all levels. This penetrating book of photographs and text will haunt and challenge the viewer."
—Roger Ballen, on Streetwalkers

ACKNOWLEDGMENTS

Thank you to Ruth Hagopian for perusing an early draft and sharing your valuable insights.

Thank you, Amy Tipton, for being the coolest agent anywhere and for the best advice at every stage.

Thank you, Linda, Sturges for reading this manuscript line by line, over and over, and spotting what is there that shouldn't be and what isn't there and should be.

Thank you to Melinda Freudenberger at Stalking Horse for your eagle-eye editing.

And thank you James Reich and Stalking Horse Press for making this book a reality.

BIGCITY

ALSO BY SCOT SOTHERN

CURB SERVICE

SAD CITY

AN AMERICAN LOWLIFE

STREETWALKERS

LOWLIFE

SCOT SOTHERN

BIGCITY

STALKING HORSE PRESS
SANTA FE, NEW MEXICO

BIGCITY

www.stalkinghorsepress.com

Design by James Reich

Stalking Horse Press
Santa Fe, New Mexico

Stalking Horse Press requests that authors designate a nonprofit, charitable, or humanitarian organization to receive a portion of revenue from the sales of each title.

Scot Sothern has chosen Homeless Health Care, Los Angeles.
www.hhcla.org

BIGCITY
CONTENTS

SUMMER - 15

WINTER - 261

SPRING - 387

THIS ONE IS A LOVE STORY
FOR LINDA

BIGCITY

PART ONE

SUMMER

Chapter One

Caterwaul Alley

A girl without a proper name grinds her teeth. A harsh contraction jabs her below the belt and jimmies her cervix. She yelps like a horse-trampled dog.

Nine months ago a mucousy seed found fertile ground in Girl's uterus. For three dark trimesters the seed has gestated. Now, it is fighting its way to the light, battering its tormented host in the process. Girl pounds the ground with her fists and cries for mercy.

Next to Girl, on a mat of rotted wood and dirt, her little sister, Snooks, joins in, her lament a morbid sing-along. Girl takes her sister's hand and holds it tight. Six years earlier, cast in the role Snooks now plays, she held her mama's hand. She helped Mama huff, puff and push Snooks into the stale air of a ramshackle tool shed, somewhere else, far away.

Snooks emerged wrinkly-pink and angry. She gulped oxygen and cried between heaving hiccups of distress. Now, six years later she is still angry and her crying lingers on.

Girl remembers the murky wash of blood that puddled the dirt floor. She remembers her mama's last sad intake of oxygen and then her face gone waxy and blue. In a fluster, Girl cut the cord with a sharp stick, thinking the blue would spread to Snooks, leaving her with no one except her no-account daddy.

Girl catches her breath and builds steam for the next natal eruption. She wonders if she's going to die like her mama. When Snooks gets to Girl's age, will Daddy rent her to a slobbering tosspot that throws her to the ground and plants a new baby sister? Does life work that way, over and over?

The three of them, Girl, Snooks, and Daddy, walked centuries from their bleak beginnings to this monstrous city, just to lie here repeating the past in a burned-out turned-over fire escape at the dead end of an alleyway. Daddy is gone now, off somewhere pursuing his American dream, but that matters little to Girl who is preoccupied with her own impending death. Girl recalls little she has to live for, but she is not ready to die. It is too soon to die. Girl is still growing.

Girl locks her knees together and laces her ankles, but she is nine months too late. Her body betrays her and pries open her legs for a look inside.

Girl tells her sister what to do: "Get down there between my legs. Get aholt of that baby's head and help pull it out before I split wide open and bleed out like Mama done."

Snooks is a mean-spirited and obstinate little girl who sometimes confuses her own imagination with reality. She crawls over dry leaves and kneels between Girl's legs. She covers her eyes with her hands and looks, peek-a-boo, through finger gaps into her sister's opening. Two slippery baby-doll feet and ten pink little piggies have wiggled out, testing the air.

Snooks thinks it's a demon coming out of Girl. "You got feet a comin' out your tinkler, Girl. Do something! Make it stop!"

Girl remembers Snooks coming into the world head first, but maybe this is a boy and boys come out feet first.

"You gotta grab him by the feet," she tells Snooks. "Grab him by the feet and pull him out while I hold my wind and push like a hard shat."

Snook usually does as Girl tells her to do, but pulling a demon feet-first out of Girl's pee hole is a lot to ask. "It's a demon, Girl! It got a tail and goat horns and I can't grab no demon by the feet."

Snooks' face is as red as the day she came out of Mama and her cheeks are rouged with dirt. A mucous leech crawls from her nostrils and naps on her upper lip.

Girl takes a deep breath and stifles her tears. "It's not a demon, Baby Sis. It's a baby boy and you gotta pull it out. There's nothing to be scared of. You just do what I tell you. You grab that baby boy's feet and pull him out."

Girl clenches and a green vein rises on her forehead. The baby boy, tight in the canal, curled like a blow to the abdomen, advances inch by inch. Girl pushes like a weightlifter. Hemorrhoids bloom.

Snooks closes her eyes, holds her breath, and grips the

wrinkled little feet. She tugs the human plug as it slips from her sister's canal like a foot in a muddy river.

Girl hollers in relief.

Snooks lets go of the baby's feet. She screams and then screams again.

Just above the demon's little peeney, a slimy tail curls upward, looping a tight noose around his neck, then slithers up into Girl's tinkler. His eyes are closed. He is quiet and he does not move.

Girl knows the baby is dead. She says, "You go and stop all that yelping, Baby Sister, nothing is gonna hurt you."

She feels a final eruption rumble from her core. She pushes with everything she has and holds her breath until her cheeks are ready to explode. The afterbirth, a grisly loaf of innards, spills out onto Snooks's lap. Snooks screams again.

Girl is calm now. She waits for the rush of blood that killed her mama. She tells her sister, "I'm gonna be going pretty soon. You come up here and sit close and bring me that baby boy."

Snooks doesn't want to pick up the still-born boy and she pokes it with her foot, making sure it's dead. She takes it by the ankle and drags it and its bellybutton-tail up to Girl, on her pillow of crushed mortar and dirt.

Girl holds the dead baby boy in her arms. Snooks cradles her head on Girl's shoulder but keeps a vigilant eye on the demon. Girl strokes Snooks's dirty blond curls. "There, there, it's gonna be all better."

Girl looks up through the charred iron grates at a smear of sky. Girl closes her eyes and waits for death to lift her and BabyBoy above the miasma of this dark metropolis.

Backdoor Byway

Charlie Debunk drops two lead balls, plunk-plunk, into the flared mouth of his flintlock Blunderbuss. The balls tumble down the rusty barrel like fishline sinkers. He sets the antique weapon across his legs and picks up a red clay jug of cornjuice. He takes long happy drinks that scorch his gullet and muddle his head.

Charlie Debunk has been loading his Blunderbuss for a week and has yet to pull the trigger. He is waiting for something special to shoot. Five days and a hundred miles ago he and his two partners made a trade with a big lunking Polack who calls himself Big Polack. Big Polack gave Charlie the gun, along with a pouch of lead balls, a pouch of powder, a pouch of flints, a twenty-inch ramrod, and a pouch of gold nuggets easily worth five hundred dollars. Charlie and his partners, Eddie Plague and Skunk Brewster, in turn, gave Big Polack a ten-year-old aborigine girl they had liberated from a starving tribe of Chickasaws. Charlie figures they got the better end of the deal. The girl had not even been old enough to noodle and had whooped like a warrior when Charlie noodled her anyway.

Charlie pours powder into the long muzzle of the black-iron red-rust rifle, rips a piece of rag and rams it with his ramrod, in and out. It makes him think about noodling, which makes him think about Bitch Bantam, the fully grown woman he has chained to a tree.

Charlie's youngest partner in the white slavery concern, Eddie Plague, is preoccupied with other things, none of which has anything to do with noodling the savage bitch. Eddie prefers people who are free of stink. He would no more consider physical relations with the bitch than with either of his two idiot partners. Very soon Eddie will be done with them all. They will sell the pit-woman, split the take and sever ties.

Eddie looks to the horizon. He has seen cityscapes in his years, but he has never seen what he sees now, camped here alongside the Backdoor Byway. On a backdrop of smokestack black, mysterious giant white rings of smoke float like fuzzy donuts up above the city. Spheres and steeples sprout from bridges and buildings above the tree line. Eddie smells sweet sewage, oil refineries, factories and steel mills. He smells poverty and waste, opulence and passion. Eddie soars into this fabulous city where other dandies like him have their own saloons, where gayblades and kinky babes appreciate Eddie's good looks and groove to the same alternative beat, thump thump thump.

Other than the price that she will bring, Eddie Plague has little thought for the shackled woman at the edge of camp. The sooner they rid themselves of Bitch Bantam the better. Charlie Debunk takes another long drink of corn and feeds a couple more lead balls to the mouth of his musket. Makes sense to Charlie: just as each drink makes him feel a little better, the more gunpowder, lead and wadding he puts into the gun, the bigger hole it will blow. He rams his ramrod with passion.

Charlie has worked up an intense hankering for poon. Problem is, Charlie has an intense fear of Eddie Plague. Along with his clean good looks, Eddie Plague is intensely scary and Charlie does not want to piss him off. Maybe he should check with his true partner, Skunk Brewster. Maybe Skunk is wanting some poon too. Maybe together they can get some bitch nookie.

Charlie says to Skunk, "I reckon if we was to hold down Bitch Bantam jus right we could get us some mighty good puss."

Skunk is smarter than Debunk. He is not as ready to follow his dick into a danger zone. He is not as likely to forget why this woman is worth more than any ten of the women they have sold in the past. Skunk does, however, agree with Charlie: Bitch Bantam would be mighty good poon. Skunk needs to give the situation some thought. "Hand me that there juga bugjuice," he tells Charlie. "I need to think." Skunk furrows his brow as though thinking hurts his head.

Unlike Eddie Plague, Skunk and Charlie are caked with filth. Charlie passes the jug and Skunk drinks a dizzying gulp. Charlie crams another load into his rifle. Skunk takes another drink and eyeballs the woman. She glares back from behind a jungle of ash-blonde hair, her eyes, through the tangled vines, opaque violet, firing blank rounds of antipathy.

Bitch Bantam has thus far spent her relatively short life in iffy, but still legal, servitude to others. Born nameless and fatherless in Joplin, Missouri, Bitch had been dumped by her mother and found by an enterprising gambler named Dicey Deucey. Normally Dicey would never have bothered with a two-year-old garbage-heap orphan, but Bitch was special.

Dicey found the thirty-pound tot already so toughened by life that she sat gurgling and cooing amid a pile of savagely exterminated and partially eaten terrier-sized rats. The kid had a talent for killing.

Dicey Deucey took Bitch under his wing and went to work, setting her up as the first ever pit-bitch. Initially he pitted her against as many as ten rats at a time, drawing such enormous crowds that soon, along with the wagering, he began to charge admission. As Bitch grew, she graduated from rats to cocks (thus the name Bantam) to pit-bulls and wild hogs.

At twelve years of age, Bitch was five-nine, one hundred and fifty pounds. Her baby teeth had been replaced with a set of permanent choppers Dicey had filed to sharp fang-like points. Her fingernails were long and hard and sharpened like daggers. In a pit against anything short of a grizzly bear, Bitch was likely to bring even money.

The thing Dicey Deucey never figured was that Bitch was not just a dumb woman; she was smarter than he and she held no loyalties to a man who would lash her with a horse whip, kick her like a dog and call her a worthless skank. The thing that always puzzled Bitch was the surprised look on Dicey's face when she leapt from the bloody guts of a dead Arkansas razorback to ringside, where she ripped out Dicey's throat with her teeth and nails. Dicey Deucey looked at her as though his best friend had turned on him. He had expected eternal gratitude for his guidance and care. Dicey earned his violent death and was too oblivious to know it before taking his final breath.

Afterward Bitch ran from the crowd, hoping to hide away in the woods, make her way to another town where no one knew who she was. Unfortunately, her escape brought hysteria to the townsfolk, as though a full-moon werewolf was stalking their young.

The local sheriff, along with a gun-toting posse and a kennel of hysterical hounds, hunted her down, chained her and put her in a cage. The sheriff was a law-abiding entrepreneur; slavery had been abolished yet he found legal ways to hawk feminine wiles to a buyer's market.

It took seven of the sheriff's men to hold Bitch down and force her hand to sign an X to a contract. The agreement was a ditto of the forms the sheriff used in his China-girl whorehouses. The girls were employed at a dollar a day. They agreed, unknowingly, to pay back a week's wages for every day they were sick. A woman's nature is to bleed a few days each month and this, according to the contract, was classified as an illness keeping them from work. The girls were thus indentured by debt for life, which mercifully was usually short.

Now Bitch Bantam is twenty-years-old. She has grown six-feet high. She is hard, cut like a superhero. She conceals great pulchritude beneath a curtain of dirt and animosity. The contract means nothing to her. But still she is chained, when not center ring, and sold and traded time and time again. She is legally the property of Skunk Brewster, Charlie Debunk, and Eddie Plague who keep the nine-year-old contract, with Bitch Bantam's squiggly X, folded up in an oilcloth haversack along with their pouch of gold nuggets and Bitch's clothes.

Bitch is accustomed to indignity but these three shitheads are the worst yet. Skunk, Charlie, and Eddie have clubbed her, stripped her of clothing and dragged her chained and naked halfway across America. Much of her time is whiled away with castle-in-the-sky fantasies. At this moment, however, Bitch Bantam is plotting escape, murder, freedom.

Charlie Debunk stands, torques his skinny frame and points his musket at Bitch. Bitch knows what Charlie wants. All she has to do is get him close enough to grab. Chains or no chains once she puts a grip on Charlie Debunk he will never buy or sell another woman. Bitch sits butt on heels, balls of her bare feet in the dirt. She opens her legs to Charlie.

"Looky there, Skunk," Charlie says. "The Bitch is in heat."

Skunk is not so sure. "I ain't so sure. I doan think we oughta be gettin too close. I think maybe we oughta club her down a little first."

Charlie takes a couple of baby steps toward Bitch. "Hell's bells, Skunk. We club her first, she woan do no humpin."

Bitch is shackled, at the wrists and ankles, with maybe two feet of play in the heavy chains. She begins to growl deep in the back of her throat.

Eddie Plague is getting irritated, distracted by his imbecile partners and their penis-motivated hijinks. Eddie is tall and muscular; his face is symmetrical and his nose is perfect. Eddie is a literate sociopath with homicidal tendencies and a loud whisper voice. He packs a cutthroat razor and a two-shot derringer in his polished boots. He carries a bottle of patchouli oil with which he douses himself two or three times a day. His pants' pockets are filled with peppermint drops which he sucks nonstop. He wears a black slouch hat with a low brim that grays his hypnotic blue eyes with shadow.

Unlike his idiot partners, Eddie is only eighteen. Skunk and Charlie have been slavery vendors since back when it was legal. Eddie entered the flesh trade as a barefoot preteen selling suck jobs to a trail of horny yokels expanding westward. Soon he added gigolo to his résumé then pimp and from there built a stable where he sold and bartered in fine quality boys and girls. But Eddie wanted more culture and so teamed with Skunk and Charlie as a means to travel east to BigCity. Now, he just wants to get back on the road. He wants his partners to leave the woman alone. Bitch Bantam could dispose of Charlie and Skunk with a well-placed bite. Yet, these idiot associates are

24

risking life and limb for a space between her legs. Eddie would like to kill Bitch Bantam, Charlie Debunk, and Skunk Brewster, but that is not what he does.

"Leave the woman alone," Eddie demands. "If you don't, I'll shoot her dead. Get your things together. It's time to go."

Skunk hasn't slept well since Eddie joined them. Eddie gives Skunk creepy dreams. Skunk screws up his courage. "Crud sake, Eddie it ain't nothin personal. Sides, ifn you shoot her we ain't gonna be able to sell her no more, an ifn I club her we still got our vestment intact. An, me and Charlie ain't had us no real poon since forever. We ain't ready to go yet." Skunk is hoping Charlie will back him up.

Charlie's fear of Eddie is also well developed, just not as developed as his craving for poon. Charlie's peter has gone stiff and he's thinking maybe he can poke Bitch while Skunk is clubbing her. That way she will be jerking around and such. It might make it more better. He takes another baby-step toward the woman.

Skunk is up now. He and Charlie have silently voted to ignore Eddie and go for the woman. Skunk removes his rosewood truncheon from under his canvas bag. He ventures within a few feet of Bitch Bantam.

Bitch knows what is coming. She flexes her body and the tight iron bracelets cut into her skin. She watches the men, closely.

Skunk takes a quick step forward, swings the club, which bounces hard across Bitch's shoulder blades. She winces and grabs at the polished cudgel. Skunk jumps backwards and gives a whoop.

Eddie Plague is disgusted, he doesn't like his partners,

but he hates Bitch Bantam, hates all women. He wants assurances that she will not enjoy Skunk and Charlie's assault. Eddie's opinion being that bondage and rape are enjoyable experiences.

"Give me the club," Eddie tells Skunk.

Skunk grins, shrugs like an idiot and hands the club to Eddie.

He pulls down his grimy pants and long-johns and calls first dibs. His peter is stiff and curved like a boomerang. "Shit," Charlie says, "It was my idea, I oughta get first dibs."Eddie readies himself to crack the woman's skull when he notices that she is no longer looking at him. She's looking beyond him up to a hilly crook on the dirt byway. Skunk Brewster, Eddie Plague, and Charlie Debunk turn together and look up the road at a most unusual sight.

Slab Pettibone and his bear FuzzyWuzzy have materialized from around the bend. Slab is singing and playing a ukulele. FuzzyWuzzy is dancing along in a four-footed two-step.

> *"My Lulu hugged and kissed me,*
> *She wrung my hand and cried,*
> *She said I was the sweetest thing*
> *That ever lived and died."*

Slab Pettibone and FuzzyWuzzy stop in the middle of the rutted road and look down a hundred yards at the three men and the shackled woman. FuzzyWuzzy stands on his hind legs to his full six-foot height to get a better look and taste the air.

Technically, FuzzyWuzzy is an American Black Bear, *Ursus Americanus*, but FuzzyWuzzy's hair is not black. FuzzyWuzzy is a rare bear, an *Ursus Americanus Kermode*, also known as a Ghost Bear. FuzzyWuzzy's fur is buttermilk yellow.

Slab Pettibone has no legs. Years ago they were cut off, mid-thigh, a couple of inches above a hungry gangrene monster. FuzzyWuzzy serves with honor as Slab Pettibone's legs. Slab is harnessed to FuzzyWuzzy's back, just above FuzzyWuzzy's front shoulder bones. His hair is long and silver. He has a gentleman's face with a curly triangle of chin hair and a thick handlebar moustache. He wears a black tuxedo coat with long tails and a red sombrero hat. When FuzzyWuzzy stands on his hind legs, they look to be nine feet tall.

FuzzyWuzzy smells the gathering of humans, their scents a cartoon jet stream of windowsill pie. The woman's bouquet is tastier than the usual odoriferous stench of homo sapiens, almost like a she-bear. She is naked and in chains. Before Slab Pettibone, FuzzyWuzzy had been in chains. It is an image that bristles his scruff and lays back his ears. He curls his lips in aggravation and issues a low moan from the back of his throat.

Below them, at the campsite, Charlie Debunk and Skunk Brewster seem frozen in incredulous mouth-breathing stares, as if neither has the brain power to digest the song and dance team of Slab Pettibone and FuzzyWuzzy the bear.

Charlie is the first to break the spell. He picks up his musket and grabs for his flints and powder horn. He puts powder in the firing cup and two flints under the hammer. Charlie has shot people before and he has shot animals before. But he has never shot anything like these two. Charlie Debunk is about to shoot himself the trophy of a lifetime.

Slab Pettibone takes in the scene, the woman in chains, the man with a club, and the other man with an old-fashioned blunderbuss, pointing at them. He tweaks FuzzyWuzzy's ears forward, the command to hit the deck. FuzzyWuzzy irons-out flat like a fluffy beige carpet. Charlie Debunk pulls the trigger.

The old flintlock's hammer clicks, sparking the flints which ignites the spoon of gun powder, which lights up the nine loads of powder, wadding, and lead balls, which explode the barrel, the stock and Charlie Debunk's head. Charlie's headless corpse lists from side to side. He takes three rubbery steps like a vaudeville comedian's drunken pantomime then collapses to the ground.

Skunk Brewster's pants are still at his ankles. His peter has deflated. He goes for his pistol, a thirty-eight-caliber small-frame automatic which unfortunately is not loaded. Skunk frantically digs bullets from his drooping pants' pocket and shoves them into the five-shot cylinder.

Eddie Plague is ahead of the situation. He knows all about Slab Pettibone and his pet bear, FuzzyWuzzy. They are nothing to run from, just another ten-cent pulp novelty, white-hat heroes not known to strike the first blow. Eddie steps back a couple of feet to avoid splatters of Charlie Debunk's blood and bone-fragments. He's calculating his cut of Bitch Bantam now that the take has changed from thirds to fifty-fifty. Eddie forgets for a moment that he has moved closer to the woman.

Slab Pettibone looks up from FuzzyWuzzy's furry back and assesses the situation. While it is true that Slab and FuzzyWuzzy never start a fight, getting shot at is deemed a challenge. Slab gives FuzzyWuzzy a command, "Go get em, FuzzyWuzzy!" FuzzyWuzzy takes off like a fubsy rocket. Slab holds onto his hat and yells, "Yaaa hoop hoop hoop yahooey!"

Skunk has two shells loaded and no time for more. The bear/man is closing in at an alarming rate.

Eddie Plague backs slowly away from the action, closer still to the pit-fighting woman. Bitch Bantam grabs him by the ankle, pulls him to the ground and takes a bite, through his cotton twill pants, out of his thigh. He struggles to hit her with the billy-club. She grabs an arm and an ear and pulls his face close enough to kiss. She spits his hunk of thigh and tattered pant's fabric in his face then bites off his nose.

Slab Pettibone and FuzzyWuzzy screech to a standstill in front of Skunk just as he raises his thirty-eight. FuzzyWuzzy rears back on his hind feet and roars a challenge into Skunk's face. Skunk turns white. He smells berries and grub-worms from FuzzyWuzzy's lunch. He attempts to point and shoot but his hands are shaking out of control.

FuzzyWuzzy has been given the signal for a round of fisticuffs. With the heel of his right front paw, FuzzyWuzzy rabbit-punches Skunk in the chest.

Skunk lands hard to the ground. He sees above him an enraged beast poised for attack. He comes to a rash and irreversible conclusion: death by a bullet is easier than death by mauling. Skunk Brewster grins up at Slab and FuzzyWuzzy. He puts the pistol to his head and pulls the trigger. The gun pops and Skunk drops dead. It is the most peculiar thing Slab Pettibone has ever seen.

Eddie Plague has used the truncheon to successfully batter his way free of Bitch Bantam. He is discombobulated and he scuttles onto the road and keeps going until sometime later when he falls unconscious into the brush.

Slab Pettibone diverts his eyes from the two dead men. Slab hates when all manners of creatures die, even no-account slave-traders like Skunk Brewster and Charlie Debunk. Slab is as well embarrassed to look at the naked woman. He is shy around the opposite sex, they make him nervous. And, this woman is not only naked, but she's the most magnificent gal he has ever seen. She's near big as FuzzyWuzzy. Slab Pettibone embarrasses himself with his thoughts. He flushes red behind his whiskered face and his heart thumps his head. He averts his eyes from everything outside of the back of FuzzyWuzzy's crown and begins to sing.

> *"If you monkey with my Lulu gal*
> *I'll tell you what I'll do*
> *I'll carve your heart out with my razor,*
> *I'll shoot you with my pistol, too."*

FuzzyWuzzy sways with the song and sings along in a low slow soulful bellow. He looks at the woman and senses a primitive kinship. He wonders if she will wrestle with him. FuzzyWuzzy loves to wrestle and this feral woman is just the right size. He bows and does a do-se-do.

> *"I seen my Lulu in the springtime*
> *I seen her in the fall*
> *She broke my heart last winter*
> *Said, Good-by, honey, that's all."*

Bitch Bantam watches the shy singing legless man and the dancing bear. She smiles at the bear and cannot remember the last time she smiled at anyone, man or beast. It feels strange and happy on her face. She spits Eddie Plague's nose into the dust and wipes his blood from her lips.

Duchy Hall

Duchy Hall is three floors high, three rooms across, three rooms deep. The façade is brick with arched double-doors, iron staircase railings, eight-foot-high windows with masonry trim. On the roof a great billboard depicts a short-skirted Indian maiden fanning a campfire with a multicolored blanket. Wheel-sized smoke-rings puff upward into the brown air.

> *SIGNAL*® Cigarettes
> *Apache warrior*
> *Him take squaw bride*
> *Her get-um fat*
> *Him run and hide*
> *Smoke Signals*
> *10 cents*

Left of Duchy Hall, the NorthSide, is pristine. Brass hitching rails and electric street lamps, stately neighborhoods with banks, churches, schools, museums, and ice cream parlors.

To the right of Duchy Hall it all goes crumbling downhill into ScourgeTown. Public opinion decries: There is no such thing as a hard-worker or honest John south of Duchy Hall. Salvation is not to be found.

Across the boulevard a man wearing a mashed fedora

makes three aborted dashes into the horse-and-carriage traffic before finally sprinting across, slipping twice in horse shit and clipping his hip on the steel wheel of a hansom-cab. His name is Daddy Smithy and he is out of breath when he walks up the front steps and into Duchy Hall. The dark-wood hallway is bright. Electric bulbs buzz and crackle from above. Open doorways invite entrance without knocking. First room on the right is filled with men and clamor. Tobacco smoke hangs like storm clouds. A rough and tumble group of men are drinking, shooting snooker, playing cards.

Daddy Smithy is prone to nervousness and panic. His knees knock and his stomach gurgles. From his coat pocket he takes a bottle of Doctor FixUp's Opiated Celery-Malt Compound, a brain tonic for nerve disorders. He uncorks the fly-green bottle and pulls a long hit. The oily liquid burns and smells like kerosene. Daddy stands unnoticed and alone in the roomful of men. He fades into a medicinal rush and attempts to look into the future.

"Pleased to meet you, Mister Draper," Daddy conjures Shag Draper, a man he has not yet met. "I'm in the moving-picture business and I'm sure a man like you has seen moving-pictures before. And I don't mean like them Edison Kinetoscope penny machines, I'm talking about movin pictures big as a wall." Daddy throws up his hands to demonstrate how big a wall is.

The rousing roomful of men no longer exists. Daddy is alone in his zone. Do it in your head, the sales book told him. Make it happen before it happens, then it's sure to happen. Three times he has read JJ Wellington's instructional sales manual, *Making It Happen*, and now he visualizes Shag Draper, the boss of BigCity's SouthSide and he goes into his pitch.

"Now I already have a suitcase fulla moving picture shows, but I'm temporarily short of the funds to set em up somewheres. And, I know you're probably thinking, so what?" Daddy taps his head with a digit. "Well, I'm here to tell you what. I have something nobody else has. Along with my moving pictures I have what I like to call, projected French postcards." Daddy gives a sly wink to the imaginary Shag Draper. "These are the kind of pictures for men only, if you know what I mean. The kind of pictures men will stand in line to buy a seat up front."

Daddy sees it clearly through his celery-malt haze. His physical self and his real self are in different rooms.

"Now, what I need from you apart from your friendship is a small investment. And I guarantee you, your money is gonna double and triple with me because soon as I get the equipment I need, I'm gonna invent the biggest moneymaker yet. Are you ready to hear it?"

Daddy is beginning to draw attention in the crowded room but he remains oblivious. He can see Shag Draper, now out of his seat in anticipation. Daddy unveils his kicker with a flourish of theatrics.

"Moving picture stories of a naughty nature," he shouts to his invisible patron. "I'm letting you in on the ground floor of a whole new business gonna revolutionize the moving picture business!" Daddy Smithy sticks out his hand for a hardy shake, sealing the deal.

"You okay, buddy?"

"Huh?" Daddy's imagined scenario fades to a smirking square-jawed face puffing a Signal Cigarette.

"Who ya talkin to pal? Maybe you better sit down, you look like your head is about to split open."

"My head?" Daddy gives his head a hard shake. "Shag Draper, my good man, I'm here to see Shag Draper."

The guy is big and solid and friendly. "Shag's upstairs, chum. But if you're a salesman I wouldn't bother. Shag's a hard sell."

The guy's sudden appearance has drained the Doctor FixUp from Daddy's resolve and set off an anxious wave. His stomach juices boil in protest. "Th-thank you," he manages to spit out.

"Sure," the guy says. "Good luck."

Daddy walks a jittery gait down the long hallway, up dark walnut stairs. At the top of the stairs he drinks another dose of Doctor FixUp. He stands in front of a closed door, sticks out his hand and says to the wall, "Pleased to meet you, Mister Draper. My name is Daddy Smithy and I am in the moving picture business."

Sunshine Avenue

Sunshine Avenue is drenched in midday sun. Plank sidewalks buzz with an eclectic stew of kinetic humanity. A cursing mass of animal, cart and trolley traffic jams the cobblestone street. Commercial structures, arrowhead pinnacles, fade up into the cloudy bright sky. Above the awnings elevated-trains rumble like wooden roller-coasters, hot cinder teardrops drizzle from the rails. An immutable roar pounds like a migraine.

Nineteen-year-old Dooley Paradise loves Sunshine

Avenue. It offers the best of everything, goals he can aspire to. Dooley is tall lean and handsome. He has a dimple in his chin. He is dressed in department store finery. A green-felt derby, worn with pride, identifies Dooley as a member of the youth gang, the Brusselsprouts. He wears the bowler with a cavalier tilt emphasizing his rakish edge. He leans on a lamppost and takes a nonchalant pose, like a masher on the prowl.

Dooley has been advancing through the Brusselsprout ranks for nine years. Soon, he will move up to, or beyond, the adult corps, the Mooks. The Mooks run the SouthSide. Dooley has big ambitions and a natural political savvy. Someday he will run BigCity like his hero and mentor, Jones Mulligan. It is a done deal. Dooley has a future.

Two fresh-faced girls, petticoats and curls, bustle by on the coattails of their austere top-hatted pater. They steal shy peeks in Dooley's direction. Dooley strikes a match on a spot of lamppost rust, stokes up a store-bought Signal Cigarette and blows smoke rings. He gives the girls a wink and a smile. He appears a picture of cool, though he balls his hands to hide his trembling fingers.

From a corner of his vision Dooley finds his best friend, Gulper Mooney, racing a stolen bicycle, weaving in and out of sidewalk traffic, peddling toward a well-rehearsed collision. Gulper has buck teeth, orange hair, and a splatter of new-penny freckles. He is dressed in his uniform of choice, a Confederate-gray suit with a collarless shirt. His green derby is two sizes too big and padded for battle with leather wadding. Gulper digs combat. He likes the smell of other people's blood and covets full-scale war. He has anger issues. It is Gulper that has brought them here today for a little memory-lane pilfering.

On Dooley's right, next to a confectioner's shop, Adelina Brown stands looking through the glass at a display of candies and cakes while keeping a covert eye toward Gulper and Dooley. Adelina is eighteen. She wears a dress with a velvet ruffle yoke and buttons down the back. She looks like a midtown girl. Her hair is high, curled and pinned like a pretty picture. Her delicate face is silver with shadow, like a graphite sketch.

Adelina stands five-foot-seven, weighs in at one-hundred-and-one. She has little meat on her bones, zero body-fat. She has no curves and a flat chest. Adelina has self-image issues; she wants to look like a Gibson Girl, but lacks the plumage.

At this moment Adelina is highly irritated with the boy she loves, Dooley Paradise. Dooley has buckled to a sophomoric dare, is in fact into phase-one of an act of petty lawlessness. Adelina is here not to applaud Dooley's daring-do. Against her better judgment Adelina is here to watch the love of her life do something stupid. A moment ago she watched Dooley wink at the two uptown girls. She came close to picking up a brick and throwing it at his head.

Two double-breasted coppers stroll the sidewalk, swinging clubs, keeping the peace. They spot Dooley puffing a butt, idling his precious time. Dooley takes a carcinogenic drag, exhales walrus-tusks from his nose. He tips his political hat to the cops. They turn and walk away.

Dooley needs to pee. He has not done what he is about to do for five years, back when they were still kids and their next meal depended upon it. It made Dooley nervous then just as now, though he keeps it to himself. Dooley has always been a leader, his strong point; brains, his weak point; physical altercation. His fears are hidden, crouched and trembling within.

Today's question for Dooley is why is he here now, gambling his future on Gulper Mooney's whim; his double-dare. Why is it a boy of such promise and achievement is bent on affirming his manhood, and for whom?

The elevated train rumbles above. Gulper Mooney grins like a cartoon kamikaze and times his collision with the rickety racket, adding a layer of cover and confusion. A woman, Missus Wilhoit Brandonburger, sweeps the dusty walkway with her hemline and twirls a parasol. Missus Brandonburger is a BigCity dowager with roots to the founding fathers. Her face is curdled with general disgust. She wears a straw hat with pheasant feathers.

Gulper has locked onto his target. He howls like a wounded cur and crashes into Missus Wilhoit Brandonburger who falls on her bustled rump. He somersaults over the handlebars and lands in her lap. He jumps to his feet and yells, "Me Bean! Me Bean! I has suffered an injurious blow to me bean!"

Indignant, Missus Wilhoit Brandonburger pulls herself up and swings her parasol at Gulper's red head. Gulper takes the blows to his padded green crash-helmet and staggers around in comic circles of feigned injury.

At the apex of a back-swing Missus Wilhoit Brandonburger accidently pokes the tip of her parasol into a gawking bystander's eye. The bystander grabs his eye and wrenches backward as Dooley slips by and removes the fat wallet from his back pocket. Dooley transfers the wallet to his own pocket as he bumps another guy, tells him, "Excuse me, sir," and adds another wallet to the collection.

Adelina has not moved. She is thinking that the adage, boys-will-be-boys, is a threat to the future of civilization. She keeps her eyes on Dooley as though keeping watch provides him with a blanket of protection.

Gulper is still dancing, he staggers backward from Missus Brandonburger's swinging bumbershoot, into a plus-sized square-shouldered gent holding a gold-handled walking stick and wearing a silk worsted suit. The gent's name is Sinclair Kissick. He flicks Gulper away, without regard, like swatting an insect. Gulper stumbles and his hair-trigger temper flairs. Dooley walks behind Sinclair and filches his money clip. Gulper winds up a swing and aims it at Sinclair's nose but pulls his punch when he sees the gold fraternity pin on Sinclair's lapel, two crossed swords, and a snarling-tiger head. Gulper hesitates just long enough for Sinclair Kissick to plant a hard low fist into his gut. Gulper sinks to his knees.

Sinclair Kissick turns and whistles his walking stick across the top of Dooley's head knocking Dooley from his feet and his hat to the wind. Sinclair takes a revolver from beneath his coat, leans down, and with his free hand yanks his money clip from Dooley's grip. He cocks his pistol and points it between Dooley's eyes.

Sinclair Kissick is a muckamuck in the SnarlingTigers who, under the direction of city boss, Jones Mulligan, runs BigCity with the Mooks and the Brusselsprouts under thumb. Whether Sinclair shoots Dooley or not, a grave political faux pas has been committed.

Dooley looks up into the snub-nosed barrel and sees the bullet in the chamber. He struggles to pause time, to rewind the reality and correct the mistake. The scene however plays forward beyond his control. Dooley covers his face with his hands and screams, loud and harsh like waking himself from a recurring nightmare. Sinclair Kissick smiles but then scowls as he suddenly arches backwards, fires his pistol wild.

With both hands Adelina Brown has grabbed the SnarlingTiger by the back of his shirt collar, scaled up his broad back, and pulled him off balance. Back up on his legs Gulper Mooney pulls his thirty-two caliber five-shot and caps the SnarlingTiger bang-bang twice in the head. Sinclair falls dead with Adelina riding his back. Blood splatters dot her face like patches of acne. Adelina is not wired for violence. She hyperventilates.

The rush of midday people moves quickly away from the fray. Dooley brings his eyes from hiding to see that Missus Wilhoit Brandonburger is back on her bustle. Sinclair Kissick's wayward bullet has put a black hole in her chest. She takes harsh gurgling breaths, her bewildered eyes are focused and scolding on Dooley.

Gulper retrieves the bicycle and quickly helps Adelina to her feet. Adelina looks to Dooley who nods that he is okay, says to her, "Go! Now, hurry!" She climbs up on Gulper's handlebars and they speed away. Missus Brandonburger's eyes are still on Dooley though unseeing and without the flicker of life. Somehow Dooley's green hat has found its way onto the dead woman's lap. Dooley grabs the derby, pulls it low over his face and runs off into the traffic on Sunshine Avenue. The El-train, a creaky mechanical caterpillar, rumbles away.

Chapter Two

DreckRiver

A beam of light passes through Girl's eyelids, capillaries like cracks on a red wall. She opens her eyes to a blinding light edged by the blackness of night. She feels around for Snooks and finds instead the cold shell of her baby boy. A wire slides up her spine, sparking synapses. She listens to the voices behind the light.

"Her jest anutter mudlark, Wilbur. Her look like sick mess."

Girl is naked. She searches through the white blindness, locates her ragged dress, her wad of underclothes. She dresses quickly without words. Snooks is gone. Girl can feel the void, like a phantom limb.

Another voice says, "Dun know, Wilbur. Yuz tink us can dicker her at TumbleHouse, fur moolah?"

"Could haps be, we dunt tell no one her rupture tween legs."

Wilbur Good and Wilbur Szedvilas are BigCity cops on the beat. They wear navy-blue frock coats with double-breasted rows of copper buttons. They wear plain cloth-covered steel helmets. They carry clubs and guns and battery-powered arc-lamps.

"That good, Girlie," one of the Wilburs says. "Get yuz dressed real quick now, we go for skedaddle."

Girl turns her back to the men. Blood and birth extracts are caked to her thighs. Trickles of fresh blood tickle her pudendum. She makes a shallow grave of crushed brick and dirt.

Wilbur and Wilbur watch in silence, giving her a brief respite to bury her dead.

The Wilburs are large men, layered with fat from a steady diet of beer, cake, pickled pig-knuckles. Both men thrive on violence.

Wilbur Szedvilas has a softer shell than Wilbur Good. He leans forward and watches the drama, Girl and her dead baby boy. Tears well in his eyes, his nose runs. This presents Wilbur Good with the opportunity to tiptoe behind his partner, reach between his legs, and flip him a quick one, through his trousers, in the testicles.

Wilbur Szedvilas straightens and grabs his scrotum. "Whoo-yee," he yammers. "I me tank yuv broken me gajoobies."

Wilbur Good clutches himself in laughter. "Huzzah fer me. Huzzah fer me!"

The source of jovial laughter eludes Girl. Laughing men sometimes signal sadistic men. Girl is leery. She is dressed now.

She tears a square of cloth from the apron of her dress to stuff in her pantaloons. Otherwise, she will be leaving a blood trail.

In spite of their shenanigans Wilbur and Wilbur keep a close eye on Girl. Wilbur Szedvilas massages his nut-sack and says, "We all goink now, girlie. Step on here out now."

Girl takes nothing, which is everything she owns, and crawls into the night proper. She leaves BabyBoy to the elements, to God, to the Devil. Shadowy high-rise walls tunnel them forward. Above them, a sliver scar of moonlit sky.

Girl had come here in the light of day with Snooks and Daddy. She doesn't care that Daddy hasn't returned, but Snooks's absence jangles her nerves and pummels her with dread. Without Girl, Snooks will be lost. She needs Girl to guide her, to keep her in check.

Out of the alley now, Wilbur Good gives Girl a knuckle-thump to the back of the head. "Dis way, girlie. Yuz goink tween me and Wilbur."

Girl takes her place, walks in stride, Wilbur Good in front and Wilbur Szedvilas at the rear. They march into a field of weeds and follow a pathway. Girl has to walk-run to keep in pace with the men. She does not want to anger them. Her girl parts sting like a pealed scab. She needs a dose of her father's Doctor FixUp. Her guts burn and gurgle. She wonders if the coppers can hear the rumbles.

The flashlights throw flickering carpets across the nightscape. To their left they walk parallel to the back doors of ScourgeTown. Crumbling five-floor carcasses spilling garbage and humankind from uneven rows of windows. Yellow kerosene lamplight blinks from the pores of swayback structures. A vociferous jumble vibrates like flies in a bottle.

To the right of Girl, the narrow Dreck River flows like a funeral dirge. The tenements, grog shops and eateries housing this fat mass of futility are without plumbing. Two-foot wide sluiceways lead from the bowels of these precarious structures across the road into the stream of fetid sludge. The air is muggy with an ammoniac effluvium that burns Girl's eyes and lungs.

Wilbur Szedvilas begins to giggle. While keeping in step he takes his billy club from his belt, leans forward, over Girl's head, and plants a powerful thump on the top of his partner's helmet. Wilbur Good staggers a step then falls to his knees, then stands, then again sinks to his knees, then stands and continues forward in a scissor-step gait. "Huzzah," he shouts. "Yuz wacked me thinker a silly bit. Next round is by me, ya dunderheaded hog flogger."

Wilbur Szedvilas laughs, har-de-har-har, until he begins to snort. "Yull haffin to catch me guard off first, Wilbur, me sorry friend."

Girl feels she's walking to the gallows. She cannot escape the policemen, she can only stay with them and hope they port somewhere safe, before they turn savage.

Wild pigs run with dogs through the offal. A skinny cur barks and nips at Wilbur Good's feet. Wilbur Good has barely recovered from the blow to the noggin. He kicks at the animal. "Goink get, doggie-doggie." He takes his shooter, a six-shot police revolver, from his holster and shoots the dog in the head. The dog howls and runs, mocking Wilbur's scissor-stagger, then tumbles into the ooze of the Dreck River.

The gunshot echoes and for a moment silences the night, sending chills of paranoia through the guilty populace. Girl starts, from the sudden gunshot. She trips and falls to the ground. Wilbur Szedvilas takes her gently by the arm and helps her back to her feet.

"We there now almost, girlie. Yuz be okay-doke when we there already."

They make a sloping turn through a dirt playground. A swing-set sits slant and rusty as though flinching against a Herculean wind. A wood merry-go-round creaks and turns slowly.

Wilbur Szedvilas walks Girl to the back door of a four-floor structure. Hurdy-gurdy music and the sounds of many come from within. Wilbur Good bangs the door with his nightstick.

Mongrel Flats

Being an animal born to nature, FuzzyWuzzy is ill-at-ease in BigCity. He has, in the company of Slab Pettibone, performed through a number of municipalities, but never has FuzzyWuzzy seen a city of this enormity.

More than the humans, who hardly register in FuzzyWuzzy's bruin brain, it is the animals that seem unbalanced. The air is filled with the vapors of territorial piss. Horses pulling cars and wagons go wild-eyed as FuzzyWuzzy tromps onto their turf. Wild pigs squeal and root for garbage. Dogs are everywhere, barking, fighting, scavenging. It puts FuzzyWuzzy on edge.

In spite of the unease of BigCity streets, FuzzyWuzzy is in a good mood. He has a new friend, Bitch Bantam. In the hours of walking, after her liberation from the white-slavers, Bitch talks to FuzzyWuzzy like a childhood chum. She scratches his neck and ears and drums his flanks and rump with the flat of her hands. Once, when FuzzyWuzzy deposited Slab Pettibone behind a bush to do his dailies, Bitch wrestled FuzzyWuzzy to the ground where they gamboled about like playful pups. Now, FuzzyWuzzy loves Bitch Bantam. Ditto Bitch, FuzzyWuzzy.

Slab Pettibone is also enamored of the big woman. He would prefer to crank up the charm, but finds himself babbling like a love-smitten youngfry. As a result, he opts to keep mostly quiet.

Slab has a mushy heart for big women and Bitch Bantam is the biggest he has ever seen. In addition, like FuzzyWuzzy, Bitch Bantam displays pure innocence and the ability to rip a man's head off. She is the perfect woman.

Slab can however see that Bitch is half his age. An old codger like him cavorting with a fresh flowered woman such as Bitch Bantam would be highly improper. He considers Bitch in a fatherly fashion yet shames himself with runaway erotic musings. His brown sun-basted face flushes red.

Bitch Bantam is a range of concerns, uppermost being her newfound freedom. Back at camp where Skunk Brewster and Charlie Debunk met their maker, Slab Pettibone found, among their possessions, the keys to relieve Bitch of her chains, her clothes (men's overalls, work shirt and boots), a pouch of gold nuggets, and the contract that held her in servitude. He tore the contract into pieces and scattered it. The gold he gave to Bitch, refusing any for himself. Bitch has never known a man who is free of evil. Slab Pettibone is a first.

They go northward through hobo camps, CoonBorough

shanties, and immigrant tenements into BigCity where the night lights grow bright. Foot-traffic totters about, crisscrossing the muddy streets. Inebriated and afflicted BigCity denizens beg for pennies. Tattered citizens stand on grog-shop corners watching the peculiar threesome, as they would a delirium tremens. Bitch Bantam, Slab Pettibone, and FuzzyWuzzy are accustomed to drawing out the curious.

Slab loves the attention and counts it as good press. Bitch Bantam wishes she could become invisible. FuzzyWuzzy is hungry and does not consider much else. Bitch watches her feet go forward. Slab and FuzzyWuzzy brought her here but have not discussed a final destination. Bitch follows along because she feels safe with Slab and FuzzyWuzzy. But she wants to learn to think ahead. She needs to learn to live on her own like other people do.

Bitch turns a shy eye to Slab Pettibone bouncing along on FuzzyWuzzy's back. She tells him, "I doan know what to do, Mister Pettibone. I doan want to sleep in no alley or eat no dogs. I want to be like other people and I doan know how."

Bitch Bantam is the most fragile person Slab has ever encountered. "I think who you are is already better than most other people and I wish you'd just call me Slab. You got that bag o gold and you can sleep and eat anywhere's you want."

"If you'd take half of that gold, you could sleep and eat anywhere too. I could follow your zample," says Bitch Bantam.

"Me and FuzzyWuzzy here got us a grubstake saved up. How's about you keep those nuggets and me and FuzzyWuzzy treat you to a fancy dinner and help you get a room in a nice Hotel? How's about that?"

Bitch Bantam is overwhelmed by the kindness. She

has always hated men and never known any women. She feels tender toward the legless man even though, like all men, his appearance is off-putting. But still she remains reticent and searches for Slab's true intent.

"That'd be awful nice, Mister Slab, an I am terrible beholden to you and FuzzyWuzzy, but I caint give you nothing back."

What Bitch wants to say is that she appreciates Slab's kindness but since he's a man, sooner or later he will want to use her for his man-needs. Bitch will not do that, never again. She will just go her own way if that is what Slab Pettibone wants. But, if he's not going to do that way and he is all-the-way-through nice, then she doesn't want to embarrass him. Bitch is facing a social conundrum.

Truth is, Slab Pettibone does have a bit of a stiff frigamajig, but outside the lewd pictures in his head, Slab really is all-the-way-through nice. He would never take advantage of a lady and is ready to pick up a rock and bang his head free of the sexual images.

"Doesn't nobody in the whole world owe me nothin," Slab wants to call her by name but would never say the word Bitch. "You specially don't owe me nothing." He wonders if she would take offence if he calls her by an endearment, like sweety, a term a father might use. "Me and FuzzyWuzzy we discussed it and FuzzyWuzzy thinks we oughta do what we can to help you get started in the world. And, guess I never could disagree with nothin FuzzyWuzzy thinks, ah...Miss Bantam."

The near future is settled, Slab and Bitch go silent. FuzzyWuzzy hasn't eaten in hours. If they don't find an eatery soon, he may have to snag one of the yapping dogs. He huffs out a sentence to Slab.

Slab answers, "Just hold on to your horses, FuzzyWuzzy. We gonna be a stoppin soon. I'll buy you a big ol cow steak and a barrel o tap-beer. You just hold your horses a little while longer and me and you and Miss Bantam is gonna have us a big BigCity feast."

A feast sounds good to FuzzyWuzzy. He purrs like a kitty-cat.

TumbleHouse

The ground floor of TumbleHouse is spacious and open. Along the south wall a long bar of unpolished wood serves drinks to anyone with a penny for a stale beer, three pennies for a whisky-shot, or six for a spiderbite, a concoction of whisky, hot rum, camphor, benzene, cocaine.

Hurricane lamps on gimpy tables murmur light and shadow. Forty-three people in the room, playing, socializing, drinking. None are older than eighteen, some are in diapers or toddle naked across the warped floor.

Before the Civil War, TumbleHouse was a hotel, the Augustus Arms. Now the building is a nonprofit cooperative, an orphanage operated by the Brusselsprouts. TumbleHouse provides home and family for BigCity's displaced and discarded youth.

Children, some towing children of their own, are in for the night from a day of peddling flowers, songs, newspapers, hot corn-on-the-cob. Others are home from a twelve-hour sweat-shop, sewing buttons, assembling fake flowers. Little boys, filth-encrusted from shoveling coal or cleaning pig sties, stand on tiptoes to reach the bar where they fritter away a day's wage for shots of spiderbite.

Older boys and girls are throwing back six-cent shots of courage before going out to the night-shift. Everyone is puffing on Signal Cigarettes. Smoke-Signal placards are tacked to the walls along with Coca Cola, Budweiser, Uneeda Biscuit, Dr. Willaims' Tablets, Pink Pills for Pale People.

The second floor of TumbleHouse houses the pint-sized castaways. Everyone has required duties and everyone is guaranteed a meat sandwich, a dill pickle, and a bed for the night.

At the back entrance a boy of ten stands on a chair cranking hurdy-gurdy, music like sour violins. A group of pubescent girls dance a freeform cakewalk.

Dooley Paradise, the TumbleHouse boss, has everyone's respect. When he enters from the front he is sighted by many admiring eyes. Dooley put together the sandwich and pickle program. After reading Oliver Twist, he started up a Fagin school where kids can learn self-respect and a dishonest trade. Dooley has a knack for administration and a pronounced empathy for his underlings. He wants to create a future for the unwanted youth of America. Dooley is idealistic and ambitious.

Dooley Paradise casts an eye to all corners, smiles and charms his way to the bar. The bartender is named Zeph Riley. Zeph and Dooley have grown up together. Zeph is an aspiring vaudeville comedian. Dooley saddles up to the bar.

To a gathering of thirsty boys, Zeph says, "It was a while ago a pretty miss from upstairs comes ta me and sez 'Zeph, I ave a problem I ave. My key dassent work my bedroom door.' So I tells her, 'Not a problem pretty miss, tis probably the lock. You go on to yur room and undress for bed and I will be up directly to look into the keyhole.'"

Zeph receives a rousing round of blank stares. He leaves the boys and walks, hangdog, over to Dooley.

Dooley commiserates, "That was a good wheezer, Zeph. You're just too advanced for the audience."

"Ahead of me own time, you might say." Zeph pours Dooley a shot of spiderbite.

"That's a good attitude, Zeph. You just need to give yourself some time for everyone else to catch up." Dooley drinks the shot hard like a fist going down, then sets the glass down for another. Zeph pours Dooley another shot and sings a ditty as he does so,

> *"How dry I am*
> *How wet I'll be*
> *If I don't find the outhouse key."*

Dooley drinks then pays for the jiggers and sets a greenback dollar on the bar. "Get me a bag of burny would you, Zeph?"

"Sure thing, chum." Zeph Riley disappears behind a door behind the bar.

Dooley leans into the bar and takes in the activities. Normally, he would be chatting up the other inn-mates, doling advice, administering admonishments, approbates. Tonight Dooley's mind goes elsewhere: The killing of an innocent woman and a SnarlingTiger. Killing is not something Dooley

51

takes in stride. He replays the murders and he attempts to edit the scenario to make a happy ending.

Dooley needs to shake the mistake and begin working on the correction. Somebody will have to pay for the dead. Dooley will be held responsible to the Mooks, just as head Mook, Shag Draper, will be held responsible to the SnarlingTigers. Dooley needs to talk to Shag Draper and straighten out this unfortunate matter of murder. He takes another shot of spiderbite.

He watches a group of boys in torn knickers sitting in a circle on the splintered floor, each with a little fist-full of pennies, clicking dice, winning next to nothing and losing the same. Political reformers regard TumbleHouse as debauched and godless. Dooley disagrees. He sees a community of displaced urchins fighting to survive. He sees the hope underlying the despair. Of course they are godless for how could they believe in a god who would abandon them here.

Dooley's gaze falls upon two Brusselsprout soldiers stationed at the back entrance along with two coppers and a girl he has never seen before. She is a mess, but pretty and out of place. The coppers are even more out of place. Policemen are not allowed in TumbleHouse. They make the inhabitants nervous.

"One bag o Bernice, Dooley, me pal." Zeph has returned to the bar, retrieves Dooley's attention with a paper pouch of noseburn.

Dooley puts the drug in a pocket. "Thanks, Zeph. See you later."

Zeph says, "Later potater," then polishes the bar with a wet rag and whistles "My Bonnie Lies Over the Ocean".

Wilbur Good and Wilbur Szedvilas are arguing with the two boys stationed at the back entranceway. Girl stands between them but hears not what they say. Girl is awestruck. Everywhere are children. Other than the two slap-happy policemen there are no adults. Girl's fear of Wilbur and Wilbur fades. For the first time ever she is a member of a majority. And now the handsomest boy she has ever seen walks into her periphery. Like many of the others he wears a green bowler. He looks at Girl and smiles. He takes control.

"Wilbur and Wilbur," Dooley Paradise says, then plants his hand for a shake. "How's the life treating you?"

Wilbur Szedvilas shrugs, life is okay but could be better. He takes Dooley's mitt and shakes it.

Wilbur Good grunts.

The two young sentries wait for orders from Boss Dooley. Dooley addresses the tallest of the two boys, "Urick, what's the situation here?"

"Like dis, Boss. Dese coppers want money for da girl, see. We tol em we dunt buy orphinks. An de girl she ken stay."

Wilbur Good has grown impatient, he does not like kids, and he stands ready to snap some necks.

Wilbur Szedvilas has known all along that TumbleHouse will not pay for the girl. He has manipulated his partner to the TumbleHouse backdoor where he knows the girl will be safe from the harsher street elements. He steps forward, "Me I making mistake, Dooley lad. The girlie she already here now so Wilbur and me I be skedaddle."

Wilbur Good has a different view. He wants a gratuity payment for the girl and will not leave without it. He knows his partner is a pushover but he knows his partner will stand and fight beside him if violence breaks out. His partner is still his partner.

Wilbur Good says, "We here for boodle, little mister Boss. Yuz dunt pay fur girlie, me, I trow her in da slammy."

Dooley takes off his hat and places it on Girl's head. The brim falls to her eyebrows.

"You must not have noticed, Wilbur, she's a Brusselsprout. She lives here and you have no jurisdiction over Brusselsprouts inside of TumbleHouse."

Girl does not know the meaning of jurisdiction nor does she know what a Brusselsprout is. She knows however that this boy, Dooley or Boss, whatever his name is, is taking her under his wing. This boy full of charm and arrogance and power has designated her as a member of his tribe.

Girl watches another boy and a girl walking quickly toward them. The girl wears a pretty dress though it hangs without shape as on a clothes-hanger. Her face is pleasant and her complexion is hidden beneath a dusting of cornstarch. The boy is thick and angry. He walks with a swagger and puffs on a cigarette.

Wilbur Good is standing pat, waiting for his money. Wilbur Szedvilas is ready to go but waits with his partner, searches his mind for an easy way back out the door.

"So, I guess I'll be seeing you Wilburs around," Dooley is trying to keep it light and at the same time rid the house of the boolydogs.

Wilbur Good reaches down, puts a vice grip on Girl's upper arm. With his other hand he takes out his billy club. "Five kopek, Boss Paradise. Or Girlie go so long."

Girl tries to pull away. The copper holds firm.

Adelina Brown has joined the group, she stands next to Dooley, holding him by the arm, making sure the girl, and everyone, can see he is hers. Now Gulper Mooney barges in from the sidelines, joins the fray, "Yoodel loo, Dooley, me chum. Can you tell me what pennies are made of?" Gulper is having a fine time and primed for a good fight.

Dooley says, "You don't need to be here, Gulper, I've got it under control."

Gulper ignores Dooley. He smiles up at Wilbur and Wilbur, tells everyone within earshot, "Dirty copper, pennies are made of dirty copper."

Girl laughs out loud. This is the boy that will steal her heart, the rough and tumble blustery boy with freckles, buck teeth and a cruel smile. Gulper tips his hat to Girl, "Welcome home, miss," then replaces his bowler and gives a scowl to Wilbur Good. "I tank you to unhand me girl, ya dirty copper."

Wilbur Szedvilas sees a fight brewing. Given his and Wilbur Good's stature, experience, weapons, and high tolerance to pain, he figures they can wipe out a couple dozen of the raggedy muffins without breaking a sweat. He takes out his billy-club, though he hopes not to use it. Wilbur Szedvilas likes kids.

Wilbur Good tightens his grip on Girl. He needs only one hand to inflict damage on this little smart-mouthed feck. "Me I take me five kopek from this one's blood," he says to Gulper.

Gulper puffs his chest.

Girl wants to show this boy that she is worth fighting for. She wants to show the coppers that she is not afraid. She smiles at Gulper, and then blushes when he smiles back.

Dooley has lost control. He needs to diffuse the situation. He has troubles enough without a riot in his house. He notices the silence that has come upon them. The hurdy-gurdy boy has stopped playing and stepped down from his chair. The two sentries—Urick and the other boy, Mike, a frail twelve-year-old—have both taken their slug-shots from back pockets and stand ready to fight. Others throughout the house have brought out weapons of their own and are crowding around.

Wilbur Good is rethinking his stance when Girl surprises everyone by turning and biting with all her might into Officer Good's hand. Wilbur is slow to react; it takes a while for the pain impulse to caterpillar from his hand to his brain. He releases Girl. He holds out his tooth-printed paw to his partner Wilbur Szedvilas. "Looky dare, Wilbur. Da girlie she bitten on me hand." Both Wilburs giggle.

"I tank we let er stay now," Wilbur Szedvilas says. "She done eaten bad tasty meat." He laughs, pretends all is well, even though he knows his partner's hand has gone to his gun.

Girl is radiant with pride. She has shown everyone that she is one of them. She looks again at Gulper Mooney, he has brass-knuckles on his fists, admiration on his face.

Dooley can see through the laughing coppers, can see that Wilbur Good is ready to erupt. Dooley proffers a five-dollar-piece from his pocket and tosses it to Wilbur Szedvilas who catches it and says to his brother-in-blue, "Looky dare, Wilbur. Young Dooley haff paid da boodle." He hands the coin to Wilbur Good. "Time we be skedaddle."

Wilbur Good grudgingly takes the coin and pockets it.

Dooley Paradise has buckled to Wilbur Good's extortion, has surrendered the respect of those under his care.

Adelina Brown has watched this scene with held breath. She has not surrendered an ounce of respect for Dooley. Adelina holds diplomacy and sensitivity above brawn, bluster, and violence. Adelina holds Dooley Paradise above everyone.

Gulper Mooney still wants a fight; he gives his opinion by spitting on the floor between the Wilburs and Dooley. His bravado turns Girl on. She admires his bad attitude, his belligerent grin, his anger.

Wilbur Szedvilas ignores Gulper, says, "Bye-bye tally ho," to Dooley. Dooley also ignores Gulper, says, "See you around," to Wilbur Szedvilas. Wilbur and Wilbur leave TumbleHouse and walk back into the night. They switch on the electric lamps. Wilbur Good walks beside his partner and soon forgets the TumbleHouse encounter, he says, "Heyo Wilbur, yuz knowing how to playing squirrel?"

"Squirrel?" Wilbur Szedvilas wonders aloud. "Do tell, Wilbur."

Wilbur Good takes a quick fist-full of Wilbur Szedvilas' testicles and gives them a brutal squeeze. "Grabbing the nuts and running," he chortles.

Wilbur Szedvilas doubles like he is going to vomit. "Yuz done me a good one this time, ye palsied-face focker."

Wilbur and Wilbur have a good laugh as they continue their nightly beat.

WhiteWay

Daddy Smithy is so excited his legs are throwing sparks. He's going to be rich and famous. He has a rich and famous benefactor, Warner Quackenbush. Things are finally working as his daydreams predicted. His lifelong string of failure is just a fading memory of minor setbacks. Somehow he made his pitch to Shag Draper who somehow set him up with Warner Quackenbush who just happened to be looking for an independent film maker with a vision of the future.

Perspiration crowns Daddy's head, pasting his oily hair to his hatband. The effort of pushing a large wheelbarrow, plus his natural adrenaline-fueled anxiety, has Daddy a tad frazzled. His brain is running to keep up with his thoughts and he needs a spoonful of liquid therapy.

BigCity's WhiteWay is blue-white with generated light. Through doorways men are bent over hand-cranked Kinetoscopes, eyes masked in viewers, celluloid loops, Peeping Johnny, Madam Bowery's Bustle, Dancing Coon's, Mississippi Lynching.

The sight of men emptying their pockets for a few seconds of titillation fills Daddy Smithy with a glorious panoramic of his destiny. Daddy sets the wheelbarrow down. He walks to the front and sits on the pneumatic rubber wheel.

Signal Cigarette magnate, Warner Quackenbush, has entrusted Daddy Smithy with two-thousand-five-hundred dollars. Daddy Smithy has used these funds to purchase everything he needs to immortalize his name. He takes his bottle of Celery tonic from his vest pocket and doses himself with a celebratory taste. He goes dreamy. Daddy can picture each item in the wheelbarrow with his eyes shut. He takes inventory, one combination Optigraph and Stereopticon complete with a newly invented incandescent vapor lamp and acetylene gas generator, along with ten pounds of carbide in one-pound tins. Daddy already owns a Magic Lantern for projecting glass slides as well as a Sears moving-picture projector. But, they are nothing compared to this. Now he can project moving films forward or backward, in a dark room at thirty feet.

Daddy Smithy has also updated his still-camera equipment by purchasing a new eight-by-ten camera and tripod along with two lenses, a darkroom set-up, and five pounds of magnesium flash powder. He doesn't need all this new equipment but his financial backer has been generous. While Warner Quackenbush expects much in return, Daddy is not concerned, payback will be a cinch. Especially, now that Daddy has his most prized possession ever, a Cinématographe motion picture camera.

There are plenty of chaps making the rounds with projectors, but they are limited in the films they can show. The corporate inventors of the cameras and films produce and distribute their own reels. They don't sell the cameras or long-roll film to independents. Monopolies control production and content of the silver flickers. Daddy has paid one-thousand-five-hundred dollars to an unscrupulous sales representative, for the Cinématographe and twenty cans of unexposed 1,200 foot reels of George Eastman's celluloid film. True to the inventive nature of the times and the licentious spirit of men, Daddy Smithy is inventing independent filmmaking, trail-blazing an unexpurgated pre-Hays future.

Daddy takes another comforting hit of Doctor FixUp. He has two long city blocks, to his plush hotel room. He stands, blinks himself back to his surroundings and notices two young boys in green bowler hats milling about a red fire-plug. They remind him of the two children he has abandoned, his daughters.

Daddy has no reason to feel guilty, after all, he had been even younger than the oldest girl when he had been put out on his own, and he has done just fine. And the youngest girl, well certainly he can't feel bad about her, he has done right by her. "She will be fine and dandy," he says aloud. Heck-be-damned, he has arranged for her to have a better life than he ever had and knowing what she's like, he almost feels sorry for the people who took her.

Daddy gets distracted from his rationalized speculations, by a scene across the thoroughfare where an enormous woman along with a man riding a yellow bear are causing a stir. He steps away from his wheelbarrow to get a better look.

Slab Pettibone, Bitch Bantam, and FuzzyWuzzy have walked from the derelict outskirts of BigCity into the cultural district. Theaters with sky-high storybook spires yield nervous volts of electric light. Posters, marquee lights, slouch-hatted barkers invite and entice, Shakespeare, Gilbert and Sullivan, vaudeville, melodrama, freaks and geeks, t & a. Sidewalk vendors sell hot corn-on-the-cob, flowers, cigars. Ragamuffin kids sing spare-change ditties and dance nickel jigs. An organ grinder cranks "A Bicycle Built for Two", peddles candied-apples while his spider monkey solicits coins of the realm.

"I'm gonna stop here for a minute, Miss Bantam," Slab reigns FuzzyWuzzy to the candied-apple cart. "I think Mister FuzzyWuzzy wants a snack. I'd buy one for you also, if you think you'd like one."

"No thank you," Bitch says, even though she would like to say, "Yes thank you."

FuzzyWuzzy is quivering with anticipation. He loves candied-apples. The vendor is taken aback by the unique customers, but this is BigCity and a customer is after all a customer. Slab digs two pennies from his vest pocket and exchanges them for two candied-apples. Slab holds his by the stick but FuzzyWuzzy puts his, stick and all, into his mouth and crunches with delight.

While the people of BigCity are cynical enough to not raise an eyebrow at Slab, Bitch, and FuzzyWuzzy, the animals don't do as well. Dogs, horses and monkeys are just naturally afraid of bears, even nice bears like FuzzyWuzzy. The organ-grinder's spider monkey screeches at FuzzyWuzzy, pulls its leash until it snaps, then scrambles into the street under the hooves of a horse pulling a single passenger in a two-passenger buggy. The horse, already on edge from FuzzyWuzzy's presence, rears and lets out a horsey scream. The buggy tilts sideways to a single wooden wheel then goes over, spilling its passenger. Frothing and irrational the horse drags the tumbled carriage and charges FuzzyWuzzy. FuzzyWuzzy chews his candied-apple, puts his ears back and braces for a fight. Slab Pettibone scrunches down in FuzzyWuzzy's thick fur, getting course hairs on his sticky candied-apple. Bitch Bantam dives through the air and grabbing the horse by the neck, she brings it to the ground. She holds the horse pinned and talks softly into its ear. "It's okay, horsey. Nobody is gonna hurt nobody. Be a good boy. There, there horsey, everything is gonna be jus fine."

The horse quiets and Bitch helps it back to its feet then puts the cab back up on its wheels and the passenger back in his seat.

FuzzyWuzzy wants another candied apple. Slab is only half done with his and the other half is all hairy. He gives it to FuzzyWuzzy who smacks his lips.

Without comment FuzzyWuzzy, Slab Pettibone, and Bitch Bantam walk onward through the busy night. Slab looks for a suitable hotel and restaurant. From the high branches of a tree the spider-monkey jeers down at the exasperated organ grinder.

Daddy Smithy watches the enormous woman, the man, and the yellow bear walk away. He is impressed by the woman's feat of derring-do. He sees showbiz potential in the strange threesome. He thinks maybe he should follow them, talk to them before another enterprising promoter grabs them up.

Daddy is excited and nervous all over again. He tips his bottle of opium mix and takes a taste. He turns to his wheelbarrow of technological treasures to find that it is gone. The two Brusselsprouts have used the commotion of the monkey, the horse, and Bitch Bantam, as cover. While Daddy Smithy's back was turned, they absconded with his future.

Daddy Smithy stands looking at the empty space on the sidewalk. "I'm so stupid!" Men and women detour around him without a glance. "Stupid! Stupid! Stupid!" His gut clenches, gastric enzymes surge upward, burn his pharynx. Daddy folds to his knees and regurgitates the mélange of a sardine lunch and a half-bottle of Doctor FixUp. Marquee lights blink. The busy entertainment center and the whole of BigCity promise passes him by.

TumbleHouse

Dooley Paradise has earned the top floor of TumbleHouse Orphanage. His blood pulses through the TumbleHouse veins. Without him, the BigCity urchins would splinter into urban Dickensian tribes. Under Dooley's reign, TumbleHouse breathes easily. The third floor of TumbleHouse is the throne from which the boy presides, King of the guttersnipes.

Originally, twelve rooms, one water closet, and a main kitchen branched from the long hallway. Dooley commissioned a young crew of wage-earners to eliminate the inside walls on the kitchen side creating a large private living space. Across the hall, his bedroom is stacked alongside six other bedrooms which he awards to a privileged few, friends and lieutenants.

Lighting below deck is a smokey blaze of John Davison Rockefeller kerosene. Only Dooley's penthouse is wired for direct-current. He has running water, a white-crock-flusher, and a claw-foot tub. He has a pot-bellied coal-burning heater. He has linoleum floors and cloth-covered couches and chairs. He has a floor-to-ceiling bookshelf of bestsellers and a stack of Slab Pettibone adventures. He has an Edison phonograph machine and a stack of platters.

Dooley taps a couple of lines of noseburn onto the white enameled kitchen table. He rolls up a greenback and snorts the cocaine into his head. His face twitches. Liquid euphoria fuses with rocky anxiety. Dooley closes his eyes and conquers the universe and then for a fleeting moment he realizes that his drug euphoria does not befit his stature, does not in fact put him at his best. He has a house filled with young innocents that depend on him to be sharp and sober. But then he opens his eyes to his addiction and acknowledges paranoia for what it is.

Dooley considers Adelina Brown, his number one confidant who is far from happy with the events of the day and rightly blames Dooley. He guesses he loves her, as she loves him, but when Dooley thinks about girls, in his sexual reveries, it is not the serious, skinny, and bossy Adelina that brings him to self-spurting satisfaction. Sometimes he wishes Adelina would just leave him alone.

Now Dooley unwittingly conjures visuals he would rather avoid. He sees the woman with the peacock hat sitting on the Sunshine Avenue sidewalk. Dying. Dead. He shakes the vision from his head. His neck is tight and his fingers shake.

Dooley blots his troubles with another shot of spiderbite. He spins a disk on his Edison juke, "At a Georgia Camp Meeting", a ragtime performed by the Edison Grand Concert Band. Thick music through a blooming brass speaker spills slaphappy jazz. It soothes Dooley with hipster delirium, carries him across the rocky divide, into the cool mix. He absorbs the music like a shot of dope. When the tune completes, he cranks it for another go. He sways and taps his toes, closes his eye and rolls his head.

Gulper Mooney strikes a lucifer on a buck tooth and lights a table lamp. He tweaks the wick animating the walls with shadow pictures. Girl stands in the open doorway, peering into her new room. Gulper takes her arm, escorts her in then closes the door.

The schoolyard chorus of children in the hallways and bedrooms follow them through the door. But, in this little room, single bed, chamber-pot, wall-mirror, straight backed chair, Girl is isolated from the activity. She can be alone or, she can be alone with Gulper Mooney, as she is now.

Gulper leans into the wall, strikes another friction match, this time on his thumbnail. He uses the flame to activate a Signal Cigarette. He drops the spent match to the floor, blows smoke, and crows, "Dem udder Sprouts they all gotta share rooms, see. But, you dunt cause I sez so and what I sez goes."

Gulper is advertising for Girl's affections. He wants her for his own.

Girl does nothing to discourage him. She likes his pugnacious nature. Girl needs a tough boy. She needs shoulders and muscle and unflinching nerve. She needs someone to love and trust. Gulper fits the bill.

"I kilt a SnarlingTiger this day earlier, I did. Capped the vomitus feck in the nut, see. Like this," Gulper takes his two-shot pistol from his pocket and pantomimes his derring-do. "Bam-bam, me gun went and down the tiger he goes."

Girl is impressed with Gulper's macho but she does not believe he killed a tiger.

"I didn't know tigers lived in BigCity. Are there many?"

Gulper pauses. "Huh?"

"You said you killed a tiger and I was asking if there are many tigers in BigCity."

"Tigers? Was a man I kilt. A big man. Never again will he wrong Gulper Mooney, see."

In Girl's opinion, Gulper has grown in esteem: he is a killer. She thinks of all the men who soiled her. She had wanted to kill each and every one. She needed a boy like Gulper then, as she needs him now.

Girl takes a seat on the bed. "I don't think I am gonna need any doctorin. I'm not bleeding any more. I'm just kind of sore." She puts her hand between her legs, rubs at the pain through thin layers of tattered cloth.

Girl's lack of inhibition is a quick jab to Gulper's manhood. He assumes Girl to be an innocent. Girls are, after all, whatever he thinks they are, or wants them to be. He is stymied by her brazen behavior.

Girl has not read Gulper's script nor will she play the innocent for anyone's benefit. Her daddy pimped her, sold her time and again like a dirty picture, like a mouse to an alley cat. Now he is gone and she is in charge of herself. Nobody is going to play Pygmalion with Girl.

Gulper is trying to regain his cool pose. He watches Girl as he would a hypnotist's pocket-watch. She is dirty and disheveled. Her long blond hair hangs in clumps. Yet, she fills the little room with such thick sexuality that Gulper can taste it, smell it, feel it. His cock has sprung, like a spring-loaded blackjack, revealing his intentions through the thin twill of his pants. He hopes Girl does not notice. He does not want to seem overanxious.

"I yav ad lots of girlfriends, I yav, see. Iym th best ketch any girl got. Everbody knows who Iym. You just ask, they tell ya. An, ya know what they tell ya?"

Girl does not know or care what anyone will tell her about Gulper. She does not care if he talks or not. She can see the rise in his pants and she knows what it is and how it works. Girl wants this boy, Gulper Mooney. And, she wants him all for herself.

"...They will tell ya Iym a chum, lest Iym crosst, see. Someone crosses Gulper Mooney, they never again..."

Girl leans forward, takes the loose cloth at Gulper's pants pocket, pinches it and pulls him close.

"You had lotsa girlfrien's. You know all about girls. You can have this girl. But you have to be my man and just be with me an nobody else." She brushes her hand across the worsted wool covering his erection.

If at this moment Girl were to ask Gulper to run and jump through the little second story window, he would dive headfirst through the glass without a moment's consideration. Gulper has little experience with girls. He is readily agreeable to monogamy.

"You be my patootie forever, understand. Nobody will nay sez different lest they lookin..."

Girl pulls Gulper by the hand, sits him on edge of the bed. She kneels, like a bedside prayer, between his legs. Girl has been with many men but never with one of her choosing. Gulper is her first. "I am too sore in my other place, so I am gonna deliver you with my mouth."

Gulper finally stops talking.

In the hallway on the other side of the door, Adelina Brown paces a groove into the creaky floor, paying little attention to the troops of ragamuffins heading for beds, waiting in line for the pump-handle, filling wash buckets, dumping chamber pots to the trestle sluices.

Two boys are pushing/pulling an overflowing wheelbarrow of motion picture equipment up the steps. Adelina watches them struggle but does not register the wheelbarrow or its contents. She makes an about-face, trenches between the fourteen rooms on the right and left. Children six deep occupy the rooms like tinned sardines. Some sleep soundly wrapped in straw-stuffed roll-ups like Sunday morning pigs-in-a-blanket. Others toss, turn, cry, whisper, fart, and giggle.

At the end of the hallway Adelina looks through the open window to the stars above and ground below. Two dearth ravaged dogs are sexually conjoined in the fluttering light of a ground-floor doorway. Skeletal mutts fucking in garbage-strewn alleys is a common sight. Adelina knows what a better world should be and this is not it. She searches for ways to bring it here to the orphanage. She needs a crusade. She needs a nonviolent weapon. She has no idea that she is about to get both.

Below the window, a coil of rope is fastened tight to an iron u-bolt. A black-ink sign, IN CASE OF FIRE THROW ROPE OUT WINDOW. This is a Dooley Paradise innovation. Dooley has outfitted every second and third floor window with a safety-rope. This is the idealistic Dooley that Adelina loves not the illogical Dooley who holds fast to the drugs and drinks that do not belong here among children. Adelina strives to accept Dooley's dichotomy, though her preference would be bringing him around to her way of thinking.

Earlier, Adelina had a hand in the two deaths on the street and even though it is not her finger that pulled the trigger she is washed with guilt. Adelina abhors violence, sees it as a solution to nothing and the cause and effect of society's ills. Yet, when she saw Dooley in grave peril, she did not ponder her pacifist ideals. When she heard Dooley scream of fright, her nature overtook her idealism, and she jumped the bad-guy like a mama panther.

Now what she remembers most is looking at her blood splattered face in the mirror, the blood of a dead man who likely leaves behind him a family to mourn his passing. People who love him, depend on him, people whose lives are forever changed by a senseless moment of violence. Washing another's dried blood from your face is not a task Adelina can justify.

Adelina walks again to the stairway. The two boys and

the wheelbarrow have trundled to the landing. The wheelbarrow spills cameras, like a Christmas sleigh of toys. The boys stand in the stairwell and pant. Adelina looks to the up stairway. One final flight to Dooley Paradise's domain. She wants to climb up and bed down in the comfort of his arms. To her surprise the two young boys began to tackle the steps.

"Where are you going with that stuff?"

The boys know who Adelina is. She is the teacher and she has the ear of Boss Paradise. She is a girl to be respected. The younger of the two boys is named Bug. He has dirt and snot caked from his nostrils to his upper lip. He says, "We gots a barrel o boodle ta sell ta Boss Paradise."

Adelina puts authority in her voice. "You can't just walk up to the top floor without an appointment. You ought to know that. What have you there? Let me take a look."

The boys tilt the boodle to her view. "Tis tangs like what Thomas Edison makes. Wurf a bundle."

Adelina inspects the equipment, cameras, a magic lantern, moving-picture gear, brown chemical bottles. She does not know how or where the two sprouts boosted it. But she knows they are right about its worth.

"I'll give you five dollars for it, right now."

The boys can hardly speak. This is good fortune like they never dreamed. A finiff can buy a lot of spiderbite with enough left over to share with an affectionate young TumbleHouse girl. They take Adelina's money, the single green bill she proffers from her pocket book, and leave her alone in the stairwell with her boodle of pop technology. She goes to her knees and examines her treasure. Coincidence has presented her with a key to her destiny. She hardly hears the hubbub surrounding

69

her, the fighting and fucking mongrel dogs outside, the stray children inside.

Halfway back down the hallway behind a closed door, Gulper Mooney is short of breath from the exertion of orgasm. Gulper is new to the sex arena. While he likes to boast a harem, he has not yet kissed a girl. Other than a long string of knock down fights Gulper has never had physical contact with anyone, male or female. He has never experienced intimacy and it has caught him off guard, stripped him of bombast, his soft psychic underbelly is suddenly tender to the touch.

Gulper is deep in love with Girl and even though she serviced him with sex that goes beyond a virgin's intuition, he deems her chaste. Gulper has never felt the love or snuggle of another, but this, the way he feels now, is what he images it to be. He holds Girl tight in his arms.

Sex is not new for Girl. Sex by choice, however, is. Girl is also infatuated. But for Girl, there is an agenda. She cuddles into Gulper. "You make me feel good and safe, Gulper. You can do anything, can't you?" Girl unbuttons Gulper's shirt exposing his polka-dot skin.

"That I can, my Girl. That I can."

Girl tickles her fingers over Gulpers surface, across his soft belly. It is a feel-good game she plays often with her sister. Soft erotic tickles they call fairy fingers. Gulper falls into a spell.

"Gulper?"

"Yeh, Girl."

"I've gotta find my sister, Snooks."

Gulper monotones from a fluffy dream, "Snooks?"

"That's her name, I gave it to her. Something happened to her, someone took her. She needs me. I have to find her. We need to find her."

Gulper will say anything at this moment to prolong the pleasure, he says, "We shall find her, see. I shall find your little sis. I am all ready making a plan for tomorrow."

Girl hopes Gulper is true to his word. She needs to find Snooks. Her sister is not smart, not right in the head. She needs Girl to care for her, she cannot do for herself.

Gulper is not really making a plan to find Girl's sister. He already has a big day planned for tomorrow. He has accepted a clandestine freelance gig from Mook boss Shag Draper. With the proceeds of said gig Gulper will buy a better life for himself, for himself and Girl. The job requires Gulper to sell out his best friend Dooley Paradise and, in turn, TumbleHouse. The job requires Gulper to assassinate a public figure. The job pays three thousand dollars. Gulper sees no wrong, has no guilt, already has the money spent. At this very moment, in the reaches of his sociopathic mind, he is buying diamonds and mink for his girl. Girl.

"I am gonna love you forever," Girl tells Gulper.

Gulper closes his eyes. He shivers from the fairies dancing across his freckled façade.

Domino's Steak & Seafood

Domino's Steak & Seafood is a source of wonderment. Crystal chandeliers twinkle with yellowed electric light. The walls are flocked with red florals and the windows look out at BigCity's cultural core like a modern-art diorama. The people coming in and the people going out are jovial and celebratory. Bitch Bantam sits in the cushy seat of a high-backed chair, pulled up close to the table. Before her are sparkling goblets of seltzer-water, bone-china plates of bread, steak, chops, and oysters on ice. Bitch follows the lead of others, eating with the aid of the polished silver utensils. She enjoys the freedom to eat as she pleases, without pressure. She savors every morsel and between bites she covers her mouth and quietly belches with pleasure.

The table is round where Bitch, Slab Pettibone and FuzzyWuzzy dine. A group of gentlemen are laughing, yelling, shoving to the front lines for a closer look at the inimitable threesome. Bitch understands spectacle, she has always drawn a crowd, but this bunch is different than the bloodthirsty shitheads at the fighting pits. These men are clean, cultured and moneyed. They wear top hats of beaver skin and lacquered silk, black frock coats with starched white collars, and necktie scarves. They are men of education and culture and like all men they are evil bastards. Bitch growls when they get too close, she wants to be civilized but she's conditioned to lash out, to maim and murder.

FuzzyWuzzy is as well a bit testy in this boiling stew of humans. But FuzzyWuzzy mostly ignores the men, who occasionally take rude and risky feels of his thick fur. FuzzyWuzzy is occupied with great bowls of green salad, mounds of raw oysters and his personal favorite, baked salmon with sides of caviar. Like Bitch Bantam, FuzzyWuzzy is happy to dine in a leisurely manner. Unlike Bitch Bantam, FuzzyWuzzy does not bother with the silverware. He prefers to lay his padded paws on either side of the plate and eat with his lips, teeth, and tongue.

Slab Pettibone is at ease in this boisterous atmosphere, he created it. Slab well understands the workings of celebrity; he uses it to capture the spotlight. Unlike Bitch and FuzzyWuzzy, Slab Pettibone is not impressed by the food. After the first two porterhouse steaks Slab lost his hunger. While Bitch and FuzzyWuzzy scarf a dozen dinners, the group of men bolster around slapping backs and downing mugs of spirit. Slab takes out his ukulele, tickles the catgut and baritones a musical yarn.

> *"I was born almost ten thousand years ago,*
> *And there's nothing in the world that I don't know,*
> *I saw Peter, Paul and Moses,*
> *Playing ring-around-the-roses*
> *And I'm here to lick the guy what sez taint so."*

Slab is savvy to the city. An amputee astride a bear accompanying a giantess in overalls would never be allowed in a ritzy joint like Domino's Steak and Seafood. Slab Pettibone, FuzzyWuzzy, and Bitch Bantam are special. Men and boys all across the great nation read the exploits of Slab Pettibone and FuzzyWuzzy in pulp books that Slab himself pens and sells through a BigCity publisher.

Slab is savvy to Bitch Bantam's celebrity as well as his own. Blurbs and tall tales featuring the fighting female have preceded them. Bitch Bantam is an adventure-story commodity. This is the first Bitch Bantam has heard of her fame. Everyone wants to shake her hand which she finds creepy and difficult, especially while trying to manage the silverware.

> "I taught Solomon his little A-B-C's,
> I helped Brigham Young to make Limburger cheese,
> And while sailing down the bay,
> with Methuselah one day,
> I saved his flowing whiskers from the breeze."

Across this sparkling castle Bitch sees, through the haze of testosterone, a table where sits a group of women. They are bedecked in a panoply of feathers, jewels, dazzling gowns, like storybook queens. They talk together without a glance toward the men, or Bitch, the single lonely woman. Bitch is glad they don't see her. She is dressed in ragged overalls, barefoot and hatless. Her hair is tangled and clumped with hardship. She is bigger than any of the men and she has ugly shark teeth. She lacks in femininity and social grace.

While attempting to chew a venison quarter-pounder with her mouth closed, Bitch sneaks peeks at the women. They appear humorless, stern, intent with right. Bitch stops chewing when her eyes fall upon the eyes of a woman, looking at her. The woman's name is Helen Beck. Her age is thirty-seven. She's tiny, five feet tall. Her face is fierce and honest. She sits within the group but is lost from the others, enraptured in Bitch Bantam's eyes. Helen Beck smiles at Bitch Bantam and Bitch nearly wets her pants and screams. She quickly turns back to her food, the raucous cachinnate of the men. There is not a man in the place that Bitch would fear in a knuckle fight but she's afraid to lift her eyes from her plate, afraid to look at the tiny woman.

> "Queen Elizabeth she fell in love with me
> we were married in Milwaukee secretly,
> But I schemed around and shook her,
> And I went with General Hooker
> To shoot mosquitoes down in Tennessee."

FuzzyWuzzy is feeling fine. He has dined like a king on the finest cuisine any bear ever consumed in a single sitting. Sitting on his tail FuzzyWuzzy leans back in his human chair with all paws outward, exposing his engorged and fluffy round tummy. He compliments the chief with a roaring bear burp. For fifteen seconds the patrons and staff of Domino's Steak and Seafood dissolve into total silence. FuzzyWuzzy falls forward, his front paws on either side of the licked-clean plate, his face in the dish. He begins to snore. The uproar resumes. Slab strums a final verse.

> "I saw Satan when he looked the garden o'er,
> Saw Adam and Eve driven from the door,
> And, behind the bushes peeping,
> Saw the apple they were eating,
> And I'll swear that I'm the guy what et the core."

Slab Pettibone's bruin companion is ready to bed down, and Bitch Bantam is nervous and uncomfortable. Slab feels the fool for bringing her here; he can see that she wants to escape the spotlight. He should have been more considerate of her needs. Slab has quickly acquired the need to take care of Bitch Bantam, she has captured his heart and not as a dirty thought as he feared. There are people in the world who you love because how could you not? Slab will help Bitch and FuzzyWuzzy procure shelter for the night but first he has business needs attending.

Sitting in a chair, atop his haversack, Slab looks like a guy with legs. From his haversack he takes out two dozen copies of his latest adventure story, *Slab Pettibone and FuzzyWuzzy the Bear Battle Genghis Khan on the Mysterious Island of Pango Pongo.* With a hydraulic reservoir fountain-pen he begins autographing the hundred-page books and selling them for four-bits each. Along with the books he has brought out a stack of three-by-three, heavy stock cards with cuts to hold dollar-sized tin coins. The cards are printed, *For all my friends who never get around to it.* The coins are stamped, the head side with a head and shoulders portrait of Slab Pettibone, the tails side with a hind view of FuzzyWuzzy. The coins are labeled on both sides, 1 ROUND-TUIT. He hands these out with the books and a few words, "Hope you enjoy the story and this is to make sure you get a Round-Tuit."

Through the crowd of back-slappers and high-handers, Slab notices, from the corner of his eye, a nervous looking man with a smashed fedora bumbling his way through the congregation.

"Good evening to you, sir," Daddy Smithy presents his hand for a shake. Slab is too busy, signing and selling his storybooks, collecting greenbacks, to give Daddy his hand.

"Best o the evening to you, sir. Should I sign this to anyone special?"

Daddy Smithy is sweating profusely. His eyes are

rimmed red and his hands shake. "Scuse me a second, if you please." He takes a medicine bottle from his vest pocket, uncorks it and sucks down two quick hits. "Got me a case of the jitters, is all," he explains to Slab. "Nothing serious. In truth I am on top of the world." He corks the bottle.

Slab Pettibone doesn't care if this guy is on top of the world or not. Slab is down to his last three books and ready to close shop. He ignores Daddy Smithy and signs and sells two more ten cent novels at fifty cents each. The place is beginning to clear out. Slab puts away his Round-Tuits and holding his last copy of *Pango Pongo* he turns to Daddy, "I'd be happy to personalize your copy of my book real quick like, before I close up shop."

"Ah, well you s-see, I ah don't really want a uh... That is, I don't mean to infer that I wouldn't like a c-copy of... uh, your adventures..."

"Do you or don't you?" Slab doesn't want to be discourteous, but it is getting late and this guy is frazzled and unable to get out a complete sentence.

Daddy takes a deep breath, "Uh, yesser sure, give me one a those, I'd be honored to purchase one of your storybooks. Two bits, I believe I heard you say."

"I've been sellin em for four. What should I be inscribing here?"

"Anything you wanna say is fine by me, Mister Pettibone, sir."

Slab forgoes sentiment and signs only his name to the flyleaf.

FuzzyWuzzy snores.

Bitch Bantam takes a venturesome look around. The

dining hall has cleared. The women have disbanded. The tiny woman is gone. Bitch's worn-thin emotions are tested as she experiences relief along with an intense sad longing. Only one woman remains at the table, settling accounts with the hangdog waiter. Her face is sad and she wears diamonds that gleam. Next to the woman's bustle a girl of six years stands impatiently fidgeting and stroking the long curls of a toy baby-doll. The girl has baby-doll curls of her own, long, blond, sparkling like silk ribbon. Bitch can only imagine the clean fresh smell of the child.

The girl's name is Cuteness Delaware. She wears frilly petticoats with ruffles above her shiny black boots. She wears elbow length silk gloves and a dark red cloak with a chinchilla collar. She wears a pink chambray bonnet. Bitch sees in the girl a gentle world of beauty and privilege. She sees what she can only experience if she dies and comes back different. Bitch likes to imagine that she can do that, die and come back.

Cuteness Delaware talks to her baby-doll and scrolls the room. She meets, and holds on to, Bitch Bantam's open gaze. She looks at Bitch without the fear and revulsion that Bitch has seen in the eyes of adult women. Embolden by misinterpreted vibes, Bitch smiles at the child, just as Helen Beck had earlier smiled at her. Cuteness scrunches her face and sticks out her tongue. Bitch is mule-kicked. She has never seen a scornful tongue, only the wagging tongues of lewd men. Never has she taken to heart anything as hurtful as this assault from a six-year-old girl. She turns her eyes back to Slab Pettibone. Snot floods her nostrils. Water fills her eyes, spills to her cheeks. She hides behind the linen napkin, behind her matted weaves of hair.

Slab can see that Bitch is upset. He doesn't know why, sometimes women just get that way. He's protective, but knows not how one protects a magnificent woman/child like Bitch Bantam.

Slab quickly signs the book, hands it to Daddy Smithy and takes the man's quarter. He gives his snoozing bear a shake, "Wake up now, FuzzyWuzzy. It's time for us to get goin."

FuzzyWuzzy wakes groggily. He yawns and scratches his butt. He puts four on the floor.

Slab saddles up.

Daddy Smithy has not moved. His sweaty hands smudge the cover illustration on his copy of Pango Pongo. Daddy knows what he needs to say. He has already said it twice to himself, once in his head, once out loud to the wind. "Excuse me."

Slab buckles his driver's seat, his ears turned away from Daddy Smithy. Bitch hears the nervous little man but pays no heed. She stands ready to leave; ready to follow Slab Pettibone's each and every example.

Daddy Smithy is losing them. He needs to lasso Slab Pettibone, with his words, with his sales-book personality. He needs to plant pictures in the man's head. He needs to call up his sales sermon, fast.

"WAIT!"

Slab pauses, gives the man another look. "I am sorry, mister. I am all talked out. Maybe some other time."

Daddy blurts, "I got something to say won't take a minute. It's about your future."

Slab is fully saddled, ready to go. FuzzyWuzzy is waiting for the command.

"One minute is about all I got," Slab tells Daddy. "You go ahead and use it and tell me about my future."

Daddy Smithy takes three deep breaths then begins. "My

name is Daddy Smithy and you may not have heard of me, but in some ways I'm just like everybody else, and I have sure heard of you and your bear and Miss Bantam." He tips his smashed hat to Bitch. "But, in other ways, I'm not like nobody else you probably ever known. You see, as it happens, I'm in show business, not the way you are mind you, but I'm in the business of managing and producing entertainment ventures. And, right here and now I can guarantee that under my management, right here in this the greatest city in the world, I can make you a star like you never dreamed. You and Miss Bitch Bantam and FuzzyWuzzy the Wonder Bear can make a million and one dollars with my idears and help. Your names will be writ in electric light at the biggest entertainment houses on the great WhiteWay Boulevard, the busiest boulevard in the whole dang country. And I have yet to mention the biggest and most spectacular idear of all. I should probably explain, at this time, that there is a matter of monies atween you an me. I'd say probably what is fair would be, oh, say, sixty percent for me, twenty percent for expenses, leaving the extra twenty percent for you, which, as you can imagine, is gonna be worth money of the kind that robber barons like Warner Quackenbush make. Anyway, I think that would probably be fair, and I would, of course, have the same deal with Miss Bantam." Again he tips his hat.

"So, now I guess I shouldn't keep you all waiting, but before I tell you the one thing that's gonna make you come aboard for the most fantastic thing ever before sprung on the American masses in the area of entertainment, just to make you all aware of how serious and dependable of a guy I am, and how much you all can trust me, I have taken the liberty of making the arrangements for your lodging at a fancy hotel right here in the district. I got a room there myself, and I got and paid for a suite for you and the bear, and a suite for Miss Bantam. You don't have to thank me for it, hell, er, that is heck, it's the least I could do. Now I don't want you thinking that you owe me nothing if you decide that you don't want me working in the capacity of you all's ahh...*entertainment agent*, then you just go ahead and enjoy your rooms at the hotel and I'll see ya all around, as they say. But, I'm positive sure that you're gonna want to pair up with me and my agenting, and now I'm gonna tell you the reason why:"—*Dramatic pause*—"I make moving-pictures!"

Daddy momentarily squelches the rap, lets the moving-pictures sink in, then with another gulp of air, "And now, and this is the most exciting part, I can make moving-picture shows like you never seen before. And, I can show them on screens the size of a double barn door, and I can take these here storybooks of yours and I can turn them into moving-pictures with you playin the parts of your own selves. And I'm including Miss Bantam here too. Why everybody knows bout her deeds. Heck, I will tell you right now I just happened to be out walkin a couple of hours ago and I seen for myself when Miss Bantam here," again the tip of the hat, "wrestled a wild horse to the ground and I'd bet my life right here and now, lots and lots of people with coins in their pockets would surrender them coins inna dash to see something like what I saw a couple of hours ago."

Daddy Smithy finds himself at the end of the pitch. He's out of things to say. It is time to close the deal. "So, what do you think? Just a couple of weeks of live performances and we would have enough to start a-makin moving-pictures."

Slab Pettibone looks to Bitch Bantam. "What do you

think, Miss Bantam?"

Bitch stifles a yawn. Too much has already happened. She's still grappling with freedom. "He sure can talk a lot," she tells Slab. "But I doan think I know what he's talkin about."

"That's quite all right, Miss Bantam. We will get you a good night o sleep and I'll explain everything tomorrow."

"How bout you, FuzzyWuzzy?" Slab asks his ursine buddy. FuzzyWuzzy grunts, huff huff. "I see your point, FuzzyWuzzy."

To Daddy Smithy, Slab says, "FuzzyWuzzy says he thinks twenty percent is plain stupid. He says that he thinks we oughta get seventy-five percent and the expenses be taken out of the gross."

Daddy Smithy is suddenly drained, ready to collapse, but his luck is changing, his pitch has worked.

"Done," Daddy says in regard to percentages. "What do you say we all head to the hotel so we can get this partnership generating first thing tomorrow? I trust that as trustworthy and honest men this is all that is required to seal the deal." He thrusts his hand forward to Slab. "Shake," he says.

"Hey, FuzzyWuzzy," Slab Pettibone says, "shake."

FuzzyWuzzy stands on his hind legs and shakes and shimmies. Slab Pettibone sits high in the saddle and doffs his sombrero.

Chapter Three

Quackenbush Manor

From his thighs to his neck Warner Quackenbush is round as a globe. His head sits atop his northernmost point like a pink snowball. He has asterisk eyes, a question-mark nose and steam-rolled ears. His pursed lips look ready to blow a tune. He stands four-foot eleven-inches, weighs two-sixty-three. He is fifty-three years old. Other than the blankets of blubber insulating his otherwise petite frame, he has not physically matured since childhood.

Warner suffers from a glandular condition known as Fröhlich's Syndrome, adiposogenital dystrophy, the result of both an anterior pituitary deficiency and a lesion of the posterior lobe or hypothalamus. The outcome is stunted growth, obesity and retarded sexual development. Warner Quackenbush is lodged in a pink prepuberty cocoon, like an editorial cartoon of a capitalist tycoon.

Warner's bed is vast, thick slabs of dark wood, a four-poster canopy. He wakes in the early morning and descends a step ladder to the floor. He waddles naked to a picture window where he looks out at a wide-screen panorama of BigCity and beyond to the new day. Warner shares this view with no one.

The retiring moon illuminates Warner Quackenbush's naked skin and shadows his fleshy craters. From a small round table, he picks up a gleaming silver spatula and begins slapping his flab. Red welts arise like despised birthmarks. This is phase one of Warner's morning disciplines. He has specific ideas regarding health and success and his enormous wealth and rosy cheeks validate these philosophies.

Warner Quackenbush began life wealthy. His father Wilhelm *Tabaccy* Quackenbush owned forty-two-thousand acres of tobacco land in Virginia. He owned three-hundred and sixteen Negroes. Business was good.

Warner, the first of two Quackenbush children, came into the world fat and lucky. His mother, Beauty Quackenbush, squeezed him out, like an obstinate pimple and swore she would never birth another. Tabaccy Quackenbush, however, was both horny and persuasive and thus Beauty found herself, six years later, once again with child. This time a daughter, Empress, was pushed into the world after which, to Tabaccy's dismay, Beauty steadfastly closed and locked tight her legs and never opened them again.

Little Warner was enlivened with foresight and brilliance,

yet physically he grew out rather than up. By six he controlled most of his universe yet he remained a beach-ball underfoot and unimposing. Looking to bring his eyes up to level, Warner commandeered a six-foot-six Swahili slave who carried the fat boy on his shoulders for ten years, before his back gave out. Warner was now imposing enough to go it on his own two marshmallow feet. Now, people bent to his level.

In his early teens, when other boys were sprouting facial hair and having nocturnal emissions, Warner's body refused to mature. He interpreted these faulty mechanisms as an act of grace, of purity. He would not be distracted by the carnality and corruption of normal striplings. He was destined for bigger things.

In Warner's sixteenth year, he joined his father in the tobacco business. In two years their acreage and profits tripled and their Negro population had been downsized to half. A smaller core of slaves works twice as hard under harsher disciplines, with fewer to feed. Warner bought more land. He became a millionaire before reaching maturity, which in fact he would never reach. Then the War Between the States started blowing bugles.

Wilhelm Tabaccy was a Southern gentleman who stood proud behind the succession of the Dixie states. Even if he had believed otherwise he had no choice. Abraham Lincoln was not giving consideration to the landowners with a financial dependency on slave labor. Leaving his teenage son to run the plantation, Tabaccy Quackenbush joined, as an officer, the Confederate Army. En route to his first battle Wilhelm Tabaccy Quackenbush fell off his horse, snapped his cervical spine, and died.

Warner, the avaricious entrepreneur, was quick to undermine his father's Southern patriotism. He opined that an America united offered the maximum profit. He believed that the future would come from the conquest and domination of foreign soil. A country divided would lose power over world commerce. Warner wanted access to that power. He knew that it would not come by way of the rebel yell.

Warner Quackenbush sided with the Unionists, thus becoming the most vilified individual in the South. He freed his slaves and gave money to the Union cause. His property was soon guarded and sometimes used as a headquarters for the Northern army. As the other tobacco plantations were dismantled by Lincoln's men, Warner bought up the properties, or in many cases simply took them over, putting his neighbors in the hands of their enemies.

As for the slave labor the tobacco growers had depended on, Warner simply employed them at a cost less than what he had previously paid to keep them alive and working. While a number of the newly emancipated took flight to the North, there were plenty remaining, as well as a whole new work force of poor whites. Freedom was often a penurious life of financial servitude to Warner's evil American empire.

After the war, Warner Quackenbush went into manufacturing and packaging. With his now enormous land-holdings in the south he moved to BigCity and opened massive cigar and chewing tobacco factories. His wealth grew like creeping kudzu. All this before his true genius took flight.

As Warner Quackenbush stands naked at the picture window, he dwells little on the past. He is a man of the future, a man of discipline, which is why he is now slapping, with the shiny silver spatula, his little prepubescent penis. Warner's lack of development insures that he will never ejaculate nor will his unmanly manhood grow beyond two dinky inches, nevertheless, he wakes each morning with a throbbing stiffy. And, each day he batters it down. Concupiscence is a fruitless distraction that Warner banishes from his life. He lies back on the plush carpet with his legs to the air providing a better shot at the useless grapes in his crumpled scrotum. He welcomes the thuds of pain. It is the lust and sex of men that makes them slow. That and the feces they allow to back-up into their brains. Warner Quackenbush maintains his brain with a daily spatula spanking and, more importantly, a ritualistic enema.

While the Civil War established Warner as a capitalist force to be reckoned with, the real stroke of fortune came with the Spanish American War. With an unflinching belief in the manifest destiny of the United States, Warner once again put his money on the winning nose. He paid for transport ships to carry fighting men, as well as artillery, guns, and horses, to Cuba. He even went along for the ride. In return for his generosity the United States Navy catered him, along with a horde of American journalists, to the front lines. From battle to battle Warner would sit on the nearest hilltop, in his favorite chair, watching the Spanish, the Cubans, and the Americans, kill each other. He had a ringside seat when the Rough Riders charged Kettle Hill. He clapped his hands with glee as media-hero Teddy Roosevelt, like a touchdown-making jock, nullified his quota of Spaniards.

When the winner was announced, Cuba was unbound from Spain, and in the hole to the United States. Warner wasted no time laying claim to the better tracts of land. While the new Cuban government was put into place, Warner simply appropriated the tobacco plantations as his own. He set up packaging plants and introduced the newly liberated but still impoverished Cuban work force to the American way. He established himself as the world's leading tobacco grower as well as top cigar and chewing-tobacco producer.

While other corporations attempted to cash in on the worldwide addiction to tobacco products, they were unable to compete with Warner's bottom dollar. He quickly weeded the competition and gobbled the struggling independents into the belly of American Quackenbush Incorporated. Warner Quackenbush now had riches beyond the dreams of kings and queens, yet still he was just warming up.

Warner sets aside his 24-carat slapping implement. Next to the window hangs a velvet rope. Warner pulls the rope three times. On the first floor a buzzer buzzes three times. Two kitchen maids wake the new enema girl from her cot in the servant quarters and usher her to the elevator. Warner's morning enema is a most important part of his day. It washes away the muddle of sleep, refreshes his brain, and disinfects his guts. Warner closes the window drapes.

There were still a few hold-outs selling their own brands of cigars, chaw-plugs, roll-your-own cigarette tobacco. Some were selling ready-made cigarettes. This was good for Warner. After all he pretty much owned all the tobacco grown and distributed. The other companies were buying raw product from him.

Advertising was in its infancy and market packaging did not exist. Newspaper adverts were seldom looked at and usually consisted of public notice displays or small campaigns for patent medicines. There were billboards that graced walls and wood fences: Coca Cola, Uneeda Biscuit. Eateries and dram shops displayed elaborate murals, seminude maidens with logo plugs for Miller brewing and Budweiser beer. Ready-made cigarettes were sold like sticks of candy in general stores. For the creation of his newest product, Signal Cigarettes, Warner concocted a plan.

Though he seldom ventured to social functions and never had social discourse with the lower classes, Warner had an acute understanding of human nature. People are lazy and stupid. They need to be told what they need. First Warner removed his name from the product. The masses love to hate the rich and anyone living in the south already hated the name Quackenbush. Plus, he wanted a catchy name, something that would hook into the public consciousness. The name Signal Cigarettes came to Warner along with a vision of an Indian Squaw.

This is how the package came together: Warner hired a team of artists. Rather than exploit them with slave wages, he hired and paid for the best. A picture was chosen, an American Indian squaw in a short fringe skirt and feather headdress, a campfire puffing puffs of smoke spelling Smoke Signals. These visuals began to appear everywhere along with catchy pop-culture jingles.

> *Injun Princess Name*
> *Running Bear*
> *Her Got Um No Clothes*
> *Just Pig-Tail Hair*
> *Smoke Signals*
> *10 Cents*

Now, the only thing missing was the cigarettes. While creating a demand for merchandise as yet unseen, Warner worked on the product. Most tobacco users either chewed chaws or smoked cigars. Warner needed to create a reason for these users to switch to cigarettes as well as a reason to begin tobacco use for the uninitiated. At great cost to the Signal Corporation, Warner put together a blend of tobaccos, burley, along with a strain his staff of scientists nursed into being. This blend in cigarette form was supposedly soothing to the throat with a sweet taste akin to prunes, and was said to aid regularity.

A cardboard package was designed to hold twenty ready-made cigarettes, along with an ingenious innovation, an inner-seal of wax-paper to keep the tobacco forever-fresh. Now, Warner was ready to unleash his product on the populace at large, almost.

The six-year-old enema girl has been pushed into the elevator to the third floor and instructed in the intricacies of opening the elevator door. As today is her first day, no one, least of all Warner Quackenbush, truly expects her to meet the task without difficulty. The orphaned children Warner has procured through the years are stupid and lazy with criminal hearts. They have to be watched at all times. They are, however, key to his success in business as in life. Warner can hear the fumbles of a child from within the elevator.

Heaven is a castle in the clouds. Inside are plush carpets, royal draperies, rainbow fairies from crystal chandeliers flutter through the air, golden framed gothic gods are slathered across canvas, peering down at Snooks Smithy, judging her withs dour expressions. Snooks figures she must be dead and strains to think back to the moment she died. She remembers pulling a demon out of Girl's tinkler. She remembers Daddy prying her from her sleeping sister's arms and carrying her, without words, without waking Girl, to the arms of a man in a tallyho-coach. Daddy told her goodbye then walked away quickly without turning. The man in the coach smelled of lilac water. He delivered her in the night to the gates of heaven.

A dour angel, in a white uniform takes Snooks by the ear and pulls her down long hallways to a large bathroom like nothing she has seen: Golden faucets with running water, a great white tub with ornate fixtures, cold marble floor, and a porcelain crapper with a flush chain. Snooks sits and shits and the angel gives her a clean rag to wipe with. She wipes her bum and then throws the rag at the angel. "Eat it; eat it, yum, yum, yum."

The angel smacks Snooks across the side of her head with the flat of her hand but Snooks refuses to flinch. The angel undresses Snooks and throws her clothes down a chute. She puts Snooks in the bath and scrubs, with soap and brushes, two years of grime until her little body is pink and hot. The angel dries her with thick towels scented like a rainy day. When she rubs a little too rough Snooks hisses and kicks at the angel. "Ouch, ouch, ouch, dumb butt." The angel gives Snooks a hard pinch on the thigh and Snooks grits her teeth. The Angel dresses Snooks in white muslin umbrella drawers, without ruffle or embroidery. She takes Snooks to a small room with bare walls, a single table with a kerosene lamp, a canvas cot, a lone blanket.

"You sleep here," she says. "Someone will wake you when it is time."

"No you sleep here, dumb-butt pig-nose," Snooks tells her. The angel closes the door and the room goes dark. Snooks tries to open the door but it's locked. She pulls the bedding from the cot and throws it in a corner of the room where, after a while of pacing, she settles and falls into a fitful sleep. Occasionally she growls and throws her arms and legs about like she's fighting her way to the surface of a deep well.

At first light a new angel, equally stern, wakes Snooks. "Come with me," she says. "I hear you're a troublemaker but you had better watch your step with me." She takes Snooks, half asleep, to a steel closet and pushes her inside. "When the car stops you slide it open with this," she demonstrates but Snooks does not comprehend nor does she understand the notion of vertical travel. The doors close with a pneumatic sigh and the closet hums and chugs. She guesses maybe instead of heaven she's going to Hell. The doors will open to fire and brimstone. The red Devil will be there, poking her with his pitchfork and Snooks is kind of looking forward to it.

Warner Quackenbush slides open the door and in his authoritative little boy voice says, "Get in here!"

Before Snooks stands the Devil.

Warner Quackenbush's naked body has fiery self-flagellated splotches staining the pink expanse. Other than his height, only a few inches taller than Snooks, Warner is everything she ever thought Satan would be. His face is without expression like a hydrocephalic child, but the skin is old, loose like dripping wax. He is hairless and smooth. His breasts are large and round like a woman's, yet his nipples are brown and tiny, much like Snooks's. His blubbery girth is balanced on short tree-stump legs. A dwarfish penis and nut sack dangle from between his thighs like a purple turkey wattle.

Warner Quackenbush is not Satan, though this not the first time the comparison has been made. Not even Prince of Darkness could devise a marketing plan as devious as Warner's Signal Cigarette campaign.

After six months of sowing Smoke Signal jingles, songs, and visuals into the consciousness of anyone not living in a cave, Warner delivered three million packages of Signal Cigarettes to the unsuspecting public, free of charge. Markets, dram shops, blind pigs, were stacked to the ceiling with the pocket-sized forever-fresh decks picturing the pretty squaw. They were in turn handed, one per customer, to anyone looking for a quick easy fix. After six months of ballyhoo everyone was looking to smoke a Signal. Newspaper kids were paid twenty-five cents a day just to pass out the freebies. Across the country bulging train cars and delivery wagons guaranteed that no man or child was left out. Everyone was sampling a Signal.

Financial experts predicted doom for the Quackenbush Empire, not even Warner Quackenbush's wealth could afford to throw money to the street. The front page of the BigCity Times headlined, WARNER QUACK'S UP. In political cartoons, Warner was an oblong Humpty Dumpty sitting precariously on a narrow wall of packaged Signal Cigarettes. The public inhaled free coffin-nails and waited for Warner Quackenbush to fall from the wall. But Warner never fell.

For those who already had a tobacco jones, Signal Cigarettes tasted better and smoked smoother than any other brand. Early on Warner had observed the addicting effects of smoking tobacco as well as the mild euphoria it produced. More importantly Warner had observed the euphoric and addictive effects of the period's more popular patent medicines, specifically the concoctions containing derivatives of opium and cocaine. Opium, his research found, along with being a downer, was costly in mass quantities, given to the climes where it was grown. And, because of its association with the Chinese, opium was fast becoming a yellow stain on the bottom of the white, xenophobic and patriotic, melting pot. Cocaine seemed the logical choice. It kept people up. It kept people happy. And, in small amounts it left people ignorant of its existence. Another million acres of productive land to grow the narcotic in South America was but a trifle. From American border to border and well beyond, everyone was puffing on gratuitous cocaine-laced Signals. And, for some reason, no one was content with just one.

When the price of a one-score deck of Signals went from free to a nickel, then from a nickel to ten cents, consumption did not go down as predicted by the naysayers. Everyone was smoking Signals, singing the jingles as they laid out their hard-earned ten cents. Warner Quackenbush is not Satan but has proven he is equal to the popular supposition.

Snooks refuses to come out of the moving closet. The round devil speaks, "Move on out here and do as you are commanded." He whips at her legs to move her forward with a leather crop. She grabs at it and tries to bite his hand. "Ouch, ouch, stupid fatty. I can see your peeney."

Warner herds her across the room through an open door into a room that could only exist in the Hell's afterlife. The ceiling, walls, and floor are white and seemingly made of glass. The floor is damp. Spigots and knobs, exposed pipes, flexible rubber hoses dangle from the walls, dripping water to the floor. In the center of the room, on the floor, a round drain. Next to the drain a low silver table with foot stirrups rising a foot from the edge. Above the table a large rubber bladder from which dangles a tube of three of four feet with a metal clamp fastened midway. Warner closes the door sealing them inside.

Twenty minutes later, refreshed from his morning ablutions, Warner dismisses Snooks, sending her back to purgatory on the vertical trolley. The chores she preformed for the little twisted tycoon amounts to depraved humiliation with the bar set high, but Snooks is immune to the negative aspects of humiliation; Snooks has passed through a distorted looking glass into a sadistic Wonderland, she feels right at home and looks forward with enthusiasm to her next encounter with the fat Devil.

Chapter Four

The Paramount Hotel

Once upon a time, in a dank corner of a backwoods blind-pig, chained to the wall, Bitch Bantam found a tattered reproduction of a palatial Arabic mosque. The image was covered with dog-shit which she wiped off with her hand. Dicey Deucey, Bitch's master, took the picture, tore it into pieces, threw it in her face and laughed at her distress. But the image remained. Bitch could close her eyes, in the idle hours of captivity, and ride a magic-carpet to the mosque, a kingdom of her imagination. There she had lady friends. They laughed together, drank tea and ate cookies. They wore golden bejeweled crowns. They hugged, cheek to cheek. The other world, where your hands stank of dog-shit was only a bad dream. Now, something strange and confusing has happened. Bitch Bantam is inside the foreign palace, her eyes are open and the nightmare is over.

The Paramount Hotel is BigCity's most luxurious. The rich and famous the extravagant and eccentric lodge in elegant and pampered comfort. The lobby has carpet thick as marsh grass, stout tables and armchairs, dark wood gargoyles. Hirelings in uniform cater and kowtow. Bitch Bantam's suite, living room, bedroom and bathroom, is a storybook illustration. Her door has a lock. Last night, alone for the first few minutes, Bitch stood clicking the lock, open, shut, open, shut, open, then a final click, locked. She sat on the floor in the center of the room and she cried.

It is through these tears that Bitch Bantam first saw herself in a full-length looking-glass. She stood a head taller than the stretch of oval reflection. She stooped and walked close to inspect herself, suspicious, as though sizing up a challenger, a stranger. She removed her ragged clothes. She was filthy and ugly with muscle and sinew, far removed from the refined ladies bustling about BigCity. Bitch is no lady, she's a pit fighting animal. She will never have a genteel woman as a friend.

The hotel room frightened Bitch, it was too otherworldly. She needed to look out at the solid world and ventured to the double-wide windows. Alas, through the window, three floors below, runs the busiest and brightest thoroughfare in the America, another Otherworld. Bitch was verging on panic when she happened to sniff in the air the scent of a friend. She opened the windows wide and stepped out to the fire-escape. Four windows and one fire-escape leftward FuzzyWuzzy was also feeling itchy. Slab was inside snoring soundly. FuzzyWuzzy needed the moon and stars to sleep. FuzzyWuzzy and Bitch found comfort in each other's company. They slept together yet four windows and one fire-escape apart, fitfully, through the night.

In the morning, before the light, Bitch goes back inside. At nine o'clock help arrives with a knock on the door. This is a first and she is not sure what to do. Still naked she wraps herself with a chenille blanket from the undisturbed bed and speaks meekly to the door, "Who is there?"

A friendly female voice says, "Maid service, Missus."

Bitch is as unfamiliar with maid service as she is with friendly female voices. She meets her fears and cracks open the door. The woman in the doorway lets out an involuntary whoop which in turn startles a whoop from Bitch.

The woman's name is Fritter McTwoBit. She composes herself and pushes open the door. She wheels in a cart piled with towels, sheets and soaps. She is tall and zaftig with soft rolls of hazelnut flesh. Her eyes are golden and her face is beatific and exotic. She smiles at Bitch and laughs for no reason, she says, "Yall be a crazyass sight fo sure, Sista. I'm here ta clean yalls room."

Bitch finds Fritter immediately likeable, though she is unable to do other than stare. She tries to smile, her mouth closed, hiding her ugly eroded teeth. "You doan haff to clean nothin, ain't nothin dirty. I stayed on the floor and dint touch nothin. I ain't even been in the other room."

Fritter forms a quick fondness for Bitch, for how could she not? White women at the Paramount seldom give Fritter more than a distasteful harrumph. In turn, Fritter seldom gives them more than a well-directed middle finger and a lugie in the silver tea service. Bitch Bantam, though, is no ordinary white woman. Fritter says, "My name is Fritter. What a yalls name, Sugar?"

"My name is Bitch Bantam. Everybody mostly calls me Bitch."

"Thas a toughass name, sista Bitch. When's the last time yall had a baff?"

"I washed in a river but I didn't have no soap, that was back some."

Fritter becomes saintly in the company of underdogs and innocence. "Know what we is gonna do Miz Bitch Bantam?"

Bitch has no idea what they are going to do but she's eager to find out. Fritter McTwoBit's manner promises fun. Bitch is nearly jumping in place with anticipation.

"I doan know...Fritter." This is the first time Bitch has ever addressed anyone by their forename, her emotions bursting. "What are we gonna do?"

"We gonna take yall inna that room you ain't been in yet and we is gonna give yall a baff. And, we is gonna wash and comb yalls hair. And we jus too crazyass girls gonna go and get prettied up like Saturday Motherfuckin night."

Fritter McTwoBit has other rooms to clean. Hanging out with Bitch Bantam jeopardizes her job, but she doesn't care. She's done working for rich honkies. Selling pussy at the grog dives is better than cleaning white-people rooms. Fritter will be fine without this hotel job and fuck em anyway. There is something about Bitch Bantam that is more immediate and more important than any job. Fritter takes Bitch's hand into her own.

Bitch is shocked and delighted by this friendly stranger's touch. Slab Pettibone and FuzzyWuzzy delivered Bitch to the doorstep of her daydreams. And now this jolly woman is ready to lead her through to the next transition. Bitch can no longer contain herself. She wraps her arms around Fritter McTwoBit and hugs. "Crazyass girls," she says a couple of times, "Crazyass girls."

"Sheeit, Sista Bitch," Fritter pinches her nose shut. "Yall gonna be all friendly, we gone haff to get yalls bigass in the bafftub real quick."

Fritter smiles at Bitch. Bitch smiles back, though she covers her teeth with her hand.

TumbleHouse

At eight in the antemeridian, TumbleHouse is no less quiet than eight in the postmeridian. Children crawl out of beds to strive through another day. Others crawl into beds, seeking a reprieve. Gulper Mooney hits wakefulness in the middle of a violent dream, at the inhalation of a scream. He crosses his arms and holds himself until he calms. He needs to urinate and has an erection.

Beside Gulper, woven in a muslin sheet, Girl is sleeping, naked to the waist. She is the prettiest girl Gulper has ever seen. Her smallish breasts are swollen with wasted milk. Fresh stretch-marks swim, like translucent polliwogs, across her soft belly. She wears these battle scars with grace, dignity and determination. Gulper is lovesick and unsure, he believes his swagger is his most attractive feature, yet he is in awe of Girl, as though he should garb her, kiss her, let her go, then run away.

Gulper quietly climbs from bed. He has his own quarters on the top floor, but has opted to stay with Girl. Later today he will move her to his room. In two more days, his dirty deeds done and paid for, they will be headed west, in style. Gulper takes the brass chamber pot from under the bed, makes it ring with a hard string of urine. He empties his bladder and his erection droops.

Within the polyphonic racket of a hundred kids arising and retiring, it is the singular tinkle of Gulper's piss that awakens Girl. She sits and looks at Gulper's broad shoulders, his working-man's back.

Girl is sort-of-in-love with Gulper, but her waking thoughts go quickly to concerns more immediate than Gulper Mooney. Snooks. Girl is invaded with nauseous pangs of anxiety. Snooks is slow and strange, she needs nurture and care. Girl feels the tremulous brunt of hardship Snooks might face and it takes her breath away. She has inherited Daddy Smithy's bugaboos, the nervous spells, the reproach of runaway thought. Her body flexes with nervous disorder triggering physical pain, the residual damage of childbirth. Girl needs a doctor, a pain killer, a mood enhancer, more rest.

Gulper turns and greets his sweet patootie, "Morning to yur, me sweetest Girl. Today yur to rest easy whilst Gulper Mooney serves yur the world." Gulper stands naked, his skin white in the window light, a paper lantern stained with rusty freckles.

Girl must love this blustery boy. She wants to hold him like her lost sister, like her lost BabyBoy. "I don't need rest, not until we have found Snooks. I can't rest, Gulper. Not yet."

Last night, before sleep, they professed everlasting love. Gulper knows Girl is his, for the keeping, but he is dismayed that her first words are not about his favorite subject, Gulper Mooney. "Iym Gulper Mooney, number one swell here bouts and anywheres else, see. I sez what me sez whens I sez it." He puffs his chest, struts standing still.

Girl sees Gulper's manhood requires stroking. "Come sit here with me. I want to feel you close to me. I wanna squeeze you and never let go."

Gulper moves to the bed. His cock refilling with turgid promise. He lies back like a king, waiting to be done as a king should be done, though what he really wants is to hold Girl in his arms, tenderly, like a newborn pup. Yet, here he is, pointing his tumid penis at her like he expects service with a smile. Gulper is awkward with sensitivity.

Girl puts her fingertips on Gulper's chest, tickles them downward. Gulper closes his eyes and thinks happy thoughts, altruistic tenderness.

Gulper's face is hard, battered, and even with his eyes closed, arrogant. Girl watches the flutters of skin and muscle where she pads her fingertips. Her hands are dirty, her nails chewed, broken and lined with grime. She needs clean clothes and a bath. She is sore and torn between her legs and needs to clean herself.

Gulper is afraid to open his eyes; afraid the pleasure will cease. He is powerless to do anything, afraid to even moan with pleasure as though it would show weakness.

Girl kisses Gulper on the mouth and reaches for his penis. There is much she needs to do, and so, she gets Gulper's immediate needs out of the way quickly and efficiently. "I love you, Gulper," she whispers into his ear. "I love you. I love you. I love you."

Paramount Hotel

Bitch Bantam sits through three tubs of hot water while Fritter McTwoBit, on a stool beside the tub, scrubs her with a stiff horsehair brush and a brick of rose-scented soap. Bitch is reborn. She's a rocket of exuberance. She has machine-gunned her life story to Fritter; she has even talked of her dreams.

Bitch is out of the tub and wrapped in clean towels, sitting on a plush padded stool. Fritter is behind her with a hairbrush with which she brushes away ten-year-old tangles in Bitch's squeaky clean hair. Now Bitch listens, like a best-girlfriend, while Fritter shares.

"I was born with mo brothers and sistas than I know how many. We lived in the ricketys over to CoonBorough. We never had no schools but I can read a newspaper. I been humpin for money far back as I remember. It ain't so bad. I like hard peters. They ain't nothing good in no man and they is all dickhead assholes. But, I still likes peters. Likes em big and long.

"This job here cleaning rooms is just about the first real job I ever had and I guess I probably ain't got this job no mo by now. But that doan matter, girlfrien, I doan like white people nohow. Cept you and you ain't no real white girl. I had two chillen that died, and I had me a buncha men. But, I got nothin much now, cept yall as my new best frien."

In a patch of silence Fritter continues to brush Bitch's hair. Both women trance out. After a while Fritter says in a soft voice, "I like to sing is what I like to do. Sometimes I sing for coins over to the colored gin-mills. I like singin bettern hard peters."

Bitch Bantam is realizing the extent her brain has been shut down, absorbing the punches like a simpleton. Now, her mind is buzzing. She's having ideas. She's creating her own future. She's rocking with excitement. Her body is clean and pink and smells of flowers. The minor pain to her head, as Fritter applies muscle to pull the brush through ropey locks, is pure pleasure. "Know what, Fritter? I gotta idear. I got a bag of gold and Mister Slab Pettibone tolt me it's worth least five-hundred dollars. If I share it with you, you can stay with me. An, know what else? Mister Slab and FuzzyWuzzy is in show business and there is this guy name Daddy that wants to put me an Mister Slab an FuzzyWuzzy to performing. Maybe you could sing songs and you could do performing too." She turns and looks at Fritter. Fritter has never seen such joy on a face. The future has never sounded so bright. Bitch Bantam and Fritter McTwoBit are busting with vibrancy that lights up the room.

TumbleHouse

Adelina Brown has an eight-by-ten still-camera atop a spindly tripod, aimed from her third-story window at a dramatic scene below. Seeking distraction from the guilty fact of yesterday's double killing on Sunshine Boulevard; she has applied her obsessive nature to a crash course in photography. From the magic wheelbarrow brimmed with state-of-the-art camera gear and supplies, Adelina found three plump volumes of instructions. She burned two oil lamps, reading through the night. Now she is readying her first trial run.

Adelina hides her head beneath a black cloth. She looks at an upside-down-reversed image, a group of well-soiled toddlers playing, running wild, screaming with youthful enthusiasm, along the toxic Dreck River shore. Adelina locks focus, closes the lens, cocks the shutter and sets the exposure at two seconds. She inserts the film holder, with a sheet of Kodak Pan, and then removes the slide. She waits. A hefty garbage-chugging hog plows into the picture frame. A boy, maybe five-years-old, carries a hand-me-down slug-shot, he swings it like a bolo and bloodies the hog's snout. The hog bites, fights and squeals. Adelina holds her breath, frees the shutter and makes the exposure.

Someone is knocking at Adelina's door, shave-and-a-haircut. Adelina returns the dark slide to the film holder. "The door isn't locked," she says. "Come on in."

Gulper bounces in like a pimp. Girl follows, cautious and quiet. Gulper smokes a Signal which has burned to the nub. He lights another with the cherry, drops the butt to the floor and snuffs it with his boot-heel. Adelina picks up the spent cigarette and throws it out the open window. "I've had this room to myself for a while now, Gulper. I keep it clean. I wish you'd have some regard for that."

It bugs Gulper that Adelina carps at him. It really bugs him that she is doing it in front of his girl, before he has even said anything. He spits on the floor with defiant flair. "What I does, I always does, see. An what's all this we ave?"

Girl likes the way Gulper scorns everything and everyone. She wonders if he will slap Adelina, show her who he is. Girl back-steps the conversation, inspecting the camera equipment and, with sly peeks, Adelina Brown. Adelina has no hips or bosom. She looks as though her branches would break in a strong wind. Her hair is done in a homemade Marcel that makes her head too big for her body. Her face is almost pretty and puffy from lack of sleep.

Adelina says, "You want to know what we have here, Gulper?"

"Yeah, ats what I said."

"Fuck you, Gulper. All this is what I have, Arsehole! Not we. SEE!"

Gulper does not approve of foul-mouth girls, he counters, "Would be mine if I sez so."

Adelina has known Gulper forever. She gives him zero tolerance. "Shut up, Gulper. You wanna talk big, go yell to the wind. What are you here for anyway?"

Girl is startled by Adelina's manner, but more so she is intrigued with the techno-gear strewn throughout the room. She says to Adelina, "Where did the cameras come from? Where did you get a moving-picture camera?" Girl treads to the bed where sits a Cinématographe motion picture camera. "This one here is a Cinématographe. How'd you come by it?"

Adelina does not care for Girl's forwardness, her questions. She says, "I don't know if it's any of your concern.

Why do you ask? And how do you know what kind of camera it is?"

Girl means no disrespect. She does not want Adelina as an enemy. Adelina has been nice to her, just as Dooley and everyone else at TumbleHouse have been. "Somebody took my little sister and my daddy probably knows who. My daddy makes regular pictures an sometimes moving-pictures. I thought that if you knew where all this equipment came from, it might help to find my daddy."

Adelina dials down her attitude. "Do you know how these camera's work?"

"Yeah, sort of, I could show you."

"Where did it come from?" Gulper asks.

"Two boys sold it to me last night. They liberated it but I don't know from whom. Second floor kids, Bug and Flopears." Adelina knows the names of all the kids at TumbleHouse.

Adelina is warming to Girl. "Why don't you go talk to them," she advises Gulper. "And while you're gone I can show Girl where she can clean up. And, I can help her find something nice to wear. And, why are you even here, Gulper?"

Girl's mind, as always, is on her sister, but a bath and clean clothes is an offer she will not turn away. She is beginning to admire the way Adelina stands to Gulper's wind. She is awed by Adelina's attitude, her smarts.

"Ave you seen Dooley?" Gulper asks Adelina.

"No. I think he went to see Shag Draper about what happened yesterday. In case you don't remember, two Midtown people were shot and killed. Somebody is going to have to pay the price and it's not going to be cheap. Personally I blame the whole thing on you, Gulper. But Dooley is the one who has to fix it."

Gulper is thinking maybe, in the next day or so, before he collects his blood money and leaves BigCity forever, he will knock Adelina on to her skinny butt. It is Adelina's influence, after all, that turned Gulper's best friend, Dooley Paradise, into a wimp.

"Like brothers we are, Dooley and me, but it was him what mucked up the pocket snatching. I saved his life, I did."

"You're a fucking idiot, Gulper. You and Dooley shouldn't have been picking pockets in the first place. I don't think this is something you and I can discuss. Why don't you go talk to Bug and Flopears, see what you can find out to help this girl? We have other things to do."

Gulper's face flares red. With his tangle of flame-orange hair, he resembles a struck match. Girl cannot help herself, she giggles. She takes him by the arm, leans in close and blows softly into his ear attempting to cool him down. She walks him to the door, tips to her toe-tops and kisses him full on the lips, says, "Hurry back."

Gulper walks out into the hallway, lights a cigarette and spits on the floor.

Duchy Hall

Shag Draper possesses crystal ball prescience. From his office at Duchy Hall, Shag is privy to all the grease and grime in the BigCity gears. If a local politico expires in a tragic fluke, Shag knows it before the final fact. Shag is the subcontractor of skullduggery for the powers that be, most irritating of these powers being Jones Mulligan.

Jones Mulligan runs the SnarlingTigers. He works with the BigCity mayor, Solly Gosterman, and police chief, Dempsey Moon. He rubs elbows with businessman Warner Quackenbush. Jones Mulligan has the glory. Shag Draper supplies the muck and muscle. Shag feels that the glory should be his and has hatched a plan to put things right. Unbeknownst to anyone, young Dooley Paradise is furthering Shag's cause.

Yesterday, Dooley Paradise and his second-in-command made a big mistake. No one has a clue that Shag paid Gulper Mooney to shoot a bystander, to set in motion Shag's master plan. That a BigCity matron and a SnarlingTiger were killed is a bonus. Shag Draper already knows the future of the Brusselsprouts, the SnarlingTigers, Dooley Paradise, Jones Mulligan, and BigCity. Shag Draper is quietly and methodically shimmying up the totem.

Shag takes his watch from his pocket, opens it and looks at the time. Dooley Paradise is due in five four three two one seconds. Three solid knocks on the door.

"Open it and follow yur nose."

Enter Dooley Paradise. There are chairs in front of Shag's massive desk but Dooley does not sit. It is uncomfortable having Shag Draper looking down at you, yelling, and Shag Draper yells a lot.

"Take a seat."

"Thanks, I'll stand."

"You will take a seat when I tell ya to. Or I'll throw ya through the window and break yur fecking neck. And, then, my friend, I'll make sure yur dead body lays there and rots so that everybody can see what can happen to an insolent brat!"

Shag Draper is a jerk. A very dangerous jerk. But, Dooley has only to bide his time. Dooley knows something of the future himself. Shag will never rise above his status, but Dooley will. No more than two, three years before Dooley is telling Shag what he can and cannot do. Dooley already has the ear of Jones Mulligan. Jones has plans for BigCity. He has plans to bring BigCity above the current level of corruption. Jones Mulligan, like his young disciple Dooley Paradise, has ideals and intelligence. Shag Draper has only brutality and misplaced ambition. Dooley takes a seat. He has no desire to go through the window.

Shag begins at a mid-tone, works up the volume as they go. "Twas yur little green hat chums what yesterday killed a SnarlingTiger. He was nay anyone important but still was a member of the Tigers. Someone must pay for his demise and yur the one takes heat for the green-hats. You are also, one way or the other, responsible for the death of Missus Wilhoit Brandonburger, a woman involved with a lace-pants group of reformers. Personally I hate the reformers, but Warner Quackenbush's sister heads this group and we would like to keep Mister Warner Quackenbush happy, because as you know, Mister Warner Quackenbush makes generous contributions to some of our own worthy causes." Shag takes a breath to let Dooley absorb the information. But since none of the information is news to Dooley and because he cannot help himself, he says, "Warner Quackenbush has never made any contributions to TumbleHouse. You'd think if he was someone we should care about he would be helping my cause."

"YUR CAUSE," Shag bounds from his chair. "Yur cause, you little pissant. You don't nay ave a cause, and real soon you won't ave a TumbleHouse..." Shag stops suddenly, sits back down, withholding information Dooley Paradise need not know. Shag sputters for a moment, says nothing.

Dooley knows, in this moment, that TumbleHouse is in jeopardy. He is suddenly very scared of Shag Draper.

Shag begins again, "Just never mind Warner Quackenbush and a clique of lady do-gooders. This is where we are, the police need someone in custody, and the SnarlingTigers need a confession and a lawful hanging. I'm not a hard fellow, Dooley. Mayhaps yur involved, mayhaps not. Either way, twas green-hats done the murderous deed, making you the one with debt to pay. I have meself pulled strings and padded pockets, making yur repent an easy one. I need a young body, dead or alive, though a live prisoner would the best be, as a confession is preferred, as well as guaranteed by our stout and trustworthy police force. Nevertheless, you will be needing to bring me a lukewarm body, which I can surrender to the proper authorities. The SnarlingTigers have agreed to accept this as payment-in-full. You should ave plenty of little arseholes around yur precious orphanage that are guilty of something anyway. I heard you got a new girl last night. I would think she is of no value. Make it easy on yurself and give her over. However you decide is all the same to me. Two days and nights is what yur granted. Tis not done by this time you will see a force of coppers at yur TumbleHouse door and yur very own name on a warrant. Is this understood?"

"Yes."

"Good."

Shag has geared down, has enjoyed yelling at the boy. He says, "I ave a luncheon appointment. Stay and enjoy the view if you want. But I would nay spend time fecking off, you ave work to do." Shag Draper leaves the room with a smiling face.

On Shag's desk is a telephone. Dooley picks it up, tells the operator, "8449 please." A few blocks away Jones Mulligan picks up the receiver and speaks into the mouthpiece, "Ahoy, Mulligan here."

"This is Dooley. Can you give me some time?"

"I will not be helping you Dooley me boy if this if about the unfortunate happenings yesterday. Tis not the way we work."

"I know that, sir. It's not about that, that is my problem and I will fix it, somehow. I wanna talk about TumbleHouse. Shag Draper has some kind of plan for TumbleHouse. I can't see any good in that."

"There has been nothing I ave been hearing, lad, but maybe I should be hearing something. BigCity's in trouble when Shag Draper knows things I don't know. I'll find out. See me tonight at nine o'clock and we can talk."

"Okay, thanks."

"Dooley, lad. Is this other thing going to be settled?"

"Yeah, one way or the other."

"I knew Sinclair Kissick. He was a good man."

"I'm sorry. Things just got out of control. I said I will fix it and I will. If I could bring back the dead, I would."

Dooley cradles the phone, walks to the window. Below, he can see Shag and his burly group of Mooks bullying their way down the plank sidewalk. Dooley sticks his index finger between Shag's shoulder blades and says, "Bang bang, you're dead." He blows the gunsmoke from his fingernail. He quotes a catch-phrase from his collection of Slab Pettibone adventure stories, "Yaaa hoop hoop hoop yahooey."

Paramount Hotel

Fritter McTwoBit has tossed Bitch Bantam's raggedy wardrobe into a rubbish chute headed for the Paramount Hotel incinerator. Fritter has outfitted Bitch's muscular frame in a snug maid's uniform of thin muslin. Bitch hunkers low to view her full length in the standing looking-glass, takes a jolt of flabbergast when she sees the woman looking back. Real time has shifted to cyber speed, Bitch knows not who she is. Fritter walks to Bitch's side, digs the twosome in the mirror, gives Bitch a friendly slap on her round rump, says, "Sista Bitch, yall too hot fo the oven, cause you be fryin in the pan."

In spite of Bitch's identity crisis, she's having fun. Bitch Bantam loves Fritter McTwoBit. Fritter is providing the happiest experience Bitch has ever had.

"Sheeit, Sista," Fritter points at their mirror images, "Ifn we ain't coupla whack bitches then I doan know nuffin." Fritter boogaloos her sexy bulk and sings a song. Bitch imitates Fritter and boogies along.

> "Doan want no hogs a rootin all round my ho
> Uh uhh, honey doan want dem hogs
> Rootin all round my ho
> Cause if de hogs keep a rootin the dogs
> Won't sniff round no mo."

Daddy Smithy, Slab Pettibone and FuzzyWuzzy, walk down the third-floor hallway of the Paramount Hotel. Daddy carries a heavy suit of piebald buckskin with fringed sleeves and a beaded bib-front, red stars and a yellow crescent moon, and a pair of matching boots. The hotel walls are in silk brocade, dark paintings and boastful gold-leaf frames. Scrolled wooden pillars hoist fabric awnings above carved walnut armchairs. FuzzyWuzzy stops to stretch his bristly body and buff his nails on a pillar. He yawns wide and voices a grumpy grunt.

Daddy Smithy freaks, "By Jesus, what's that cur doing?! Don't let him scratch the wood. This hotel has already cost me a fortune. I can't be billed for damages."

"A cur is a dog, Sir," Slab informs Daddy. "FuzzyWuzzy is a bruin. He just needs to take a minute here. He won't scratch up anything. He knows not to do that when we're indoors. He's just letting us know he would sooner be outdoors."

Slab is feeling a bit cooped as well, too many walls, too low of a ceiling. He needs to find himself and FuzzyWuzzy a place with elbow room, possibly not an easy task in this densely compacted city.

Slab would also like to ditch Daddy Smithy for a while. Daddy Smithy bugs Slab. Slab tolerates Daddy because he likes the show business rap. All management types are corrupt as a government treaty, but, Slab wants to see what this fella can do. He likes the idea of being on stage. He likes singing and dancing, playing his ukulele, telling tall tales. He will give Daddy some time, see what happens.

Daddy Smithy's compass needle is in a spin. He has a zillion things he needs to do and it is coming on noon. He has already rented a theater space on WhiteWay, hired a couple of cops for an afternoon performance and ordered a batch of hand bills and business cards at a print shop. As usual Daddy is overtaxing himself, flinging on extra blankets of anxiety.

Assuming he can talk Bitch Bantam into signing a contract he spent his final fifteen dollars to purchase, for her, a show outfit. Daddy is staking everything on little of concrete value.

In two days and one night, Daddy Smithy has spent two-thousand-five-hundred-dollars. Other than an empty theater (and that for only a week) he has nothing. The reason he has nothing is because he was robbed of his new moving-picture equipment. The cause of this effect is Bitch Bantam. Had she not created a stir on the street he would have never taken his eyes from his prize possessions. Bitch Bantam owes Daddy. The very least she can do is to perform on stage, maybe even wrestle the bear. Otherwise, Daddy is deep in debt to Warner Quackenbush who expects his vigorish on demand. Daddy has signed a risky dotted line. His hands shake as he breaks the seal of a new bottle of Doctor FixUp.

As this crew of three continues down the hallway, Slab's thoughts go to Bitch Bantam. Slab took on a responsibility when he rescued Bitch from the white slavers. From his point of view Bitch Bantam is as fine as any woman ever lived. She needs help finding her way and for that matter finding herself. Slab has a big mushy spot for Bitch Bantam, much like he has for his bear. He will help and watch over her and expects nothing in return.

The two men and the bear stop at door number three-zero-five. Daddy Smithy knocks.

Fritter McTwoBit opens the door. She's laughing and grooving to a ragged beat only she hears. "Goodday, mister mens. What be yalls bidness? Yall here ta see Miss Bantam?"

Daddy Smithy, Slab Pettibone and FuzzyWuzzy are struck dumb. Slab can hear Bitch, giggling behind the door frame. He is dismayed that it hasn't been he to egg these delightful trills from Bitch Bantam.

FuzzyWuzzy also hears Bitch, his friend, and wants to play. He noses his nose through the doorway past Fritter. Fritter to everyone's amazement gives his snoot a friendly thwack. "Caint come in till yall been nounced by me, Mister FuzzyBear."

FuzzyWuzzy looks at the big brown woman. He takes a couple of her fingers with his lips and gives her hand a shake, Howdy-do.

Daddy Smithy needs another drink of celery malt. Blender-blades are spinning in his gut. He knows not who this happy maid is, but she best not be getting her meathooks into Bitch Bantam, at least not before he gets his percentage. He needs to get the meaning of all this and fast.

He begins, "Would you please relay to Miss Bantam that the esteemed Daddy Smithy and Mister Slab Pettibone are here requesting her presence."

Fritter laughs at Daddy's manner. "How bout the bear, bro?"

"The bear?"

"I gots to nounce the bear too."

"Would you please relay to Miss Bantam that the esteemed Daddy Smithy and Mister Slab Pettibone as well as Mister FuzzyWuzzy are here requesting her presence."

"Yo, Sista Bitch. Two men and a Fuzzybear come a callin." She opens the door wide and steps back for the threesome to enter. Again the men are dumbfounded.

Bitch Bantam's make-over has uncovered a vision of beauty. The maid's uniform is sleek and tight and emphasizes every curve. Her hair is clean, shiny as sunlight and shoulder length. FuzzyWuzzy sniffs the air; Bitch has lost some of her tasty scent. Daddy Smithy, on the other hand, is greatly relieved that Bitch Bantam has washed away nature's scent. It is bad enough with the bear and Slab Pettibone who probably washes only once a year. Daddy is also pleased to see that she had dispensed with her rags, even though the maid's uniform will never do. He has properly invested the last of his coinage on the piebald buckskins. Bitch Bantam will make a splendid stage appearance, like a female Buffalo Bill Cody.

Slab Pettibone has a stiffy. It was bad enough trying to hide his lust from Miss Bantam trying to think of her in a sisterly fashion, now he has another big magnificent woman to contend with. The sassy Fritter McTwoBit has drained his brain and pressurized his dingus like a shook bottle of seltzer. Even though his erection hides below FuzzyWuzzy's fur line, Slab turns red from embarrassment. He takes off his floppy sombrero and holds it over his heart. To Bitch he says, "Miss Bantam, you look a lady o distinction. I am at your service."

"Sheeit, Sugarplum," Fritter says to Bitch. "Man be at yalls service. If this ain't the most crazyass thing I ever seen, and I seen some damn crazyass things."

Slab gets a stab of hurt; this luscious honey of a woman has called Bitch Sugarplum. Oh, what he would give to call a woman Sugarplum. He addresses Fritter, silently, Sugarplum-Sugarplum-Sugarplum.

Daddy is ready to get down to business. "May I inquire as to who you would be?" he asks Fritter McTwoBit.

Fritter has made a vertical move, befriending Bitch Bantam. Here she is getting respect from an obstinate white man and Bitch, it seems, is the prize everybody wants in on. Fritter is thirty-three and has born two children - neither lived beyond a year. Bitch Bantam is a child more durable than an infant yet just as vulnerable. Fritter has signed on as full-time surrogate mom.

"Who I be? I be Miss Toughass Bantam's personal adviser. Who be you?"

"I'm here, along with Mister Pettibone to discuss business with Miss Bantam..."

Slab interrupts, "That isn't entirely true, Miss Bantam. I'm here to let you know that you should do just what you want to do. Ifn you'd like to maybe work with me and FuzzyWuzzy along with Mister Smithy here, then that's just as fine with me as not. Me and FuzzyWuzzy are here to help you, whatever you wanna do. You got some money now, and if you don't feel like doin nothin except to get a quiet place somewheres I'll sure enough help you out. But, I just want you to remember, you don't owe nobody nothin."

Daddy Smithy wonders whose side is this sawed-off man on? What the hell is he trying to do? Of course Bitch Bantam owes him something, cripes, had not she been responsible for his loss of equipment? What the hell is wrong with these people?

Bitch has so far said nothing, has watched instead the play before her. She has spent her life watching brutal men of low character lay out her future without so much as a look her way. Now, here she is transformed to a woman of freedom and even some wealth. And everybody is still making her plans for her. Daddy Smithy is the easiest to understand, he's a shithead. Slab is the enigma. Slab Pettibone is a man, and men are evil. Only thing Bitch can figure is maybe when a man loses something, in Slab's case his legs, it changes them, makes them so they are not shitheads anymore. She can see that Slab is trying to help her make her own decisions. But, he is never-the-less trying to control her concerns. Also, Bitch is starting to notice a part of Slab Pettibone that he has not lost, the simmer of sex near steaming out the top of his smokestack sombrero. She hopes it will not hinder their friendship.

Bitch as well ponders the other new presence in her life, Fritter McTwoBit. Fritter, like Slab, wants to protect Bitch from the evils of the world. It is nice having people who suddenely want to watch over her, but, Bitch is a quick study. In a night and a day she has morphed into a real person who wants to pull her own strings.

Bitch Bantam tells Daddy Smithy, "I'll do your show jus like Mister Pettibone and FuzzyWuzzy, and you kin pay me jus like Mister Pettibone an FuzzyWuzzy. But I won't sign nothin. I got no contract with nobody. You jus make sure I get mine jus like Mister Pettibone, an I kin wrestle FuzzyWuzzy or do whatever I'm aposed to do. And, my frien here is Miss Fritter McTwoBit and she's a singer and you gotta find a place for her in your show. And, that's what you gotta do."

This is not what Daddy Smithy had hoped for, but it is close. He holds out the buckskin costume and boots, says, "You need to wear this, the maid's uniform is not right. And, you'll have to learn to trust me on matters of business. I know best."

Bitch likes wearing the dress. She has never worn women's clothes before. She has never looked like a woman before. She looks at Slab Pettibone and solicits his opinion.

Slab knows full well that Bitch needs to ditch the dress for the cowgirl getup, showbiz is, after all, showbiz. But, dadblamed if he has ever seen a sight like Bitch Bantam in a tight thin dress. Sadly, he nods conformation to Bitch. "I'd have to agree with Mister Smithy, Miss Bantam."

Bitch takes the armload of buckskin show-duds.

"Now, Miss Bantam," Daddy proceeds. "I understand that you may not feel comfortable about signing a contract. But, it's for your own protection. As your manager I'm just trying to look out for your best interest."

Bitch says, "No contracts, period."

"Okay." Daddy remains unflappable, even though his insides are flapping away. "No contract. Now, we should discuss for a moment, Miss, I'm sorry I didn't get the name, your ahh... friend."

Fritter hardly needs Bitch to do her negotiations. She can talk just fine. "Fritter McTwoBit, be my moniker. Yall go head and talk, mista Daddy."

"For starters, Miss Fritter, you'll need a costume, something with feathers would work nicely."

Fritter looks to Bitch who gives a nod that says, no problem, we can buy a costume. Daddy takes in the gesture as well. "Alright, next, and you have to understand I have never hired a singer before without first hearing her sing. And, it could be a problem, you being a nigger an all. We'll have to look into that aspect."

Slab interrupts, "This here woman friend o Miss Bantam's is a woman o color to you and to everybody else. There ain't no reason to use that other word."

Bitch told Fritter something of Slab Pettibone's unusual sensitivities. Now Fritter sees with her own eyes and hears with her own ears that indeed Slab Pettibone is unique to the gender.

She takes a long look at Slab; he sits tall on the bear's shoulders. He's kind of good looking in a backwoods peckerwood sort of way. She gives him a smile that reinstates his bashful blush and throbs his hard but hidden wiener.

Daddy Smithy is aghast. Why, if Slab Pettibone wants more fame and money, does he not work with Daddy, as opposed to making everything harder? Daddy suddenly needs to defecate. His bowels hurt like a nail in the navel.

To Bitch and Fritter, Daddy says, "Ladies, I beg your pardon if I have used offensive language. I shall watch myself in the future. One thing more to get through here and I'll leave everyone alone for a bit. I have much to do, and, I hope you realize, much of what I do is toward your future and well-being." Daddy takes a business card from his pocket. He had waited at the printers for the first twenty or so cards, so he would have something to go calling with. He hands the card to Slab Pettibone. "This address is the theater where we will be working, all of us. It is of utmost importance that we all are at this exact address today at two o'clock for a little impromptu performance. I have even hired a couple of coppers as shills to help us get some needed publicity. Can I count on you for that?"

Slab scratches between FuzzyWuzzy's ears. He can tell that FuzzyWuzzy is tired of contract negotiations. He wants to go outside. He wants to roll around in the dirt with Bitch Bantam. He wants to scratch the bark off a tree. He wants lunch, maybe some grub worms or a tasty dandelion salad. Slab looks at the card:

> THE HONORABLE DADDY SMITHY ESQUIRE
> MOVING PICTURE SHOWS & LIVE ACTS
> 500 NORTH WHITEWAY, BIGCITY

"We will be there," Slab says, after looking to his contemporaries and receiving affirmative nods. "Two o'clock."

Daddy is now in a hurry to get out of the room, out of the hotel, into the nearest privy, outdoors or in. Magma boils in his intestines, ready to erupt. He could use Bitch's bathroom but feels it would be improper. He could run to his own room, but he has checked out already which brings to mind another small detail. "Miss Bantam," he says, "I'm sure that you're probably feeling beholden to me after the way I have provided you with this luxury room, but, don't give it another thought. I was just happy to do it. However, now that we're all in this business together I think it best if you checked out of this room and found a nice but less expensive place to stay. I'd be happy to pay for your lodging any place you find but, for the moment, it might serve our enterprise better if you were to use your own money. That is, unless I'm mistaken. You do indeed have money?"

"Yes."

"Fine, fine. Then I guess that's all settled for now and I just want to say I'm looking forward to a long partnership as well as friendship. And, though, I'm not usually a man of emotion, I'd like to say that I'm feeling a bond of friendship here." He wipes a faux tear from his eye. "And, now I bid you all a fond farewell, until two o'clock." Daddy makes a quick bow and hastens from the room, runs down the hallway taking long pulls from his bottle of patented poppy-juice.

FuzzyWuzzy opens wide and voices a near human sounding cry. Time to blow this place for the great outdoors. Slab is at a loss for words, in this room with the two ultra sexy women. He hangs his head in thought. He needs to get

FuzzyWuzzy some fresh air. He needs to lead Bitch Bantam to the nearest bank exchange where she can cash in her gold for paper money. He needs lunch. He needs to help the women as well as himself find lodging. He needs to get moving.

Bitch is also a bit lost, after her outpour of speech with Daddy Smithy, her head is swelled with pride. But, she's not too sure of what comes next.

Fritter McTwoBit is having the time of her life. "Tell yall what be, Miss Toughass Bitch, yall go head in the other room an dress up in that fancy costume, whilst me an Mister Slab an Mister FuzzyWuzzy, gets acquainted."

Bitch Bantam takes a long look at herself as a woman, in the standing mirror, then goes to the other room and closes the door.

Slab looks at FuzzyWuzzy's back, but what he sees in his mind's eye, is Bitch Bantam in her form fitting dress. He shakes that image only to replace it with another visual, this time Fritter McTwoBit, naked. Tarnation, he wishes he could control his sinful thoughts. He is painfully aware of the silence in the room. He is aware of Fritter McTwoBit watching him. "What kind o songs do you sing, Miss McTwoBit?" he asks, without looking up.

"I sings em all, an yall can call me Fritter and I be callin you Slab and maybe sometime Sugar."

Slab Pettibone looks up for a brief moment. Fritter McTwoBit winks at him. He quickly lowers his gaze. Once again his penis is blimped. FuzzyWuzzy stretches his height, bumping Slab Pettibone's Sombrero on the ceiling.

Chapter Five

Tumble House

Ceiling-high ground-level windows put tiles of light onto the basement/schoolroom floor. Six days a week at one o'clock Adelina Brown reads stories to a group of Brusselsprout kiddies. She has been reading of late a new book by Stephen Crane, *Maggie, A Girl of the Streets*. Adelina chooses the books at a Sunshine Avenue bookseller. Her choices are most often sociopolitical.

Dooley Paradise prefers adventure stories, Jack London, H.G. Wells, or pulps, Slab Pettibone, Horatio Alger. But this is Adelina's class and Dooley trusts her judgment better than his own. In fact, Dooley needs more like Adelina at his side and less like Gulper Mooney. Like his mentor Jones Mulligan, Dooley is finding less need for soldiers, more for leaders and organizers. BigCity's orphans should not be drafted into homefront wars. War puts them at mercy to those who are stronger, which when you are a child is just about everyone. Book-learning will plow the route out and pave way the status quo. Dooley needs to delegate and organize his troops, forge beyond survival skills and Fagin-schools. He needs to legitimize the orphanage and straighten himself out.

Dooley takes the steps down to the basement classroom which is also a storage room, Barrels of spiderbite are stacked beside the blackboard. No one is there. This is a puzzle, Adelina and the kids should be here. Dooley goes back to ground level, two steps at a time.

The TumbleHouse main-room is quiet. No one is at the bar, though Zeph Riley is tending. In the back, a group of young mothers with toddlers, sewing and mending, playing quiet games and tending their young. Dooley walks to the bar.

"Hey, Zeph, how you doin? You seen Adelina or Gulper?"

"Fair to cloudy, Bossman. Lina took her class to the roof. Gulper and the new chickie went off somewheres a while back."

"You talk to the new girl?"

"Nah, Gulper's got her surrounded." Zeph does mediocre impressions, "She tis me girl, see, cause Iym Gulper the big tough guy, see. And when I farts I stinks, see."

"Shag Draper thinks I should give up the new girl for what happened yesterday."

"Gulper Mooney will nay see that happen."

"Yeah, I know. I wouldn't do it; she didn't do anything. You know anyone that deserves to grow old and die in the Tombs? I need a sacrificial orphan."

"I ave heard there is a bad duck on a rage at the SodomHeights docks. I shall keep me flaps and peepers alert."

"Thanks. As long as I'm here how about pouring me a bite?"

"The bite ye shall have." Zeph bends a bottle of venom over a shot glass and imitates the sound as he pours, Bllubb paloopp paloopp.

Dooley takes the shot like a punch in the nose, says Sayonara to Zeph then walks upstairs. His gait has slowed and acquired a sway. He snaps his fingers and becomes invisible. He snaps his fingers again and he can float through the air. He goes quickly to Shag Draper's place and floats unseen around Shag's head stinging him with stingers taken from his bag of bumble-bees.

Dooley climbs the ladder up through the hatch accessing the roof. His head arrives first. To the south, all manner is squat, haphazard, inebriated. Horseshit byways. Dead trees. Slouching daub-and-wattle houses. Swayback steeds, whipped forward by brokeback peddlers. Everything is brown.

On the roof pigeons coo and flap about, whitewashing the rooftop floor as though they own the place. Twenty kids from seven to seventeen sit on the tarpaper covering, powwow style. A young girl of seventeen, Mabel Scott, sits reading aloud from Stephen Crane. Mabel has been with TumbleHouse for two years. She shows promise and leadership skills. She takes on extra work including reading to the other kids. All present steal sly peeks at Dooley, the bossman.

At the northwest corner, Adelina Brown looks through the viewfinder of a tripod mounted Cinématographe moving-picture machine. Her right hand turns the film crank. She looks through a rectangle view of the Dreck River and beyond to the spires and domes of City Hall, the Anglican cathedral, the towering skyscrapers of BigCity commerce. At the right edge of the viewfinder industry smokestacks spew ash into the ozone. At the center she can see airborne smoke rings from the Signals Cigarette billboard.

> *Injun Chief*
> *Smoke Peace Um Pipe*
> *Him Sleep All Day*
> *Live Lazy Life*
> *Smoke Signals*
> *10 Cents*

Adelina interprets the finished product in shades of silver. She stops cranking, turns and spies Dooley Paradise and smiles. She is happy to see Dooley, though apprehensive due to the events of the day before. Beyond all else, Adelina is into her filmmaking. She has found her calling as well as a vehicle of expression and obsession.

"Hi Lina," Dooley smiles back. "What have you there?"

"It's a motion-picture machine. I'm making a motion-picture. I look through the viewfinder, that's what the thing is called that you look through, and I can see more than just what I usually see, as though I can capture meaning for the first time. It's kind of hard to explain. But, what I'm doing is going back and forth between the kids' faces to different parts of BigCity. I'm trying to make a document of what is here along with my opinions. I want to change what people think about the proletariat with images that demand truth."

Dooley's politics are strictly local. "Sounds pretty ambitious, Lina. Most people are too stupid to change what they already think. Anyway, I'm having kind of a hard time following you." He steps closer to the camera for a better look. "How's it work?"

"The film is inside here. You have to process it with chemicals in a light-tight room. Then you show it on a white wall with a gaslight projector. I have one of those too."

"Oh. Where did it all come from?"

"A couple of Sprouts, Bug and Flopears, liberated it on WhiteWay. I paid them for it."

"How come you know so much about it?"

"It came with instruction books. I stayed up and read all last night. And the new girl, Girl, she knows all about it."

"Oh. You talked to her? You seen Gulper?"

"Gulper's in love. He and Girl are on a mission to find her missing sister."

"So I hear. I guess he already forgot he killed a guy yesterday and I'm in a world of trouble because of it."

"I think Gulper Mooney is a fucking idiot, I always have," Adelina says. "But I don't think you should be blaming him for something you were in just as deep as he. The worst of it is that I was there too, and for that I blame myself but I blame you too, Dooley. You put me there in the middle of your goddamn mess. You and your asshole idiot playmate Gulper."

"Yeah, okay, Lina. You're right. I'm wrong. Sorry I brought it up. I was stupid. I can admit it a thousand times and it doesn't change the problems we have now. Shag wants a live body for the coppers. I'm supposed to just hand over some poor sap for the police to molest."

"You shouldn't be making deals with Shag Draper and you shouldn't be making deals with other people's lives."

"It's not like I had a lot of options, Lina. Tell you the truth I've been having trouble figuring a way out of this whole mess. And I keep seeing it over and over in my head. I almost got myself killed and I watched two people die and it was my entire fault. I keep imagining that I can go back in time like in a Slab Pettibone story and change the outcome."

"Jesus, Dooley. I don't want to make this harder for you and I don't want to be angry at you and I don't want you to get angry at me, but I've got to say this: Maybe if you weren't so filled with shots of spiderbite you could keep your thoughts in the real world where they do the most good."

"This isn't the time for that, Lina! Let's just save that one for later, alright?"

Mabel Scott has stopped reading. She and those under her tutelage are watching and listening to Boss Paradise and Adelina Brown. Dooley looks their way. Mabel turns back to the book and reads aloud. The kids turn their attentions to Mabel. Dooley and Adelina lower their voices.

Dooley says, "I'm sorry I got you involved. You shouldn't have even been there. You should have been here running things, we both should have been here running things. It was my fault for letting you come along."

Dooley is under the impression that he is apologizing and is therefore flummoxed by Adelina's next outburst.

"It was your fault for letting me come along? Is that what you're saying? You're the one that tells me what I can and cannot do? Maybe you should have listened to me in the first place and none of this would have happened! Maybe you shouldn't have put yourself in harm's way so I wouldn't have had to get involved by saving your stupid life. Maybe you should just go to fucking hell!" Adelina has gone red faced. Tears spill onto her cheeks. She is having difficulty breathing.

Dooley wishes he had never climbed up to the roof. "I'm sorry, Adelina. You're right about everything. I gotta go. I'll see you later." Dooley turns to walk away.

"Dooley," Adelina whispers then speaks again with a bit more verve, "Dooley."

Dooley stops and turns. "Yeah, Lina?"

"I'm sorry I got so angry."

"Yeah, I know."

"Can I come to your room tonight and listen to music?"

"Yeah, that would be great. I gotta see Jones Mulligan at nine. I'll be back by ten or so."

"Okay."

"Bye, Adelina."

"Bye, Dooley."

Dooley takes the ladder down to the floors below. Adelina walks to the group of kids. "Don't stop reading," she tells Mabel Scott. "You," she says to a ten-year-old girl, freckled cheeks like pinpricks of blood, a world of worry on her brow. "Come with me for a minute." She takes the girl and stands her about six feet from her moving-picture camera. Just stand there for a minute, she tells the girl then swivels the camera on the tripod. She frames the girl's head and shoulders in the viewfinder. "Just look at me," she says from behind the camera. The girl looks into the lens. Adelina turns the crank and records the hardship and stress on the little girl's face.

Orpheus Theater

The Orpheus Theater sits at the bottom of WhiteWay, just above the border of Division Street, dropping down into ScourgeTown. The better theaters replete with the more opulent productions and refined theatergoers are a half-mile north. Daddy Smithy prefers the more rambunctious clientele; they are better attuned to his mode of entertainment.

Inside the Orpheus Theater, Daddy Smithy has found a wobbly picnic table. He walks backward and pulls it, legs scraping the floor like a staccato tuba solo, from the stage and through the gallery, then outside. He sets the table below the empty marquee at the front entrance. He climbs to the tabletop, stands looking out at the hats, the ticket-buying public. Showtime is near. Daddy bolsters his courage to assault the pleasure-seeking sidewalkers, COME ONE! COME ALL!

Daddy is surprisingly calm for a man who is seldom calm. He's Zenned into the windup, suppressing his depressing obsessing. He ignores the anxious cankers that munch his brain and instead pumps himself with the power of positive thinking. He says to himself, "If I can put a show together in a couple of days, I can be making some dough. No, that is not right," he corrects himself. "I will put a show together in a couple of days and I will be making good dough. I will I will I will I will."

Daddy Smithy looks to the southeast, then looks at his

watch. His performers should show soon as he's ready to pull the switch and shout out the pitch. He wishes they would hurry. It is getting near three, he did say three o'clock, or two? Shit, he did say three, didn't he? My Christ, he's losing his head again. It was three o'clock! They will be here soon!

All stripes of type zip past Daddy Smithy's knees. He looks down at their heads and wills himself to equate the hats as dollar sign$. His stomach is beginning to hurt and he suddenly needs to pee. He finds some relief when he sees, across the throughway, the two coppers, Wilbur and Wilbur. Daddy has hired these two as shills. He gives the two eggs a nod, then takes from his pocket a bottle of Doctor FixUp and chug-a-lugs a couple of slugs.

Wilbur Good and Wilbur Szedvilas have just finished a thirty-six-hour shift as BigCity's finest. Earlier this morning while patrol-strolling WhiteWay they noticed a new tenant had taken residence at the Orpheus Theater. They stopped to welcome Mister Daddy Smithy to the boulevard and to explain the intricate workings of police protection, ten dollars a week. Daddy reasoned, to the most reasonable coppers, funds were momentarily scarce, but, if they were to help him launch his show and garner a little publicity, he would happily pay them triple their asking price after closing time this coming Friday night. Wilbur and Wilbur assume they can trust the little man with the squished fedora to pay up, after all, he knows they are men of violence.

Wilbur Good grumbles, as he just wants to get his money and go home. Wilbur Szedvilas is stoked, eager to make his show biz debut. Wilbur Szedvilas says to Wilbur Good, "Me thinking yuz shoe be unlaced, Wilbur me friend."

Wilbur Good is not going to fall for that, he's way too smart for that one. Rather than look down at his shoe he looks up to the sky. "Bgolly, in the sky I spies a Merican Eagle burddy."

Wilbur Szedvilas knows that Wilbur Good is too smart to look at his shoe. Rather than look upward at the fictive burddy he stomps his boot-heel on Wilbur Good's toes. Wilbur Good lets out a hoot and hops about holding his stomped foot in his hands. They both guffaw and Wilbur Good swears a good-natured revenge.

Across the way it strikes Daddy Smithy that he hasn't clued Slab Pettibone and Bitch Bantam in on the act with the coppers, or maybe he did, he can't seem to remember. He wonders if he has screwed up again. He takes another drink of celery-malt. To his left he sees a crowd, like a dust cloud, billowing around his stars, coming his way. He clears his throat of malty phlegm. He practices deep breathing and begins his countdown.

It seems that everywhere Slab Pettibone and FuzzyWuzzy, Bitch Bantam and Fritter McTwoBit walk in BigCity they collect a swarm of vicarious thrillseekers. Men and boys traipse in and out of their swath like matadors, vying for a hello from Slab or a furry pat of FuzzyWuzzy's hindside. Always at the front of this queer parade Slab Pettibone sits high on FuzzyWuzzy's shoulders, and at times removes his sombrero and waves to the gadabout stew. He plunks his ukulele and entertains with witty ditties. Now and then he tosses out his Round-Tuit coins, says, "Glad to meet you, been meaning to get a Round-Tuit." He leads his loyal troupe, Bitch, Fritter, and FuzzyWuzzy, through the confusion and apprehension.

Slab is high, as if the oxygen in his stratum is speedy

pure. He has been busy and now he's ready to have some fun. Earlier he escorted Bitch Bantam to the local exchange where a cashier weighed the gold and offered six-hundred and twenty-three dollars which Bitch took in cash and trucked away.

From there they moved onward to lodging. At Slab's request Fritter McTwoBit led them south to the north edge of CoonBorough. Slab prefers this atmosphere; he regards the colored folks as neighborly types. Also, the area provides more open space. Bitch Bantam as well as FuzzyWuzzy needs outdoor space. Slab followed his instinct to a dead-end dirt road where two pre-Civil War two-story houses stand ill-repaired but sturdy behind a white-picket fence. The house on the left, 33 KeroseneRow, has a barn in the backyard and a few acres of woods behind the barn where FuzzyWuzzy can roam. Slab paid the owner of both places, an old Gael who owned much of the neighborhood, eighty-seven dollars to purchase the house on the left for himself and FuzzyWuzzy. Bitch paid the same guy eighty dollars for 35 KeroseneRow, for herself and Fritter. Both houses are unfurnished but have coal burners for heat, a pump for well water, a wood stove, and a two-hole privy in the backyard.

Before trekking upward to WhiteWay the group stopped at a CoonBorough chopjoint, where Fritter sang a couple of racy songs to the rowdy clientele. They have eaten well and are in celebratory moods. Now, for Slab anyway, the best part is the upcoming performance. He can see, a short distance from his elevated seat, Daddy Smithy, also elevated. It looks as though Daddy is winding up a pitch. Slab hopes Daddy has some genuine talent, all he has shown so far is a healthy line of baloney. It is apparent that Daddy Smithy is a fellow of shallow scruples and likely a virtuoso screw-up. But Slab can see that Daddy Smithy is driven with ideas and prone to work twenty-hour days to launch a show with pizzaz.

It is the two women that perplex Slab. Bitch Bantam and Fritter McTwoBit are more complex than Slab's male/female ciphering abilities. Slab wishes he could find a book somewhere that would explain how exactly a woman works. All he understands about Fritter McTwoBit is she gives him a perpetual boner. Slab takes off his sombrero and gives Daddy Smithy a wave. He gives FuzzyWuzzy a hardy scratch between the ears and adjusts his tumescent penis.

FuzzyWuzzy is in a pretty good mood for a bear surrounded by stinky humans. He enjoys the songs and dances with Slab and he especially likes the two new women in his life, Fritter, who gives him funny hugs and pats, and Bitch Bantam, who wrestles with him like he wrestled with brother and sister cubs many years before. Not that FuzzyWuzzy really remembers his cub-hood but the feeling has been reactivated in his bruin brain.

Above all else, FuzzyWuzzy endures the polluted morass of BigCity because of his love and loyalty to Slab Pettibone. Given druthers, FuzzyWuzzy would remain in the American West to roam among his own under a blue sky. The city is enclosed within a dome of manmade poison, FuzzyWuzzy longs for the natural world. Slab, however, revels in the city and unfortunately thinks FuzzyWuzzy does as well. FuzzyWuzzy and Slab communicate far better than most human and bear unions, but FuzzyWuzzy doesn't have the communication skills to tell Slab how he really feels. It would be a grave blow if Slab were to find out that his understanding of bears is not much better than his understanding of women. FuzzyWuzzy nods his head like the answer yes and gives a loud huff. The humans whoop and step back quickly with a combination of apprehension and glee.

Fritter McTwoBit is elated. This is better than a whitegirl fairytale. Fritter befriended Bitch because the woman needed a friend. Her motivations were unselfish. Now, good karma is her reward for a simple kindness. She has a house that she lives in with Bitch, along with a job in show business. She is wearing an elegant dress, shoes, and a hat, from a department store where Bitch had footed the bill. Bitch Bantam is unlike regular ofay shitheads and Fritter hopes her uniqueness will spread to others.

At first, as Fritter and the peculiar threesome had started out from the hotel, onlookers had crowded the celebrities, pushing Fritter aside. Bitch has since taken her new friend by the hand. They walk palms tight through the throng. No one comes between them, or shoves Fritter. Everyone is respectful of Bitch Bantam.

And on the subject of ofay non-shitheads, Fritter McTwoBit can't keep her eyes from tiptoeing up to Slab Pettibone. She ponders his other leg, the middle one. Fritter likes Slab and Fritter likes middle-leg skinbones. Most honkys have dinky doodads, but maybe Slab is as different there as he is in other respects. He blushes when their eyes meet. Fritter likes this white man. She hopes he still has a middle leg and assumes he does. A man without a skinbone would never blush.

Fritter can see Daddy Smithy standing atop a table. Excitement hums through her veins. She gives Bitch Bantam's hand a squeeze. She wants Bitch to enjoy the moment as much as she does. Her new friend has supplied her with a new happiness and she wants to return the favor.

Bitch Bantam is conflicted. She can see that Slab and Fritter are excited about their future prospects in show business. Both seem to be fulfilling lifelong ambitions, singing, dancing, and storytelling. And, while show business holds no appeal for Bitch, she feels a great debt to Slab and Fritter and she will do as they do, for them. In truth Bitch feels that on-stage-spectacle is no different than she did under the confines of white slavocracy. She does not yet know what she wants from her new freedom, but she doesn't want to perform for a shouting group of men. Earlier, Bitch had been, for a fleeting few moments, a woman, albeit stuffed like a bloated sausage into the maid's uniform. She had been a person, not unlike the women she saw last night in the restaurant. Now, in her new buckskin uniform she feels more at home. Home, however, has always been the fighting pits. Home is not where Bitch Bantam's heart is.

Bitch feels the care and concern telegraphed from the soft squeeze of Fritter McTwoBit's hand. She can see, under the shadow of his sombrero, the kindness in Slab Pettibone's hirsute face. It is the trained animal, FuzzyWuzzy, that Bitch exchanges knowing glances with.

Daddy Smithy watches the group approach. Following Slab's lead, they line up in front of the table facing the crowd. Daddy is counting down, his voice scaling up, "Ten-nine-eight-seven-six-five-four-three-two-ONE!! Good afternoon to all and don't be afraid to gather round folks. Step up close for a once in a lifetime glimpse at the real-life storybook heroes, Mister Slab Pettibone and his bear FuzzyWuzzy."

Slab waves his hat to the crowd, which is gathering to gander.

"I'm sure you have all heard of the famous exploits of Mister Slab Pettibone and FuzzyWuzzy. All over the world they have been, brushing with danger and exciting adventure. Now normally tis a cost of one whole US dollar just to see this famous duo. And, you all come back this Friday and you'll see and hear these adventures right up on stage where Slab Pettibone will his very self tell the tale of his and FuzzyWuzzy's exploits for the bargain price of just fifty-cents." Slab cues FuzzyWuzzy up on his hind legs. FuzzyWuzzy does a two-step trot. Slab pulls and spins his silver six-shooters.

Daddy is hitting his stride, his stomachache has passed, and he no longer needs to pee. "Now in just a little while you will be allowed to walk right here and shake mister Slap Pettibone's hand and maybe even shake FuzzyWuzzy's paw..."

Slab thinks Daddy Smithy is maybe overstepping, offering up a FuzzyWuzzy paw shake. But, what the heck, a crowd is clumping up.

"And, now, before I go on to the ninth wonder of the modern world, the indestructible Bitch Bantam, I'd like to introduce you to the heretofore unknown, the newest discovery of yours truly. The famous Princess Fritterich Exotica from the far away kingdom of Sexonia. Born to royalty, the Princess is known throughout the world for her famous oyster dance and songs that, well, I don't want to spoil the surprise, let me just say, when she sings and dances entire countries blush, if you know what I mean."

Slab Pettibone knows what Daddy means. Slab is impressed. Theaters on BigCity's WhiteWay play a lot of darkie shows, but most of these are white guys in blackface. There is no such a thing as a black female performer outside of CoonBorough. Daddy Smithy is showing his smarts, by dubbing Fritter McTwoBit a princess from another land he's erasing the line between white and colored. Fritter is not a colored woman, she's an exotic princess.

Fritter catches on as well. The name change is fine; the McTwoBit moniker has never been worth more than twenty-five-cents. Playing into Daddy Smithy's pitch, Fritter begins a slow hip roll. She knows what to shake and how to shake it. She likes making men blush, she casts a sly eye at Slab whose face is red as an invigorated glans. She bumps and grinds and throws eye contact into the hat-brim shade of the horny gawking white guys.

Daddy is yelling now, "Watch closely as she demonstrates the moves that she used to conquer kingdoms and countries. The very same dance that put the king of England to his knees."

Wilbur Szedvilas and Wilbur Good are working their way through the crowd to the front. Wilbur Szedvilas says to his partner, "Me thinks, the darkie princess feels all yummy to watch." Wilbur Good agrees with a nod, Princess Exotica is indeed yummy good.

Bitch Bantam is confused. She at first did not understand who Princess Fritterich Exotica is and only realized it after Fritter released her handhold to better shake her moneymaker. Fritter's lewd dance dismays Bitch. Fritter McTwoBit is a free woman and Bitch would gladly share her fortune with her. She doesn't need to cater to the shitheads with her sex and Bitch can't understand how Fritter can enjoy it.

"And now, for anyone who has been deaf and dumb

and never heard of this here man-sized woman, I'd like to introduce you to Miss Bitch Bantam, the toughest and strongest woman alive."

Fritter unplugs the shimmy and steps back to give Bitch centerstage. Bitch dislikes the spotlight, she stands straight and stoic. She looks out at the mass of faces, Men in top hats, skimmers, derbies. A tight cluster of women in flashy finery, feather boas, flamboyant hats, festive floral festoons. Bitch recognizes these women. She has seen them all her life, the demimonde around the all-male places where Bitch has fought the rats, dogs, hogs, and men, in the dirt pits. These women are from BigCity's ScarletSquare. They live and work in the houses of assignation. They laugh and look to be happy in their finery. But Bitch knows better. Like her, in her never-to-be-repeated past, these are not free-women. Bitch watches the sad women laugh and she hates the men.

Things are coming together for Daddy Smithy, he has the crowd, he has the act, the two coppers have moved up front, and here comes the reporter and photographer from the BigCity Times. Daddy had earlier gone to the newspaper office and promised the reporter a story that, with a rotogravure from a photograph, could make the front page. If everything goes as planned the reporter will go away happy and provide Daddy with publicity worth a fortune. As always, Daddy is gambling on his own shrewdness. He watches from the corner of his eye as the photographer sets up his tripod.

"Now you all will get the chance to see the great Bitch Bantam fight not only all comers, but starting this Friday night, as long as you're here early enough to get a ticket before they are all sold out, which I assure you they will be, Miss Bitch Bantam,

141

the toughest and meanest woman in all America will wrestle the bear FuzzyWuzzy. And to show you how confidant I am that there is not a man anywhere equal of this magnificent woman, I am right now right here making the offer of fifty dollars to any man that can pin Bitch Bantam in the ring."

Daddy has said all that needs saying. He is ready to start today's free performance. He gives a secret nod to the two Wilburs.

"I me," Wilbur Szedvilas yells out, "Thinks woman-fighting be against the BigCity laws. Me and me pertner Wilbur shall now handycuff and arrest the woman and skedaddle her to the clinker." The two Wilburs walk forward with handcuffs out.

Daddy did indeed tell his players about the two uniformed shills he has hired to help drum up a little publicity but Bitch had not really paid attention or understood. Now Bitch sees the coppers coming and she's again confused. She looks to Slab who gives her a wink, then to Fritter who also gives her a wink. Bitch thinks the coppers are planning to take her to jail. Her friends, Slab Pettibone and Fritter McTwoBit, have not noticed and both seemed to have something caught in their eyes. Bitch Bantam begins to growl. FuzzyWuzzy picks up her growl and he too gives a guttural challenge.

"What's this!?" Daddy Smithy cries in mock disbelief. "We have broke no laws. Miss Bantam has the right to fight in BigCity. We'll not allow BigCity boolydogs to take Miss Bantam to jail. I demand an explanation!"

"Are against the breaking laws, a woman fighting," Wilbur Szedvilas delivers his lines like a born thespian. "To clinker we must her go."

The two Wilburs are cautiously approaching the

big woman. Both Slab Pettibone and Fritter McTwoBit are attempting to send signals to their friend. Fritter says to Bitch, "It ain't for reals, Sista Bitch. Nobody tryin to do you no bad. It jus a big show. Doan nobody wanna take you to no jail."

Bitch only half understands. The only thing she really knows at this moment is that show business is just about the stupidest thing in the world.

Wilbur Good makes a quick lunge at Bitch. Before he has even reached her, he finds himself flying through the air and landing on a group of onlookers ten feet away. Whoo hee, Wilbur Good thinks, he has never tangled with anyone so quick and powerful before. Maybe this will be fun after all. Wilbur Szedvilas, meanwhile, bends at the waist and charges Bitch like a buffalo. Bitch stands planted to the ground. Wilbur Szedvilas plows into her, barely pushing her back more than a foot or two. Bitch brings her right fist up into his jaw. He flies up and back and hits the ground laughing.

Like Bitch, FuzzyWuzzy is a bit confused. He doesn't like watching Bitch tangle with the two uniformed men. FuzzyWuzzy wants to play too. He begins to bounce on his four legs. Slab can feel FuzzyWuzzy's desire to join in, Slab wants to play as well.

While Wilbur Szedvilas brushes himself off before charging in for another dose, Wilbur Good has his arms around Bitch Bantam's waist, attempting to squeeze her into submission. Bitch grabs the copper by the seat of his pants and pulls him off the ground, then begins squeezing him around the waist. His grip loosens, as his breath is strangled from his body.

"What will become of Miss Bitch Bantam!?" Daddy is yelling over the shouting adrenaline-fueled crowd, shoveling coal to the fire. "Is this fair?! Unhand that woman you unruly boolydogs!"

Wilbur Szedvilas is in a run to join his partner when he's encircled by a rope. The rope is pulled tight over his arms at his chest. He stops and follows the rope with his eyes up to Slab Pettibone. Daddy Smithy is only paying the two coppers for fighting Bitch Bantam. Nobody has said anything about the legless man and the bear. But that matters little to Wilbur Szedvilas, a good fight is a good fight whether with a giant woman or a bear. It is all the same good fun.

Slab Pettibone has lassoed the copper like a steer. He pulls the rope tight and attaches it to the horn at the top of FuzzyWuzzy's collar. "Swing and roar, FuzzyWuzzy. Swing and roar."

FuzzyWuzzy rears to his full height and swings his upper half. Wilbur Szedvilas, at the end of Slab's rope, goes airborne. "Whoo heee! Huzzah, Huzzah!! Me a flying burdy! Tweet tweet!"

Bitch Bantam has Wilbur Good over her head where she twirls him like a pinwheel. He also yells gleeful huzzahs.

Just for the sake of showmanship and excitement, Slab Pettibone takes his twin blank-loaded six guns from his holsters and begins firing into the air.

The photographer from the Journal takes a picture then reloads and takes another.

Bitch tosses Wilbur Good into the now frenetic crowd. Slab unhitches the rope from FuzzyWuzzy's collar and Wilbur Szedvilas lands in a jumble twenty feet away on top of his partner. The two Wilburs know that the show is over, though they both would prefer to keep going. They stand together and shake their fists for good drama.

"Being back, we will be, at showtime next," the dramatic Wilbur Szedvilas proclaims. "And shall taking be the Bitch woman to clinker locking up!" They walk off laughing and head for the nearest blind pig for a cup of grog before calling it a day. The crowd cheers with approval. The reporter and photographer head back to the newsroom to write the story and develop the photos.

Slab Pettibone re-holsters his six guns.

Bitch Bantam sits on the edge of the table next to where Daddy Smithy stands. She's not even winded by the ordeal. She watches as the crowd, realizing the show is over, dissipates. She watches the whores walk away. She looks to her friend, Fritter McTwoBit. "Sista Bitch," Fritter says, "Yall done gooood. Yall is one toughass fightin sista." Bitch smiles at her friend. Something new has nested in her head, in the center of this clownish violence. A new world of thought has presented itself and Bitch Bantam knows, finally and absolutely, who she is. She has only to bide her time in this silly show business, and repay her debt to her new friends. Then as a free woman she will do what she will do, as dictated by no one. Bitch looks at Daddy Smithy and smiles, like the other shitheads he is not even worthy of her disdain.

Daddy Smithy climbs down from the table. He takes three long pulls of Doctor FixUp and closes his eyes. He has done it; everything has worked exactly as he planned. Daddy Smithy hasn't screwed-up. Maybe things are going to change after all.

Daddy Smithy leaves the table and walks into the Orpheus Theater. Slab Pettibone and FuzzyWuzzy, Princess Fritterich Exotica aka Fritter McTwoBit, and Bitch Bantam follow Daddy inside.

TigerCage

Uptown, north of Division Street west of Boone Avenue, City Hall and BigCity Courthouse sit on the north side of State Street known as Municipal Row. Across from City Hall, between a new steel-vertebrate building owned by the Quackenbush empire and the Stars&Stripes Saloon, a three-story brownstone known as TigerCage houses the SnarlingTigers.

Jones Mulligan is firmly seated on the third floor of TigerCage. He sits in a recliner behind a brawny oak desk. Along with pen, ink, and other business nick-knacks, Jones' desk is set with edibles. Two baked pheasants on a platter, cracked lobster claws on a bed of ice with a bowl of melted butter, a sterling bowl of radishes, onions, carrots, two greasy platters with the skeletal remains of chicken and rabbit, a silver champagne bucket filled with mashed potatoes, a platter of baked potatoes, a bowl of boiled red potatoes, and a two-quart pitcher of buttermilk. Jones Mulligan is a man of voracious appetite. At this moment he is eating lobster meat, wiping trails of butter from the sluices of his chin with a linen cloth. He smacks his lips with passion and greed.

As a youth, Jones Mulligan sailed steerage, across the Atlantic, to the BigCity docks. It was on this deathship of starving pilgrims that he developed his polyphagian hunger. Thirty-five days below deck, damp, dark, standing room only, meager hoards of foodstuff, triggered Jones' pathological urge for sustenance. It was after he had eaten his shoes that his ambitions became ravenous.

Jones waded ashore and went to work assimilating with the politicos and thugs that plotted BigCity's future. He scaled the hierarchy with quiet charm and before anyone noticed he was controlling BigCity's on/off switch. Now he is forty-four years old. He has more than he set out for, yet not nearly enough.

Jones Mulligan runs TigerCage in much the same manner that young Dooley Paradise runs TumbleHouse and Shag Draper runs DuchyHall. TigerCage is the grownup version of politics and muscle. Unlike Dooley, the flashy young Brusselsprout, or Shag, the mouthy thug, Jones is reserved and unassuming. While he daily eats his weight in fodder, he has never gone to excess fat. He maintains a jovial portliness of the kind associated with wealth and power. His face is drawn with thin expressionless lines and he has smallpox scars on his cheeks like a spray of buckshot.

Jones Mulligan sucks marrow from a pheasant bone and deliberates his place in history. Jones would never presume sainthood, but would like to be remembered as a contributor to the good of BigCity. Not, as he fears, as a man of selfish and vile conscience. Jones wants the murder and mayhem that has propelled him to the top of BigCity's totem to fade in the murky shadows of his past. To induce historians into editing the bad, Jones needs to create a magnanimous and historic good.

Jones Mulligan plans to bring the SnarlingTigers into legitimacy and benevolence. The core of SnarlingTigers have become businessmen. Strong-arm tactics are nothing more than a reminisce over a couple of beers. These businessmen will follow any lead Jones takes. And Jones is leading them to

TumbleHouse. By turning TumbleHouse legit (removing the alcoholic beverage bar and Fagin School) and heaping it with contributions, Jones Mulligan will be remembered as The Man Who Saved The Children.

Jones stacks probable obstacles through the corridors of thought and approaches them one at a time. Dooley Paradise is his first and most personal hurdle. Dooley is locked into a political imbroglio of his own creation. He, as well as his lieutenants, Gulper and Adelina, should have been years beyond pick pocketing. Jones understands, probably better than Dooley himself, what took him to the street for a little petty larceny. It was the druggy high of chance that accompanies youth. The same high that sends boys off to war. It is Dooley Paradise's only failing, he likes to get high.

Jones Mulligan has left young Dooley on his own to straighten the tangle. All the boy needs is a body, warm or cold, for the murders of the SnarlingTiger, Sinclair Kissick, and BigCity dowager, Missus Wilhoit Brandonburger. For the prior two nights a youth from the west has been on a murderous rampage in SodomHeights. Since nobody cares, and the newspapers do not cover SodomHeights, Dooley and his henchman Gulper can either track down the killer or snuff and frame a random SodomHeights homo and hand the faux-guilty corpse over to the police. Dooley can then, with Jones running the machine, become a newspaper hero, putting TumbleHouse back in good light.

Inadvertently, Jones' next obstacle also involves Dooley Paradise. Jones has done too well of a job building his BigCity organizations. Rather than delegate, Jones has ruled. Now he is without a proper chain of command. Without Jones Mulligan, the SnarlingTigers and TumbleHouse would cease. The only organization within his dominion would be the Mooks. And Shag Draper and his Mooks are on Jones' list of things to be dismantled. Dooley Paradise is being groomed by Jones to inherit his control. But he needs to grow yet and until he does Jones Mulligan is alone on his throne.

The bigger problem, since Jones is not planning to die anytime soon, is Shag Draper. While the Mooks still kowtow to Jones they are nothing more than a gang of killers, pimps, thieves, and corrupt glad-handers. It will do Jones' legacy no good to be connected to the Mooks. It will however, look good on any résumé to be the guy to rid BigCity of lowlife gangsters. It is going to take time and finesse but Jones will clean the city of the riffraff infestation that has in fact helped to seat him where he sits.

Black Alley

Girl's health has taken a turn for the worse. Driven by obsessive anxiety to find her sister, she hides her ills from Gulper Mooney. She wants to appear resourceful and tough. Gulper's eyes filled with admiration last night, when she sank her teeth into copper Wilbur Good's arm. Gulper's love comes from his respect for her hardshell resolve and she will not let him down. But she is sick, weary, febrile, and dyspeptic. The lacerations at her perineum have yet to scab over. It hurts when she has a bowel movement and burns when she urinates. She has not relieved herself in hours. She needs a drink of Doctor FixUp opiated malt. The only good memory of her father, his generosity with patented medicines.

Girl and Gulper walk together down a twilight darkened alleyway. She holds Gulper's hand and follows his lead. The alleyway is quiet. She can see only the faint outlines of the backs of steel and mortar buildings. The area is cleaner than the alleys whence they have come. It does not smell of death, pestilence and piss.

If only she could hurtle the physical discomfort and pain of her missing sibling, Girl would be happy beyond compare. She is away from her no-account father, she is in love, and she is clean and well-dressed, maybe even pretty. She has bathed, in hot water, in the privacy of Adelina's bathroom. She had scrubbed the grime of her debauched childhood with washing rags and Ivory soap until her skin turned pink and tender. Adelina gave her a near-new dress with an apron front along with stockings and underclothes. She walks in shoes that have never been scuffed, though they are a size too small and bunch up her toes. She has washed her hair with liquid soap and brushed out the tangles leaving a cascade of thick soft curls framing her pretty oval face. She has many reasons for happiness and ditto for sad. Her interiority is an emotional typhoon.

Gulper Mooney seems neither happy nor sad. His emotions as well as his mental dialogues are hidden away, or disguised by verbal vaunts of self-promotion. He bounces and huffs his chest as he walks in single-minded strides, like an onward soldier. Gulper knows where he is going and what he is going to do when he gets there. It is not information he volunteers. Girl will know soon enough. She will see first-hand the true value of Gulper Mooney.

The street-side façades, lining State Street, are grand displays of architecture boasting both panache and muscle. The alleyway backsides are substantial yet unadorned. It is in the backalley shadows of these mundane slabs of high-rise that Girl holds tight to Gulper's hand.

"Jear tis," says Gulper. He walks them to a single-story shack hunkered between buildings. He takes a large key from his pocket and unlocks the door. Pulling Girl inside he closes the door behind them. The dark is absolute. A shooting star flares in the quick scratch of a struck Lucifer. Gulper lights a cigarette then shakes out the fire. A sulfurous ghost burns Girl's sinuses. Gulper takes a drag, his face evanesces the void, the smoldering fag a fuse sizzing down down down.

"A minute me Girl, I shall be having us the answer of yur missing sis," says he, then disappears into the black ether. The Signal ember floats through the pitch like a gnat with a headlight. Girl is afraid. She holds that she loves Gulper, but wonders about his judgment. She wishes she knew where they were, and why.

Earlier at TumbleHouse, Gulper had interrogated the two boys Bug and Flopears. They had described to Gulper a man with a smashed fedora which fit Daddy Smithy. Girl cannot imagine how that information has led them to this place. She listens to Gulper skulking about in the darkness. The acrid stink of mildew and decay overpowers her soapy-fresh redolence, pushes her back in time, to places she does not want to go. She hears the moan of a rusty hinge, the snap of a switch. Yellow electric light suddenly washes upward from a trapdoor in the floor. Gulper stands at the edge of a fiery rhombus; otherworldly shadows demonize his face.

"Twill be best without talk till I sez different, me Girl. Foller me down."

Gulper climbs down a ladder into the tunnel. Girl wonders, as her eyes adjust to the anomalous glow below, if she is climbing into hell. She is leaving the mortal world for molten limbo where suffer vanquished souls. In the future, Girl will look back and still wonder if this moment had been her last before sacrificing her remaining virtues to Hell. She follows Gulper into the sepulchral burrow and closes the trap door above her.

TigerCage

Jones Mulligan picks up a fork, and captures a pillow of mashed potato. To his left, the floor-to-ceiling bookcase squeaks like chalk on slate. Jones moves fast. He opens the top desk drawer and grabs for his gun. He is not fast enough.

Gulper Mooney gives him a warning, "I will cap yur melon, if yur picks up the gun."

Not wanting caps in his melon, Jones slowly closes the desk drawer. He chews mashed potatoes and swallows. Only two people have keys to Jones Mulligan's secret escape tunnel, Gulper Mooney is not one of them, nor is the girl standing by his side.

Gulper keeps his short-barreled pistol aimed at the

SnarlingTiger. Jones takes his time. He picks up a pitcher of buttermilk and pours a glass full. "I shall be with you children momentarily." He picks up the glass and drinks.

Gulper crosses the room and puts the gun to Jones' head. "I wull not be waiting a moment. Gulper Mooney dassent wait, see."

Jones continues to drink down the thick milk. Even with a gun to his head he remains superior to this snotnose whelp.

Girl has never seen such a room as this. Everything, corner to corner, floor to ceiling, is brightly illuminated with clear and odorless electric light. Elaborate curls and swirls are carved into the mahogany wainscoting, above which is paved with white flocked flowers on red silk. The floor is carpeted with thick Persian rugs. There are armchairs of dark wood and leather. In the center of the room is Jones Mulligan's massive desk. Behind the desk, Jones finally sets down his glass of buttermilk. "And what brings you to my office, lad?" Jones is casual, relaxed.

Gulper keeps the little gun aimed but backs up three paces. Jones Mulligan seems a mild man, but is nevertheless ruthless, and has faced guns before. It is best to keep from his reach.

Gulper says, "I needs information, see. And that's what yur gonna give me."

"Information," Jones scoffs. "You don't need a gun for information, Gulper boy. You've never been on my enemies list. That isn't why you're here. You've come here to kill me." Jones swivels to Girl, addresses her, "Did you know that, young miss? Do you even know where you are? Are you a willing accomplice to an assassination that will keep you running until exhaustion

153

takes you? Did you think you were here for information? Did you think you could come in here through a secret passage with firearms and then leave me alive to hunt you down?"

Girl's insides are twisting into anxious knots. This man, an obvious man of power, is making her vertiginous with words that churn her stomach acids. She looks to Gulper, the boy she loves, for relief.

"Yur talk is malarkey, ya vomitus feck, I wants only ta know what I come ta find out."

"And what would that be, son? I will gladly tell you whatever it is you want to know."

"Someone took me girl's sis. Yur the one knows everthing what happens. Sos yur to tell me where is me girl's sis?"

Jones knows nothing of any lost girls, though he knows that Warner Quackenbush has taken in a new girl; he had even used the information to play with Warner's mind. Jones is good at playing with people's minds. He lies to Gulper and watches the girl's reaction. "Your girlfriend's sister is dead. Raped and murdered by Shag Draper. Shag will tell you, just ask. I assume you are under his employ at this time, is that correct, child? Only Shag and young Dooley have access to the secret passage. And, it wasn't Dooley sent you here."

Information sledgehammers Girl in the gut.

Snooks is dead!

Girl will not believe it. She is dizzy, the boiling upset in her stomach spreads like splitting amoebas. She sits in a chair gasping like an asthmatic.

Gulper says, "The feck is fulla falsities, me Girl," then to Jones, "Yur to pay fur this, see. Tisnt no man upsets me Girl."

Jones is composed. He puts a potato in his plate and

fills it with melted butter from a gravy boat. He says to Girl, "You are looking ill, little miss. Would you like a bite to eat? Or maybe you would like to leave here before you have gotten into something you will never get out of. You're free to leave; you owe nothing to this boy who has only lied to you. He is not here to find your sister he has come for me and he works for Shag Draper, the very man who murdered your sister. Run now, while you can."

"Yull shet yur yap about me working fur Shag Draper and fillin me girl's head with lies. Yull be runnin this town no more." Gulper moves in closer. He takes a set of handcuffs from his pocket. "Me thinks we said all that needs be, see. I will ave yur hands behind you now."

Jones makes a show of tasting a bite of potato. "Are you sure you wouldn't like a bite to eat, son? You're looking a bit underfed and weak."

"I wull be showin yur weak, now do as I sez and put yur hands behind yur."

"I'll do no such thing. I will not make my killing easy. If you are to shoot me, you better do it and move fast, before my boys charge in. And, this young lady doesn't look ready to move fast. She looks to need a doctor."

Girl does indeed need a doctor. She has drained to a pale white. Her limbs shake as if sub-zero. Her breathing is slow coming. She is bleeding again.

Gulper considers Jones' theory that a gunshot would fill the room with loyal SnarlingTigers. He backs to the fireplace where he picks up an iron poker with a dueling sword handle.

Jones Mulligan sets down his fork and wipes his mouth. He considers the odds. The boy is fueled with youth and scorn that Jones has given up years ago. But Jones has experience, strategy and confidence. Neither man nor boy shows fear. Life and death fighting is a thrill fix for Gulper and a nostalgic stroll for Jones. Jones stands and faces the boy.

"Come on now, son. Let's show your little miss what a weak pathetic little nothing you are."

Girl is ready to go. She does not want any more information; she does not want to be here. She is paralyzed and sick, and cannot move from the chair, cannot even speak. She needs to explain to Gulper that nothing is important anymore, Snooks is dead. A stab of pain chews at her from within. She holds herself and buckles like a jackknife, yet she keeps her eyes upward, watching Gulper Mooney and Jones Mulligan circle and growl like dogs in a territorial pissing contest.

For the first time since Girl has known Gulper, he is not talking. His eyes are locked to Jones Mulligan's eyes. He puts his little pistol in his pocket and raises the iron poker, ready to strike.

Jones Mulligan is smiling, his ever present charm shines like his white teeth. He holds a silver butter knife in his hand. He speaks to Gulper in a quiet tone through the tense air.

"I ave supplied you with your information, child. I will give you this chance to run along home with your little girl. You should have told her, lad, you should have told her you came here to kill me. Now, she feels betrayed. And she looks to be sick." Without taking his eyes from Gulper, Jones casually uses his free hand to pick up an oyster and slurp it from its half-shell.

It is in this slice of a moment that Gulper glances at Girl, who indeed is sick and confused and feeling betrayed. It flashes in Gulper's head that he has done her wrong, he has hurt the girl he loves. He sees tears in her eyes, agony screwed into her face.

It is also in this slice of a moment that Jones Mulligan strikes with uncanny grace and speed. He takes three steps and, with his left-hand, grabs Gulper's raised wrist and twists the boy's arm. With his right, Jones swings his arm like a rock on a rope and runs the table knife through Gulper's cheek, breaking a molar in the process. Jones continues the twisting pressure on Gulper's wrist until Gulper drops the poker. Jones takes a step backward giving the boy the opportunity to appreciate his disadvantage.

Gulper Mooney's head spins from pain and obfuscation. Gulper has never lost a fight, has never left himself open to a bushwhack. He tastes blood and silver and butter. He spits tooth chips onto the carpet. He has to clear his vision, regain his authority. He is without a weapon. If he loses this fight, he will die. This is not a backyard scuffle.

Girl watches. She takes a startled stab of pain when Jones opens Gulper's cheek with the dull silver blade, as if the knife has gone twisting into her abdomen.

Jones Mulligan is back at his desk, still smiling. He sets the butter knife on a plate and picks up a baked potato. He speaks in a tone associated with calming a dumb animal.

"You were not paying attention, were you, Gulper my boy? Maybe you want to try again. Or have you realized that you're overmatched? Maybe it's too late for you, little boy. Maybe it's time for you to give up and die. But, let's not do that, let's play some more. Alright, sonnyboy? To show you what a sport I am, pick up your weapon and try again. As for me, I think this potato should be all the weapon I need against a little nobody like you."

Gulper is enraged. Perspiration drips from his forehead and under his arms. His cheek throbs and he cannot keep himself from exploring the gash with his tongue. He has been humiliated in front of his Girl. He wants to kill Jones Mulligan and make the man suffer in the process. Gulper quickly bends to pick up the fire poker and with his head down he charges Jones Mulligan.

Jones anticipates, and indeed controls, Gulper's moves. Like a surprise ending, Jones falls flat to the carpeted floor. Gulper whistles the iron bar, connecting with nothing and losing his step. From the floor, Jones kicks Gulper in the solar plexus. Gulper buckles to his knees, his mouth agape. Jones shoves the baked potato into Gulper's mouth and down into his throat. Twice more he hits Gulper, with all his weight behind his doubled fists. He twists the iron rod from the boy's hand and uses it to smash Gulper's right arm. The bone cracks like a gunshot.

Girl is in a spin, watching the performance, like one of Daddy's out-of-focus moving-pictures. She is shivering from cold. She nearly screams when the door behind her begins to pound.

"Ya alrighty in there, Boss!?" Jones Mulligan's platoon of soldiers yell from the next room.

Jones has Gulper on the floor. He has his knee on Gulper's left arm. Gulper is unable to use his right as it is broken at the wrist. Jones continues to push the baked potato into Gulper's braggart yap. He reaches over casually with his other hand and pinches Gulper's nose shut. Gulper is struggling for breath. His red face is draining to a cyanotic hue.

Jones is composed when he yells to his henchmen

behind the door, "Everything is dandy as should be, fellows. Twas just the sound of the champagne cork. No need for the help, and my thanks for your vigilance!"

Gulper is beyond understanding, swinging his broken arm to no effect other than his own pain.

Jones smiles at Girl. "I shall be giving you another chance now, young miss. If you can find you own way back to the tunnel before your unfortunate fellow expires. I will be happy to let you go your way."

The girl means nothing to Jones. She is only a dupe, her punishment is not necessary. "Be gone now," he tells her, "and forever remain clear of my path."

Jones returns his attentions to Gulper. He unclasps his forefinger and thumb from the boy's nose and loosens the potato plug, for a quick moment, giving him a hint of needed oxygen. Jones wants the boy to enjoy enough consciousness before death to realize the severity of his mistakes. The boy has wronged the one man that could have made his life better. He has wronged a man some think to be a saint. But now the fight is over, and as always, Jones has won. He has done only what is necessary. He takes no joy in ending young Gulper Mooney's life.

Gulper can see Jones Mulligan's face looming above him. He looks gentle, almost sad. Gulper thinks surprise in his life is over, but, in his fading state, he is astounded when the great Jones Mulligan begins to softly whisper a children's song, as though rocking him to slumber.

"Where is Stannie? Where can he be?
Where is he hiding away from me?
I've looked in the closet and out on the stair,
Under the table, behind the big chair.
Where is the scalawag? Where has he gone?
Leaving his poor papa all..."

Jones is zoned into the throes of murder and has forgotten Girl until he sees her suddenly out-of-focus and up close. In the blink of a tearful eye his senses are knocked abstract. Girl has picked up the fireplace poker and fractured Jones Mulligan's skull. She falls to the floor from the strain. The man is sprawled across the floor on his back in a semiconscious state, whispering, "Where is little Stannie...where...can he be...?"

Gulper rolls to his knees and coughs out the potato. He looks at Girl but says nothing. He finds way to his feet and without talking he takes the poker from Girl with his left hand, his right twisted, broken at the ulna, useless. Girl sits on the floor. She can feel warm blood that has begun to trickle from her woman place. Her teeth chatter like wind-up chattering teeth. She watches as Gulper swings the fireplace implement again and again, smashing Jones Mulligan's head into muck. He offers Girl a pull-up and they go quickly to the secret passage and down into the tunnel.

Chapter Six

TumbleHouse

Dooley Paradise's nether-sleep is infused with cocaine and spiderbite. He wakes with a start, flat on his back, his neck muscles tight and sore. His brow is pimpled with perspiration. Gunmetal twilight blues the white bed clothes. Next to Dooley, Adelina Brown lies snoring in the cool light. Dooley wonders why the snoring does not wake her. He wonders how someone so fragile can snort like an enraged hog. He also wonders why it is his bed she chooses to be in. Most of the time she acts like she does not even like him. Yet here she is, snoring butterflies across the hair on his forearm.

Dooley wants to love Adelina, does love Adelina, but is

not swept into passion with Adelina. He can hold her and caress her. He feels tender and safe. But, he has a softie for skinny girls with attitude. And Adelina is all bones and self-righteousness. Dooley does not want to lie about his feelings, but he does.

Earlier, before snuffing the final wick, Adelina had accused Dooley's spiderbite and noseburn of leaving him limp in her hands. If Dooley agreed, he admitted to his addiction but if he disagreed he was dangerously close to admitting she was a big turn-off. He ended up saying little of anything. He feigned sleep and took fantasy field trips and held her in his arms as though he cared.

Now Dooley carefully frees himself of Adelina and tiptoes to the living room. TumbleHouse is quiet. Everyone except Dooley seems to be sleeping. At the dining table Dooley taps out a line of noseburn. He rolls a greenback and snorts the drug into the back of his head then taps another line and burns the other side. His heart palpitates. He takes a Signal from the corral and strikes a shaky kitchen match on his thumbnail. He closes his eyes and inhales then exhales dopey smoke. He wears a green silk top-hat and rides in an open two-horse calash behind a uniformed coachman. He performs magic like a character in a Slab Pettibone story and he changes piles of horseshit into silver dollars. From the sidewalks people cheer and shout salutes of gratitude. He opens his eyes and shakes his head then walks to a low cabinet and takes out a brown bottle of spiderbite. He takes a hard pull then recorks the bottle, puts it in his pocket and walks from the room up the stairs to the roof.

The stars are melting from the sky. The moon is blanched by the rising sun. Three floors below, a door opens and spills lamplight onto the dirt pathway. Dooley walks to the edge and looks down to see Doc Slips walking out, black medical bag in tow. He climbs aboard his horse and clip-clops away. Dooley stretches his arm and holds his hand out before him. He can cover Doc Slips and his horse with his thumb. He marvels that he can swoop his giant Godhand to earth and pluck bug-sized people from their narrows. His fascination with perspective wears away as his mind, kicked by the appearance of Doc Slips, reviews his troubles.

Eight hours earlier Dooley walked into TigerCage for his appointment with Jones Mulligan. Jones was upstairs, dead on the floor. The main room was filled with mournful SnarlingTigers, Chief of Police Dempsey Moon with his squad of boolydogs, BigCity mayor Solly Gosterman, as well as Shag Draper and an army of press reporters. Shag Draper was unable to keep his mirth contained, his face hurt from wrestling down a smile. A handful of higher echelon SnarlingTigers stood about debating the organization's future. Jones Mulligan's demise may well mean the demise of the SnarlingTigers. No one wants, nor is anyone qualified, to fill Mulligan's shoes.

Outside on the white granite steps Dooley sat and mourned for Jones Mulligan. Jones had not been a saint, nor had he been a malevolent political thug. He had been a man of complexity. Much of his good side had trickled down to Dooley. Now, Dooley could watch his future and the future of TumbleHouse evaporate like a spring thaw. He wished he were a boy instead of a man. He smoked a Signal and cursed his lot.

Shag Draper sauntered into the night and sat beside Dooley. "I'd hope ya dassent be thinking this takes you from the hook, yur cutting close yur deadline for bringing in responsible parties for the murder on your docket."

Dooley looked at his feet and spoke his mind, "It was you behind this assassination, you bloodrag jerk. I hope it comes back at you in spades."

Shag hit Dooley in the ear, knocking him from his seat, filling his head with static. Before Dooley could process the blow, Shag was on his feet. He shot the arrow of his shoe into Dooley's ribs.

"You will not be wanting to disrespect me with name placing, Dooley me boy. I could kill you now, place yur carcass with the blame of poor mister Jones Mulligan, and walk home the hero. But, only as I have a great surprise coming yur way that I will nay have you missing another day of yur wretched life. Meanwhile I still expect you to bring me the boy responsible for Missus Wilhoit Brandonburger and the SnarlingTiger. Elsewise it will be yurself we lock into the city prison."

Dooley fought for his breath and huffed out, "I'd think you'd have bigger kettles to contend with now that Jones is dead. Why do you care about a woman and man that you never even knew?"

"I don't care, you little shite speck. But you better care." Again he kicked Dooley. "Now, you wull excuse me, I ave the mayor and police chief to consult with, and little time for you."

Dooley walked from the orange gaslit glow of Senate Center to the dark of ScourgeTown and home to TumbleHouse where he found Doc Slips arriving on horseback. A TumbleHouse visit by Doc Slips signals the imminent death of an infant, or a birthing young mother, or a stabbed, shot, or beaten urchin, or a case of the ague too extreme for a child to fend. Doc Slips is a kindly man and Dooley would be pleased to see him if only he were somewhere other than TumbleHouse.

Dooley had gone inside with Doc Slips and met Adelina who had summoned the doctor. As the threesome walked upstairs, Adelina explained, Girl was hemorrhaging, from a still birth the night before. Also, as an aside, Gulper Mooney broke his arm and has what looks to be a knife wound in his left cheek. Doc Slip set and splinted the arm with wooden barrel stays and cleaned the wound with alcohol.

Upstairs Adelina and Doc Slips had gone into Girl's room and as they did Gulper came out. Dooley wondered if the girl would live. He chewed the bullet of his guilt and hoped she did not. He wanted to wish well of the sick girl, but he instead wished her to die. Her death would not solve, but would help to ease his problems. He could give her carcass to Shag Draper and the boolydogs as payment in full.

Gulper was subdued yet still he was Gulper, "Dooley, me best pal. Me gal Girl has fallen to jeopardy. Iym hoping the best from ol Doc Slips. He wull save me girl or answer ta me, see."

Dooley was feeling little tolerance for Gulper.

"Leave the bragging for someone else, Gulper. Doc Slips will do what he can and in the end you'll thank him, whatever happens to the girl."

"Me girl is not just the girl, tis her name, Girl. And now yur tellin Gulper Mooney when and to who he gives his thanks. We have come to where we are together, me chum. I dassent remember askin for yur please an thank-yous."

"That's right, Gulper, we came up together, but it seems we are walking different roads. How'd you break your arm?"

"Stumbled and fell like a washed-over inebriate, whilst helping me poor sick Girl."

"I need your help tomorrow. We need to go to

SodomHeights and find a guy to turn over to Shag Draper. Can you do that with a broken arm?"

"Only if me girl is well, lest I be grieving. I wull be at yur side, as always I ave been."

"Good. Oh yeah, somebody killed Jones Mulligan."

Gulper put on an unconvincing mock surprise. "Tis a sad day, Chum. A sad day. But the devil with it. We dassent need any Jones Mulligan ta boss us. We does quite well ourselves, see."

"Yeah, we're doing great, Gulper."

Dooley left Gulper and went to his room where he checked his wall safe for the key to Jones Mulligan's secret passageway. Only two people other than Dooley knew the combination, Gulper and Adelina. It was Gulper he suspected, though the key was there where it should be. A while later Adelina joined him, then after an hour of cuddling, and frustration, she fell into slumber at his side. A while after that Dooley went from the bed to the rooftop, which is where he stands now, watching Doc Slips ride away in the quiet steel morning.

Quackenbush Manor

The nine women seated in the first-floor sitting room of Quackenbush Manor are as elegant as the lavish surroundings. Some twirl silk parasols the size of hats, others wear extravagant hats the size of parasols. They are sealed, neck to ankle, in envelopes of puritanical yet fashionable dress. Across the dark walls oilpaint-slathered renditions of quiet American landscapes are framed like windows into wilderness. Beside each woman sits a curvy-legged coffee table with sugary iced petit fours and glazed porcelain cups of tea, which they hold with white gloved hands, ballerina pinkies gracefully plié.

All of these women are of wealth. Three are widows. Five are married to community and industry leaders. One has never married. Together, all the women, but one, set the standards for taste and culture in BigCity. They are gathered today for the purpose of reform and salvation of BigCity's orphaned youth.

Empress Delaware is one of the three widowed women. She walks to the center of the room and stands behind a walnut podium. She tings her teacup with a dainty spoon. "Good afternoon, ladies," she says. "It is indeed a heartfelt pleasure to see you all here today."

Empress Delaware is Warner Quackenbush's sister. She and her daughter, Cuteness Delaware, reside at Quackenbush Manor. Empress's late husband Jinx Delaware had been a southern gentleman of vast inherited fortunes. He had been a man of idle ambitions who whiled away his time with travel and social whoring. He collected racing horses and mistresses. He gave Empress a girl child, Cuteness, now six years of age. He died, just as Empress's father had died, in a fall from a horse. Rumors have persisted that his death was financed by Warner Quackenbush. None of these rumors have ever progressed beyond a harrumph from law enforcement.

Shortly after Jinx Delaware's fatal fall, Warner had moved Empress, with Cuteness in tow, from their southern plantation to BigCity, where she presides over the megalopolis as the first lady of the Quackenbush empire.

"While an introduction is hardly necessary," Empress tells her guests, "I would like to bring to the podium Missus Biddy Wrinkle, who will be sharing with us a talk that involves us all. She will also be introducing our special guest. I present Missus Biddy Wrinkle." Empress takes a seat and Missus Biddy Wrinkle takes the floor.

Biddy Wrinkle, a cockatoo-faced dowager, says, "Good morning, ladies. It is with heavy heart that I talk to you today about the tragic death of one of our own, Missus Wilhoit Brandonburger."

Biddy Wrinkle's family was among the first to settle in BigCity. For four generations BigCity has grown under their care. Biddy Wrinkle rallies relentlessly against poverty and degradation, not from empathy but from a sense of duty. Her family built BigCity from the floor up, they are honor bound to keep it pristine and Godfearing. "Tomorrow, we will give our love and say our goodbyes to Missus Brandonburger, who many of us knew simply as Peach. The funeral is at ten at the Anglican Cathedral. We will all be there." She lowers her head for a ten-count pause then continues, "Today, our topic pertains to how a crime of this enormity could happen in our fair city and what we can do to guarantee it never happens again.

"The sidewalks are on perilous ground indeed when one of our beloved cannot safely shop the marketplace of Sunshine Avenue. It is we who must bring back strength and decency to the city that is our home. It is we, the daughters and granddaughters of the founders of BigCity and the mothers of the future of BigCity, who must step in to return our ever-expanding city to a city that honors our pride. It is our families that pay the salaries of the mayor and the police chief and it is therefore we who must take charge.

"A few startling facts have recently come to my attention which I would like to share with you now. We are all aware of a group of businessmen called the SnarlingTigers, a fraternal organization that has existed with our approval as a link to those less fortunate. While the SnarlingTigers and their families were not of our echelon, we could depend on them to work with us in our battle for decency. As some of you are already aware, last night SnarlingTiger chairman, Jones Mulligan was brutally murdered."

A shiver or two as well as a gasp here and there tiptoes through the sitting room.

"We believe that this crime, this assassination, could only have come from within the SnarlingTigers and therefore an organization who kills their own is not one that we can support. Also, I am sorry to report that we ladies have been bamboozled by this same organization. For some years now we have known of the SnarlingTiger orphanage, sometimes referred to as TumbleHouse. We were led to believe that it stood as a high mark of worthy causes and were considering a charitable donation.

"It has come to light that TumbleHouse Orphanage abducts youngsters of questionable background and holds them captive with liquor addiction and terror tactics. They train these children in the wiles of thievery and prostitution and put them to test on the streets where we live. It was three of these children who cruelly and without conscious took the life of our friend Peach Brandonburger.

"In striving to do what is best for BigCity there are times

when we must make concessions. I am afraid that this is one of those times. In addition to working with the city police and mayor's office, I find that we are in cahoots, as one less refined might say, with a lower echelon group known as the Mooks and represented by a Mister Shag Draper. It is through Mister Draper that we have come by much of this information. While we are indebted to Mister Draper, and will be in fact working alongside he and his men, we are not ready by any means to place him on Municipal Row. We do what we must.

"Tomorrow, ladies, we go into battle and we are indeed fortunate to have a famous leader with us to guide us and show us the way..." Biddy Wrinkle continues with a toplofty introduction of the famous guest, Helen Beck.

Helen Beck is a five-foot high eighty-pound stick of dynamite. At thirty-seven years old she has done more in the name of goodness than anyone twice her age and weight. She has traveled coast to coast leading her minions of wealthy Christian ladies into the slums, dins of sin, pockmarking these United States. Helen carries with her into these battles a five pound sledgehammer, The Hammer of Justice, with which she has smashed countless bottles of hootch, gambling devices, doors, windows, hard skulls. Newspapers follow her raids across the land and sensationalize her dramatic victories over sin and corruption. Helen makes good press.

Today, Helen Beck is in BigCity to lead a raid, tomorrow. But she is thinking about two nights ago and the strange woman she saw at Domino's Helen knows what men can, will, and have done to women. She has helped many a sister find her way to the light of goodness, away from male domination. It is the inhumanity of men that spurs her indignation and indeed her crusade. Helen Beck has never looked into the eyes of anyone quite like the primitive yet beautiful woman she had seen, sitting alone, in the middle of a blusterous crowd of men. It is Bitch Bantam's melancholy eyes that haunt Helen Beck.

"...And that said, it is my pleasure to bring to the podium, Miss Helen Beck." Biddy Wrinkle steps away from the podium. Helen Beck stands and walks forward to the polite applause of BigCity's leading ladies. She is petite and attractive. A small round black patch, like a beauty mark, covers an acne scar on her cheek. There is fire in her eyes. She holds the sledgehammer in both her tiny hands. "This hammer," she tells her captive audience, "is The Hammer of Justice. And, tomorrow, all of us together, will strike a blow for decency and righteousness in BigCity."

Snooks Smithy pads her bare feet quietly along the soft hallway runner. Heaven is a maze of confusion with a zillion doors, some open to wonderland rooms, others closed, harboring dark mysteries. Though Snooks has been instructed to remain in the rooms behind the kitchen, she has wanderlust. She sneaks from her quarters whenever she can, to explore the vast hereafter.

Snooks has access to both Heaven and Hell. Heaven is a riddle. Hell makes more sense. In life Snooks had been bad and therefore belongs in Hell, where she has perverse frolics with the portly manboy. In her addlepated and undeveloped state of mind, she looks forward to these play dates with the devilman. He excites her spirit.

For now, she is free to scout Heaven's acres. She stops

and quietly listens to voices coming from nearby. A door she has opened exposes a small stairway curling upward, away from the adult voices. Padding both feet and hands up the steep steps, Snooks quickly crawls up and out onto the second floor. She stands next to a table with spider legs and below a dark portrait of a long dead soldier. His eyes follow her. She runs for a shadow and again stops to listen. She hears a child's voice, "I can do whatever I want just because because."

Snooks goes to all fours and quietly inches toward the open door. She has seen into the room before. It is a special room for children that belong in Heaven. It is filled with toys and bright window light and today it has a voice. "I can marry anyone I want to and I'm going to marry the Prince of the world."

Snooks, flat on her stomach, puts her forehead and eyes into the room's view. She growls softly like a mountain lion stalking prey. Inside the room a beautiful angel girl sits playing by herself on the floor. Snooks is dressed in cotton bloomers and a plain cambric nightdress. The angel girl wears wonderful frills and ribbons and magical shiny black shoes. In her hand she holds a rag doll with a smiling blackface porcelain head. She has a loop of string around the doll's neck. The angel girl is lynching the golliwogg. "I can count to ten," she informs the lynchee. "An you can't because because." She holds the string and twirls the doll like a lariat. "Stupids are bad because they spit and I don't say bad words."

The girl sees Snooks, releases the string, the doll crashes into a wall and cracks his bright-red smile.

"My name is Cuteness Delaware, and this is my house."

Snooks crawls into the room proper. She whispers to the angel, "Are you deaded or was you always an angel?"

"I know the word for you," Cuteness explains, "because I know the word is Poor and that's a bad word."

Snooks stands and walks to a rocking horse. It has a mane of real horsehair. She pushes its nose and watches it rock. "I ridded a real horse oncet. It was itchy."

Cuteness walks to a tea-set table and picks up a black plug of licorice. "You want some licorice?"

"What is it?"

"It's licorice. Don't you know what licorice is?"

"Uh uh."

Cuteness takes a bite. "It's candy, see." She chews with exaggerated chomps. Her teeth turn blue-black.

"Give me some."

"You're supposed to say please. Don't you know that?"

"Uh-uh."

"That's because you're a bad word."

"I know."

"You can have some anyway." Cuteness strains her muscles and tears off a hunk for Snooks. "Here," she hands Snooks the chaw. She straddles the horse's saddle.

Snooks puts the licorice in her mouth. She imitates Cuteness' embellished chewing procedure. Black tinged spittle drips from her mouth and onto her shift.

"You were supposed to say thank you. And you're not supposed to slobber and you don't even have on any real clothes. You're not supposed to go anyplace in your underclothes."

Snooks likes the licorice, it is better than anything. She wants more. "Gimmie more a that?"

"You're supposed to say may I." Cuteness gives Snooks the remainder of the plug. "Here."

Snooks takes it, again without a thank you. "Do you have a mommy and a daddy? I hadda sister. But I died."

"My daddy went to heaven."

"So did I, an sometimes I go to the other place."

"What other place?"

"Hell."

"You're not supposed to say that word. If I scream, one of my nannies will come and punish you and take you someplace else because you're not supposed to be here."

"Know what?" Snooks remembers a mean game.

"What?"

Snooks reaches out with her thumb and first finger and gives Cuteness a painful titty-twister, through her pretty shirtwaist.

"That's what."

Cuteness screams and continues screaming until the morning shift nanny comes running in, discovers Snooks, and takes her roughly back to her quarters in purgatory. Snooks puts the remainder of the licorice in her mouth and chews with great satisfaction.

Warner Quackenbush is basting his roly-poly backside with a warm creamy sheen of sunlight from the third-floor window. He looks at his shadow across the rich Persian carpet. His flat grey twin is long and thin. Warner is a man of great power, yet he lacks in areas beyond his control. He will never perspire. His body will never grow course curly hair. He will never grow long and thin, though he will continue to grow richer and more powerful.

There is no business like show business and Warner

Quackenbush has been looking for young pioneers in the entertainment market. Young disposable men with visions he can exploit. He has found one of these men in Daddy Smithy.

He has been generous with Daddy Smithy—wrote him a check on the spot, though half of everything the frantic man said was fabrication. Warner was however inspired by a couple of things Daddy said—moving-pictures with stories and true life heroes, and moving-pictures of a sexual nature that excite the basic mind of men. It is easy for Warner to see the billion-dollar potential of motion pictures and he wants to be the mogul who owns it all.

Warner drags his skinny shadow across the room to the standing safe. It is taller than he by two-feet and is, with its double doors, his width. He turns the combination lock, five right, fifty-eight left, seventeen right, and opens the double doors spreading his arms wide. Inside green paper money is stacked and banded top-to-bottom, side-to-side, front-to-back. Chairs, stools, tables, and everything other than his bed and the safe, are specially crafted down to Warner's unusual size. He takes a seat on a low settee and views his petty cash like a Maxfield Parrish sunset. He sits posed like a king and considers the wheels of government.

Jones Mulligan is dead and good riddance. If Jones Mulligan had his way, the masses would be socialized, unionized, educated, and fed; a concept that goes beyond Warner's thinking. Jones Mulligan had slipped backward in time, his goals had become personal. He had not been keeping with the times. BigCity is a better place without powerful liberal thinkers.

Also in Warner's thoughts is his sister, Empress Delaware. Empress has always been his responsibility and he arranges her happiness and protects her name. Rumors suggest Warner's snap of a finger was the same snap of his dead brother-in-law's neck. Warner needed a first lady to represent him socially and politically. He stands proud behind her silly political stands, pulling the strings that guarantee her successes. Empress provides their family with respectability. She demonstrates their charitable side.

Warner employ's Mook boss Shag Draper to mesh the gears for Empress and her reform-minded hens in their quest to sanitize BigCity. Draper will bring the police and the mayor's office into the admixture to applaud and expedite the noble deeds of these women. Shag Draper has as well been employed to keep an eye on Warner's investment with Daddy Smithy, using whatever tactics he deems useful. Warner hopes Daddy Smithy doesn't develop scruples, because the new girl is Daddy's daughter and she was part of the deal, and Warner has grown very fond of Snooks Smithy. In fact, he has been overwhelmed with emotions that he has never felt before, something like what he understands love to be.

Warner smiles at his money, closes the safe and twirls the combination lock. He goes to his dressing table and from it he picks up a hank of soft blond hair and holds it to his face. Never in his life has he done a thing that so defies explanation. He should be perplexed, instead he feels like yelling gibberish to the high roof-beams. He wants to dance though he has never done so. He wants to strip naked, lie on the floor, laugh and holler, flail his gleeful extremities like a turned-over turtle. It shocks him to find his steel mind digressing so yet he throws caution to the wind for that's what one does in the throes of love.

For years Warner has used the little mudlark females to

aid his morning cleansing. When they grow large enough to be a threat, they are discarded with the daily trash. They are born of near subhuman beginnings. They have no worth. Warner has remained detached from these nameless whores' daughters. In his presence they whimper and cry or turn catatonic. They go about their duties in fear and without personality. They are poorly-made disposable machines. Warner can remember none of their faces. Until now, with the new girl's face embossed into his every thought.

It has crept to him, this love. At first it rankled, her lack of fear, her intuition, as though she were on a play date, as though she were a real person. Slowly his anger has subsided, has been overpowered by new pleasures. The enthusiasm she demonstrated as she went through the paces of his perverted morning ritual has put him on a cloud of bliss.

With her hank of hair still in his puffy dinner-roll of a fist he climbs the three-step accommodation ladder and rolls like a beach ball to the center of the bed. He tickles his pendulous breasts with Snooks's hair.

After Snooks's first visit before he was truly stricken he was somewhat shaken by the queerness of his sensations. She did her tasks without prompting, with pleasure and zeal. Unlike most men of great wealth Warner has never insulted himself with thoughts of divine coronation. What he professes in public, and what he knows he is, is opposite poles, one repelling the other. He is neither fanatical nor pharisaical. He knows not why the girl has fevered his libido like a nympholeptic influenza, nor does he care.

The second day the elevator had delivered the girl she had come to Warner like a schoolyard recess. She had tackled the serious business, his inner cleansing, as a playtime. As an adult, Warner's physical being is that of a child. As a child he had always behaved as an adult. Now, suddenly, he is compelled to put the serious facets of adulthood on hiatus. He wants a playtime for himself. If the girl is a gift from Hell he accepts it and dash the consequences.

The jolt of an inordinate action comes into his head and sits him up, shivering with excitement. Across the room, next to his window with its view of the world, the velvet signal-cord hangs in a manner that suggests pulling, a summons to playtime. Never has Warner pulled the cord at any time other than his morning ritual. Would he dare? Would he be so brazen as to use this valuable work time to tug on the cord that rings the bell that brings the girl? "Yes," he says aloud. "Yes, I will." Warner Quackenbush bounces his middle-age babyfat from the bed like a pillow-fight and runs to the signal-cord. He pulls down and holds onto the velvet jungle-vine like an obese chimpanzee in a faraway jungle.

Tumble House

Girl's head lolls, a helium balloon through webs of cigarette smoke, a hazy saloon with dreamy laughter, a freefall of distorted musings. Girl is dopey with drug. The most wonderful Doc Slips has diagnosed dyspepsia and neurasthenia, nervous exhaustion and gas, as well as a badly torn and infected perineum. Doc gave her a snort of ether, a jab of morphine, then cleaned, medicated, and stitched her up. For her frazzled nerves he has prescribed and supplied a green-glass bottle of Doctor FixUp's popular elixir, astonishingly good luck for Girl, as she has been nursing the green bottles since toddlerhood, Doc FixUp is the only old friend she has.

Next to where she lies, on her bundle bed in her little room, her new friend, Adelina Brown, sits in an armless girl's chair reading aloud, *The Adventures of Huckleberry Finn*, Chapter Six, 'Pap Struggles with the Death Angel'.

Girl relates to Huck Finn, so much so that she cannot stay with the story. Huck will do or say something that sends her back to a time, place or situation, where she wanders, helpless, until Huck comes back into focus with Adelina's schoolgirl voice...*Pretty soon he was all tired out, and dropped down with his back against the door, and said he would rest a minute and then kill me. He put his knife under him, and said he would sleep and get strong, and then he would see who was who.*

So he dozed off pretty soon. By and by I got the old split-bottom chair and clumb up as easy as I could, not to make any noise, and got down the gun. I slipped the ramrod down it to make sure it was loaded, and then I laid it across the turnip barrel, pointing towards Pap, and sat down behind it to wait for him to stir. And how slow and still the time did drag along...

"And that's the end of that chapter," Adelina tells Girl. "Would you like me to go on?"

"Not yet. I'm still kinda thinkin about the part you just read. Huckleberry Finn should shoot his daddy dead while he sleeps. That's what I'd do."

"I'd never want to shoot anybody. But I never had a father, maybe if I had, I'd feel different about killing."

"Sometimes I wanna kill my daddy an sometimes I think I just want to see him messed up, you know. I just wanna make him hurt. Gulper's gonna help me look for him tomorrow. But I don't know what we're gonna do when we find him. Gulper says he's going to kill him."

"You should just forget about your father. He's fucked-up. You shouldn't trouble yourself. I know it's not my business, but you might want to rethink your relationship with Gulper. He's probably more fucked-up than your father."

"You just don't like Gulper but I love him and he loves me," Girl says without true conviction.

"I'm sorry, you're right, I don't like Gulper, I never did and I never knew why Dooley does. I know you love him and I understand what it's like to feel that way about somebody. But if Gulper kills your Daddy an says it's because of his love for you, then that's the same thing as if you did the deed, and I think that feels pretty awful."

"I do know what it feels like. I don't even know if I should say anything about it. I helped Gulper kill a man. I had to. I hit him with an iron stick then Gulper killed him. He had to."

"Maybe he had to but I'd bet he was smiling when he did... I'm sorry. I don't mean that. Mostly I'm pissed-off at Gulper for being a traitor. The man he killed was probably Jones Mulligan and Jones Mulligan was Dooley's friend and TumbleHouse's only real supporter. I think Gulper killed his best-friend's other best-friend. And I don't know why. Do you know?"

"I didn't know you knew about it."

"It wasn't hard to cipher, though I don't think Dooley has allowed himself to figure it yet."

"I think when I get better, Gulper and I should go

someplace else. I just wanna find out first for sure about my sister. I don't know why Gulper killed that Jones guy, but I knew he was going to as soon as we got there. Gulper says he has some money and we might go live in the West. He won't kill anybody in the West. He said we can even have a house."

"Boys are partial to big dreams, Girl. You shouldn't put too much stock in Gulper's promise. I guess a house sounds nice, but I will never leave BigCity. Even if Dooley wanted to get married and move somewhere I don't think I would do it. I'm going to make moving-pictures and I'm going to leave my mark. I think I can communicate the good and the bad of where we live, like when Mark Twain writes about Huckleberry Finn, he is also writing about how wrong everything is. That's what I want to do. I wish you could stay here and help because you already know about film and cameras, besides I could use a new friend."

"Sometimes you're kinda hard to follow. This might sound strange to you, but I've never had a friend before. I really want to be your friend, Adelina."

A few moments of soul-searching silence and smiles of camaraderie, then Girl says, "What's the next chapter called?"

"Chapter?"

"Huckleberry Finn."

"Oh, let me see. Chapter Seven, 'I Fool Pap and Get Away'. Should I read it?"

"You don't mind?"

"'Git up! What you 'bout?' I opened my eyes and looked around, trying to make out where I was. It was after sun-up, and I had been sound asleep. Pap was standing over me looking sour - and sick, too. He says, 'What you doin' with this gun?...'"

$ - $ - $
MAJOR ENTERTAINMENT VENTURE
DADDY SMITHY PRODUCTIONS
* * * * * * * * * * * *

PAYING TOP $$ FOR TOP TALENT
SONG - DANCE - NOVELTY ACTS
AUDITIONS: THURSDAY - AUGUST 3
8:00 AM TO 4:00 PM
THE ORPHEUS THEATER
500 WHITEWAY - BIGCITY

Orpheus Theater

Daddy Smithy is running seven directions at once and crashing into himself in the process. Tomorrow night he will stage his first BigCity show. What an extravaganza it will be. He gets jittery just thinking about it. In fact he has become so jittery, while running between auditioning acts and talent rehearsals, that he trips over his feet, falls and bangs his nose on a theater seat. Without pause he sits on the floor, retrieves his bottle of Doctor FixUp, takes a soothing drink, and yells to a man on stage, "You may begin anytime, my good man, I am all eyes and ears."

The man, Captain Ignatius Alexander, Injun Killer, is not yet ready to begin. "Nother minute, she'll be all ready," the captain says. Captain Alexander has a display that accompanies his act. To a great degree the display is Captain Alexander's act.

"What you need to understand, sir," Daddy explains to the Captain. "Is that this show depends on a continuous pace. Bam!-Bam!-Bam!-Bam!-Bam!-Bam! That's how I want it to go. You understand, Bam!-Bam!-Bam!-Bam!-Bam!-Bam! What I'm creating here is what I call wall-to-wall-entertainment. Spectacle without pause. We're doing mostly without sets and displays as they stop the action. So what I'm saying is if you need extra time to set up a display maybe we'll have to do without your act. Though don't get me wrong. You are a man to be admired. Tis just, you know, I need everything to go Bam!-Bam!-Bam!-Bam!-Bam!-Bam!"

"Just one more minute and I'll have it all set," Captain Alexander is working up a sweat. Once assembled, Captain Ignatius Alexander's exhibit will display one-hundred-sixty-four American Aborigine scalps, twenty-seven skulls in all sizes from newborn to great-grandpa, and, for sale after the show, a case of souvenir tobacco pouches made from Injun body parts, most notably teats and scrotal sacks, a dollar each.

Daddy is perplexed, he has a hundred things to do and Captain Alexander can't seem to take a hint. From a backstage door Fritter McTwoBit enters the auditorium. Daddy climbs to his feet. Fritter is heading his way, which can only mean she has something to say. Probably as an emissary for Miss Bantam, probably something he doesn't want to hear. "Miss Exotica," he addresses her by her stage name. "How's the rehearsal coming along? Have you worked your songs out with the accompanists?"

Hiring an orchestra, a small band, or even renting a piano is out of the question. Daddy has instead hired a couple of Civil War vets, twin-brothers Pete and Repeat Kirby, with a snare-drum and a bugle.

"The songs is fine. Thay is sompin more pressin I need to call to yalls attention. Me and Miss Bitch got a problem wit that suckass cracker up on stage."

Daddy's not surprised, Miss Bitch has problems with everything. She's becoming a spokesperson for humane causes that have not yet been invented. Daddy looks up at Captain Ignatius Alexander and then back at Fritter. "That guy? He's an American hero, just like Miss Bitch and Mister Slab."

"Sheeit, Bro, yall can be one thick mofo."

"What? I'm sorry, I just don't see what your objection could be."

As if on cue, from center stage, Ignatius Alexander announces, "She's ready to go, sir. Would you like me to start?"

Daddy says to Fritter, "Let's give the man a chance. Hear what he has to say." Daddy then says to Ignatius, "Go right ahead, I'm listening."

The Captain projects from his diaphragm. "My name is Captain Ignatius Alexander. To quote a great American, 'The only good Injun is a dead Injun...'"

Fritter has heard all she needs to hear, "Yall tell Capn Butthole he ken go on home now."

Daddy doesn't like the guy anyway. His exploits may have been adventure-packed but his stage presence and timing suck. He megaphones his hands and yells upstage. "I'm sorry sir. Your act isn't right for our show. But good luck to you elsewhere. I'm sure you'll find success."

The Captain is not discouraged, "That is quite all right, sir." He is however somewhat irritated. "I understand you need more bang-bang-bang-bang."

"Exactly, I'm glad you understand."

Ignatius Alexander tries again, "Perhaps I could set up in your lobby, before and after the show. I could sell my souvenirs. With a generous cut for you, of course."

No matter how you look at it, money is money. Daddy looks to Fritter for an answer.

"Yall tell, that mister Capn he best hightail outa here real soon, else Sista Bitch Bantam gonna rip off the motherfucka's head and use it fo a cookie-jar."

"I'm sorry, no, Captain. I have a strict policy regarding peddlers in the lobby. Now if you would please pack up, I need the stage for other additions."

Captain Ignatius Alexander flips Daddy Smithy the middle finger, and begins packing his dead Indians.

"Would the next act please proceed to the stage," Daddy Smithy yells into the air, and then to Fritter McTwoBit, he says, "Would you do me the favor of rounding up Mister Pettibone, Miss Bantam and the animal? I need thirty minutes of their time to take publicity photographs. I'd like them center stage as soon as the next audition is finished."

This picture idea had come to Daddy in a flash of inspiration, an idea he knows he can sell to his benefactor, the world's richest man, Warner Quackenbush. He will take individual photos of his famous troupe which in turn the cigarette tycoon can include as trading cards in the packages of Signal Cigarettes. Everyone will win.

The next audition is walking in from stage right. He's just a boy, no more than seventeen. He comes out singing.

"Me name is Zeph Riley
I yam here to entertain
And when I ave done a song or two
You may think meself insane."

Zeph has talents that far outweigh his TumbleHouse bartending skills. He turns his back to the empty audience and bends forward with his head nearly touching the floor. On the seat of his britches a white handkerchief is pinned like a flag. A face has been drawn on the handkerchief. He takes his hat, a green derby, from his head and places it on his tailbone. In long soulful notes he farts, "Wait Till the Sun Shines, Nellie".

Fritter McTwoBit laughs out loud and, to Daddy Smithy, she says, "Ise seen lots a assholes, but I never seen one play music afore. Yall gonna put im on the bill?"

"I don't know," Daddy is thinking the pros and cons of a flatulence act. "I really don't know. What do you think?"

Fritter is flattered he's asking her opinion.

"Do I think stubholders gonna preciate a boy what poots a tune? Sheeit, Bro Daddy. Sign the boy up."

"Yeah? I don't know. Maybe. I don't know. You think so?"

"I said I did. Yall got a wax ear?"

"Yeah, I guess. I mean no I don't. But I guess so, about the act. I think. I don't know." Daddy dips into his Doctor FixUp to assists his decision making. Fritter walks backstage.

FuzzyWuzzy is a well-groomed bear. In the enclosed alleyway behind the Orpheus he has combed and cleaned his plush coat with his claws, tongue, and teeth. He sits in the sunlight like a fat pampered kittycat. He licks the backs of his front paws, rubs his snout up to his ears with spittle and styles his whiskery face. He expresses little huffs of contentment.

Slab Pettibone sits on a barrel next to his bear. His pant legs are cut and sewn closed, with leather padding, at mid-thigh, like mittens without thumbs. He puts his hands flat on the barrel-top, to the side of his hips, and pushes himself up and down, supporting his body with his arms. Slab sets aside an hour each day to exercise while FuzzyWuzzy primps.

Slab also uses this time to rehearse the recitation of his written stories, with great dramatic flair.

"So there we was, face to face with the evil Commander Shenanigan. To the left o us the fair maiden Purity Purty had sunk to her ample bosom in the quicksand. To the right, Purity's Papa, Percival was perched in a tree throwing coconuts at the humongous White Bengal tiger, to little effect as the ferocious tiger was slowly climbing the tree, closer and closer to the brave little man.

"It was then that I spotted the twenty-foot-long cobra snake dangling from above. 'It's now or never FuzzyWuzzy,' I told my trusty bruin friend then I grabbed aholt o that serpent by the head, swung it like a lariat and lassoed Sweet Purity by the shoulders and began to pull her free o the deadly African muck. 'You will never defeat me and FuzzyWuzzy with your evil magic,' I said to Commander Shenanigan. 'Not as long as we still have fight left. Right, FuzzyWuzzy?'"

FuzzyWuzzy who is biting out a tangle on his tummy, raises his head and gives a gruff growl. He knows his cues. When Slab is attached to FuzzyWuzzy, during this particular scene, he twirls his lariat and cues the bear up onto his hind legs.

"To my startled surprise," Slab continues, "Commander Shenanigan laughed an echoing laugh, 'Ha ha hee hee, hee hee ha ha,' that chilled and quieted the jungle, even the great white tiger. Then he turned into a thick black wisp o smoke and disappeared. 'Just as well,' I told FuzzyWuzzy. 'We have a tiger, a cobra, and quicksand, to contend with. We will have to save the defeat of Commander Shenanigan for later. Your time will come! I yelled to the dissipatin smoke. We have scores to settle.'"

The backstage door to the alleyway is open. Fritter McTwoBit is standing in the opening. Off in exotic locals, Slab hasn't noticed Fritter. FuzzyWuzzy, however, sniffs then spies Fritter and rolls to his back exposing his fat fuzzy abdomen and gives Fritter his most seductive pose. In bear language he pleads, "Scratch my tummy, please please, pretty please." Fritter is a sucker to his charm. She goes to FuzzyWuzzy and scratches his belly, far and wide, with her nails. FuzzyWuzzy says, "MMMMMMMMmmmmm MMMMMMMmmmmm moooooorrrr moooooooorrrrrrrr."

Slab is momentarily startled and a bit embarrassed as he always is when not saddled to FuzzyWuzzy or situated on a chair with his disability hidden beneath a table. He feels as he does in his dreams of being on stage, naked, and without his fuzzy companion. Fritter likes Slab Pettibone, she doesn't care that his legs are missing. She can feel his chagrin and out of kindness she keeps her eyes to Slab's face, without veering downward to his gloved stubs.

"Thas a toughass story, you wuz tellin, Slab. An I like how yall tells it."

In actuality Slab would prefer Fritter look just about anywhere other than where she's looking, which is into his eyes. Her dark eyes are soulful and sexy. Her gaze travels through his peepers into his head, sends an electric charge directly to his dingus, which, springs vivaciously upward and, because he's positioned on a barrel, wigwams his trousers. Slab Pettibone has been without female companionship for too many years, as a result his body responds like a horny adolescent.

"I thank yee for the compliment Miss Fritter. And, just between you and me, those stories are not really real. I just make em up."

"So yall ain't jus handsome but clever too. Got-damn, Yall gonna make me swoon into a puddle." Fritter can see her effect on the bashful Caucasian. She has never jonesed for a white man before. But, like her friend Bitch, she can see Slab's goodness. And, beyond what her friend can see, Fritter sees Slab's creative side. She can think of nothing more attractive than a kind and creative man. Once he overcomes his shyness, he could be a garden of pleasure on the bedsprings.

Slab removes his floppy sombrero and holds it over his heart, hiding his telltale boner behind the hat-brim. His flushed-red face crinkles into a beatific smile.

"I never reckoned myself too much on looks. It's real nice a you to address me as handsome. In return I'd like to say that you yourself are a stunner, in the lookin-at department." Suddenly Slab's head is ablaze. He can't believe he has said what he has just said. Miss Fritter carries a good-sized handbag. Slab hopes she doesn't hit him with it for his brazenness.

"Damnation, Sugar," she smiles at him, "If ya ain't the most suave and debonair mofo I ever heard."

Slab is in the clear. She's not going to hit him. In fact, and it slaps him like a bucket of ice, he's gonna score.

All along Fritter has been scratching and playing tom-toms on FuzzyWuzzy's soft tummy. When she removes her hands FuzzyWuzzy quickly captures them, one at a time, with his prehensile lips and puts them back on his midsection. Again Fritter takes her hands to herself. "FuzzyWuzzy, honeybear, I ken only handle one man atta time. I get back to you."

Slab's nerves tickle his brain. Fritter is closing in. He needs another clever remark, but is cautious of opening his mouth for fear of stuttering idiotically or worse, howling like a moonlit coyote.

Fritter speaks instead, "If it be all the same to yall Ima gonna give yall a big kiss on the mouth, jus outa pure sweetness."

Slab manages a sentence, "I would be right honored for the pleasurable pleasure o kissing your lips."

From where he sits, Slab and Fritter are eye-to-eye. She walks in close. She reaches under the sombrero and sets her hand on Slab's penis where it strains against his button-fly. They lean into a nice fit and connect lips. She opens her mouth and canoodles his tongue with hers. He can see into her open eyes. Slab drifts into a world of wanton rapture and everlasting love.

Fritter massages his erection and soul-kisses him with true passion and affection. She breaks the kiss slowly and removes her hand. She keeps her face in close to his. He can feel her soft breath. Fritter says, "I think me n yall gonna haff ta find us a nice private nest real soon, Mister Slab Pettibone honey."

"It seems you have read my thoughts, Miss Fritter... Sweets."

Slab Pettibone suddenly has a new freedom. Fritter's kiss has cured the insecurities and bashfulness he had formerly exhibited in her presence. He feels a newfound closeness. He feels a kinship where he can speak his thoughts without hiding his true feelings.

Fritter, though more open of nature to begin with, feels all of the above and more. Slab Pettibone has put her heart to thumping, and her thoughts to humping.

"Ah doan much wanna be leaving yall, but we got work gotta be done. And, anyways, I just stopped by to tell yall Mister Daddy wants you an FuzzyWuzzy up stage to take some pichers. An me an yall got a date for later."

Slab puts his hat back on his head. "I'll be a counting the minutes, Fritter my lady. I would also like to give you my humble thanks for being just who you are."

"Yall keep that sweet-talk commin, sugar, yall can just bout put a brand on my booty." She gives him a quick-but-sweet pucker-kiss on the lips then gives FuzzyWuzzy one on the snout, then makes her exit with a wink and a wave.

Slab closes his eyes and replays the kiss. He says to FuzzyWuzzy, "Come on over here, FuzzyWuzzy and let's get saddled-up. We got some pictures to get took and I do believe I ain't gonna have no trouble a smilin to the camera."

FuzzyWuzzy licks his paws, slicks back his brow, then ambles over to Slab. He imitates Fritter, puckers his lips and gives Slab a kiss. Slab Pettibone buries his face in FuzzyWuzzy's fur, wraps his arms around FuzzyWuzzy's neck and gives his bear a heartfelt bear-hug.

Bitch Bantam is too tall to sit in the chair at the dressing-room vanity. She sits instead on her knees and studies her face. The looking-glass is rimmed with electric bulbs. She has never seen herself in this light. Her eyes are violet, near purple. Depending on who is looking, they are freakish, or exotic, or scary, or melancholy, or beautiful. It is the beautiful that Bitch searches her reverse image for. Finding beauty snuggled fast across her face, even for a moment, would exceed all the dreams of her past. Bitch Bantam has, from the beginning of time, dueled antagonistic beaks, fangs, claws, yet her face bears no physical scars. Her greatest accomplishment has been the saving of her face. She has high edged cheekbones. Her skin is tight and rosy without lines of exclamation. Her lips are drawn into a soft sensual sneer. Though Bitch cannot find it, great beauty is there.

Bitch swirls her finger pad in a white jar of red rouge. Earlier she had watched Fritter apply makeup. She strives to imitate her friend. She rubs a red war-paint circle on her cheek.

Bitch needs to practice the lines that Daddy Smithy has prepared for her act with FuzzyWuzzy, *There is no beast alive can wrestle me to the ground!* She has however found that practice in front of the mirror is not possible. She can't face her open mouth, her teeth, iron-grey, pointed, carious and ugly.

The dressing-room door opens. Fritter McTwoBit enters, says, "Knock-Knock," then closes the door behind her. She sashays across the little room shakin her jam and singing a tune,

> *"Slab Slab bo bab*
> *banana bana bo bab*
> *fe fi fo fab, Slab."*

Bitch covers her mouth with her hand and laughs. "You're singin bout Mister Pettibone. You like him like girls and boysr sposed to do, doncha?"

"He be a sweetheart, sista Bitch. Ah kissed em like a ho and felt like a little girl. Ifn that ain't whack, I donno what."

"You kissed Mister Pettibone?"

"And felt it down to muh toes."

"I doan understand kissin a man, but I like that it makes you silly."

Fritter pulls a chair up next to Bitch, "Lemme, help yall with prettyin up yalls face." She puts a cloth over her index, wets it with her tongue and goes to work removing most of what Bitch has put on.

Bitch says, "Did you talk to Mister Daddy-Shit-For-Brains?" Fritter has been coaching Bitch in the art or irreverence, assigning names to the likes of Daddy Smithy is part of the homework.

"Ah tolt I'm we doan go on no stage with no human killer. He sent the mofo packin. Daddy-Shit-For-Brains gots somthin nasty somewheres inside em, but he knows show bidness."

"I guess. Ken you tell me somethin, Fritter? How come you're not a scared a nothin?"

"All things is different, Sista Bitch. I ain't scairt of kissin and I ain't scairt of performin. But, I'm plenty scairt, babydoll. I'm a colored woman in a white man world. I stay good and scairt, but ah feel safer round you an Slab Pettibone an FuzzyWuzzy than I ever felt before."

"I wisht I was brave instead a scared alla time. Sometimes I wanna talk to everbody and learn all about everthing and be a real person. And sometimes I just wanna hide where doan nobody haff to look at me."

"Doan you never hide, Sista Bitch. Yall got all-that and more," Fritter snaps her fingers. "Yall the muthafuckin second comin."

Fritter puckers up and gives Bitch a big kiss, not like the one she gave Slab Pettibone but just as full of love. "I just a membered, sweetchops, Daddy Shit-Fo-Brains wants yall out to the stage for some pichers."

Bitch Bantam demonstrates her irreverence: "Daddy Shit-for-Brains can shit in his squished hat." She laughs and looks at their mirrored reflections. She still can't find the beauty. She does, however, see the happiness.

Chapter Seven

The A-Train

The A-train clatters northeast toward the water, the end of the line, SodomHeights. Dooley Paradise prides himself with high morals yet the debauched preoccupation of SodomHeights excites him. He is anxious, his ideology is in peril.

Through crud-blackened windows BigCity rattles by like a flip-book. The landscape is sketched with small doses of great wealth and long panoramas of abject poverty. The whole of the dark earth is brought to light with a moonlight mix of gas-flame and electric-filament. At each screechy stop, a multitude of languages and customs, a worldly mix of mutts.

Next to Dooley sits Gulper Mooney. Across from Dooley sits a man in a band uniform, brass buttons, golden epaulets, a bright visored military cap. He holds a trombone to his mouth, but does not blow. He slides the slide fore and aft in a silent marching-band pantomime. Dooley spins a corresponding rag in his head, an inebriated Sousa. He closes his eyes for a while and when he opens them again, nothing has changed.

He says to Gulper, "This is stupid. I don't even know why I'm doing this."

"Tisnt stupid, tis a duty we do, us together like the years done. Best pals."

"Best pals? Jesus, Gulper. I don't think I even like you."

"Be there a speech yur to be makin to Gulper Mooney, save it, see. When we ave done our good deed and found our dupe, we shall ave us a go round."

Dooley agrees, he needs Gulper now, for the dirty work. He's deep in hock to Shag Draper and he needs to find the rumored killer without a nose. He needs to nab the guy and give him to the police, dead or alive. Dooley needs Gulper for this mission and when it's over, he hopes to never see the bastard again.

The train screams to a stop, deposits the trombone player and replaces him with a pretty boy in a ruffled shirt and a large square-jawed man in overalls who buries his face in his hands and sobs like a hungry baby.

Dooley says, "You know there is a good chance we won't find this guy. There are a lot of people in SodomHeights."

"Worry not me pal, forget the villain what has no smeller. Dassent matter who we nab, frits are all the same. We could end it all now if I grab this one," he nods across the aisle to the pretty boy. "Wouldn't take a moment to slice off the frit's pretty nose and we're back on the homeward-bound with our bounty."

"No way, Gulper, people up here are more like us than Shag Draper and his stupid Mooks. They're more like us than the corrupt BigCity-shots that run Shag. You go randomly fighting with this community, you're on the wrong side."

"I av nothing the same as these cocksuckers, they're worth no more than nobody else, see."

"Actually, I think they are worth more than we are. I don't think you and I are worth much of anything right now."

"Yur problem is yur too much always thinkin."

"No argument there."

Across the aisle, the weeping man continues to share his despair in loud impassioned bawls. The pretty boy moves to a different car.

33 KeroseneRow

Slab Pettibone's little house is brightly lit with flickering wicks. On his leather-padded stubs he sweeps the linoleum floor with a straw broom that stands taller than he. He dances a pigmy jig. He cannot recollect feeling as goofy as he feels now. He has a glorious erection for the object of his affection. Dashing though he is, Slab is painfully self-conscious around the opposite sex. He was a virgin when he lost his legs and as a half-man has never pursued a sexual relationship nor had the moxie to go to a whore. He has mummified his sexuality, buried it in a cortex tomb. Fritter McTwoBit has unraveled and pulled away the gauze strips, spinning his libido like a top.

Fritter's skin is deep sweet-caramel. Her face is carved with subtle beauty and fierce with passion. Her body jiggles with soft mounds of blissful flesh. Her smile is hot and sinful. She could smile a man to orgasm. Just thinking about it wrinkles Slab's face into a powerful grin.

Slab sweeps a puff of dust out the open front door then ambulates on his padded stubs to the kitchen. Shortly after arriving home, before unsaddling from FuzzyWuzzy, Slab had started a fire in the cook stove then pumped and heated buckets of water with which he filled a galvanized washtub. He detached himself from FuzzyWuzzy, who went out back to explore and play, then stripped jaybird-naked and lowered himself into the steaming tub. He soaped and scrubbed his epidermal casing exposing new, clean, blanched-white skin. Sitting in the warm suds with a hand-mirror, a razor, a scissors, a comb, he had shaved, trimmed, and groomed. He winked at his noble reflection and practiced sexy faces.

From the barn Slab has brought in a soft pile of hay, carried it upstairs to the bedroom, piled it on the floor, covered it with an oilcloth then two bedroll blankets, and made a comfy and welcoming bed. Also in the barn he found an old wicker love-seat which he has cleaned and set in the living room. He has slicked his long silver hair with rose-scented pomade, dressed in his fancy clean shirt and collar, and eaten a stick of horehound candy to sweeten his breath. He sits in the love-seat in front of the open door and practices debonair poses while awaiting his ladylove.

Earlier in the day, Daddy Smithy went to a little WhiteWay costumers shop and purchased an outfit for Fritterich Exotica's song and dance number. He paid for it with money borrowed from Slab. As Daddy saw it, Fritter needed something alluring to enhance her exotic princess persona. It is this new costume that Fritter McTwoBit is wearing when she says Knock-knock and walks into Slab Pettibone's living room.

Slab nearly levitates from his seat. "Gadzooks," he proclaims to the heavens above. "Mine eyes done seen the glory."

Fritter McTwoBit sashays, shimmies and smiles sexy megawatts. "Ain't yall just sweetness and honey, Mista Slab the flatterer."

Her hair is natural, in a short fro, with a tiara of colored glass across skeins of silver alloy twig. Her soft fleshy protuberances, tits, ass, belly, are nestled into a muslin two-piece Egyptian enchantress costume, upon which bright flowers and palm-fronds are drawn. She is without undergarments. Her hard nipples are embossed in the silky cloth, her navel a soft crater in a pillowy landscape. Her face is picture postcard perfect, wide sensual lips, eyes flecked with gold, the color of cigarette tobacco. Slab can do little more than stammer and whoop.

"Fritter, my flower... Tarnation, woman! I believe you've done stolen my heart as well as my repose. I am bowled backwards by thoughts o sinful glory."

"Ain't nothin sinful bout us. We down with each other, and when you down with someone, they ain't nothin sinful bout good fuckin."

Dadblamed, Slab's bashfulness melts away when Fritter says dirty words. He has never heard a sound so sweet as the word Fuckin from Fritter's lips. Say it again and again, he wants to tell her, but instead opts to say nothing, as he is not au courant with boudoir talk and doesn't want to botch the mood.

Fritter saunters to Slab, kneels to the floor with her heavy breasts in his lap, and leans in, face to face.

"Kiss me, Handsome. Make muh cootche coo."

They lock lips and touch tongues and Slab enters heaven through the pearly gates. Fritter's kiss is better than a thousand pipe dreams. His hands begin to explore, her neck, shoulders, breasts. He wants to grope hungrily yet he wants to pleasure her as much as she pleasures him. He has heard that there are ways of pleasuring women but he is not sure how it works and too shy, thus far, to ask.

Fritter has no problems with shyness. When the time comes she is prepared to coach Slab on the finer points of sexual favor. But first she will do him and do him she does. She breaks the kiss and says, "Less get a gander at that big jimbrowsky, sugarplum."

Slab's heartbeat pounds the walls. His emotions, a pinball, ding, lust, ding, love, ding, desire, ding, bashfulness, ding, brazenness, ding, and cowering behind it all, ding-ding-ding, orror. What if she is repulsed by his ugly stubs?

Fritter unbuckles Slab's belt and unbuttons his fly. She pulls his pants (outer and under) off and sets them on the floor. Slab closes his eyes away from the abhorrence her face will surely show.

"Sheeit, that be one big mofo jammy, Slab honey. Open yalls eyes sugar booger, I want yall ta see me aworkin yalls skinbone."

Ding-ding-ding, Fritter is far from repulsed and she is talkin dirty again. The terror evaporates. Slab Pettibone is seconds from spontaneous combustion. He opens his eyes and looks at Fritter. She winks at him, moves from side to side and gives a tender kiss to each of his calloused and scar-tissued thigh stubs.

"Ahm a do yall like stick-candy," Fritter says, then does.

Tears of joy drizzle Slab's cheeks. His dingus telegraphs unsurpassed pleasure to his head. He caresses Fritter's face, her neck, her everywhere he can reach. He could revel in this erotic rapture forever. If, that is, he could control the school of spermatozoon surfing the tube. The onrush of orgasm begins in his coccyx, spreads through his body. Pleasure spasms quake the control from his limbs. It has taken years to get here and only seconds to ejaculate. "Yaaa-hoop-hoop-hoop YAHOOOEY!"

Fritter uses her hand to squeeze out residue laggers, giving Slab multiple pleasure jolts. She smiles up at Slab.

Land-O-Goshen, Slab thinks, (or maybe says out loud) this beautiful magnificent African-Queen has emptied him and at the same time made him whole. This is the apex of life, an experience of this nature. Now, even though he is spent, he wants to return the favor, if only he knew how, if only he can find the voice to ask.

Fritter reads his mind. She stands before him and pulls her thin costume over her head. Slab has never read anything in a storybook or elsewhere that comes close to describing a vision as exquisite as Fritter McTwoBit stark naked.

"Did yall like what Ah did fo yall, Mista Sweet-man-lover Slab Pettibone?"

"I do believe, my radiant beloved dove, I never in my born days felt nothin so dazzling and heartfelt. If only I could serve you as well."

"Yall can, babydoll. Just let me lead the way. Ah ma show ya how to use yalls face for pleasurin even more better than fuckin."

Again with the dirty talk. Slab loves this woman with all his might. Fritter and Slab trade places. She sits on the love-seat with her bare feet on the edge, her legs open. Slab stands on his stubs, leans in and takes his first ever gynecological look into a woman. She is more beautiful than all nature. She smells of sweet forest musk. He is drawn forward into the tangled web of pubic hair and with a sudden brazenness takes a nibble, a taste, allows instinct to kick-start.

"Sheeit, doan nobody need a tell yall how make a girl feel fine."

Slab needs little coaching. He performs like a professor of pussy. He improvises cunning tweaks here and there, a finger in and out of there.

"Oh, Baby-baby-baby! That be it, oh yeh. Ohh, Slab, baby, yalls sooo goood. Bring it all home to Mama."

Slab stays with it, gets lost in it, until Fritter pushes her sex into him, squeals passionate delight and rocks through a double-triple-quadruple orgasm.

Slab lays his head to rest on Fritter's velvety thigh. Fritter runs her fingers through his long wavy locks.

Slab wonders aloud, "Where you been all my life? I never done thought I would love nothin as much as I love my bear, FuzzyWuzzy. But, I never knowed about this kind o love. Not never."

"Sheeit, mista Loverman. Ain't never in my own damn life Ida thought a whiteman could be nothin but a shithead. They is black men that er good for fuckin, but theys all shitheads in the end. Yall, Mister Exception. Yall gonna get alla my love."

"Tarnation, my angel, look at that. My ah...dingus is all blowed up again. I got a nice soft pallet all set up upstairs. We still ain't done the ah... you know... part."

Fritter takes his hand and kisses it. "Yall can say it, I like the word."

Slab Pettibone takes a deep breath and fills himself with courage. "Fritter, my love. What say we adjourn to the upstairs parlor where I shall fu--fornicate you, ah, good and ah, give you all my love?"

"Ohh, baby," Fritter titters. "I love a man knows how to talk that talk."

KeroseneRow Woods

FuzzyWuzzy is lounging, stomach to egg-yolk moon, like a fluffy recumbent snowman, licking grub-worm and berry residue from his lips. Behind Slab Pettibone's house a miniforest sighs in the quiet. The dark sky is fish-belly silver. FuzzyWuzzy says, Uhmppp uhmppp and smacks his lips.

He rolls to his paws and walks to a young tree, thin and twenty-feet up. He stands on his hind-legs and attacks the tree with his upper-body, shadow boxing. His claws gouge the skin and take hold, going up. He climbs five feet and hugs the trunk like a dear friend then decides to shake it up. He rocks his four-hundred-sixty-seven pounds back and forth. He moans happy, mmmmmyaammmmm. He flaps the tree, whipping its tip like a fishing rod, and then continues his climb.

At fifteen feet, the tree resembles a catapult. FuzzyWuzzy puffs out vowels, aaaaooouu, rips off a limb and brushes his teeth. He points his puppy-dog profile to the tippy treetop, wondering how it might taste. Onward he treks as the treetop bows under his weight. With his claws in a secure grove, FuzzyWuzzy begins to spin. The tree thawks around like a loaded spring.

FuzzyWuzzy hits the brakes when he hears the crunchy cracks of the trunk below, Timmmberrr! Perplexity replaces the playful glee across his buttermilk babyface. The tree snaps, crackles and breaks. FuzzyWuzzy vocalizes the ursine equivalent of Oops. He falls to the ground and bounces like a bag of clay. The foliage shutters.

FuzzyWuzzy rolls around in horseplay, wrestling limbs and branches. He freezes when he hears an unwoodsy noise, goes to all fours and takes a radar sniff. FuzzyWuzzy is practiced in staying out of sight when not with Slab Pettibone. People carry guns and don't think twice when it comes to shooting bears and minorities. FuzzyWuzzy is cautious. He relaxes when he determines the scent of a friend. He smells Bitch Bantam but cannot see her in the spectral lunar light. It is a little spooky for FuzzyWuzzy.

Bitch Bantam jumps suddenly from the bushes and yells, "BOO," then leapfrogs over FuzzyWuzzy, spinning and landing, facing him. FuzzyWuzzy shits three pounds of recycled berries, grubs, termites, and greens. He huffs a startled sentence, Hhhuuugggg!

Bitch Bantam is laughing through guilty feelings. FuzzyWuzzy looks faint like an old woman with the vapors.

"I dint mean ta asceer ya so much. I was jus playin." She goes to FuzzyWuzzy, snuggles in under his legs and hugs him. She dances him away from the pile of scat then rolls them both to the ground. She sits astraddle his belly and gives him leg-fibrillating scratches.

"I like nighttime bettern day," Bitch tells FuzzyWuzzy, "It's quiet here. Mister Pettibone and Fritter are kissing and stuff. I looked in the winder. Men are even more ugly when they doan wear clothes. Fritter says she thinks Mister Slab is handsome. If handsome is being nice then I think he's handsome too. But I doan think that's what it means. I can do things now. I'm gonna learn how to read books. Fritter says we can have chairs and beds and tables and chromos in our house. Fritter and Mister Slab likes to do all that show stuff. I doan. I doan like when people watch me. But I wanna stay close to Fritter and Mister Slab. Did you know that ifn I get smarter, I can find out how come people are the way they are. Remember when I saw that lady and she smiled at me? If I ever see her again I'm gonna be brave and smile back, then I bet she will talk to me. Wouldn't that be somethin, FuzzyWuzzy, if that lady talked to me? It's good about Mister Slab and Fritter kissing and liking each other because they like it. Sometimes Fritter is real funny and she's pretty too. If I was pretty as Fritter, I'd be funny all the time jus like her."

FuzzyWuzzy has drifted into a dream of a clean icy stream, spawning salmon. Bitch Bantam leans back into his cozy fur and looks up to the moon. She says, "This is nice."

SodomHeights

SodomHeights sits on a declivitous hillside overlooking the shoreline. Single-story buildings draggle up and down the muddy roads like cockeyed tombstones. Fiery red-lanterns attract swirling areolas of sputtering bugs. Music rolls downhill from shanties and pubs and loops, night and day, day and night. Below this askew village a thick fog has drifted in from the north shore, a wispy white cover refracting the quivering lights from above. It looks to Dooley Paradise that he could climb a tree and jump to a soft landing on a floor of cotton.

Unlike the other specialized ghettos of BigCity, the spectral SodomHeights does not exist. Politicians, reformers, historians can never, will never, acknowledge the degradation born of this rockin little hillside where men are women, women are men, where public debauchery reigns without shame. It is better to close one's eyes to such raffish shenanigans and look instead to bible-story phantoms. Dooley Paradise's eyes are open wide as he checks out the mad denizens of SodomHeights. Dooley feels a kinship that frightens him and confounds his morals.

At the bottom of the Heights, a vast body of water trickles against the shore like background music. Just above the hightide line, next to a ghostly weatherbeaten pier, a row of squat shacks peddle sin from crooked doorways.

On the tail of the pier, Dooley Paradise and Gulper Mooney shimmer in the light of haphazardly placed kerosene torches.

"This place is no good," says Dooley. "I'm about ready to give up on this whole thing."

"Yur is sometime like a gurl, me friend," Gulper says. "Taint nuttin here can't be killed er beaten, see. Me ownself could never be creeped by no pufferboy."

Dooley knows better, there is more down here than pufferboys. Hard-trade men and women, meaner than Gulper, are armed, dangerous, and void of compunction. It matters little to Dooley if Gulper thinks he acts like a girl. He says, "Let's just do what we have to do and get outa here. I'll take the pier and the first couple of shacks on this side. You take the beach pathway and we can meet back here in a half hour."

"Yur makin it more than need be, me frien. I'll be pleased to grab up a pufferboy and slice his throat and we be on the way, see."

"Just shut up, Gulper. We're here to find one guy. Leave the others alone."

"Always the caring one yur are, like a puffer yur own self. I spit," Gulper spits, "on dem all, see."

"Think what you want. Just do me this favor and look for the guy without a nose. Thirty minutes we meet back here."

The boys check their pocket watches and go opposite directions, Gulper with brass-knuckles, a gun and a knife, Dooley with a small pistol and a slug-shot.

Dooley goes into a slapdash structure at the waters-edge. A great lily-pond pool is carved into the earth. A fire burns bright, heating caldrons of water, dancing the shadows of unbridled perversity to the warped wooden walls. Men are everywhere naked, conjoined like astrological signs. On a small stage a quartet sings, "Mary's A Grand Old Name".

"My mother's name was Mary
She was so good and true
Because her name was Mary
She called me Mary too
She wasn't gay or airy
but plain as she could be
I'd hate to be contrary
and call myself Marie."

Everyone in the joint is looking at Dooley, who after all is a teenager and generally feels that everyone is watching him anyway. He looks quickly through the steam around the room for a guy without a nose; as if he knows what he would do if he found the guy among this orgy of men.

From out of the mist a naked muscleman runs in slow motion to Dooley, calls first dibs. His penis is large and hard, bouncing like a high-dive. Dooley turns tail and runs back into the night. Tarzan sighs, turns, runs, jumps, and cannonballs into the drink.

Outside Dooley is woozy, conflicted. From his pants pocket he takes his flask of spiderbite and anesthetizes his nerve-ends. He is finished, that's it, the mission is ridiculous. Dooley hardly cares, at this point, about some noseless maniac. Shag Draper is full of shit. Dooley is an administrator and budding politician. He is not a bounty hunter. He looks off to the smell and sound of the waters teasing the shore, sees the thick wispy white of low clouds. Dooley walks out onto the rickety pier, his cocky strut busted to a tail-drag.

On the pier, cool mist nibbles Dooley's skin like a glass

of seltzer. His thought process, a fuzzy amalgam of sickness and spiderbite pays no heed to his forward motion feet. Suddenly he is blind, in the teeming advection fog, beneath a dirty white sheet. "Shit!" he says aloud. "Goddamn and double goddamn what the hell am I doing?!"

"Maybe what your doin is lookin for me," says a raspy voice that brings a startled cry from Dooley. He jumps, slips on the wet-wood surface, stumbles and falls.

A hand from the white blindness offers a pull-up. Dooley declines the hand, pulls himself up and nearly falls again when he sees a boy not much older than he, underexposed in the grainy bleached haze. He is dressed like a westerner, vest, boots, slouch hat, denim jeans. His face absorbs the ambient light and emerges from a muffler of shadow. His scent is thick of patchouli. Below his black snake-eyes and above his sneered trail of lips, he wears the smiling gash of a red silk scarf twisted and tied in the back like a bandana. His name is Eddie Plague. In his right hand he holds a smoky-white straight razor, loose with implied threat. "You're very pretty," he tells Dooley, "like I used to be."

Dooley is petrified. The weapons in his pockets are not a consideration. He would run, but to where? He and Eddie Plague stand together in a white-walled box, without direction. He opens his mouth to speak but says nothing. He is horrified by the razor in Eddie Plague's hand and the psychosis in his eyes.

Eddie is heavy-breathing through the open sore where once he had a nose. He inhales snotty bubbles of blood that punctuate his syntax. "I know what you want," he says in a nasty whisper. "But do you understand what I want?" He reaches his left hand and feels Dooley between the legs.

Dooley knows this is the killer. He knows his life hangs,

like the fog, on thin air. His brain screams Go away, but he says nothing.

Eddie feels a little something extra in Dooley's pants. "Is this what I think it is?" He brings his razor up to Dooley's eyes and with his other hand removes Dooley's gun and slugshot from his pockets. He drops them clunk to the sodden plank floor.

"Maybe I was wrong. I thought you were cruising but I don't know why a pretty boy like you would need a gun unless you were going to do a little mugging. Is that what you were going to do? Take my money?" He grabs and squeezes Dooley's penis, gently like a lover's touch.

"Of course it no longer matters what you had planned to do because now you belong to me." He brings the razor to Dooley's Adam's apple and breaks the thin skin.

Dooley closes his eyes and begs everything to go away. Below him he can feel the concussion of waves, can hear the water against the pilings, can smell wet wood, dead fish, sour marsh. Somewhere beyond the white blindness, across the impenetrable forest of water, a man yells, "Raise a glass, to me mudder's fat arse!" then all goes quiet, all except Eddie Plague's whispers.

"Open your eyes," Eddie brings his face in close. "I want you to look at me. I was pretty like you. I want you to look at me and tell me how pretty you think I am. Unless I'm too ugly for a handsome young man such as yourself." He screams in a harsh whisper, *"Open your eyes!"*

Dooley opens his eyes. Inches away, the gash of scarlet covering Eddies nose-hole puffs in and out like fish gills. Dooley remains silent but tears begin to coat his cheeks. He looks into the killer's eyes, black, reflecting gravestones of white fog.

"You like this, don't you? You like my hand, you like the feel of the razor. And when I cut your throat and your blood pours out, will you like that as well? You know, you have a nice mouth, cruel but nice. You have a mouth I would like to kiss. Is that what you want? Would you like to kiss me?" He goes cheek to cheek and puts his ear next to Dooley's mouth. "I can't hear you, beautiful, and I'm waiting for an answer. Do you want to kiss me?" Eddie increases the push of the razor. Dooley can feel the blood, the same as his tears dribbling down his cold skin.

"Yes? No? Am I too ugly for you? Is that it? You better hurry up and tell me what you want."

Dooley lets out a sob and with it a mournful word, "Yes," though he does not know which question he is answering.

"Well then pucker up, pretty boy." Eddie puts his mouth to Dooley's mouth, the scarlet scarf wipes across Dooley's nose. Eddie puts his tongue in Dooley's mouth. Dooley cannot breathe, cannot cry, cannot scream. He tastes peppermint.

"Yoodel loo, Dooley me chum. Are yur out here in the soup?!" Gulper Mooney hollers.

Eddie pulls away from Dooley, gives him a kiss on the forehead and a wink then disappears into the blinding white mist. The thick scent of patchouli clings to Dooley's face like a spider-web.

"Yoodel loo, yoodel loo!" Gulper emerges from the low cloud, nearly bumping into Dooley. "Wha dey feck?!"

Dooley's gun and slugshot are at his feet.

Gulper looks at Dooley with curiosity and a degree of disgust. He reiterates, "Wha the feck?!"

At this moment Dooley hates his childhood best friend. He hates Gulper Mooney even more than he hates the manboy who has just molested and nearly murdered him. He hates Gulper for putting them here on this wild goose chase, hates him for his betrayal. "It's nothing, Gulper. Let's get the hell out of here."

Dooley picks up his gun and slugshot. He takes from his vest pocket the flask of spiderbite and drinks.

Gulper smirks. He is perplexed as to what has happened, but he has an idea. "Methinks I heard yur talkin to someone, me pal. Did yur make a little friend out here onna boardwalk?" Gulper is smoking a Signal. From his nose he exhales a white Fu Manchu.

"Fuck you, Gulper. Cmon lets go home."

"Home? We ave yet to find our bounty, chum."

"Forget it we're not going to find anyone. The guy without a nose is just story."

"Tis not my neck but yurs, so if yur wantin to go then go we shall."

This infuriates Dooley even more. He wants to scream at Gulper, call him names, and confront him with his crimes and betrayal. But what Dooley needs now at this moment is the protection of their number. He is scared to be alone in the white blindness. "I'll worry about my neck later." He casually feels the razor cut on his Adam's apple. "Lead us the way out of here. I'm turned around. I just want to go home." Dooley strikes a match, suckles a Signal and feeds druggy nutrients to his brain.

Saying nothing, Gulper walks down the boardwalk out of the fog and back to the pathway. Dooley follows close behind.

33 Kerosene Row

Slab Pettibone's arms are wrapped tight around Fritter McTwoBit's middle; he can almost touch his own fingers at her spine. He wraps himself in her naked flesh, a luscious foam-padded security blanket. Together they canoodle in languid repose, catching the breath they have blown in robust intercourse. At the open window, fireflies blink amatory dispatches.

Slab cradles his head between Fritter's bouncy boobs, his goatee teases a nipple, hard and wrinkly as a sweet prune. He speaks in a whisper as though he might wake sleeping mice in the squeaky floorboards, as though he might startle his truelove into flight.

"Would you marry me and be my wife?"

"Yall whisperin to mah titties, Honeybun. Mah ears caint here yall up here."

"Would you marry me and be my wife!?"

Fritter gives Slab a big sloppy kiss on the top of his head. "Looky up a mah face, ya hot and handsome Slab a loove. Sheeit! Will ah marry yall?! Goddamn! Sheeit! Lordy-Muthafucka!"

Slab is getting worried, unable to decipher her reaction. Damnation all, he has blown it! Fritter McTwoBit does not love him the way he loves her and now he has blown what they have by asking for too much. Why oh why couldn't he have been happy with what he had?

"Yall still ain't lookin at me," Fritter coaches his gaze upward. He raises his eyes slowly, her breasts, two fat sepia cheeks framing his consternation which metamorphosis into jubilation when she says, "Sheeit yas, mah main man. I marry yall tomorra, yall want. Ah been meanin to tell yall, Mister Slab Pettibone, I loves yall like nuttin afore an ever after."

Slab says, "Yaaa-hoop-hoop-hoop YAHOOOEY! God o thunder mighty!" With the aid of two digits he whistles a shrill but happy cheer that wakes all manners of animal in a half-mile radius, including FuzzyWuzzy and Bitch Bantam.

"Yall sho knows how to make a girl feel preciated."

Slab has shinnied up to a face-to-face. "Fritter," he likes saying her name, "Fritter-Fritter-Fritter. I believe it to be plain fact that you are the perfect girl. How could any man not appreciate that?"

Fritter could at this juncture explain how most men are jerks but why would she? Slab Pettibone is not most men. There are concerns, however, that live at the periphery of their romantic love. She does not want to break the spell, but... "What about FuzzyWuzzy and Miz Bitch?"

The spell is not broken; the question has been at the edge of Slab's lips as well. His love for Fritter only grows with her concern for the others concerned. Ditto Fritter.

"FuzzyWuzzy has never been the jealous type. I reckon he'll be hunky-dory. He likes you an if we stay here, in BigCity, and then he has the woods out back where he can roam and such. I think FuzzyWuzzy will be just fine. But, I must to tell you, Fritter... Fritter-Fritter-Fritter, I cannot much figger Miss Bantam. What I think, is she needs both you and me to help her along. She's a fine person who hasn't had much good before now. Soon as I met her I was feelin all gooshey about her, like with a baby or FuzzyWuzzy. I guess sometimes I don't do so good sayin what I mean to say."

"Ah thinks yall talk real good. We can get us hitched

214

together and we ken watch over Bitch Bantam. I doan be knowin Bitch, or even yall, cept a couple a days, an here ah loves everbuddy like a big ol happy family. We ken stay close to Bitch and hep her when she needs us. She's gonna be all growed up real fast, smart cookie like her. What we gotta hope for, is she doan grow up and go away. Ahd be missing her real bad, if she went an gone away."

"Me too, Fritter, Fritter-Fritter-Fritter. Gadzooks my princess, take a look down yonder. My ahh... My big hungry dingus looks ready for another helpin o your sweet pudenda." Slab is finding that intimacy and familiarity has assuaged his stammers. He gives out an enthusiastic Whoop-whoop-whoop.

"Ohh Slab Pettibone mah husband-to-be. Gimmie that big ol hunk a skinbone. Stick it in, baby! Oooh ooh, stick it in, stick it in, stick it in!"

TumbleHouse

At the TumbleHouse bar Zeph Riley is practicing jokes on his girlfriend Mabel Scott. He lights a Signal cigarette and says, "I used to be a chain smoker but they got too heavy to carry around." Across the room a boy is standing on a chair cranking a hurdy-gurdy. Girls dance with other girls. Boys with Signal butts plugged into their mugs, talk tough, pretend they do not care about the girls. Behind the bar, a mouse teeters across a picture frame, rappels down to a dusty shelf, poops turd pellets next to a pickle jar and sniffs for crumbs.

A circle of preteen girls sit sewing, talking about boys they will marry, houses they will live in, families they will have, dreams they will realize. They will in fact live through wars, epidemics, scientific breakthroughs. Some of these girls will die young while others will live to see atomic bombs, television, Disneyland.

On the second floor a boy of ten in a room of six has awakened to find his ticking sopped with urine. He lies still and watches a crane-fly navigate ceiling shadows. His bottom itches, squishy against the bedwet straw. He does not scratch or otherwise move for fear of waking others, pointing fingers, chanting hurtful bedwetter rhymes,

> *"Stupid boy*
> *don't mean maybe*
> *Wets his bed*
> *just like a baby."*

The boy imagines he is grown with a child of his own, a child that wets the bed. He whips the boy with a hickory switch.

Outside, along the DreckRiver, a hog is firmly rooted in a marshy bog. His hind legs churn in slow-motion through sucking sludge. He squeals operatic pleas of distress. A dog perks two parabolic ears and slink-bellies to higher ground. Two teenagers, a boy and a girl wearing Brusselsprout Derbys, stand in a patch of dirt watching the struggling pig. The boy says, "That pig is dead meat," then puts his arm around the girl's shoulders and casually rests his hand on her budding bosom. The girl blushes and smiles and the amber moon shines.

A slice of lunar cheese falls into a top-floor window where Girl sits in Gulper Mooney's bed with an open book, *Huckleberry Finn*. She slides her index finger below the words, the ones she can and cannot read. Girl's wounds are healing, but the news of Snooks's death and the homicidal nightmare at Jones Mulligan's, plays heavy on her head. Girl whacked Jones Mulligan to the afterlife with a fire-poker and she watched the boy she loves in a murderous rage. Gulper spit on the dead man with a satisfied coolness. Gulper likes killing people. Girl hates it but she wants vengeance for Snooks, her murdered sister. Girl blames Daddy, Showbiz Smithy. She wants him dead and Gulper is the man for the job. Afterward she can live here at TumbleHouse and be a part of something good. Hopefully she can make a clean break from Gulper Mooney and hopefully, Gulper will go west without her.

Girl gets a chill. She drinks from her medicine bottle of Doctor FixUp and goes to the window to warm herself in the summer breeze. In the backyard below a little group of preteen boys are smoking and cussing. Girl turns her back to the window, closes her eyes and twirls through space and time.

On the floor above Girl, Adelina Brown is in Dooley's room waiting for him, making sure he is okay. She looks into Dooley's shaving mirror over the sink and checks out a volcanic zit on the tip of her nose. It's grown since she last looked thirty minutes ago. She wishes she looked more like Girl and less like her. She wishes Dooley would look at her like all the boys look at Girl. But maybe, Adelina tells herself, her appearance is more suited to her quest as a journalist-photographer-filmmaker. Maybe this new passion will supply her with reason and self-possession. Maybe her future efforts will negate her propensity to measure her worth by the appraisal of pop culture and Dooley Paradise. Adelina says, "Fuck it," and turns her back to the mirror.

Adelina is not sleepy and decides not to wait for Dooley but to instead go to her room, gather her equipment, and take a few trips down to the cellar where she has more room for her cameras and darkroom. Maybe she will develop her first reel of film. Adelina gathers herself up to go and as she is about to open the door going out, Dooley Paradise opens it and walks in.

Unlike Adelina, Dooley's appearance measures up to, maybe even defines, popular standards. People fall in love with Dooley at a glance. Tonight, though, at this moment, Dooley looks ruined. His charismatic halo is charred. The handsome boy, normally a rigorous machine of kinetic cool, appears broken. He looks at Adelina and says, "Gulper Mooney is no longer a part of TumbleHouse. He's not a Brusselsprout. Tomorrow I'm going over Shag Draper's head and I'll tell the chief of Police that it was Gulper who killed the SnarlingTiger on the street, as well as Jones Mulligan."

Adelina knows better. Whatever Gulper has done, and indeed Adelina knows the things Gulper has done, Dooley will never sacrifice the boy that has long been his brother.

"You talked to Gulper about this," Adelina says not as a question but a lead-in for Dooley's diatribe.

"We talked. Gulper told me everything like it was no big deal. He assassinated Jones Mulligan for five thousand dollars from Shag Draper, which he has not yet been paid.

Five thousand dollars to forget about me and you and TumbleHouse. Five thousand dollars to throw away everything I thought we wanted."

"You know, Dooley, Gulper never really wanted what you wanted him to want."

"He's taking the girl, Girl, or whatever her name is and going west. He thinks he's going to be a rich cowboy or something. He thinks he's going to kill Indians and buffalos. He's an idiot and he sold out the only person that ever loved him."

"That would be you."

"Yes, that would be me."

"I'm sorry, Dooley. I really am."

Adelina has been talking with her hand casually hiding the blemish, a murky soap bubble, at the tip of her nose. Dooley has not noticed but suddenly his hyperactive head grabs at another subject altogether. He looks into Adelina's eyes with a mad gleam in his own.

"I want to make love to you, Adelina, right now. I love you and I love your womanhood and I want to make love right now."

Womanhood? "How about if we get in bed together and snuggle, Dooley. You need to calm down. Let's just snuggle and relax for a while and see what happens. I love you too." Adelina puts her arms around Dooley and holds him. His body shakes like a freezing dog.

Dooley has been seized with an urgency to assert his manhood, the result of his emasculating encounter with Eddie Plague. He grabs Adelina roughly and kisses her not with love or passion but desperation. He walks quickly near dragging her along to the bed. "Get undressed; I want you naked."

"Dooley..."

"Don't talk. Can't you see that I need you?"

"Dooley..."

"Show me your breasts."

"Fuck you, Dooley," Adelina is up off the bed. "If it's a quick poke you need, you'll not be getting it from me. I hope you feel better tomorrow. I'm sorry about you and Gulper. If you want to apologize to me, I'll be in the cellar with my photography equipment. Goodnight!"

"Adelina..."

Adelina is gone out the door, a passing storm. Dooley goes to a cabinet and retrieves a bottle of spiderbite.

DADDY SMITHY PRODUCTIONS PRESENTS
A STIMULATING SPECTACLE
A TANTALIZING ADVENTURE
SONG – & – FIGHTIN' – MANIA
AMERICAN HERO SLAB PETTIBONE
& HIS FEROCIOUS PET BEAR FUZZYWUZZY
ADVENTURE RE-CREATIONS – SONG & DANCE
THE MOST DANGEROUS WOMAN IN THE WORLD
BITCH BANTAM
– FIGHTS ALL COMERS –
$ 50.00 TO ANYONE THAT CAN STAY
3 MINUTES IN THE ON-STAGE RING
PLUS
BITCH BANTAM VS FUZZYWUZZY
– TITLE BOUT FOR WORLD'S FIERCEST BEAST –
NO HOLD'S BARRED

INTRODUCING TO AMERICAN AUDIENCES
- NOT FOR THE WEAK OF HEART -
THE WOMAN BANNED BECAUSE OF HER EROTIC ALLURE
FROM PARIS FRANCE

PRINCESS FRITTERICH EXOTICA

ALSO
FOR MEN ONLY,
LIVE MOVING PICTURES OF A NAUGHTY NATURE
PREMIERE - THE ORPHEUS THEATER
FRIDAY - AUGUST 4 - 8:00PM
500 EAST WHITEWAY AVE. BIGCITY 50 CENTS

Chapter Eight

Orpheus Theater

Thirty minutes to show time. The box-office is open. Daddy Smithy has hired Mabel Scott, the young girlfriend of his opening act, Zeph Riley, The Singing Butthole, for the ticket booth. She is math proficient, adept in speech and manner, and hopefully honest. A big dumb looking guy named Sow Madden stands next to the booth swinging a slugshot. Sow is also hired help. He protects the proceeds. Next to Sow stands bartender/entertainer Zeph Riley. Zeph is stylin in a prototype checkered zoot-suit, yellow and green. He wears a matching yacht cap with a patent-leather visor. His suspenders are wide and red with embroidered flowers. He has metal taps nailed to the heels of his pug-nosed brogans. He dances a jig and kicks up a goodly noise. He delivers a spiel, "Step right up. See the show of shows. Listen to me. I'm the one what knows. Bring the ladies. Bring the old folks. Bring the babies. Bring the artichokes. Slab Pettibone and FuzzyWuzzy, his live bear, are here, with tales of deepest darkest everywhere. Step right up, tickets are here."

A crowd is gathering. A dough-faced guy with a turkey-neck goiter pushes a vegetable cart of overripe tomatoes and cabbages which he sells to critics for a pence apiece.

Down the alleyway around to the side, Negroes and prostitutes stand in the ticket line and climb the outside stairway three floors up to the balcony. The whores go down a flight to the second balcony and mingle with the randy white clientele. The Negroes are in high spirits and the prostitutes are looking at a good night of suck and loose pockets.

The front lobby, while large and stately, has fallen to disrepair. The beams are warped and plaster is cracked. High royal drapes have fallen to masticated tendrils. The wooden floor is rubberized with mildew and rolls like molehills. Two green-hatted youths, drafted into service by Zeph Riley, are selling flip-books and copies of The Adventures of Slab Pettibone and FuzzyWuzzy. The animated flip books are a Daddy Smithy specialty. The woman, fully dressed in the first photo and down to her skivvies in the final photo, is in fact not a grown woman but Daddy Smithy's oldest daughter at age ten with padding and stage make-up. The two boys hawking the art and tall-tales are Bug and Flopears, the same two Brusselsprouts that boosted Daddy Smithy's motion picture gear. Daddy Smithy has not recognized Bug and Flopears as his powers of observation are elsewhere occupied.

On stage behind the curtain Daddy Smithy is cursing the thieving Brusselsprouts as he futzes with his old projector. A week back, this old Sear's Optigraph projector was Daddy's pride and joy but now, after owning and then losing the state of the art film equipment, this sucks. Even so, Daddy moves forward. He has rigged the Optigraph with a wide-angle lens borrowed from an old view-camera so that he can rear project the moving film clips from twenty-feet back onto a stretched white muslin panel. The wide angle vignettes the images somewhat, but for Daddy's purposes it is perfect. The only problem is his light-source, an either-calcium burner which is without a cooling system, tends to produce poisonous smoke and occasionally ignites the highly ignitable celluloid film, a minor concern within Daddy's plethora of concerns.

Daddy Smithy's biggest worry is his new star player, Bitch Bantam, who is refusing to speak her lines, lines that Daddy has perfected, great lines such as, *It's smackdown time!*, and, When *I finish with that Fuzzy-beast he will be picking his tail from his teeth!* Now, Daddy will be side-stage with a megaphone and yelling Bitch's paraphrased lines for her, *Miss Bantam says there is no man can pin her and I offer fifty dollars to any man who can!*

Bitch Bantam won't speak lines because she can't face a full-house with an open mouth: freak shark-teeth for all to see. Bitch owes this explanation to no one, though she may confide to Fritter. To Daddy Smithy she has said, "I won't say no lines, PERIOD."

On the other hand, Daddy finds Fritter McTwoBit a valuable go-between in negotiations with just about everybody. She has an understanding of the biz and is a professional performer and natural manager. Daddy likes Fritter McTwoBit and wishes he could talk to her now about a number of last minute items. Unfortunately, Fritter is not available.

There is a Do Not Disturb sign on Fritter's dressing-room door. She is entertaining company in the person of Slab Pettibone. Occasionally Slab's shouts can be heard, through the keyhole and bounced around the acoustical backstage: Jumpin Thunder Almighty! Land O Goshen! Yaaa hoop hoop hoop yahooey! And once Daddy could swear he heard the man crow like a rooster. Therefore, Slab is also unavailable. Daddy Smithy needs to talk Slab about FuzzyWuzzy. Slab has set up a spot backstage with a mattress of straw, a washtub of fresh veggies, and a makeshift litterbox. FuzzyWuzzy has taken to the area like a sunbather with a hot summer novel. This would be fine with Daddy, if Slab would only leash the beast. A bear on the loose makes Daddy, as well as the troupe of second-string talent, nervous. Slab Pettibone refuses to chain the bear and insists that the animal is not dangerous. On top of that, FuzzyWuzzy's litterbox needs changing once every fifteen minutes. The big bruin seems to crap more than he eats and he is always eating, at times simultaneously masticating, ingesting, defecating and micturating.

All this is relatively minor in the showbiz scheme of things. Other than an occasional jab of angst, Daddy Smithy is pretty feeling good. In two days' time Daddy Smithy has put together a show like no other and in no time at all Daddy Smithy is going to be rolling in greenbacks. Daddy Smithy is going to pursue his greatest ambition, stag films with a story line. He puts his shortcomings aside and digs on the good vibes of his genius. He has his projector set up and ready to go. He walks to the stage curtain, looks out to the empty seats. One of the somehow-familiar green-hatted boys selling books in the lobby is taking a break, puffing a Signal. Daddy yells to the boy, "Go out front and tell the ticket takers to open the doors. It is nearly Showtime!"

TumbleHouse

Dooley Paradise is wearing his best suit sans derby. The coat is a four-button pinstripe. The lapels are high, short, cut like diamonds. The front tapers to the back like grasshopper wings. Though Dooley is still a boy, this is a suit tailored for a man. Dooley believes it gives him maturity and dash when in fact he looks like a boy in a man's suit.

Dooley is alone on the TumbleHouse roof, waiting for the world to crumble. He looks to the northwest, BigCity's pride. His eyes scan the modern cityscape but record nothing beyond his self.

After a pacing night of spiderbite and nose-mosquito Dooley had bathed, dressed in his best and walked uptown to the Anglican Cathedral for the funeral of Missus Wilhoit Brandonburger.

He waited outside, smoking a Signal below a bell tower, until ten-fifteen when the sendoff was fully launched. Inside the pews were packed halfway to the back. The ship-hull ceiling was alive with murals, geezers in white robes, flowing beards and angels. Up front a diorama, the holy cross, winged statuary, Missus Wilhoit Peach Brandonburger eternally snoozing in a box of polished dark wood, brass handles, and silky sleeping-bag innards. She looked made of wax. She wore a mask of disdain that reflected the fires of a dozen candelabrums. Dooley sat unnoticed in a back pew.

From the podium the priest did his thing, though Dooley heard not a word. Three boys, Dooley's age, were on stage with the blessed father. They wore red floor-length robes under white gossamer blouses. One lad held high a gold cross on a wood pole like a SodomHeights torch. Dooley was mesmerized by these boys. At TumbleHouse he could find his soul in the young disenfranchised boys, could see the reality of each and every one. But, these boys, dressed like angels, what could they be thinking? What did they pray for and what did they not have? Did they feign piety or were they truly pure, free of malice? Dooley thought not.

The congregation knelt and stood and sat as the priest called out the signals. Dooley couldn't remember why he had come, what he thought it would do for him. Maybe he hoped to absolve his guilt. Surely he had not come here for the scorn he had worked up observing the funeral from a back pew. Dooley closed his eyes and the cathedral began to quake and yards of stained glass cracked, broke and fell in great shards that sliced off heads and limbs of the panicked congregation. Stone walls and spires broke into boulders that flattened the already sliced worshipers. Great candelabras fell to the ground setting fire to the gossamer robes of the altar boys, they whooshed into balls of flame and turned quickly to ash. Dooley opened his eyes and slid out of the pew and out of the church. He sat on the steps and lit up a Signal. He was ready to leave when Shag Draper, along with three henchmen, came outside from the church and addressed Dooley. "Tis a sad day when we attend the wake of one of BigCity's fine ladies of standing. And, what do we ave here? Could this be young Dooley Paradise all dressed up like a dignitary? Ave ya come to pay yur respects, lad?"

Dooley said, "Eat shit, Shag," then walked south. He could hear Shag laugh even after he had walked too far to hear Shag laugh.

Now Dooley is on the TumbleHouse roof waiting, for what, he does not know. He replays last night's ordeal with a razor at his throat and a creep's hand in his pants. He bugles his hands and yells, "FUCK YOU!" His echoes commingle with a city of a thousand fuck-yous. His expression of misery is a shared community endeavor.

Dooley takes a drink of spiderbite and looks to the streets below. To the north, a phalanx of hats caterpillaring through the streets toward a point, it seems from Dooley's vantage, between his legs. Dooley knows now what it is he has been waiting for. He can see in this cortege, a quarter mile away, horse drawn paddywagons, coppers, Mooks, a flower-garden of ladies' hats, a little woman in the front, sledgehammer held like a crucifix. Dooley shakes his self-pity and hurries inside to prepare TumbleHouse for an onslaught.

Orpheus Theater

Daddy Smithy pokes the bell of a five-foot megaphone through the split in the center of the curtain. He signals to the young hireling, Flopears. Flopears flips a row of switches. The houselights fade to black. Daddy yells through the megaphone, "Daddy Smithy Productions along with Signal Cigarettes proudly presents the show of shows, SpectacleMania!"

Stage left, Pete and Repeat Kirby get funky. Pete on bugle, Repeat on snare-drum. Pete blows a rag and Repeat batters a beat. Behind the curtain Daddy Smithy runs to the projector, hits a switch and removes the lens-cap. The curtain opens to the stretched muslin sheet. The projector smokes and projects a silver-screen spectacle. Pete and Repeat lower the volume. The rowdy house quiets, awe-filled eyes to the screen. Daddy Smithy has edited a single clip from a Thomas Edison flick, The Great Train Robbery. A giant shimmering head and shoulders, a rangy black & white cowpoke meets the grandstanders gaze. He pulls a howitzer-sized six-shooter and aims at everyone. He pulls the trigger, one, two, three, four, five, six times with great white puffs of gunpowder. Repeat Kirby bangs his snare in full synchronization. The audience is listening. Some dive to the floor. The whores in the balcony have let peters go limp. A painted lady screams. The image fades to black. The stage lights come up. Zeph Riley hits the stage singing and dancing.

"Me name is Zeph Riley
Permit me a song and dance
And I'll tell a joke or two
If youse give me just half a chance."

Zeph hits center stage and yells stage-left to Pete and Repeat, "Hey, Pete me pal, Did I tell yur about the gal I met from a town in Ohio, can't remember the name, starts with a D."

Pete: "Dayton?"

"No, we're just friends."

Repeat Kirby, drum roll, cowbell, ba da ding. The peanut gallery is still a bit shell-shocked. It takes two rolls and three clangs before the wheezer sets in, at which time they laugh uproariously.

Zeph says, "Hey, repeat me pal, did I tell you about the gal I met from one of those islands to the east?"

Repeat: "Jamaica?"

"Nah. I didn't even kiss her. She was ugly."

Da da boom!

"And now ladies and germs I shall play for youse a song." Zeph turns, bends, places his green and yellow yacht cap over his sacrum bone. He pulls a string which drops a cutout section of his britches, exposing his butt. Two moon-pie eyes are drawn on his pink cheeks. Below the eyes he wears a large whiplash moustache. Pete and Repeat provide accompaniment as Zeph backfires his cover of "Beautiful Brown Eyes". The crowd goes wild.

Up top, dark faces, eyes and teeth are gleaming. Word has spread that the Orpheus opens its doors to ethnic community. Word has spread that a black princess is on the bill. Tier three

231

is brimmed with ebony cool-cats, digging the honky with the baritone butthole.

Tier Two, also full and nearly spilling over, is the more vociferous and inebriated crowd of white guys and whores. This party-hardy group of glad-timers buy tickets not so much for the show as for the pit action. They are however, at this moment, held rapt by Zeph Riley's stylish performance.

Below decks in the main gallery are the serious show-goers, including a row of critics who, based on the multimedia opening, are giving enthusiastic thumbs-up. Also, in the main room, in the shadows close to the stage, BigCity boolydog, Wilbur Good. Earlier, Wilbur along with his partner Wilbur Szedvilas had been called to Shag Draper's office for assignments. Before that, Gulper Mooney had been to see Shag Draper. Gulper had gone to Shag for payment for the assassination of Jones Mulligan. Shag stalled and promised the money tomorrow. Shag also informed Gulper of the Daddy Smithy show. Shag correctly assuming that Gulper, along with the girl, would head for the Orpheus, as they had Daddy Smithy issues. Next, he had hired the two Wilbur's, Wilbur Szedvilas to accompany him on the raid at TumbleHouse, and Wilbur Good to the Orpheus. In his pocket Wilbur Good has two arrest warrants, one for Gulper and one for Girl. He has been instructed to arrest no one. His instructions are to kill. Shag Draper does not want to pay Gulper five-thousand of his hard earned cash, nor does he want Gulper Mooney's big-shot mouth bragging about subjects that could incriminate him. Also Warner Quackenbush has informed Shag that his new ward, Snooks Smithy, has a sister, Girl, that could be a future problem. Shag has orchestrated the inevitable outcome like a master puppeteer.

Wilbur is paying little attention to the show; he is scanning faces, the girl's face he remembers well as he still has the crust of her teeth marks on his hand. And, Gulper, of course he knows Gulper's face; he has long yearned to snuff that smarty-mouth dundershit. He bides his time and taps his foot to Zeph's flatulent fugue.

Outside the box-office is quiet. The security guard, Sow Madden, is thinking about pot roast. Seated in the box-office Mabel Scott is listening for sounds from the theater interior to ascertain whether her boyfriend Zeph Riley is or is not a hit.

Mabel is startled when a fist bangs on her little window. She looks up to see Gulper Mooney and a girl she had seen briefly at TumbleHouse. Gulper does not know Mabel's name though he knows she works with Dooley and Adelina. "Gimme two tickets," he tells Mabel.

"Okay, that will be one dollar."

"Does ya not know who yur talkin to? Yur not to be charging Gulper Mooney. You will hand me over the tickets for nothing and pay the price yurself."

"I shall do nothing of the kind. I don't care if you're Teddy Roosevelt. You will pay to see the show."

Gulper's blood simmers. His ears turn candy-apple-red and give off heat waves. Girl leans into him and says, "Give the girl a dollar, Gulper." Gulper gives Mabel Scott a dollar and a scowl. Mabel gives Gulper two tickets. He and Girl go inside where the show is in full swing.

TumbleHouse

Beneath a thundercloud of hair, Helen Beck's face is a fist of determination, inkblot eyes shining like glossy vellum, transparent skin taunt over angular cheekbones. She wields her sledgehammer high and mighty like a liberty torch. Behind her is an eclectic army with a common goal and a hundred reasons.

Helen and her high-minded ladies, including Empress Delaware, are planning to save the children of TumbleHouse. Accompanying Helen and the girls are BigCity Mayor Solly Gosterman, Chief of Police Dempsey Moon, Mook Boss Shag Draper, thirty uniformed coppers, and a smattering of press reporters, photographers, and sketch artists. Police Chief Moon carries arrest warrants for two of the TumbleHouse residents, Dooley Paradise and Adelina Brown, for the murders of Sinclair Kissick and Missus Wilhoit Brandonburger. Once these arrests are made, Helen and crew, along with the army of armed coppers, will enter TumbleHouse and round up the kids. Many of these children will be taken, in the black marias, to BigCity's CentralCenter train depot where they will be deposited on the waiting Orphan trains. These trains will chug these children across the country where they will be adopted by good Christian families in need of farm laborers. The older incorrigible children will be transferred to juvenile facilities or, in the more extreme cases, put into adult prisons. This plan also includes photo ops for Helen Beck who is something of a national cause célèbre. Helen uses this publicity to alert the public to the dire need of reform.

Helen Beck's Crusade Parade turns the corner onto

GravelStreet and walks the final half block to TumbleHouse. Behind Helen, next to Shag Draper, BigCity copper Wilbur Szedvilas is possibly the only member of this group who is not filled with righteous indignation. Wilbur does not want to be here. Shag Draper is paying Wilbur one-hundred dollars to shoot and kill, for resisting arrest, young Dooley Paradise and the girl Adelina Brown. Wilbur Szedvilas does not want to shoot and kill anyone except maybe Shag Draper.

Flanking Helen Beck, the Mayor and Police Chief are smiling to the press corps. Neither man really gives a good goddamn what happens here today. Both men hope to make newspaper photos rubbing elbows and glory with Helen Beck. Both men have political aspirations as well as an absence of political ideals.

Mayor Solly Gosterman wears a pince-nez, thick lenses attached to the bridge of his bulldog nose. His magnified peepers protrude like a sockeye salmon eye.

Police Chief Dempsey Moon sports a thick walrus moustache streaked with yellow mustard from a corned-beef sandwich he polished off two hours ago.

Shag Draper has thus far directed like a maestro. He owns the police and the press. He has knocked Jones Mulligan from the ring and taken the crown. Shag is smiling. Occasionally he laughs for no discernible reason.

The thirty helmeted coppers bringing up the rear are jazzed up, ready for a fight, ready to kick some urchin ass and earn some overtime.

A couple of news photographers run ahead and set up to get a photo of Helen Beck as she strikes a blow for decency by banging her hammer into the TumbleHouse front door.

This photo op is lost when the TumbleHouse front door opens from the inside. Dooley Paradise walks out to the sidewalk flanked by two young Brusselsprouts, fifteen-year-old Urick and twelve-year-old Mike, in green rag-stuffed bowlers. These are not the soldiers Dooley would normally choose to stand beside him. His first sergeant, Gulper Mooney, is no longer a Brusselsprout, and he has been unable to find Adelina Brown or even Zeph Riley. Dooley knows what is about to happen and hopes to prevent violence upon those under his care.

Shag Draper leans forward to address Helen Beck, Mayor Gosterman, and Chief Moon, "Tis he, the criminal we are arresting. We will get this done proper then proceed."

Shag's plan is okay by Moon and Gosterman but Helen Beck is unsure. Helen cannot quite quell the bee in her bonnet. She has never second-guessed herself before, regarding her campaigns and raids, but this time something is not right. Justice seems somehow askew.

The other ladies are excited and spurred onward with unflappable morality. Empress Delaware, Warner Q's little sis, is filled with apprehension. Empress has heard tales of these feral children who, trained to kill the rich, are charged with superhuman strength from clandestine drugs. Empress slows her pace, falls back when the three boys walk out onto the sidewalk. She wonders if they carry concealed weapons. She has heard they carry bombs on their person, will blow themselves up for the opportunity to kill or maim others, especially women of her standing. Empress looks around for a large policeman to stand behind.

Dooley Paradise wishes he had a bomb strapped his body. He wishes he could kill himself along with these corrupt authoritarians, wishes he could trade himself for the TumbleHouse urchins. Dooley steps forward to meet the enemy. He ignores Shag Draper. He ignores Police Chief Moon, Mayor Gosterman. Dooley knows who Helen Beck is. He feels she is misguided yet he respects her intentions. "You're making a mistake," he tells her. "TumbleHouse is a good thing."

She takes a moment to gather herself then addresses Dooley, "How is TumbleHouse a good thing? Why is this a mistake?"

More than anything Dooley wants to talk to Helen Beck. He wants to tell her everything he has to tell. He wants to encourage this tiny woman of great influence to do the right thing. He wants to cry his woes on her shoulder.

Shag Draper gives a shove to Police Chief Dempsey Moon, pushing him forward to do his job. Dempsey Moon stifles a yawn and says to Dooley, "Are youse Dooley Paradise?"

"Yes, you know I am."

"I ave a paper for yur arrest," then to Wilbur Szedvilas he says, "Take the scoundrel away." Two photographers are set up on the periphery and Dempsey is pissed that they have not taken a picture of him arresting the kid. The photographers are waiting for Helen Beck to pick up her hammer and smash something.

Wilbur steps forward and takes Dooley respectfully by the arm. The two boys, Urick and Mike bring out weapons, a slugshot and brass knucks. They are ready to go down fighting.

"Put those away," Dooley admonishes the boys, then speaks quickly to Helen Beck, "It's okay if they take me away but don't destroy TumbleHouse."

Wilbur encourages Dooley out of the spotlight toward the paddywagons.

Helen's mind has lost its sharp edge. She wants to regroup, somewhere else, away from this house of a hundred children. She feels stupid, hoodwinked.

Inside TumbleHouse, many of the teen girls and younger boys have slipped out the backdoor to seek hiding places along the DreckRiver. A force of twenty-seven boys with makeshift weapons stands in defensive position three yards inside the front door.

Back outside, the Mayor is checking out Helen Beck's butt. He thinks she has a nice one for an old gal, though she is ten years younger than he.

Chief of Police Dempsey Moon has just discovered the mustard on his moustache and it still tastes pretty good.

Shag Draper is becoming irritated with Helen Beck. He wants to get this show on the road. He catches Wilbur's eye and gives him a wink that means, you know what to do with Dooley Paradise.

Wilbur is well aware of what he is supposed to do.

The thirty coppers are pushing against a testosterone rubber band that strains to fling them into TumbleHouse like torpedoes of mass destruction.

The two young boys, Urick and Mike, are short on self-control. Society has taught them that real men fight and die for their clan. It is too late for Dooley to stop them. Urick twirls his slugshot and hits the Mayor in the head knocking off his top hat. Mike, standing only four-foot eight, attacks the police chief. Chief Moon falls on his butt with Mike on top. He yells like a cavalry captain off to slaughter Injuns, "ATTACK!" A force of thirty boolydogs rush through the front door and charge into TumbleHouse.

Wilbur Szedvilas and Dooley have walked to the paddy-wagons. Dooley strains to look at TumbleHouse, at all the kids that trusted him.

Wilbur says to Dooley, "I me are to shooting yuz wit me pistoler as prisoner running way. But I me am not going to, cepter yuz wanting that way. Otherway, I is to cage yuz."

Dooley translates; Wilbur is supposed to kill him in an escape attempt. Prison could possibly be worse than a quick death. Wilbur is giving the boy a choice. "Lock me away Wilbur, and thank you."

Wilbur puts Dooley in handcuffs and locks him in the cage. Two cops sitting up top give the horse a whack on the ass and clippity-clop Dooley Paradise off to jail.

Helen Beck and her group have not moved. They are standing like shell-shocked soldiers listening to the mêlée inside. They hear children screaming and crying. Helen holds her hammer high and runs into TumbleHouse. None of the other women follow.

Orpheus Theater

Center stage, Slab Pettibone atop FuzzyWuzzy takes a modified bow. They have just concluded three song and dance routines, as well as an eight-minute oration of *Slab Pettibone and FuzzyWuzzy the Wonder Bear Battle the Evil Commander Shenanigan in The Village of Doom*. They are receiving exuberant foot-stomping applause. Slab draws his six guns, twirls them like batons and fires all twelve blank rounds. Gunsmoke feathers tumble down over Slab and FuzzyWuzzy as they fade from the stage. The stage lights blink to black. Suddenly, as Slab and FuzzyWuzzy slip backward through the curtains, a bright projected image, bigger than life, a jumbo elephant fills the screen. This is an Edison film demonstrating the lethal wallop of AC electricity. It is titled *Electrocuting an Elephant*. Pete Kirby is putting all his lung power into blowing distressed pachyderm sounds through his bugle. The elephant's feet begin to smoke like stoked cigar cherries. The elephant teeters. The stubholders stomp, whistle, clap, and shout. Some, following Slab's example have pulled guns and fire rounds into the air. A guy on the second tier takes a bullet in the earlobe. The elephant falls to its side in a cloud of dust that coats the camera lens like talcum. Pete Kirby blows all the anguish he can muster. The elephant dies. The projector fades to black for two beats. One. Two. The stage lights blast, eye-blinking bright. Fritter McTwoBit is center stage. Behind the curtain Daddy Smithy points his megaphone through the curtain and yells, "Introducing, for the first time to American audiences, Princess Fritterich Exotica!"

Fritter is wearing her sexy slave-girl rig, showing a lot of skin. She sings a song of her own composition.

> "The king of England was a suitor o mine
> I tolt im put your arms round me, kingy,
> Show me a good time
> He said, Cheerio, my tan honey,
> I hardly know where to begin
> I said, let me see that royal scepter, baby,
> and Stick it in, Stick it in."

Fritter gyrates through the chorus and shakes all she's got. Pete blows lush syncopated scales to Repeat's backbeat. Zeph Riley has joined the Kirby brothers. He and Repeat sing backup.

> *"Stick it in Stick it in Stick it in Stick it in*
> *Stick it in Stick it in Stick it in Stick it in..."*

The calamitous roar of the crowd has died into a single shared gasp. Fritter is a showstopping horn-dog apparition, a sight and sound treat. Hardened men are hyperventilating. Flaccid tallywhackers are turning turgid. Up top, the brothers are gaga. This is one of their own, a princess, an ebony goddess.

> *"Teddy Roosevelt axe me would I be his gal*
> *I says doan bother wit me Teddy*
> *You seem more like a pal*
> *He said Bully from his pulpit*
> *Ahm a man what needs muh sin*
> *I tolt I'm, you ain't seen no rough ridin*
> *Till ya Stick it in, Stick it in."*

Girl Smithy and Gulper Mooney are edging their way to the front of the theater. Girl knows and has told Gulper that Daddy Smithy is backstage running the projector between acts. Before, Girl had been burning with rage, seeking revenge against her no-account Daddy. Now, she is rethinking her thoughts. She wishes she had not told Gulper about her father. She does not know why she has just directed him backstage.

241

"Stick it in Stick it in Stick it in Stick it in
Stick it in Stick it in Stick it in Stick it in..."

Wilbur Good thinks that Princess Fritterich Exotica is tasty good. He is digging the tune as well as the moves and yummy brown exposed skin. Wilbur thinks that maybe he should make humpy love to his wife when he gets home tonight. Wilbur and his wife do not have sex often. Wilbur does not like his wife, plus she is ugly. Wilbur's wife hates Wilbur. Last time they did it, Wilbur had to sock her in the yap, knocking loose a couple of teeth, to get her in the mood. Maybe when Wilbur gets home tonight he will sock his ugly wife senseless and then they can make humpy love.

"Would yall be mah honey said George Armstrong Custer
I tolt im back on off, blondie
yall doan cut the muster
Sez he, Ahm a hero, a man among men
Sez I, Crazy Horse he the one what can
But you caint never Stick it in, Stick it in."

Daddy Smithy, the man behind the curtain, is changing the film in his projector. He caps the lens leaving the incandescent vapor lamp burning between clips. The acetylene gas generator is burning through a gallon of ether. Daddy holds his breath to avoid the fumes.

"Stick it in Stick it in Stick it in Stick it in
Stick it in Stick it in Stick it in Stick it in..."

Also backstage are Slab Pettibone, FuzzyWuzzy, and Bitch Bantam. Slab is in the process of detaching himself from FuzzyWuzzy's back. The next act is FuzzyWuzzy and Bitch in a choreographed wrestling match. Bitch is listening to Fritter sing. She loves to hear Fritter sing, wishes she could be out front where she could watch Fritter dance. Bitch will never understand why Fritter favors naughty lyrics and dirty dancing. She cannot find the rationale in throwing sex at men. But if it makes Fritter happy, then Bitch is happy for her.

Slab climbs down to his stubs, standing waist high to Bitch. Slab also wishes he were out front watching Fritter, though he knows that whatever the audience gets, he can get better and in private. Slab Pettibone has an exclusive on the enchantress knockin em ga ga on the other side of the curtain. Slab is the luckiest man in the joint.

> *"Warner Quackenbush got alla money inna world*
> *But he got a dinky manhood,*
> *and I ain't that kinda girl*
> *I tolt im takes mo than money fo mah favors ta win*
> *You needs a bigger shootin iron*
> *to Stick it in, Stick it in."*

The stubholders are all aslobber over Princess Fritterich Exotica. Most are up from their seats. Many are joining Zeph Riley and Repeat Kirby belting out backup. Zeph is having a swell time. As far as he is concerned, there is no bizness like show bizness. He farts a mephitis melody, dances the Mashed Potato, and sings with the soul of a black man.

243

> *"Stick it in Stick it in Stick it in Stick it in*
> *Stick it in Stick it in Stick it in Stick it in..."*

Fritter agrees, though with different consonants, there be no bidness like show bidness. She is a sensation. All her years of goodness have karmalized into a rewarding career in the entertainment biz. Fritter is living inside her richest dreams. The audience is wild with approval. Fritter moves, grooves, and croons another chorus.

> *"Slab Pettibone got a big-o sweet jellyroll*
> *Ah sez, that sho sweet cream honey*
> *Now try mah donut hole*
> *Slab know how to kiss me and where to begin*
> *He flips on mah switch, baby*
> *And Stick it in, Stick it in."*

Slab teeters like an electrocuted elephant when he hears the naughty lyrics about himself. He has tears in his eyes, love in his heart. He sits on the floor next to FuzzyWuzzy and hugs his bear's right foreleg. He leans his head into FuzzyWuzzy's soft fuzzy thigh. Slab Pettibone loves FuzzyWuzzy and he loves Fritter McTwoBit. Slab is delirious with love.

FuzzyWuzzy likes it when Slab hugs his leg. He turns his head and gives Slab a big sloppy lick that plasters Slab's handlebar moustache back to his ear. FuzzyWuzzy is awaiting his cue to hit the stage and wrestle around with Bitch Bantam. He gets excited just thinking about it. He pees a stream that foams across the floorboards. Slab coaxes him forward out of the current. FuzzyWuzzy gives Slab another affectionate lick.

Bitch Bantam reaches over and scratches FuzzyWuzzy between the ears. From the corner of her eye she looks at Slab. Bitch is glad her friend Fritter has a man like Slab Pettibone.

> *"Stick it in Stick it in Stick it in Stick it in*
> *Stick it in Stick it in Stick it in Stick it in..."*

Stage right, Gulper Mooney and Girl have ascended, unnoticed, the three steps to the stage and slipped behind the curtain. Girl needs a shot of Doctor FixUp. She sees Bitch Bantam, a giantess in piebald buckskin and fringe. She sees Slab Pettibone, a half-man wearing a sombrero and side arms. She sees FuzzyWuzzy the bear. She sees her father. Her heart falters. No one has yet seen them, she turns to Gulper and whispers, "I don't want this. I want to leave now. I changed my mind."

Gulper says, "No," and pointing to Daddy Smithy, he says, "That man has wronged me girl. For that, the feck shall die, see." He continues to walk them toward the smoldering projector.

The crowd is so responsive Fritter has decided to improvise. She tosses out bluesy phrases.

> *"Yeh, honey chile,*
> *Slab Pettibone know where ta stick that thang.*
> *Stick it in Stick it in Stick it in Stick it in*
> *Stick it in Stick it in Stick it in Stick it in*
> *Sock it to me, Slab baby..."*

Stage left, Wilbur Good has also worked his way backstage, passing behind Zeph and Pete and Repeat in the process. He would prefer to remain out front watching the sexy black princess, but he has a job to do and can use the bonus pay. Wilbur takes his gun from his holster. He can see the boy and the girl. He is somewhat puzzled by the obstacles, Bitch Bantam, FuzzyWuzzy, and Slab Pettibone, between him and his intended targets. He tippytoes through the shadows.

> "Sock it to me Sock it to me Sock it to me Sock it to me
> Sock it to me Sock it to me Sock it to me Sock it to me..."

Daddy Smithy hardly notices anyone backstage. His head is spinning with success. He is a genius, the show is a hit and he has done it without screwing up. His future is bright. He readies the projector and counts down to the next segue.

Fritter and chorus wraps the song with a flourish. She backs through the curtain just as Daddy gives the signal to Flopears who cuts the lights. Daddy takes the cap off the projector spilling a kinetic image onto the screen.

Flopears wonders what Gulper Mooney is doing backstage and where did he come from?

Daddy's blood suddenly turns cold. Is it his imagination or did he just see his daughter, with a boy, with a gun?

The screen lights-up; a life-sized locomotive, puffing smoke. A film made by the Lumiére Brothers. The train steams toward the camera. The audience, still jazzed from Fritter's song and dance, is going into shock, deliberating, and some diving out of the path of the charging iron-horse.

Backstage, the train in reverse image is also charging its source, the projector.

Slab loves the effect, like an amusement park ride. But

his eyes are on the silhouette of Fritter McTwoBit making her way back to him.

It is time for Bitch Bantam and FuzzyWuzzy to walk through the curtain to the stage. Bitch has had a couple of days to get used to Daddy Smithy's films, but they still make her nervous.

Gulper holds his gun, in his broken-arm hand, and walks quickly toward Daddy.

FuzzyWuzzy has not previously seen the Lumiére film. He sees a huge ungodly machine getting bigger, charging him, like an enemy in the wilds. He rears and cries out. He stumbles backward knocking over the projector.

Daddy Smithy jumps out of the way and in the process slips and falls in the puddle of bear piddle. Gulper Mooney starts shooting.

Bitch and Slab are both momentarily confounded, attempting to get a handle on the situation.

Gulper fires three more shoots in the shadowy fray.

The projector hits the floor. The blue either-calcium flame ignites the reel of film. The tin of ether impacts with the floor and spews a mist of flaming ether over FuzzyWuzzy. FuzzyWuzzy's fluffy fur is set ablaze.

Slab yells, "Roll FuzzyWuzzy! Roll," but FuzzyWuzzy doesn't hear or comprehend anything beyond the five alarm panic in his head. He screams like a human, frantically charges through the screen across the stage into the audience.

Wilbur Good has walked around the action. He walks up behind Gulper Mooney, puts his pistol to the boy's head and shoots him twice. Gulper falls dead. Wilbur trains the gun on Girl.

Bitch Bantam has come alive. She springs forward after FuzzyWuzzy.

Slab has lost sight of FuzzyWuzzy as well as Fritter. He is at a loss as to what to do. He does not react as the pulp-book hero Slab Pettibone would. He is up on his stubs but does not know which way to run.

Still on his ass, Daddy Smithy sees Girl, the daughter he discarded. They look at each other and forget for a moment everything else—until together they see Wilbur Good.

FuzzyWuzzy is a fiery ball of madness. Stubholders don't know if this is part of the show or not. Many of the men have pulled guns and take pot shots at FuzzyWuzzy. FuzzyWuzzy's head inside and out is afire. He understands nothing other than the pain and panic. Someone has opened a side door to make an escape. FuzzyWuzzy, runs, howling like Repeat Kirby's bugle, through the exit, out of the theater.

Wilbur Good grins at Girl. Wilbur likes shooting people. Daddy Smithy flings the smoldering reel of film at Wilbur. The reel hits Wilbur in the head, knocking off his helmet and burning his forehead. Girl turns and runs. Wilbur picks up the burning reel and holds it for a moment before realizing he is burning his hand. He giggles. The girl has gotten away. Wilbur shrugs, tosses the reel, and goes home to make humpy love to his ugly wife.

Bitch Bantam has fought her way through the crazed mob to the alleyway. FuzzyWuzzy is not in sight. Bitch runs, following the scent of burnt hair and flesh.

TumbleHouse

Inside TumbleHouse, war rages. Helen Beck is on her knees though not in prayer. She raises high her five-pound sledgehammer then swings it down on the brogan of one of BigCity's finest. The copper drops the ten-year-old he is dragging by the hair. The kid runs. The cop sits on the floor and holds his broken foot. Helen runs to the next cop she sees, smashes his foot as well. So far, Helen has smashed five feet.

The group of boys wielding makeshift weapons have been decimated to a few bloody diehards. Green hatted boys and girls from four to seventeen are being dragged, some unconscious, some fighting and biting, out to the Black Maria and carted of to trains, jails, reformatories. None are taken to a hospital.

This is not what Helen came to TumbleHouse for. Her priorities changed the moment the first cop hurt the first child. Shag Draper has used her to extract some kind of revenge. He has sicced his Goon Squad on helpless children and now Helen is saving as many as she can and looking to smash Shag Draper's foot.

Shag Draper's right foot is on the rail at the bar. He has poured himself a drink and seems to be enjoying himself. Next to him, Mayor Solly Gosterman yells above the din, "This is out of control, Shag. There are reporters here. I think we should call off the dogs. This isn't going to look good."

Shag sips a beer. "Fine with me, Mayor, except they do nay work for me. Ya wants to call off the coppers, you should talk to the chief."

Police Chief Dempsey Moon is munching a dill-pickle. Dempsey gets a charge out of watching his men kick ass. Mayor Gosterman repeats to Police Chief Moon, "This is out of control, Moon. There are reporters here. I think you should call off the dogs."

Dempsey Moon says, "Sure ting, Mayor," then he says to the air, "That'd be enough, boys. Yur to cease wit the beatins." He sucks sour juice from the pickle and tells the mayor, "They aren't hearin me commands. Best we wait till they get weary."

Mayor Solly Gosterman decides he does not want to be here. He leaves without saying goodbye and, once outside, avoids the photographers.

Empress Delaware, Biddy Wrinkle, and the group of women reformers have not gone inside but have witnessed the children being dragged out to the paddy wagons. At first Empress had been afraid of these kids but now she sees that many are the same age or younger than her own child, Cuteness. They look to her to be defenseless and sad. Empress is feeling an onset of the vapors; she feels she might faint, if only she could find a handsome and gallant copper with strong arms to faint into. But alas, this brutish squad of boolydogs seems lacking in Prince Charmings. Together with the rest of the women, Empress Delaware joins the mayor in exodus.

Walking inside TumbleHouse is Wilbur Szedvilas. He surveys the scene and wonders if he is in the wrong profession. Across the way he sees Shag Draper. He walks the opposite direction. A fellow officer walks to the door, a little red-faced girl squeezed under his arm. Wilbur notices where the cop has his hands. "Looking like yuv catched a keeper," he says to his brother in blue. "Aye," the blue brother says. "This one I may be takin home."

"And what haff happen to yuz elment?" Wilbur asks.

"Elment? Oh, yur mean me helmet." He takes his hand from under the little girl's skirt and removes his helmet to check out whatever it is that Wilbur is talking about. Wilbur beans the guy with his shillelagh, knocking him cold. The girl runs.

A couple of boolydogs have gone behind the bar and kicked up a covey of kids, one of these a nine-year-old boy, climbs across the bar-top to escape. Shag Draper grabs the little gamin by the hair and just for fun smacks the kid with his beer mug. This action is frozen in a brilliant burst that momentarily blinds Shag and just about everyone else in a ten-foot radius. Adelina Brown has just taken a flash photograph, depicting the brutality of big-shot Mook, Shag Draper. Shag blinks. The kid, though partially blinded, runs.

Adelina can do nothing to stop this slaughter but she can expose it to film with her her new camera and and gear. She fills the flashpan with magnesium flash powder then flips the filmholder and pulls the dark-slide. She aims the big camera, ignites the powder, releases the shutter, and archives Chief Moon sucking a pickle as his troops bully foundlings half their size.

Adelina is plainly dressed, she views her surrounding from outside of the mix, has in fact attained partial invisibility. This, along with the intense flashes and awkward presence of the tripod mounted view-camera, has so far kept the boolydogs confused, they have yet to approach her, though she senses it is time to collect her gear and run.

Helen Beck stands her full five feet. Her face is red with

fervor, oiled slick with perspiration. She holds the Hammer of Justice in both hands. Helen looks at Adelina. Adelina looks at Helen. In Adelina's face, Helen sees herself. In Helen's face, Adelina sees herself. Adelina's gaze is peeled away when Wilbur Szedvilas takes her by the arm and says, "Yuz must be skedaddle, elst Shag Draper will be doing your die-now."

Adelina does not wait for an explanation, she says, "This way."

Wilbur only wanted to warn Adelina. He hadn't planned to be her accomplice, yet here he is, carrying her camera, clearing a path through the other coppers. To the basement door they go, then down the stairs. The basement is lit with the flicker of a bug clouded kerosene lamp. Adelina was here when the cops first raided and set her equipment in the wheelbarrow outside the window, anticipating her need to escape.

Up top Shag Draper blinks his vision back to normal just in time to see Adelina and Wilbur going through the basement door. It doesn't look to Shag as if Wilbur is doing the job he was hired to do. To Police Chief Dempsey Moon, Shag says, "Grab ye a couple of men and follow me."

Wilbur knows Shag Draper saw him enter the basement with Adelina. "Dey commink now fastly, get goink go." Wilbur pushes her camera through the open window. Adelina climbs a chair and Wilbur helps her through the window to the back alleyway.

Adelina says, "Thank you, Wilbur. You are what a good copper should be." Wilbur is thinking he is the worst copper ever and he proves it by picking up a twelve-gallon barrel of spiderbite and heaving it at Shag Draper who has just come in the door. The barrel hits Shag in the chest, knocks him flat on his back, then hits the floor and explodes in a tsunami of ninety-nine-proof hooch. Shag is seeing stars and the spiderbite burns his eyes. He climbs, slipping and sliding, back up to his feet and leans on the wall then screams expletives when Helen Beck's sledge hammer slams down on his foot. He screams again when Helen smashes his other foot.

Orpheus Theater

The night has turned quiet. Out front, under the marquee, Zeph Riley and Mabel Scott sit on a soap box. On the street a horse-drawn BigCity morgue wagon is tied to a rail. The Orpheus audience emptied out thirty minutes ago. The show was cut short with a finale of disaster. Surprisingly, no one has asked for a refund. Other than the guy who lost an earlobe to a random bullet, the stubholders got their money's worth. They loved the show, especially the disaster part.

While the show is a hit, Zeph and Mabel look forlorn. For them the disaster was a disaster. Also, word has trickled to them regarding the demise of TumbleHouse. Zeph and Mabel have no home to go to. Their friends have been scattered, some never to be seen again. Zeph notices Bitch Bantam walking slowly up the sidewalk. To Mabel, Zeph says, "Tis Miss Bantam a coming, without Mister FuzzyWuzzy. I dassent know what to say."

Mabel does not answer. She as well does not know what to say.

Bitch walks, head down. FuzzyWuzzy has not been found. The four-hundred-sixty-seven-pound bear has vanished. Bitch does not know how she is to tell Slab Pettibone. She had herself fallen in love with FuzzyWuzzy, but Slab Pettibone has loved his bear for years. FuzzyWuzzy is part of Slab Pettibone's body. How is she ever to tell him? Where could a burning bear have gone in this dark city and how could he survive, wounded in a maze of steel and mortar, surround by bloodthirsty gun-slinging humans.

At the theater she sees the two kids, Zeph and Mabel. They look her way with sad eyes. She nods a greeting. Mabel Scott says to Bitch, "I am sorry."

Bitch walks inside. Chairs and benches are strewn about. The stage lights are on. Daddy Smithy paces, stage-left, stage-right, stage-right, stage-left. Two guys from the morgue carry Gulper Mooney's body out on a stretcher. Bitch walks up the aisle. Daddy Smithy sees Bitch but cannot meet her eyes. He walks from the stage, out of sight. Closer to the stage Bitch can see Slab Pettibone's hat, then she sees Slab Pettibone sitting on the floor in the orchestra pit. Fritter McTwoBit is also on the floor. Slab cradles her head in his lap. Fritter's eyes are closed. In the dark midst of the madness, murder, and fire, a stray bullet kicked up a foot-long wood splinter and flung it into Fritter's neck like a lance. Fritter fell backwards off the stage. Slab frantically looked for her in the stampeding crowd, unaware that she lay suffocating, bleeding, only a few feet away, below him, in the pit. Now, Fritter McTwoBit is dead.

Slab looks up at Bitch Bantam. Bitch says, "FuzzyWuzzy is gone."

Slab says, "So is Fritter."

254

Bitch goes to the floor and holds Slab Pettibone in her arms. Slab cries. Bitch Bantam has never before held a person with tenderness. She rocks him softly.

Caterwaul Alley

It seems to Girl that she has been running for hours, her lungs burn. She runs from the big copper with the gun. She runs from her dead lover, Gulper Mooney, the boy she led backstage to revenge her wounded heart, the boy who died in the backfire of her intentions.

It is nine-thirty, the sidewalk dances with WhiteWay gladtimers. Painted ladies hang to the arms of Friday-night-rich gents. Drunks stagger and grasp lampposts, laugh out loud at their own pathetic suffering. The lights are bright. Girl crosses WhiteWay, running southeast. She runs without direction, overloaded with thought. Snooks. Gulper. Daddy. TumbleHouse. She believes she should be the one who is dead, not her sister. She hates herself and she wonders how Snooks died. Was she afraid and crying? Snooks had been Girl's responsibility and now she is dead.

The crowds have thinned. The street is darker than before. Girl is out of breath. The stitches between her legs hurt. She gulps at the air. She retches. Her brain swells and pounds in her head. She is weak and sick.

Girl looks to the street and sees, a block away, a group of little kids, TumbleHouse kids. They dart about from one hiding place to the next. Girl hears horses pulling trucks. She hides behind a curtain of shadow. Soon the trucks bounce by, black-marias stuffed with kids; rolling dogcatcher cages taking mutts to the pound. The shelter Girl seeks is gone. The adults have punished the children and taken away their sanctuary.

Girl leaves this street and turns east. Shadowy men traipse the sidewalk, appraising Girl, offering lewd comment and gesture. Two tatterdemalion creeps trail her. Again Girl runs, this time two blocks east where she ducks into a dark alley. In her deep heaves of air, she can smell the scent of decayed animal and she knows where she is. Girl smells her dead baby boy.

She looks to the alley's end where the turned-over fire escape landing sits like a perverted dollhouse. The starry night lights the brick walls without color. Girl walks deeper into the crevice. How long ago was it? Three nights? A hundred years? Am I the same girl that was here? Is this where I belong?

A chill shimmies her spine and her legs shake. She feels a presence. She smells patchouli and peppermint. She turns and jumps when she sees Eddie Plague. Eddie reaches out and takes her by the wrist.

"I need to make a living," Eddie says. "You are the right age and it seems you are available."

Girl attempts to pull away. Eddie holds tight. She remembers how she had sunk her teeth into the copper, but that had been in the company of others, and she dare not do that now. Eddie Plague with his red silk bandana nose, his eyes, dark in the shade of his slouch hat-brim, paralyzes Girl with terror. She pleads, "Let me go!"

In a blink, Eddie Plague brings out a straight razor and opens Girl's cheek from chin to cheekbone. The pain is immediate. The wound is deep and bloody.

"Next time you beg freedom, it will be your throat that I slice." He rips the apron front from Girl's dress. "Bandage yourself with this and hurry with it. It stinks of death in here."

PART TWO

WINTER

Chapter Nine

The Wrinkle Baff

Sub-zero sleet falls like a swarm of bees in the night. A Cinderella brougham passes by, jumbo wheels, gold-leaf spokes. White horses in silver harness prance forward under the bridle of a uniformed coachman. His nose is red and his walrus moustache is frosted. Two large lanterns, flanking the coachman's ears, reflect flurries of ice like detonated glass.

Inside the brougham, sealed from icy winds, Warner Quackenbush says, "I'm a very naughty boy."

Next to Warner, seven-year-old Snooks Smithy says, "Naughty naughty," and whips Warner's thighs with a star-tipped wand. Warner shivers, the pain is bliss.

Wrapped in a full-body mink, Snooks Smithy is dressed

like a fairy princess. Her golden hair is set with a coronet of diamonds. Her pink satin shoes have a low heel, twelve butterfly ribbons flutter up the ankles. She wears a lacy gown over six petticoats. Gossamer wings like kissing question marks sprout from her shoulder blades. Warner encourages her bad behavior and she acts accordingly.

Warner, in black and white, tux and tails, looks like an eight-ball. His legs do not reach the floor. He has taken to escorting Snooks Smithy Quackenbush to BigCity society functions. He flaunts his injudiciousness with bold disregard to public opinion and enjoys himself. Tonight, a grand ball.

Warner tilts his eggshell sideways and cuts a fart, says, "Oops, I was naughty again."

Snooks whacks him with her wand. "Bad Baby." Warner closes his eyes and issues guttural yum-yums.

Across from Warner, the seat once occupied by Warner's sister, Empress Delaware, on these festive occasions, is empty. Unable to face her social circle of friends under the humiliation of Warner's scandalous behavior, Empress, with daughter Cuteness in tow, has packed up and moved back to the family plantation in the genteel south.

Warner doesn't give a good hoot what his sister or anyone else thinks, he is on top of the universe. Business is grand; he pulls the world along on a string of addiction and manipulation without breaking a sweat. Warner is easy to hate and his flagrant relationship with a ragamuffin child ups the enmity, but there is no one anywhere likely to confront him. BigCity is at Warner's dimpled knees. The SnarlingTigers, as a power, are history. Shag Draper and his goon squad do Warner's bidding and the mayor and police chief do nothing.

The coachman whoa Nellies the horses and stops at the grand entranceway of the Gustav and Biddy Wrinkle estate. Electric light opens the shadows and sparkles across the snow floor. A guy in a tall round-top hat, heavy cape with shoulder epaulets, opens the coach door and escorts the passengers down the gangplank. Warner steps out with Snooks at his side. A sudden sheet of magnesium-flash illuminates them and blinks their eyes. One hundred and one pound Adelina Brown is near invisible within the one hundred and twenty-six pounds of photography equipment; she wears a teepee of an overcoat with marsupial pockets, inside and out, brimming with photography paraphernalia, assorted supplies including a pound of flash powder, and loaded film holders. Her 8x10 view camera is screwed tight to the top of a wooden tripod which she rolls about on casters. A flashpan is wieled to the top of the camera. Adelina is a camera.

Another brougham is pulling up to the stop as Warner Quackenbush and the strange little girl walk the red carpet inside. Warner has been courting that little girl all over town and there is something familiar about her but Adelina can't figure out what it is. She wants more pictures. She wants to get inside and get another look at that little girl.

Adelina Brown has acomplished much since the fall of TimbleHouse, five months gone. She lives in a two-room flat in BigCity's growing Left Bank where she has discovered the bohemian call to arms. In her spare time, she is making a moving-picture documentary of the city's homeless children, *Guttersnipes*. She earns her keep by taking photographs and writing stories for the HuggerMugger, using the nom de plume Adelle Liberty.

The HuggerMugger is a small enterprise putting out a three-sheet alternative newspaper twice a week. With Adelle Liberty's input they have increased circulation. The HuggerMugger relies on contributions of ideas and essays from the burgeoning underground community. The young paper peddlers that hawk the HuggerMugger also sell illegal condoms and bootleg sheet music to help finance the leftist rag. Tonight Adelina is documenting the enemy, exposing capitalism in its most repugnant splendor.

Snowfall has lessened, yet sharp winds continue to scatter frosty splinters. The brick street is rippled with frozen slush. The mansions lining the street gleam like glass castles, the inhabitants born of steel, railroads, oil, media, and real-estate. Adelina trudges around to the side of the manse, through the vast yard toward the back, pushing her camera ever forward like a plough; watching the upsidedown backward view in the ground glass. On her left the towering wall of the Wrinkle manse seems quiet, unaware that there is a party inside. Sloshing forward, a cobblestone barn sits, snow-flocked and smiling like a luminous skull. An owl hoots three dots and a dash.

Snow squeaks beneath Adelina's feet like a cheap pair of shoes. She finds a dark unlit door at the back of the manse, opens it, and goes inside, up three steps, through another door into a storage room, through another door, up a stairway, down another hallway and antechamber and into a lavish ballroom filled with refined party animals, gowned and tuxedoed.

Adelina stays close to the walls and circles the room. She doesn't look like a guest but she also doesn't look like a crasher. She looks like a bundle of equipment, a wooden robot. To the rear, through dancing cliques of bejeweled laughter, the orchestra attempts to stay light, contrite and still cutting edge. They play a medley from The Mikado.

Adelina is breathless from the spectacle, the shoulder-to-shoulder glitterati, but she does not covet the lifestyle. She sees not a glorious existence but rather waste and selfishness. Adelina rolls through the room and the casters squeak like mice. She stops when she sees her next photograph. A small group of women, the smallest one she recognizes, Helen Beck.

Helen Beck takes a glass of raspberry punch from a silver tray and says thank you to the colored waiter who smiles and walks off. Biddy Wrinkle, the hostess of this spangled affair, rolls her eyes to the other women in unanimity: Helen Beck talks to Negroes. Maybe it's time for Helen Beck to take her pinko causes elsewhere. Biddy Wrinkle sighs of relief when Helen, without a word, walks out and away from their gossipy gaggle.

Adelina sets focus, fills the pan with magnesium. She is under the black cloth, focusing. She gasps and swallows saliva sideways when she sees the upsidedown image of Helen Beck walking toward her, morphing from sharp to fuzzy. Adelina comes out from under the cloth, coughing.

Helen says to Adelina, "Are you alright, dear?"

Between hard gulps of oxygen Adelina says, "You're Helen Beck. It was you at TumbleHouse."

"What's your name, dear? And take your time, get your breath."

Adelina takes her time and gets her breath. "Why would I give you my name? I'm not here as a guest as you are. I'm here to expose the plutocracy that keeps the proletariat starving and chained. You know, people like you."

"I hope that's not what I am. You sound quite enlightened.

Maybe I could help your cause. I'm not a part of all this. Believe me, I'm on your side."

"You're on my side? I don't think so. Why should I trust you?"

"I made a mistake with TumbleHouse. Let me prove to you that my heart is where it should be."

"Prove to me? Why should you care what I think? You don't even know who I am. You're full of rhetoric and self-pity."

"And you seem full of spite. I think I do know your name—Adelle Liberty. You wrote about TumbleHouse in the HuggerMugger. You wrote about me as well."

"You read the HuggerMugger? You read what I wrote about you?"

"Yes and I took no pride in reading my name in the context in which you placed it. I was aware of the error of my actions before reading your article. I'm trying to make amends and you seem determined to resist me. I would like to give you a better person to write about."

"Could you find out about Dooley Paradise? Do you know who he is?"

"I know who he is. He's locked away in the city Catacombs. I don't know what I could do."

"Haven't you wondered why there's been no mention of Dooley since the night he was arrested? After all, you're the one who led the hunting party. In fact, I don't know that he is in the Catacombs. I don't even know if he's alive. That is what I want to know. That's what you can do for me, Miss Beck."

"I think I can do that," says Helen Beck. "This is not the place for us to talk. Where can you be found? I will come to you."

"Adelina, my real name is Adelina. The DownStairs, in

the Left Bank—you can find me there. We'll see how it goes." Adelina's eyes spy danger. "Shag Draper!" Before Helen Beck has even registered surprise, Adelina disappears into her elaborate array of equipment and rolls away.

Helen Beck turns to see Shag Draper and his posse of three. Shag walks with the aid of crutches. It's been five months since Helen tenderized Shag's feet with her Hammer of Justice. He may never walk unaided again. Shag sees Helen and quickly shifts leftward, as far away from her as he can get. He puts Helen Beck firmly from his mind and concentrates on maneuvering through the happy mass of affluent asses. Shag hates the rich even more than the poor. The rich oppress him as he oppresses the poor.

Shag's master plan has not progressed as originally schemed. The SnarlingTigers are defunct yet Shag and his organization have not risen in stature. Shag Draper wanted to be Jones Mulligan. Jones Mulligan would have been a guest at the Wrinkle Ball. Shag Draper is here as a hired hand. Somehow, unwittingly, Shag has become a personal lackey for Warner Quackenbush, leaving him little time to run the Mooks, who in turn remain nothing more than a cadre of shiftless soldiers and petty crooks. Shag is angry and out of place, dragging himself across the expanse of ballroom like a Civil War bum. Men in formalwear turn their backs to Shag and his three pug-faced thugs as though acknowledgment admits bouts of whoredom, gambling and sin. Lavishly trimmed women do not bother to hide their harrumphs of distaste for Shag and his ilk.

Shag is looking through orchids and diamonds for Warner Quackenbush. Mister Quackenbush has requested his presence. Mister Quackenbush, the freakoid despot motherfecker that holds Shag Draper in servitude, has requested Shag's presence. Escalating blood pressure reddens Shag's face. His left foot hurts and drags behind his crutches. Chances are his left foot will always hurt and drag. Shag wishes he were one of the guests in this grand ball. Shag wishes he were someone else.

Yonder, next to a grand table of hoity-toity foodstuff, reflective silver, delicate bone china, a group has formed. Gustav Wrinkle, the Wrinkle-Ball host, stands six-feet high, six-and-a-half if you count his top hat. Gustav retains a straight back even though he is bent at the waist like a pump-handle to converse with the four-foot-eleven Warner Quackenbush.

Under this Gustav/Warner heads-together bridge, Snooks Smithy runs back and forth to and from the table of goodies. She grabs handfuls of shellfish, fruit, fowl, cookies, candies, cakes and crams them in her mouth. Her fairy-princess dress is a mess, though Snooks shows little concern. She passes under the Robber-Baron bridge and stomps Warner's toes in the process. Gustav feigns nonchalance, pretends the little girl does not exist.

Warner and Gustav talk shop and, as their respective fiefdoms include great holdings of land, people and thought, they are both smiling. Warner says, "I've been finding good labor prospects on the Eastern Providence." Gustav says, "I've had some problems in that area. I find they need more discipline and to tell you the truth, they are just too damn small."

Shag Draper halts a respectful ten feet from Warner Quackenbush; his goons stumble to a standstill, sniffing, itching, scratching, grinning like the lamebrains they are. Shag would nay interrupt Mister Shit-splatter Cooze-face Quackenbush. He rocks on his heels. His head explodes into chunks of hatred.

Warner and Gustav Wrinkle are still heads together, strategically crushing the world's underdogs. Warner sees Shag but leaves him hanging.

Snooks Smithy stands ten feet from the Warner/Gustav arch opposite Shag on the other boundary. Her cheeks are bubbled out to capacity, full of chocolate cake. Crumbs dribble like lemmings from her open mouth. She bends forward like a charging bull, winds up her legs and takes off, zoom under the bridge, toro toro, then squeals her heels to a rubbery stop three inches from Shag Draper's toes. Shag looks down. Snooks looks up, pumps her elbows like a bellows and spews wet crumbs with globs of icing up into Shag's face.

Shag's three goons giggle and snort. One nickel, that is all it would cost, five measly pennies, and you could pay it on installments. That is what Shag Draper would charge to torture and murder Snooks. Yet he does nothing other than remove a clean handkerchief from his pocket and windshield-wipe his face. His jaw is clenched, his teeth near breaking.

Snooks makes an about-face and charges back to the food table for another load of sugared shrapnel.

The combo of Snooks below, Shag and crew to the side has become too much of a distraction for Gustav Wrinkle. He tips his tall topper and bids Warner a solicitous sayonara.

Warner beckons Shag front and center and queries him regarding his show-business investment. Warner has become near obsessed in his movie-making venture with Daddy Smithy. He has been correctly predicting the future all his life and has come to realize the future of film is titanic. Warner has lavished Daddy Smithy with everything he needs to produce a feature-length blockbuster. Also, Warner is aware that Snooks, his blissful little Snooks, is of Daddy Smithy's loins. He feels a strange link to the filmmaker, almost like family. Warner has thus far kept Snooks from meeting her father and, rather than deal with Daddy Smithy himself, has been using Shag Draper as his mouthpiece.

Shag gives Warner a quick, concise and humorless report and winces each time Snooks gets near. A fat vein at the side of his neck ticks like a time-bomb.

Across the ballroom dance floor, a hundred formal couples dance a soulless cakewalk—the women are stiff and the men are stiffer. On the periphery groups are toasting flutes of bubbly, glad-handing, boasting, and laughing. Helen Beck has cornered Mayor Solly Gosterman, assailed him with Dooley Paradise questions. The mayor has not a clue or care about Dooley Paradise's fate, past or present. He points to an empty spot behind Helen and says, "By gad, I have never seen one of those before." When Helen turns to look the mayor walks quickly away. Helen cannot think of a single reason to remain here. She gathers her wrap and goes out to grab a cab home to the Palace Hotel.

Orpheus Theater

Ringmaster Zeph Riley stands center stage. He pulls a fan of thirty-six crisp five dollar bills from his lively checkered suit coat and says loudly, "Just sos you knows, I got all this dough, for the gent who thinks Bitch Bantam he can throw." Daddy Smithy is swamped with the grind of filmmaking but has continued with the Orpheus multimedia show in a producer capacity. On site Zeph Riley and Mabel Scott are in charge. Daddy pays them well through profit-sharing.

Behind Zeph, the curtain parts and Bitch Bantam takes the spotlight. The crush of stub-holders hoot and huzzah. Most have seen Bitch Bantam before and are back to see her again. A group of sporting men have brought a tank of a fighting man, a Negro with ties to no one and a killer left hook, named ProudBoy Goodwin. For the last few weeks, Zeph has been adding five dollars a day to the booty. It is now up to a hundred and eighty. The sporting men are paying ProudBoy twenty-five dollars to get in the ring with Bitch Bantam. If he loses, they lose, but if he wins, they get the hundred and eighty bucks minus the twenty-five that ProudBoy gets, win or lose. The sporting men have unwittingly failed to offer ProudBoy Goodwin an incentive to win.

Bitch Bantam steps forward to meet the challenger. She wears fringed piebald buckskin. Her hair is cut short and her mouth is closed tight. Her jaws and cheeks are swollen and bruised. Three days back, she went to a dentist, purchased a set of ivory teeth, and had all her pointy choppers extracted. She is anxious for the swelling to go down so she can insert her new white smile.

Zeph Riley is flashing the fivers, introducing the challenger, making jokes and rhymes. Left-stage, Pete and Repeat Kirby take a break; right-stage, Mabel Scott tinkles melodrama on the new piano. Bitch holds the stage like a cinematic explosion yet she remains alone within herself. She fights these daily challengers and wins without hearing the shouts, without looking into anyone's eyes, without the true antipathy she feels for men. Bitch fights solely to save up for a life without fighting.

The fight ring is the entire stage. The floor is wood and the knuckles are bare. ProudBoy Goodwin is shoeless and has stripped down to a striped bathing suit. His arms bulge with hard labor. He has been fighting for all of his thirty-three years. His neck is corded with muscle and scar. In his youth he danced from a noose, the price of a pilfered nanny goat, for three hours. He was cut down and pronounced dead, only to pull himself up and start walking toward the North Star. He stopped walking at BigCity, yet still he dangles for the entertainment of lynch mobs. ProudBoy walks center stage, shakes Bitch Bantam's hand, says quietly, "I doan need to win, but I need to put on a show."

Bitch nods her head in affirmation; she prefers a dance to a fight. Knocking men unconscious only feeds her desire to knock men unconscious. Bitch strives to delete her rage and the masculinity it brings to her surface. She sometimes feels that she is a man in disguise and there is nothing in the world as bad as a man. Still she continues to fight two shows a day, six days a week; she has come to believe that money can set her free and make her a woman.

Bitch lives alone in her little house on Kerosene Road, next door to Slab Pettibone, the one person she truly cares for. Storybook legend Slab Pettibone, the man who loosed the noose that had once enslaved Bitch Bantam. It is he who has guided her hand as she became a real person making real decisions. Now Slab has shrunk into an obsessive funk. He has vanished in a sad puff and returned a sad cripple who mourns his truelove, Fritter McTwoBit and his pet bear, no not pet, best friend, his legs, his gumption, FuzzyWuzzy. Of course Bitch Bantam also mourns, is also sad, but Bitch has always been sad. It does not slow her down.

There will be no rounds to this fight. They will fight until one goes down and does not get up. Repeat Kirby gongs a cowbell. Bitch and ProudBoy crash into one another like a freeway pileup. The very idea of physical contact with a man, any man, puts sick in Bitch's stomach. She wants to regard the contenders as objects, though they tend to prove themselves men again and again, with contact-sport feels of her female delicacies. Even in the midst of violent confrontation, they grope for sex. Bitch grips ProudBoy around the waist, spins him and drops him to the stage floor.

ProudBoy is back up fast. He projects a right hook to Bitch's forehead and she rolls with it. ProudBoy would be a challenge in a real fight, but Bitch has no pride to swell upon putting a man to the mat. Pride is learning to read and write and having ideas that are feasible. Pride would be, could be, talking to other women and having a straight white smile.

Bitch fights like she cares, grimaces like it hurts, swings and misses, swings and connects. On a higher plane, Bitch is sweet sixteen and having a birthday party. Five pretty female friends have brought presents wrapped in floral boxes with ribbons and heart-shaped bows. Her best friend is named Lulu and she looks like the woman who smiled at Bitch at Domino's Steak & Seafood, her first night in BigCity. Lulu and Bitch giggle with their heads together and talk about nice things. They don't like boys, boys are icky. One day, Bitch and Lulu are playing with her pet baby bear that looks like FuzzyWuzzy. They all three roll across the plush carpeted floor in a laughing tangle, when, to Bitch's surprise, Lulu suddenly kisses her smack on the lips.

ProudBoy Goodwin biffs Bitch in the mouth which is tender, sore and toothless. Bitch wakes up and strikes back. ProudBoy takes a jab to the chin that staggers him backward. ProudBoy is also fighting on autopilot. Like Bitch, ProudBoy can take a heavy dose of pain without a flinch. Once, in a tippling shop, for two dollars, ProudBoy hammered a nail through his foot and an hour later danced a jig for four-bits. Taking a pounding from Bitch, who is pulling most of her punches anyway, is a walk in the wind.

ProudBoy has fought before many a crowd and doesn't listen to the insults and racial slurs from the jeering white fuckheads in the stands. Tonight though he catches something he wants to hear more of. He listens through the ringing in his ears and it appears, he's the fight favorite. They are calling his name. "ProudBoy ProudBoy ProudBoy ProudBoy ProudBoy."

The peanut gallery, the swells, the sporting men yell hoot and stomp. They come here to see Bitch Bantam, though they do not shell out, night after night, to see her win. The pay to see her lose, which, as it turns out, she never does.

The stub-holders understand the true order of things. Men are men and women are women. Man beats woman, woman does not beat man. Therefore, someone needs to beat Bitch Bantam, make her understand the way things are supposed to work. And if that someone is black, all the better. The men, and even some of the women working tier two, are chanting, cheering. "ProudBoy ProudBoy ProudBoy ProudBoy ProudBoy."

ProudBoy's ears are unplugged. His pride is swelling. He does not consider his rancor toward white people. Instead, he listens to his name. The same world that lynched him, like a straw and rag effigy, now is praising him and giving him worth. And why would worth be derived from this group of honky gladhanders? Not a question ProudBoy can answer. All he knows is that he has never heard his name from so many mouths with so much near adulation. "ProudBoy ProudBoy ProudBoy ProudBoy ProudBoy."

Thirty seconds ago, ProudBoy tapped Bitch in the mouth, noted it was a sore spot and determined not to hit her there again. Now he wants to win, he wants to be sported on the shoulders of the white swells, he wants to feel the glory of a returning soldier. Bitch is sparring and, therefore, taken by surprise when ProudBoy connects her swollen jaw with two hard left-right one-twos. The impact knocks her from her feet to her seat.

The audience goes up from their seats to their feet. Bitch Bantam has never been knocked down before. A vociferous rainstorm fills the Orpheus. "ProudBoy ProudBoy ProudBoy ProudBoy ProudBoy."

Bitch is back in the wrong world. She hears hate. She looks up at ProudBoy and sees no apology. She sees the flash of his foot as he kicks her in the side of the head. She rolls but still takes a hard knock. A big-toe toenail has opened her scalp. She pulls up to all fours but ProudBoy kicks her in her ass-crack with a thud that travels to her head.

ProudBoy Goodwin is dancing a jig around Bitch Bantam. He is grinning out at the darkened grandstands, a changed man. Afterward, the swells will want to shake his hand, buy him drinks, give him respect, freedom. Respect. "ProudBoy ProudBoy ProudBoy ProudBoy ProudBoy." ProudBoy places a foot on the back of Bitch's head, pushes her face into the mat, beats his chest like a proud warrior.

Bitch is in a fog. Her gums throb. Why has ProudBoy turned? Is it because he is a man? A black man is supposed to be different. A black man should be... Bitch cannot raise her head. She can taste the warped floor, dirty feet, bug shit, bloody lava from tooth socket volcanoes. She reaches up and behind, gets a grip on ProudBoy's big-toe, twists it until it snaps. ProudBoy stumbles and yelps. A broken big-toe hurts more than a carefully placed nail.

Bitch grabs ProudBoy's other foot and pulls it out from under him. He falls and she is on him. His head in an arm lock, she pommels him with a barrage of knuckles, yet still, somehow, she holds back. Could she be mistaken? Maybe ProudBoy has not really turned on her, maybe he is just giving a good show. But Bitch does not hear what ProudBoy Goodwin hears, would not understand, if she did, the inner workings of vainglory, the thing that leads men, black or white, happily to their destruction. "ProudBoy ProudBoy ProudBoy ProudBoy ProudBoy."

ProudBoy is determined to bask in a victory and has found his opponent's soft spot. Between Bitch's rain of uncertain blows he whispers upward, "Okay, Miss Bitch. Pick me up and throw me down and I be playin knocked-out."

Dare Bitch trust this man? Does his pigment make him other than..? It is just a show, that is all, just a show. Bitch believes what she most wants to believe. She loosens her head-lock, squats on her hunches and scoops up ProudBoy Goodwin. He is heavy and her knees wobble as she stands. ProudBoy has gone limp, feigning utter defeat. Adrenaline-injected men spill from balcony rails. Hats go flying. "Wake-up ProudBoy. Shake it off and give the bitch the old what-for. Make her beg, make her cry, be a hero, be a hero, be a hero. ProudBoy ProudBoy ProudBoy ProudBoy ProudBoy."

Bitch Bantam strains her muscles, presses ProudBoy over her head, and holds him there for all to see. ProudBoy turns his head to the audience, mugs a jive-ass grin and winks at his fans. To Bitch Bantam's complete surprise ProudBoy slams his fist down into her mouth, one two three four. Bitch is knocked off kilter, drops her heavy load. ProudBoy falls on her hard, twists his legs over her shoulders and settles, as she stumbles, with a scissor-lock on her neck, his crotch in her face. His fists clang against her temples in a chorus of confusion, her equilibrium is cast from reach. Her eyes are open but see only the grey and white cloth covering his manhood. His rubbery cock and balls press into her nose and swollen mouth. Bitch feels herself falling backwards in slow motion. She smells musk and poor hygiene. She gags. She feels his cock and balls, a water balloon, in her face. His cock and balls. His cock and balls. "ProudBoy ProudBoy ProudBoy ProudBoy ProudBoy."

ProudBoy rides the woman to the ground, never letting up the brick fists, head-trauma head-trauma head-trauma. He looks out at the spectators, feels their excitement and admiration. He shows them idiotic faces and humps the woman's face, which brings a roar of approval. Bitch never would have believed that only days after extracting her cursed pointed teeth, she would wish they were back in her mouth. She suddenly wishes for the vilest of weapons at her disposal. Her head is far away. She has no legs.

Bitch Bantam closes her eyes. She does not see the charmed youth of her waking dreams. No Fritter McTwoBit,

No FuzzyWuzzy, no best friend named Lulu who kisses her on the lips. Bitch Bantam sees herself, as she is, a huge toothless freak of nature. A woman without grace, without education, a fighting machine with a fucked-up past and a fucked-up future. She sees herself using her wild-animal strength. She is a wild animal. Bitch steels herself, takes three deep breaths.

"ProudBoy ProudBoy ProudBoy ProudBoy ProudBoy."

ProudBoy's arms are tired so he stops swinging, though he does not loosen the lock on Bitch's neck, continues to stop the flow to her head, blood, oxygen. He waves out to the ecstatic swells, now pointing, laughing, whoop-whooping. "AttaBoy AttaBoy ProudBoy ProudBoy." Up from the earth below the ground swells with an unexpected temblor. Bitch Bantam rises to her feet with ProudBoy Goodwin attached to her face and neck, his cock, his balls, his cock, his balls. She reaches upward, grabs him around the waist and pulls him down. Bitch holds ProudBoy upside down, by the waist, his back against her body. She swells upward then pile-drives his head down to the floor.

Even in her rush of strength and anger, Bitch's goal is only to render ProudBoy unconscious. When she hears the cherry-bomb crack of his thick rope-scarred neck she knows she has exceeded her goal. ProudBoy Goodwin is dead, like a finger-snap. Bitch has killed a man, a black man, a survivor of lynch mobs, reconstruction, Jim Crow. She drops his body to the floor.

"ProudBoy ProudBoy ProudBoy Proud... Boy..."

Pete Kirby blows taps. Zeph Riley cues close the curtain, comes out singing and dancing, the show must go on. Bitch Bantam walks to her dressing room. Mabel Scott follows, says, "Are you alright? Do you want to talk?"

Bitch says, "No, thank you. I'm okay." In her dressing room she retrieves her heavy lamb's wool coat, bowler hat and hides inside. She leaves the Orpheus through the back door, walks down an alleyway to the street and makes her way unnoticed through the hoarfrost night to her little house on Kerosene Row.

33 Kerosene Row

Slab Pettibone's house. A pad of snow glows from the shingle roof like a light-table. The windows are dark, icy whiskers droop from the sills. Yonder a crack of lamplight hides behind a canvas drape. Through the crack, into the light, a fire-breathing lamp on a kitchen table. A stack of onionskin paper shimmers under the hula-dancing flame like crumpled foil. Sitting on his stubs, in a straight back chair, Slab Pettibone leans forward, puts fountain pen to paper.

This is a true story that took place back in 1,879 AD when I was just one-score past a whippersnapper. I remember it like it was yesterday, how I found a faithful and loving companion in a bruin cub; how I found my true love in a woman that made the stars twinkle and my dreams come true. This is a love story. But, that's not how it began.

This is not a true story. Slab Pettibone adventures are tall-tales, spun-yarns, abracadabra. This is not to say that Slab does not have true stories he could share with his readers. It is just that his true-life tribulations are not something he would put upon others. A book titled *Slab Pettibone In The Throes Of Despair* would likely flop and flounder. Maybe he should relate the story about amputating his own legs, inches above the gangrene kudzu that entwined his feet, ankles, knees. Here is a good title, *Half A Man*, the sad saga of Slab Pettibone as he watches his companion, his other half, burst into flame, vanish for all time, while the woman he loves suffers and dies only feet away. Slab figures to keep the self-indulgence to a minimum and stick to the tried and true: innocent feel-good yarns in a world void of angst, depression and reality.

Slab hears the crunch of snow and the open and shut of the gate next door. Bitch Bantam has arrived home from the Orpheus. Slab hunkers over the table lamp, hoping Bitch does not see his light. Slab loves Bitch Bantam, his only link to the recent past, a past he often retrieves and revises in his personal fictions. It was he who had been protective of Miss Bantam. Now, it is she who goes forward, it is she who watches over him. Yet he hides his light in fear of simple conversation and daily pleasantries.

Slab Pettibone no longer wears his sombrero. His handlebar moustache droops like a Fu Manchu. His silver Colt pistols are in a closet under the bundle of his best clothes. When he ventures out, which is seldom, he treads low and slow like a side-show freak and hides himself in nondescript clothing. He shudders at the thought of recognition. The big-as-life hero, twirling guns, singing songs, lassoing bad guys in black hats from the back of his ferocious bear, would surely deny his identity, in public just as in private.

Tonight offers a breakthrough of sorts. Slab Pettibone has just written his first paragraph in over a year. Last year, while touring with FuzzyWuzzy in the Californias, he had written *The Adventures of Slab Pettibone & FuzzyWuzzy the Bear in the Volcano at the Center of the Earth*. He had planned to begin the new book, *The Adventures of Slab Pettibone & FuzzyWuzzy the Bear on the Island of Lost Time*, in late August, but things had happened. Now he attempts to make up for time lost.

Slab turns his eyes inward, sees the make-believe Slab in the make-believe world. He levers his pen in the ink-barrel pool, sucks up a blue paragraph and puts nub to paper.

I was mostly walking place to place back then as I still had my legs and walking places was my favorite thing to do. Matter of fact, I walked so much and wore out so many shoes that I took to walking barefoot. Got to where my soles were so tough I could stamp out a bonfire and dull a railroad spike with the heel of my foot. I walked from the Misery Divide across the continent to the North Coast. It was there my adventure began.

Chapter Ten

Saddle Sore Productions

At the bottom edge of BigCity's Left Bank, on the right side of Beat Street, three doors down from the HuggerMugger, five doors down from the DownStairs Café, is a converted factory, City Saddle Works, now known as Saddle Sore Productions. Daddy Smithy, Filmmaker Extraordinaire, has installed, on the north wall, a bank of frosted glass panes, pulling in soft light, dawn, morning, noon, afternoon, dusk. Inside, an array of motion-picture equipment, backgrounds, scrims, indoor sets, outdoor sets. Lights. Camera. Action.

Daddy lives, works and creates in this vast space, every

living moment, even when he is elsewhere. He sits at a table and pours half-milk, half-Doctor FixUp into a bowl of Kellogg's Corn Flakes. He crunches and swallows. Somewhere a rooster crows.

Along with this space, equipment and lavish funding via Warner Quackenbush, Daddy's vision has grown. His once simple dream of making a cheap nudie flick is null and void. Daddy is now in the third week of filming his epic, The Rise & The Fall, which will run ninety minutes with a continuing story line, drama, comedy, sex.

Daddy studies storyboards and script, visualizes scenes and success. Then, in the snap of a synapse, his scenes are out-of-focus and his success is utter failure. It takes a fix of his elixir to balance his neuro-chemical imbalance as well as great self-discipline to convince himself he is not the screw-up he has always been. Once again Daddy conjures a scene for filming, thinks out the lighting and direction of the players. I will succeed. I will, I will. Will not. I will, I will.

Outside, three doors up, Wilbur Good and Wilbur Szedvilas walk by the HuggerMugger building. Wilbur Szedvilas waves through the window to Adelina Brown, working inside, inking a letterpress.

Wilbur Good says, "Yuz oughtnt oughtr being friendship to that girlie. Yuz shoulda killed her dead."

While Wilbur and Wilbur have remained best buddies. Wilbur Good blames his partner for their permanent suspension from the BigCity police force. Wilbur Szedvilas should have whacked Adelina Brown back at TumbleHouse instead of helping her escape and then throwing a barrel of spiderbite at Shag. It is not fair he should be penalized for his partners' soft-hearted failings. Wilbur Good discounts that he also botched his assignment; he was supposed to whack the other girl, the one with Gulper Mooney. Still it is mostly Wilbur Szedvilas's fault, though he also blames Shag Draper, the guy who penned his pink slip.

Wilbur Good points back over his shoulder and says, "Mudder Mary I spies a five-legged doggie-mutt." While Wilbur Szedvilas doubts the existence of a five-legged doggie-mutt, he makes the mistake of looking anyway. Wilbur Good quickly pulls an icicle from an awning above and jabs it until it breaks into his partner's ear.

Wilbur Szedvilas grabs his ear. "I thinking me hearing bell been stabbered and frosted. Next time up yuz pooter the icy she goes, me friend." Wilbur Szedvilas is glad he lost his job with the police. He did not like being a cop anyway. He knows not why his partner has been in such a mood about the whole thing. Money concerns are not a problem since they continue to wear their uniforms, continue shaking-down the same merchants they have been extorting for years. And the new job, how could anything be better than the new job?

Wilbur and Wilbur are pantomime actors currently working in starring roles on the soon-to-be-epic The Rise & The Fall. Wilbur Szedvilas loves it. Wilbur Good tolerates it. As they approach the Saddle Sore building, they see the other players, waiting for Daddy to open shop. The actresses are Annabelle Bilyeu and Sarah Heart. Hair, makeup and wardrobe are done by Billie Époque, a rabble-rousing chick-with-a-dick from SodomHeights Billie loves, passionately loves, show business, the underground feeling of independent genre busting, the dawn of an intellectual revolution. Billie is a shining bohemian star in charge of style and the avant-garde.

Annabelle Bilyeu and Sarah Heart have come to acting from bawdyhouse T and A. Annabelle thinks Wilbur Szedvilas is cute. Wilbur Szedvilas thinks Annabelle is yummy hot.

Daddy Smithy opens the door and the multiple personalities, cast and crew, file in. Daddy sails through his equipment and props, readying this and that. Four tall stools face a mirror rimmed with electric bulbs; the players sit and squint. Billie reads through today's scene list.

Scene 32

Wilbur Szedvilas saves Annabelle Bilyeu from jumping to her death from a window ledge. Annabelle, in her bloomers, dances a hootche for Wilbur S. Sarah Heart barges in and the two women fight a comic battle, ripping off clothing in the process.

Billie Èpoque goes to work on Annabelle Bilyeu, puffs out Annabelle's blond curls, affixes a black paper rose above her left ear, blanches her face with a mist of powder, accentuates her cheekbones with rouge, paints her lips into a full bow, startles her eyes with wide penciled lashes and caterpillar brows, assigns her outer and under wear, then goes to work on Wilbur Szedvilas. On her way to wardrobe, Annabelle winks at Wilbur Szedvilas. Wilbur blushes, smiles and winks back.

Daddy Smithy has the set set: wall-papered wall, double bed, chest of drawers, window to a painted cityscape. He frames the scene in the viewfinder of his Cinématographe motion-picture camera. He can see the black and white scene that, in fact, he has not yet seen. Daddy Smithy is a man of the future; there is no room in his viewfinder for the past. He has not a dead wife, he did not abandon a teenage daughter he did not barter away a six-year-old daughter. He is not a screw-up. He is a visionary genius. Daddy picks up his megaphone and calls talent to the set.

The Catacombs

On the west end of State Street, Municipal Row, two doors east of the federal courthouse, a great stone bunker houses an amalgam of law enforcement, commissioner down to jailer-trustees. Sunk deep into the clay and limestone below this mighty building, a city of bars and locks, tunnels and cages, the Catacombs, where living dead serve time for crimes they did and did not commit. Down these rubble stairways a boolydog descends, lamp in one hand, an unconscious man's foot, like a pull-string, in the other. The man's head thuds down the steep steps like a soft cantaloupe. The man is just some guy who found himself on the wrong side of the law.

Last night, after a few hours of good old-fashioned hands-on interrogation, the man confessed to a crime he may or may not have committed. Now morning, three floors below the surface, the man's head bounces down the stairway. He is not expected to live, yet still he is dragged to the deepest of dungeon cells to live out his days, hours or minutes in gothic squalor and defeat.

The boolydog has reached the bottommost landing. It is dank and shadowy and smells of mummified death. From a skinny tunnel he stops in a small cavern where, in the center of the floor, he opens a padlock, peels back the bars and looks down into a deep oubliette. His flashlight skims the flank of the prisoner below. He drags the man to the pit and, for a little sport in his otherwise drab day, he attempts to drop the breathing carcass on top of the other prisoner. Now, for a little more sport, he unbuttons his fly and voids his bladder.

The prisoner has dodged the falling body, though when he hears the splatter of urine he attempts not to avoid the stream but to catch as much as he can, in his cupped hands, in his mouth, like a baby bird. His water rations have been minimal. He needs liquid, regardless of the source. The boolydog shakes away the last drops. He buttons his fly and refastens the padlock, walks back up the damp stairways to civilization.

The flickering Tinkerbell of the boolydog's lamp, now gone, was no more real than the modicum of light Dooley Paradise finds in knuckling his closed eyelids. He crawls to the fallen body and puts his hand on the man's chest to find life, heaving and troubled. He puts a hand to the man's face, attempting to read the Braille of his features, but finds only a puffy mask of indecipherable hematomas.

Dooley says, "Can you hear me, chum? Are you going to die? If you're smart, you'll go ahead and die now, save yourself the misery. You know what I'd wish for if I could have anything right now? I'd wish for a shot of spiderbite. Can you believe that? A lousy shot of spiderbite. I wish you could talk because I have about a million questions. I don't know day from night, I don't even know hour from day. I can pace this room without bumping into walls, like I can see them coming. I get pictures in my head and I can watch the rats run from wall to wall. If you live, you'll get that way too. Do you have a lot of friends? I used to cry when I thought about my friends but I haven't done that in a while. Being here is almost the same thing as being dead. But it's hard to think about being dead because when you're dead even your memory is gone. And everything is nothing except everything is still there, all the people who are alive. If you die I might need to eat you to stay alive. That's a thing that's hard to think about. Why, if I'm already dead, would I eat the flesh of another human? How come I can't just go ahead and die? I make stories in my head about if I wasn't here anymore but they don't work the way I want them to. Sometimes I'm not even sure if I'm awake or asleep. Who knows, maybe you'll get better and I'll die and you'll be eating me. Guess it doesn't really matter either way."

An invisible black rat bites Dooley on the haunch and then scampers away with a sampling of blood. It hurts and it makes him yelp and he's terrified of the next one to come. Up from a rat-hole comes a billowing groan too big for a rat, too guttural for a human, a bear singing the blues. A thin current of clear air laps at Dooley's face. He crawls back to the man who is now dead. The man is dressed like Dooley, shoeless and hatless with thin, black & white stripped jailbird shirt and pants. The dead man's wrists are shackled with iron cuffs and ten links of heavy chain. Dooley tugs the man's body to the wall crevice. He holds the man's arm and uses the iron cuff to chip at the opening in the wall. He closes his eyes in search of light.

The DownStairs

The DownStairs sits below a three-story brownstone, has high peek-a-boo windows two feet above the sidewalk. Fourteen steps down, smoke, chatter, laughter. Up top, the air is crisp. The moon is bright. The sky is gunmetal. Stark white clouds frolic like lambs.

Helen Beck peddles a bicycle down the wintry street. She wears a straight serge skirt, low shoes with spats, a button-front shirt, a leather vest and doeskin gloves. Her head is wrapped in wool scarves that trail her like a jet stream. She sports bug-eyed goggles. The bicycle is large and clunky. Helen is tiny yet traffic stands aside like a parting sea. She bumps the wheeled steed across snowy ruts and holds to the handlebars like a rodeo cowboy. She pulls from the street onto the sidewalk then breaks and skids to a halt. Helen has come to the DownStairs in search of Adelina Brown.

Inside she finds a warm electric cavern—American moderns, hipniks, poets, intellectuals, anarchists, writers, atheists, feminists, trendsetters. A black guy jumps up and down on eighty-eight ivory keys, invents Boogie-Woogie, Rock-a-billy, Funk, Rap. Another black guy hits the floorboards dancing, invents Tap, The Charleston, The Twist, Disco. Four-passenger tables under checkered cloth ghutrahs. A long bar and open kitchen. An espresso machine. A jet-fueled staff, college educated waiters, cooks, cashiers. Women openly smoke cigarettes, though no one smokes Signals, everyone is too cool to smoke Signals.

Helen Beck wonders if she can fit into this oddball gathering without being cast out. She has spent her career converting snooty dowagers to her causes and now believes she has been on the wrong team. But this bubbling hepcat stew is possibly beyond her social etiquette and she is ill at ease. She walks through this enlightened forest to a table.

Adelina Brown comes in from the cold. At Helen's table, Adelina says, "Hello, Miss Beck."

Helen Beck says, "Won't you have a seat, Adelina?"

Adelina sits and Helen says, "I am grateful to finally spend some time with you, Adelina. I read today's HuggerMugger. It was very good."

"Thank you. What did you find out about Dooley?"

"Absolutely nothing, I'm sorry to say. I went to City Hall. It appears that, on paper, your friend never existed, which I'm afraid may mean that he no longer exists. I hope I'm wrong."

Adelina's eyes pool. Helen reaches a hand across the table, but Adelina is not ready to take Helen Beck's hand. Helen says, "You've been very brave. I've some influence in the world, though I fear I'm putting myself leftward of my former supporters, I would like to help you. I'd like to get your stories and pictures in a publication that would be more widely read."

"Maybe a better plan would be for you to write articles for the HuggerMugger and then we could increase our circulation and support ourselves."

Helen Beck says, "Admittedly, Adelina, my allegiance has changed, and I feel I've not taken my fight to the proper extremes. It's happened so suddenly that I don't know quite where I stand or what I should be doing. I'm concerned about the children living on the streets. I'm looking for a starting point."

Adelina is still filled with anger toward Helen. "I should think if I had a great deal of money, Miss Beck, I would set out to feed the hungry."

With feathers suddenly ruffled, Helen retorts, "Why is it, Adelina, that you assume I have great wealth at my disposal? You act as if I have no empathy outside of my own privilege and I resent that."

As quickly as Helen has said what she has said, she regrets it. In fact, Helen lives on the proceeds of a very substantial trust fund and, indeed, is heir to fortunes. But never before has she been ashamed of her money or attempted to excuse it. Before she speaks again, she ponders her emotions, then says, "Yes, I do have wealth. And having it has taught me not to use it in haste. Giving away what I have would be a mere patch on the wound that is poverty. You need to give me a better cause, where my donations can do the most good. I am trying to truly understand your world and only ask that you try to understand mine."

Adelina concedes. "I'll try. I'm sorry. Sometimes my passion exceeds my logic. If you really want to help me personally, I need financing for the film I'm making."

"Film? You mean moving pictures? How would a moving picture help?"

"Come with me tomorrow, to ScourgeTown. I can show you how moving pictures can be a podium of cause and change." Adelina seems to Helen like a girl who has never had the chance to be a girl and a young woman who feels obligated to right all the impossible wrongs. Of course, Helen will accompany Adelina to Scourge town.

TumbleHouse

Shag Draper drags himself forward, armpits over crutches. His face is a knot of perseverance. His shoulders nearly touch his ears which hold up his hat which covers his balding pate. His three goons follow along like vaudeville stooges, nyuk nyuk nyuk.

Up ahead, back from the eroded sidewalk, under an awning, sitting in a leaned-back chair below a wide-brim slouch hat, Eddie Plague. Eddie has found time in his busy schedule of murder and terror to build a thriving enterprise. His experience as a slaver and pimp has served him well. The TumbleHouse, well-maintained and semi-vacant, has provided Eddie with home and headquarters. After the TumbleHouse raid many of the strays returned to the only home they knew. Now they whore for Eddie, or they starve, or they face Eddie's vile temper. A few have gone off to chance life on the winter streets, most though have stayed, too afraid to run. Eddie watches Shag Draper and posse approaching. He snickers at Shag's obvious misfortune.

The one thing Shag has held onto, since his misfired political coup, is ScourgeTown. Shag still controls it, still bleeds it of hope and banks its ill-gotten gains. Now this Eddie Plague kid has moved into a building owned by the Mooks and seriously disregarded the rent. That Eddie is a vicious killer has not escaped Shag's network of information. He knows with whom he is dealing.

On either side of Eddie, sit two large-boned teenage

293

girls wrapped in thick coats, wearing murderous grins. Eddie's enforcers—girls with little talent for prostitution and big talent for harm, girls full of spite without prejudice whose fondest wish is to cause suffering to others.

Shag and the henchmen stop at the stoop. Shag says to Eddie, "I yam Shag Draper, yur parked on me property. We need to talk and I need to sit."

Eddie has yet to look up, his face cloaked in hat-brim shadow. He says to the girl on his right, "Get up, give the man a seat." He raises his face to Shag and says, "Sit."

Shag is startled backward. Eddie Plague's face is seriously messed up. A scant few months ago Eddie was handsome, irresistible. Then, suddenly, he was ugly. He had a butchered hog snout where his nose was supposed to be. Eddie has since been to a BigCity surgeon who, for the right price, was willing to experiment with rhinoplasty. The surgeon cut a forehead flap down to the fascia, rotated it down over the open nose hole and stitched it into place. He then sewed shut the gaping forehead. The result was a long suture line on his forehead, a hump between the eyes and a new nose that looks more like a duck bill.

Shag sits, steels himself to Eddie's face, and gets situated. "I ave nary a thin against a man of industry. I'm happy to have you in me town. But I ave come to let you know I own the building yur occupyin. My take is a third of all yur takin. Tis not yur option but yur due."

Eddie looks at Shag for thirty seconds then says, "What do you give me?"

It is enough that Shag gets no respect from the rest of BigCity. He will not tolerate it at a ScourgeTown bagnio, at

TumbleHouse, Shag's alma mater. "What you get is use of my building and protection and a license to work in this town."

"And if I choose not to?"

"If you do what? You dassent refuse. I'll ave ya run out and beaten or dead in a gutter."

Suddenly Eddie is holding a straight razor, stropping it on the thigh of his pants' leg. "But what of right now, Mister Draper, sir? Right now, you cannot even walk on your own legs. And I sir, mister landlord, could open your throat and watch you die before you take your next breath."

Shag quickly takes his next breath. "Try me, ya ugly feckin pimp. I did nay come by me position with slowness and stupidity. I'm not unprepared to take what is rightfully mine." Shag punctuates his speech with a two-shot derringer pointed at the bump between Eddie's eyes. "Come on, test me, ya feck. Find out if me trigger finger is slower than yur feckin razor."

Eddie folds up his razor and puts it in his pocket, rationalizes his situation. "I misjudged you, I apologize. Sure, I'll pay your cut. I'm not looking for trouble. I understand politics. Maybe you can help me with a problem I have. We can work together."

"A favor yur already askin?"

"Just one little thing and I'll pay my debt and you and your boys can go inside and take your pleasure with my girls."

Shag cannot remember the last time he got laid and feels pretty good about the way things have turned around. "What would yur little thing be?"

"Bitch Bantam. You know who she is?"

"A WhiteWay show freak, fights at Daddy Smithy's place. She should be of no concern to you."

"But she is a concern to me. I own her, just like you own this building. She's my property."

"I can nay do nothing about that. She is off me limits for now. Can you prove ownership?"

"No. But you could have her arrested. She killed a man. I read about it. She killed a man in front of a hundred or more witnesses."

"Twas an accident in a fair fight, I can nay be of help."

"Alright fine. I'll take care of it myself." Eddie has slunk back into the shadow of his hat, his mangled face fades away. He says quietly to one of his girl bodyguards, "Take Mister Draper and his boys inside, give them to Girl. When you're done, get back out here. I have an errand for the two of you."

Inside TumbleHouse, Zeph Riley is not smiling from the bar. None of the kids are tending younger siblings and offsprings. Very few wear green derbies. There is no music. Boys and girls rub up against rowdy johns, jousting for meager hits of food and drugs.

Running the show is Girl Smithy. A red chin to cheekbone scar reflects lamp flickers like candle wax. She is naked under a floor-length coat of rabbit fur and flashes body parts like a party tart. She is abandoned, adrift in a sea of brimstone. She is filled with rage.

A girl-goon comes in escorting a flashy gent on two broken feet, dragging three dimwits behind. The girl-goon says, "Eddie says to give these guys what they want."

Shag Draper is feeling pretty cool, back at the top of his game, earning respect. His back has straightened and he pushes his chest out. Girl is beside him; she takes his arm and reads his mind, "You look like a man of respect. Let's sit you down."

She leads him to a couch, along the way signaling three girls to whisk away the goons and show them a good time. Girl thinks she knows who this swell is. She sits him down, sits beside him, puts her hand on his thigh, and flashes her breasts. "I should know who you are, you look important. What's your name?"

"I yam Shag Draper."

Shag Draper puppeteered Gulper Mooney and had him killed, nearly killed Girl. Shag Draper is at the top of Girl's *People To Kill* list along with Eddie Plague. It is Shag Draper that good fortune has delivered to Girl this day. "You're a big hotsy totsy. I've heard all about you. I heard you're the boss of BigCity."

Shag has a boner. This chickie stirs his urges. Her face is innocent, pure, yet the healing slash up the left side is perverse and evil. Her body is nubile. Shag is not unaware that every word from her lips is a lie, yet still he swells in the flattery and respect.

Girl bats her lashes. "What happened to your feet?"

"Me feet were broke in this very house. Twas an army of fighting brats. Me feet will be better soon and the brats now answer to me."

Girl tickles his nuts through his pants. "Does that mean I answer to you instead of Eddie? I'd like that. I like you bettern Eddie. Eddie's mean and ugly and you're cute."

Shag knows better, he is not cute. He has a russet potato-face, pixie ears and chia-pet teeth. "Tis I what owns it all. Eddie Plague answers to me."

"But who do I answer to?"

"Plague controls this house but I may or mayent change me mind about that. Yur a fine chickie, I may want you for meself."

Girl straddles Shag's legs, opens her rabbit coat, and sits ever so gently across his thighs. "We should go to my room now. I need to take care of you; it's something I really want to do." Girl leans forward and kisses Shag and puts her tongue into his bitter mouth.

Shag Draper has just gone stupid and it feels really good.

33 Kerosene Row

Under a yellow waver of lamplight Slab Pettibone puts pen to paper.

She first appeared in a billow of smoke from the medicine man's magic peace-pipe. She was from my lifelong dreams and she was as dark as Africa with golden eyes. She wore veils that blew in the wind and changed colors. She said to me, "You are my dreamlove and I am waiting for your return to the past." This didn't make much sense to me but I knew it had to do with my future. My dream woman then faded away like a whip o fog.

While still despondent from his losses, Slab writes his adventure story with optimistic fantasy. He watches himself in an altered world where miracles are real. He plans ahead his happy ending. His ladylove kisses him. FuzzyWuzzy dances.

Bitch Bantam knocks three times on Slab's front door, walks in with an armful of groceries. She goes to the kitchen, puts the larder on a counter and says, "Ya writin fun stuff, huh? Can I take some home and read it?" Bitch, under the tutelage of Mabel Scott, has greatly improved her reading capability. She loves Slab's magical books. She loves Slab the pulp hero just as she loves the real man. Bitch wishes she could do something to bring back Slab's singing dancing rootin-tootin persona. She wishes she could do something for him other than bring groceries. She wishes she could share with him her new optimism. Bitch strikes a friction match, lights a couple of lanterns to burn away Slab's gloom.

Slab says, "It's not ready for readin yet. It's nothing special anyway. You'd be better off reading real writers like Mister Samuel Langhorne Clemens or Charley Dickens."

"I read a Mister Dickens' story about Christmas. It was hard to understand but I still understood. I like your books better. Your stories are more funner."

"Well, thanks, Missy." Slab who could never say the word Bitch has taken to calling her Missy, which she gratefully accepts.

A long silent pause.

Slab looks up at Bitch's smiling face. Her smiling face? "By thunder, you got your new teeth. You look downright purty as a picture."

At this moment Bitch could not drag down her smile with both hands. "You think so? Really?"

"You look like a woman. You look splendid like the favored lady at a grand ball."

Bitch loves hearing what she has just heard yet she knows she looks nothing like a lady at a grand ball. In fact, she no longer wants to look like a fancy lady. She wants to look like something she has not yet seen or heard defined. She wants to look like what she looks like except, except, it is all very confusing. Happily, though, she has recently made a new friend to help her with style. "Thank you. I been thinkin bout dressin up some and I met this person named Billie Époque who does clothes and stuff for Daddy Smithy and wants to help me with clothes and stuff too. And I been thinkin I could maybe save up enough money to quit Daddy Smithy's show. I doan wanna fight no more. Specially since I kilt that guy. I couldn hardly sleep last night thinkin bout that guy I kilt. I dint mean to kill em. He dint deserve to die."

"I don't guess anybody deserves to die, Missy. You meant no ill will, be best you try and not think too much about it."

"I guess so. Cept I can't not think about it, because I think I should feel bader about it than I do, you know what I mean? I don't wanna hate nobody, but when I kilt that guy I hated him. I doan even know if I kilt him on accident or on purpose. I guess I got a lot things to figger out."

"Best you stick to thinkin about all the new good things."

"That's not what you been doin. You doan think about nothin but Fritter and FuzzyWuzzy and I doan mean that that's a bad thing, I think about them too. But you can still do happy things that you like to do. You're all famous and everything. Member when we went to that restaurant, Domino's? Everbody wanted to shake your hand and I know that makes you happy. Know what I was just thinkin? It ain't, isn't late yet and you and me could go to that place tonight and you know what? I could buy your dinner jus like you bought mine that one time. Ya wanna do that?"

"Not tonight, Missy, thank you. Nobody wants to see a half-celebrity, an incomplete man. I would only rouse their pity."

"I doan mean to sound mean or nothin, but I think you think you're the only one who cain't feel nothing but pity on your self. I doan know how it happened that I'm the smart one and you're the dumb one."

"I guess maybe you were always the smart one, Missy. I can tell you one thing that makes me very happy. It makes me happy watching your metamorphosis into a smart and wonderful young woman."

"I could metaporpoise even more if you was doin stuff steada sittin all lone at home all the time. I did sumpin today I wanna tell ya bout. Sumpin that'd make me real happy. When I was gettin my new teeth I asked the guy that made em some questions and he tolt me bout this guy that I went and talked to today. He makes legs."

"I don't know, Missy. I've seen far too many veterans tottering on sticks like inebriates. I have cultivated an image that would never allow my public persona to be seen as such."

"These ain't sticks. They're legs with a left foot an a right foot and bendies at the knees. You wear shoes an everthin. An I think it'd be real good for you and since you already said that I was smarter than you, then that means that I know best and so you gotta go with me tomorrow an talk to the guy that makes the legs."

"I surrender. Missy, my dear, you are surely a miracle. Tomorrow we can go and talk to the man, though I promise nothing."

Bitch Bantam walks over and bear-hugs his half body. Slab blushes, as he always does with displays of affection, though he relishes the warmth and sibling love in her embrace. Bitch sneaks a peek at the manuscript on the table.

I knew all about Buffalo Shank's magic peace-pipe and wasn't surprised when I blew a puff of smoke that froze into a cloud above our little campfire. We watched in silence as the smoke curled into the image of a little black bear. He was only a cub and he was cuter than dimples and he was held in shackles and chains. The little pup looked at me and telepathically put these words in my head, Help me!

Chapter Eleven

NetherWorld

When Dooley Paradise opens his eyes he sees nothing. He can hold his hand in front of his face and blow into the palm but still he sees nothing. When Dooley Paradise closes his eyes tight, then tighter, he can see the night sky. He can see himself, young, energetic, handsome, and charismatic. He can see reel after reel of his lifetime. He can clearly see the past, but nothing of the present or future.

Dooley wakes from a troubled sleep, or maybe not, maybe he is still asleep, or, then again, maybe he has never been asleep. He starts to crawl because that is what he does, he crawls. Yesterday, a hundred years ago, he chipped away a rat hole with a dead man's shackles in the dungeon wall. He crawled through the hole into a black labyrinth of natural and man-made tunnels, rooms and rivers. Beneath BigCity is a vast macrocosm of sewers and hollows, rails, cables, pipes, stalactites, darkness. It is the smell that moves Dooley ever forward. Beyond the stench of waste and the gasses of ferment is the pure odor of living organisms. His nose, his ears, his knees and his hands contain the optimism that his eyes and his head have lost.

Sometimes, in moments of precarious lucidity, Dooley thinks about Existence and Death and the loss of thought. If one lives in a void, is he, in fact, not living? I no longer interact, he thinks, therefore I am not. And if I am not, then what of the rest of the world? Is it gone? Somewhere above the layers of limestone and dirt are there people standing over me, in sunshine, in rain, in conversation? Is someone, right now, high above my head, in a bed, making love? Dooley asks these questions aloud or maybe not, and because he is still just a boy of eighteen he has no answers.

Dooley is on a ledge, five feet wide, below a ceiling of fossil and clay. To his right a wall of natural brick. To his left, three feet down, a toxic stream. He creeps along carefully, his fingers testing the obsidian space ahead, avoiding head-on collisions, drop-offs, and sharp objects. Goblins and ghouls with bloody fangs lie in wait around the next bend. He can hear a colony of rats, getting closer, louder like a flock of starlings. He crawls and he crawls and he knows not which way he goes.

ScourgeTown

Adelina Brown and Helen Beck on a plank sidewalk; Adelina pans her Cinématographe movie camera and hand-cranks film past the clacking shutter: A frozen mud roadway rutted with icy shark-fins. Barbell tenements bulge at the waist, slump from the load of gravity like a defeated Atlas. Pulley clotheslines from sad-eyed windows, frozen long-johns dance in the wind like Max Fleischer cartoons. Shutters applaud the wind and fire escapes hang with loose grips. Phone poles engage like fencing foils.

Helen Beck watches the intense young Adelina Brown at work. While she cannot envision the finished product as Adelina does, she can plainly see the merit of the venture. She has already pledged her financial support. She has as well agreed to write for the HuggerMugger. And, she is preparing a speech for the BigCity bigwigs as well as the ladies' auxiliary, which she hopes to win over, though doubts she will. She teeters between her capitalist upbringing and her ever-expanding socialist views. Helen is attempting to rebuild her head, though her deep seated mien remains in charge.

Adelina cranks the take-up reel:

A ragpicker wobbles a three-wheel cart. He wears monochrome filth from the ground up, looks like an unearthed Pompeii person. Tipsy staircases climb mountains of scree to squatter shacks. People huddle outside from lack of space inside. They complain about the government and expectorate tubercular lugies. Some are drinking while others are begging drink. A skinny mud-incrusted pig shows his ribs and challenges a skinny mud-incrusted kid for a turnip the kid holds like a snow-cone. A bad-ass group of young toughs glare at the camera from alleyway shadows and posture like gangsters. A scabby-looking kid in an unblocked bowler flips the bird.

Adelina swivels and cranks the motion-picture camera:

An old crazy woman turns a circle, screws herself into the frozen ground, bangs a sheet of corrugated tin with a mallet and yells silent-movie curses at no one and everyone. A man in shirt-sleeves and without a hat pulls a faded dray horse. The horse shuffles slowly and shits in the street. A draggled fence pasted with bright placards:

Sitting Bull
Him Always Ride
Him Bottom Sore
Him Got Raw-Hide
Smoke Signals
10 Cents

A woman, infant and toddler in a doorway, a Dorothea Lange photograph. The toddler wears rag moccasins, a paper coat of yesterday's headlines, a stiff hat of her own matted hair. In for a close-up, the toddler's face, petrified abraded skin, round black eyes that cry without tears. We hold on this face, lingering, lingering still, until we can look no longer. FADE OUT.

"That's it," Adelina says, "I got what I wanted. I'd like to walk to a place close to here. Is that alright with you, Miss Beck?"

"Yes," Helen says. "It is."

Adelina leads the way pushing the camera and rolling tripod; her head looks tiny like a turtle's head on top of her vast kangaroo coat. Helen walks a vigorous pace to keep up. She would like to take this opportunity to talk to Adelina but knows not what to say. In all of Helen's travels and campaigns, she has never come across a young woman who impressed the way Adelina does. In fact, Helen has never been with other women who have had more to say than she. Helen has always been the leader and, therefore, has only known followers. Adelina is a girl, woman, with foresight and insight and possibly future greatness. Helen feels that with her age and experience she should lead Adelina to her potential. But Adelina seems angry and listens to no one's advice, least of all Helen's.

Adelina takes them past an intersection and along a rickety sidewalk to the right, Gravel Street. Helen Beck unveils a bad memory. TumbleHouse. Adelina is taking them to TumbleHouse. Maybe the tragedy at TumbleHouse would have happened without Helen's participation; maybe Shag Draper would have orchestrated the fateful raid without her. But, in fact, he did not. Helen Beck and her famous silver hammer is, in part, whether big of small, responsible for the demise of Adelina's former home, shelter for the children. Helen says nothing, makes no rationalizations inwardly or verbally. She takes full responsibility for what she is about to see.

TumbleHouse

The main room is dead at this time of day. There is no sandwich and pickle program. The children eat when they get a chance and an undeclared farthing. They do not eat on Eddie Plague's clock. Most are now sleeping or attempting same. Eddie Plague is alone in this vast empty room at the bar, drinking a mix of whisky and milk. Twelve hours ago Shag Draper and Girl went into her room upstairs and have not yet come out except to send underlings for food and drink. Eddie was giving Shag a poke on the house. He was not giving him the house or the girl. Eddie is irritated and antsy. He paces the room.

One of Eddie's guard dogs, a dyke welterweight, comes in from her station outside. "You need ta come outside and see what's going on." Eddie follows her, and, as he steps outside, he stumbles into a documentary film. On the sidewalk Adelina Brown is behind the Cinématographe cranking film. Helen Beck looks on. Eddie has never seen a moving-picture camera but he knows what a lens is and this one is pointing at him like a gun muzzle. Adelina is cranking film even though the image in the viewfinder is quite startling: the pimp has beautiful blue eyes, cruel sensual lips and a duck bill where his nose should be. Adelina has heard about this guy and she wants him on film. Eddie says, "What the hell is this? Get the hell away from here before I have you taken away." Eddie's two goons flank him with girl power. Adelina keeps cranking.

Helen Beck is lost. She does not know who Eddie Plague is and she does not know that TumbleHouse has become Eddie's Romper Room. She can plainly see that trouble is afoot. Helen steps up next to Adelina, reaches into her handbag and takes out her silver sledgehammer.

Eddie studies Helen, who is welding a weapon that is easily fifteen percent her body weight. Sunlight glints from the hammer and attacks Eddie's eyes. Eddie decides to walk back inside, give these people, whoever the hell they are, nothing. Before Eddie can turn to walk away Adelina stops cranking, comes out from behind the camera. She says to Eddie Plague, "We'll be leaving now. You can go back to your whorehouse."

Helen thinks, *Whorehouse?*

Eddie says, "And who the fuck do you think you are, girly, that you can tell me what to do and what the fuck do you think you're doing with that camera?"

"You want to know what the fuck I'm doing, you fucking pimp. I'm exposing you and your kind to the world. That's what."

Helen understands the definition of the word fuck. Though, until now, twice from Eddie and twice from Adelina, she has never heard the word spoken. She knows this is not language befitting a young woman, yet she rather likes the punch that Adelina gives it. She thinks maybe someday she will give it a try.

Eddie tells his two henchwomen, "Come on, let's go inside." He turns and does just that. Inside, out of the light, Eddie rubs his eyes and tells one of the girls, "Go knock on Girl's door. Wake her the fuck up. Remind her who she works for."

The girl climbs the stairs to the room that once belonged to a ruffian boy named Gulper Mooney and knocks on the door, only to hear Girl yell, "Go away. Don't bother me."

Through the keyhole, Shag Draper is on his back, naked on the bed, while Girl is giving him fairy-fingers across his scrotum. Shag is finding it near impossible to get up on his broken feet and walk away from the pleasure this Girl-chick has lavished upon him all night and part of this morning. Shag is not entirely stupid for Girl, he has nothing scheduled this morning and he will indeed get up and go about his slimy business when the time comes. He knows it is not his charm and good looks holding onto this chick, he knows she wants something and what-the-feck if he can do her a favor, then why not? He is delighted when the favor comes to light as it falls into his favor as well.

Girl says, "If you was to kill Eddie Plague, then I could run this place and you'd get all the profits which you shoulda been getting anyway since you're the one that owns everything. Eddie beats me. He's the one that give me this scar. And he's a faggot too. Without Eddie I could be your girl all the time."

Shag says, "Yur a smart chickie, I like that. I gotta go soon. Hows bout ya give me stem another suck?"

NetherWorfd

Dooley Paradise listens to the roar of echo bouncing about his space. He thinks he hears the screech of a subway train but, alas, as it gets closer, he determines the sounds are animal not mechanical. He is on his hands and knees as the ceiling is low. He's been rat bit four times in the last three minutes. The rats are terrier-sized and hungry, invisible in the dark. Dooley is terrified, the rats bite hard and their teeth are sharp. A squeaking mass like shrill police whistles are getting closer from all sides. Dooley crawls forward. Another bite and then another. He can't stop; he has to keep moving, he can't stop for anything. He has to go forward or surrender. He gets a surprise bite on his hand and another on his haunch and another on his right foot. Two rats climb atop his back. He wails and rises up on his knees to shake them off but instead he bangs his head on the ceiling. Hammers are pounding anvils in his head. He falls flat to the floor and lands with his face next to a five pound rat. The rat screeches like an owl and bites into Dooley's left eye with an audible crunch and doesn't let go. Dooley screams and grabs at the rat which is swinging from his eye. He succeeds in pulling off the rat but most of his left eye becomes unattached as well. Now the rats swarm onto Dooley biting through the thin cloth of his jailhouse shirt and pants. He covers his head with his arms and hands and he kicks and kicks and they don't stop coming. The pain in his eye throbs like rhythmic kicks in his head. The rats are in frenzy but they all freeze, momentarily, when they hear the roar of a beast, like a lion, or a tiger, or a bear. Dooley remains hidden, his arms over his head and he listens as something, a wild beast, is chasing the rats away, knocking them off of Dooley with its paws and teeth, huffing and growling. The rats scream and fight back but they are no match for the beast. And now they are gone and though the beast is quiet Dooley knows it is here.

Chapter Twelve

Orpheus Theater

Fourth row center sits Helen Beck and Adelina Brown. Adelina has come to see her friends on stage. Helen has seen the advertising posters around town, the fighting woman kicking male butt, furthering a cause she has never even heard of. Bitch Bantam. The savage woman who had once looked into Helen's eyes and transformed her, unhung her closeted self. One look into this giant woman's eyes has charged Helen's neurons.

But what can exist of true love from a glance? Lust maybe, lust can occur from the merest of glances. And, indeed, Helen has a buzz going. But even this seems excessive and unfamiliar. Helen is a woman of convention; she cannot give her life over to a lustful buzz. Beyond that, how can she be so cocksure that she and this fighting woman are predetermined for love?

On stage performers Bug and Flopears are joined hands to ankles traversing the stage floor like a bumpy wheel. Their act is rated poorly and the audience is winding-up to throw tomatoes and cabbages. Helen has many times been to opera, ballet, symphony, Shakespeare, Gilbert and Sullivan, Barnum and Bailey, but this is her first vaudeville. She finds the rowdy atmosphere intimidating, yet she admires the open manner of both the entertainers and entertainees. Stage-left, two lively young men providing drum and horn accompaniment. Stage-right a teenage girl tinkles piano keys with humor and finesse. It is this girl, Helen has noted, that has the attentions of Adelina Brown. Adelina has come this night not so much as Helen's friend but as a friend to the performers and ringmaster, most notably Zeph Riley and Mabel Scott. They are, like Adelina, successful TumbleHouse refugees. Helen can see the pride riding Adelina's face as she watches her friends attaining goals and dreams.

Helen feels she has reconnected to the clarity of childhood innocence and discovery. She attributes this lens-cleansing to the TumbleHouse massacre, Adelina Brown, and a moment in the eyes of Bitch Bantam.

On stage Bug and Flopears have taken their bow and exit. Zeph Riley is now center stage. He looks out on the sea of people and happens to spot Adelina. He winks at her and she smiles. Zeph and Adelina were toddlers together. They toiled through childhood as adopted brother and sister. Zeph gives a covert signal to his beloved, Mabel Scott, at piano, leads her eyes out to Adelina. Adelina and Mabel exchange happy smiles.

Zeph projects, "Tis time for the battle you ave all been waitin for. For three weeks, I ave been adding five dollars a day to the bounty for any man thinks he can go the bell with our own Miss Bitch Bantam, and looky here what it has become." Zeph brings out a fan of thirty-eight five-dollar bills and holds it high. "One-hundred and ninety smackarooneys for today's volunteer, whoever that may be, and if he wins."

Helen Beck's gaze goes to the stage but her mind wanders and wonders. No one among this herd of show-going glad-handers recognizes Helen, though her name would sound an alarm. For fifteen of Helen's thirty-seven years she has been tabloid news. Helen and her hammer, while still at the university, harbors her sorority sisters, hoisting sails of protest at the doors of administration, EQUAL EDUCATION FOR WOMEN, onward through the years, EQUAL RIGHTS, EQUAL VOTE, EQUAL ALL. And Helen wonders now if it has been for nothing. Were all her campaigns born, not of compassion, but of her own loneliness? After all this time, she has not a single friend with which to rail about the chauvinism of men, the crude rules of sex, the imbalance of wealth, birth control, child care, corruption, education, sexual orientation. And now Helen is searching for inspiration, what to do next. Where does she take her new campaigns and will the media still care enough to cover her with reportage? Is there indeed a vast underground of thought that she has somehow missed all these years, fighting the real fight, and how does she fit in?

And all the while Helen, in her reverie, is unaware of the boisterous crowd around her, hanging from the balconies, shouting boos and huzzahs, shouting, "Bring out the Bitch." Helen does not see, in front of her face, the big guy who has just taken the stage, Sow Madden, a bouncer under the employ of the Orpheus who, for five bucks, fights Bitch Bantam when the audience lacks a fighting volunteer. Helen is thinking about a word she has seen only in dictionaries, a word that contains only negative connotations. Lesbian. Helen does not know, other than naive speculations, what it is lesbians do, in public, in the bedroom. Three times, in her cotillion youth, she had been kissed by handsome young boys, boys with brains and brawn and ambition, boys on the make. One time she had even tried kissing back, but at no time did she enjoy it. Now she is an old maid by anyone's reckoning. Her maiden-head is intact. Her parents were devoid of affection and she never had close girlfriends, never kissed a girl in play. Helen is unrubbed wood, hard and alone in her consternation. Her true self, as it turns out, is that of an outlaw who is afraid of breaking the law. And what of... And what if...?

A hot shock knocks Helen from her floating jeremiad.

Bitch Bantam stands center stage. She wears fringed piebald buckskin that clings to her muscles like pastry wrap. Her hair is cut short, her cheekbones frame the exotic mask of her face, her teeth are straight bright-white and new. She looks out at no one. The crowd of men love and hate her with hisses and hoorays. She holds her hands on her hips like Superman watching over Metropolis.

Zeph Riley is into a spiel and Sow Madden is flexing his muscles, hamming it up and making scary faces. Bitch is happiest when no one volunteers; she worries what she might do, again, to the next dirty fighter. She prefers fighting this big friendly palooka, Sow Madden. Bitch and Sow have a routine: they roll through telegraphed punches; they choreograph flips and flops, Sow bites fake-blood capsules hidden in his cheeks and Bitch takes him by the ankles and spins him in circles until the both fall to the floor; and, in the end, Bitch always wins.

Zeph referees and Repeat Riley ding ding dings a bell. Bitch and Sow dance and pretend to size one another. Sow throws a haymaker right, rolls it off Bitch's chin. Bitch pirouettes in place as though the blow has spun her round to starting point, and, in that spin, that blur of audience participation, she sees, she sees... Bitch falls into Helen Beck's eyes. Helen smiles and Bitch smiles back so hard she nearly loses her upper teeth. Sow telegraphs a left, but Bitch does not get the message. His fist crunches into her jaw and moves her not a bit. The crowd cheers, Sow rubs his knuckles, Pete blows boogie, Mabel plays woogie, Repeat keeps a beat, Zeph lays down rap, Adelina claps her hands and roots for the woman, Helen Beck and Bitch Bantam fall in love.

33 Kerosene Row

Slab Pettibone puts pen to paper.

And there before me a doughy face took shape and gave me an ugly sneer. Twas the evil warlord Commander Shenanigan. First thing I noticed was the nose, it was the longest, most pointed prow I'd ever seen on a human face, and, to tell you the truth, I wasn't too sure the face was human. His eyes was black as bullet holes and

set close together. He had tombstone teeth stained red with blood.
He wore a hat made of bleached bones.

Slab sets down his pen. He needs to go to the bathroom. Elegiac depression has brought along constipation, funk = irregularity. Slab has not had a notable bowel movement since August –four, three months ago. His head aches, his neck is tight, his gut is bloated like a malnourished child. In troubled sleep he dreams of taking a crap and wakes up red-faced from the exertion. Along with clogged bowels and having his mind clamped in everlasting lament, Slab looks like crap. His proud handlebar moustache slumps like dead dandelions. His eyes are dark and sombrous. His forehead a thumbprint-whorl like that of a crying kid. He wears a union suit on top of another union suit, cut and sewn mid-thigh, his stumps tucked into feed-bags.

Slab climbs down from the writing table and wraps himself in a thick Indian blanket. He stops, on his way to the back door, and looks at the two wooden legs standing against wall in the corner. Yesterday, he went with Bitch Bantam to a prosthetics shop when he had been fitted for two legs standing nearly as tall as he. State of the art, light hard wood, polished and varnished, hinged at the knees and ankles, carved toes. Slab has yet to put them on, as though to wear them, to balance and ambulate forward like Frankenstein's monster, is more defeat than victory. Walking without FuzzyWuzzy is admission to his loss.

Slab pads his way out the back door to the outhouse. He stops, hip deep in the crunchy snow, to look at the moon and the stars. A romantic melancholy unfolds within, leaving him defenseless to the silver nightscape, the hoot of an owl, a train whistle. In the thunder-box he climbs up to the hole, lowers his drawers and pushes and pushes without reward and remains stuffed to the gills with solidified shit. Slab listens to the still of the night and hears only the moan of his bowels, the keen of his loss, then something else, outside, footprints squeaking as they fall through the crust of snow. He freezes like a forest creature at the snap of an antagonistic twig.

Last night Eddie Plague's two girl goons tailed Bitch Bantam home from the Orpheus Theater then reported back to Eddie with the address. However, last night Bitch had first gone to Slab's house before going home. Now, Eddie, with his two girl goons, his razor, two guns for him and one each for the girls, is sneaking into the wrong house, with murder on his mind.

Eddie Plague shares with Bitch Bantam a background of violence. The threat of physical harm and death raises not a glimmer of anxiety; fright was long ago scared away. But Eddie is careful, even apprehensive, for he knows Bitch Bantam's potential, just as he knows his own. The girl goons have been instructed to shoot and shoot again the first moving shadow they see. They have been offered incentives of twenty-five dollars each, even though Eddie hopes it is he who pulls the trigger. Eddie can envision shooting Bitch's legs out from under her and then slowly, like foreplay, opening her throat with his razor.

The backdoor is unlatched. There is a light flickering in the kitchen. Eddie whispers to Girl A, "Go around to the front, try the door, quietly." He gives her time to get to the front then says to Girl B, "Keep your gun at ready. Open the door. Stay in front of me." Eddie has a gun in each hand; he holds his straight razor in his teeth. Girl B slowly pulls open the door which gives a small hinged squeak, like a stomped rat, putting this murderous duo on sixty second pause. They proceed

319

through the door into the empty kitchen. Eddie motions Girl B to stay, at arms. He tiptoes away and evaporates into the dark of the next room.

Girl A has entered the living room from the unlocked front door. She sees Eddie across the room and nearly shoots him. Eddie motions her to a dark side room while he creaks softly up the stairs to the bedrooms. In the kitchen, Girl B, on edge, hears, behind her, the same hinge squeak. She pivots without thinking and fires her pistol three times, into nothing, a foot above Slab Pettibone's head. She sees a small figure, low to the ground, a gnome, a haint. It rushes her and she yelps. Slab head-butts Girl B in the breadbasket. She goes down. Two more shots are fired, one of which tears the fabric on Slab's union-suit at the shoulder. The air is full of sharp smoke. Girl A stands at the kitchen entranceway, both hands on her pistol, taking quick and clumsy aim at the dwarf. Slab dives to his stomach behind the felled Girl B, just as a poorly piloted bullet from Girl A's gun drills through Girl B's skull. Slab quickly wrests Girl B's pistol from her frozen hand, and, like a true sharp-shooting pacifist cowpoke, shoots not Girl A but shoots the gun from her hand. He says, "Just you stay right there, buster, doan be makin no moves to go nowhere." Slab hears a creak above him, knows someone else is here, maybe the leader of these hirelings. He looks at the body of the big girl prone at his stubs, sees for the first time she is not a he. He looks at Girl A and sees that neither is she. "I doan know why you're here or what you mean to do, but you ain't gonna be doin it. You take your friend here and get goin and don't come back. How many upstairs?"

Girl A says, "One, a goddamn mean one."

"Okay, now go on, get."

Girl A carries her dead friend, Girl B, and leaves by the back door.

Slab yells up the stairway, "I don't know who you are or what you're a fixin to do, but you done made a mistake comin here."

From the upstairs comes Eddie Plague's voice, "I don't know who you are either, but I believe I'm in the wrong house, so if you'll accept my apology, I'll come on out and be on my way."

"Just whose house did you think you was in? Who is it you come lookin for with loaded guns?"

"I don't think that's any your concern, sir. You gonna let me leave or not?"

"It's my house you come into, so I guess it's my concern whose house you meant to come into."

"I think you must not understand. I'm leaving here as I came and if it requires that I kill you on the way out then so be it."

"I'll tell you what, Mister Killer. Afore you start predictin my future maybe I should introduce myself. Slab Pettibone is the name, an I can out-shoot, out-rope, out-wrassle the likes of whoever you may be, any day o the week."

"Pettibone, hey, that is good news for me. I guess I'm not in the wrong house after all. You are on my list, you little half-man cocksucker."

"You ain't makin it no easier on yourself using that kind o language in my house."

And now talk has come to a halt. Slab blows out the tabletop lamp, moves forward, cautiously, into the next room, in the shadows of moon bright windows. Eddie, quietly fueled with bloodlust, noiselessly slithers down the stairs. Slab is fueled with survival and curiosity, who is this invader and why does he want blood? He edges toward the stairway, Girl B's gun tight in his hand. He smells the tense air like a woodsman tracking game. He sees through the dark with intuition and he watches a peephole of light where he anticipates a gun hand. He aims and waits and then fires, bang, when the hand creeps into the target.

The gun in Eddie Plague's hand takes flight, breaking two of his fingers in the process. Eddie falls, purposely, sideways to the bottom of the stairs while firing three shots from the gun in his right at Slab's gunpowder flash. Slab is no longer there. Slab is at the front door, which he pulls open, shielding him while spilling snow-bright light on Eddie, at the foot of the stairs. Slab shoots for the other gun in Eddie's hand, except his gun jams and doesn't fire and Eddie throws three lead projectiles into the door, tossing splinters and sawdust into Slab's eyes. Eddie tosses away his now-empty gun and takes his pearl-handled razor from his teeth. He dives at Slab. Slab swings the door, catching Eddie just above the eye with the edge. Eddie yells and rolls and slashes the inch of air between the razor and Slab Pettibone's neck. Slab jumps at the hand, grabs Eddie's wrist twisting and struggling. Slab's upper body is strong, but he doesn't carry the weight of a man with legs. Eddie hits him in the temple, one two three four. Slab is forty-six. Eddie is twenty. Slab weakens. Eddie presses his weight, continues hitting. Slab holds to Eddie's wrist but Eddie keeps control of the razor which he flicks in an arc and carves out three rounds of Slab's knuckle skin. Slab loses his grip and, in a madly frustrating second, Eddie is on top, knees speared into Slab's biceps, holding him down and defenseless. Eddie's hands are free, and, in a single deft stroke, he shaves off the left half of Slab's moustache. He says, "You're almost a handsome old man, Pettibone. When you're dead I might just use your rugged face for a cunny. How does that sound to you, me fucking your face while you're still warm?"

Slab can see clearly the features of Eddie Plague's face, the creepy, duckbill nose. He smells peppermints and patchouli. He knows this is Eddie Plague, the white slaver, the man who lost his former nose to Bitch Bantam's former teeth. Slab hardly hears Eddie's foul-mouth remarks for Eddie's words are as abstract as death. What was it, five minutes ago, ten minutes? Slab hardly cared for his life, no longer saw the value. Five minutes, maybe ten and now Slab sees the true value of his life, his muscles cannot save him, but his mind races for escape.

"How does it feel, you old cocksucker, to know that your worthless existence is over and done?" Eddie holds his razor across Slab's Adam's apple.

Slab says in a whisper, *"You will watch your language in my house, you foul-mouthed blackguard."*

"What, fuckface, what'd you say?" Eddie leans in closer, presses the razor until a long thread of blood coats the honed edge.

"I said," he whispers, "you will watch your language in my house, you foul-mouthed blackguard."

Eddie wants to hear the pleas of the dying man. He leans closer yet. His duckbill blows a hot jet into Slab's eyes.

"I said, you will watch your lang-" Slab raises his head two inches, which pushes the razor another eighth-inch into his neck, and, in a flash, he grips Eddies freshly healed platypus snout in his teeth and rips it from Eddie's face.

A lightning bolt hits Eddie between the eyes. He wails, falls backward away from the pain. Slab is up on his stubs. He wrests the razor from Eddie's hand and throws it across the room.

Eddie is blinded, defeated with pain. Slab backs away from the wounded man; he wishes him no more harm, wishes no man more harm than life has already bestowed. Eddie struggles to his feet, through the open door, and away from KeroseneRow into the night.

Slab Pettibone closes the door, lights a lantern and carries it to the kitchen where he cleanses the cut at his neck, the missing skin on his knuckles, and applies bandages. He stands on his stubs and studies the prosthetic legs. He climbs a chair and struggles for five minutes, strapping, buckling, attaching the wooden legs to his thighs. He pushes himself up, six feet tall, and wobbles like a newborn colt. He throws forward first the right leg then the left, stamping the linoleum floor with castanet feet. He teeters out the back door into the snow like a rubber-limbed drunk. Mannequin footprints following a step behind. In the privy, he sits and unlocks the knee hinges then lowers his drawers. Slab pushes with his stomach, peristalsis, and for, the first time in five months, he evacuates his bowels.

Orpheus Theater

Backstage, after the show, Adelina introduced Helen to Zeph and Mabel who, in turn, introduced Helen to Bitch, who somehow managed to work up the gumption to invite Helen back to her dressing room, which is where they are now. Two strangers in addlepated love, each aching for the approval of the other. Both in a breathless race to share the innermost corners of their never-before-spoken selves. Their lives, like a Benzedrine high, rolls from their tongues in nervous narration.

Bitch says, "So far I haven't done anything except what men made me do. Sometimes I hate men. Except funny thing is, it was a man that helped me to be all on my own. It was Mister Slab Pettibone that got me free. Do you know who that is, Slab Pettibone? He's kinda famous and he writes books and everything. And he's all sad now and I wish I could make him feel better but he lost his bear named FuzzyWuzzy and FuzzyWuzzy was almost like a real person except nicer. And there was this woman named Fritter that Slab was in love with and she died and that made me sad too cause Fritter was my first real woman friend, sort of. I had a friend named Lulu when I was just a girl except she was really just made up in my head, but when I think and remember, it seems like she was real and all the bad stuff, which was most everthing, was the stuff that wasn't really real. Then that time when I saw you at Domino's it was almost like you was Lulu except I was a scared to even look at you an I'm still kinda that way except I like talkin to you anyway. A whole lot."

Helen is reminiscing her own childhood imagination, where her girlfriend's name was Linda and she was the strongest woman in the world and Linda would pick Helen up and hold her in her arms and kiss her on the lips. Helen wishes she could share these memories with Bitch but she cannot, not yet. For she is still testing the waters and afraid of the deep end. She says, "When I first saw you I knew you'd survived your life with nothing, yet would not hate me for my diamonds and pearls. I pray this is true. I have misread too many eyes in my past and it frightens me. Once, in my college years on a slumming lark, I saw a young girl, near my own age, eighteen at the time. She was pretty, in fact beautiful, yet she was dirty and dressed in tatters. She looked at me with brash familiarity, and she spoke with broken English and she spoke like the proverbial sailor cursing me with venom and profanity. It was then I first understood why someone who does not know me can detest me. And from that moment I've lived my life in the service of those who do not want my help. And sometimes I become irate with frustration. I want to shake and rattle the teeth of those who cannot see that it is to their own benefit that I slave. Please forgive me if I seem too wound up, I'm that way by nature."

Bitch is working to decipher Helen's verbal whoosh but is momentarily stuck on five of Helen's words, shake and rattle the teeth. Can Helen see that Bitch's teeth are not real? Do her teeth rattle? Bitch wants Helen to understand that she does not want anyone feeling sorry for her, that she is not the tattered girl of Helen's memory. She says, "My friend Slab Pettibone has been callin me Missy and I'd like it if you could call me Missy too. I'm not gonna be doin this show biz stuff forever so then I won't be Bitch anymore, I'll be Missy. Right now I'm makin more money than most people do. An Mabel Scott, the girl that plays the piano here at the Orpheus, has been teaching me to read and stuff. That's kinda why I can talk to you now and couldn't before cause I dint think I was smart enough. One time Slab told me that dumb and ignorant aren't the same thing and he thinks I'm real smart. And now I'm startin to think so too."

Helen listens intently to Bitch yet she misses words, sometimes sentences, as she is fraught with unchecked emotions, improper physical urges that beg to be tapped. And, God in heaven, how can Helen be thinking like this? A woman friend is that which is thoughtful and tender yet not queer, not prurient or amatory. How is it Helen is so tempted to sin? How can she say aloud the feelings that contradict her morals? She says, "I've never married and have thus been subjected to speculation and gossip regarding my morals. And I regret that morsels of the speculations are true, yet I should, by rights and even pride, stand naked and declare to all what I am. I want to believe I'm more moral and empathic than the accusers. I don't know, maybe I'm talking out of turn, maybe I'm making assumptions about you that are incorrect. Please excuse me if I've offended you. I just want to know you. I want us to be friends."

Bitch is confused by Helen's rhetorical soft-shoe. But her confusion is overshadowed by this short strand of Helen's declaration: I should, by rights and even pride, stand naked, the key word here being NAKED. Bitch would like to see that, Helen standing naked. Bitch would like to get naked with Helen. It turns her jumpy just thinking about it. She says, "I want us to be friends too, really really good friends." Two women, strangers, grasping at love. Two lonely women searching for their fantasy mates, desperate to make them real. Missy Bantam. Helen Beck. Lulu. Linda.

Chapter Thirteen

NetherWorld

In bright sunlight, Dooley Paradise bends on all fours to drink from a sparkling mountain stream. As he nears his rippled reflection, happy Crayola salmon swim up out of the water and slap his cheeks with tail fins gently, whap whap whap, like the licking kisses of a bear.

Dooley opens his right eye to absolute darkness. He tries and tries to make his head work though nothing clicks. His left eye hurts worse than a bad tooth and he doesn't know if it is open or shut, or maybe gone entirely. He has rat bites all over. He feels warm steamy jets of breath from, from what, on his face?

FuzzyWuzzy is a bear who has lost much of his hair. He has no concept of when or how he came to be here. He remembers Slab Pettibone, and he remembers light, though now he only knows dark. He has an abstract memory of bursting into flames. FuzzyWuzzy's buttermilk fur was burnt away in the explosion of fire at the Orpheus. Fortunately, the fire burned quickly and FuzzyWuzzy survived with now-healed burn blisters across his front. New hair is already sprouting. He is guided through the tunnels by his nose which has led him to Dooley Paradise, his doppelgänger of woe and confusion. FuzzyWuzzy needs a friend and he was happy to kick a bunch of big rat's asses to help the boy out. He licks Dooley's face with tenderness.

Dooley thinks maybe FuzzyWuzzy is a dog, a damn big dog. He puts his right hand up, touches a long snout. Dooley says, "Hi, are you real? Are you tame? Thanks for chasing away the rats, you saved my life."

FuzzyWuzzy answers, Uuhhhh Uuhhhh, guttural, mournful.

"Don't get excited. I'm gonna sit up. You don't sound much like a dog."

Dooley sits with his back to the wall, he is woozy. FuzzyWuzzy picks up an offering with his lips and bumps it into Dooley's chest.

"What's this? Smells clean like dirt if that makes any sense. Is it a mushroom, is that what it is? No matter, I'm eatin it, whatever it is. Taste pretty good. I'm sure glad you're here. I hurt all over and I need to get some food to my head. I don't know what I'm eating but it's about the best thing I ever had. Is it okay if I feel around a little bit, figure out what it is I'm talkin to? Nice boy, good boy, this is one of your legs and this is your foot and Jesus, these are pretty big claws. I'm pretty sure you're a bear and not dog after all. I've never been friends with a bear before." Dooley tries to rise, slowly with his hands up above to determine head room. "I'm gonna try to stand up, okay? That's a good boy, I need to lean on you, is that okay? You like your neck scratched? Yeah, that feels good, doesn't it? You know what's weird is I don't even know if you're real. You know what else is weird is I had pretty much given up on going on, kind a no longer saw a reason. But now that you're here maybe we can get out of this place. What do you think, does that sound like a plan to you? Is it okay if I climb up on your back? I don't think I can walk right now. You wouldn't have another one of those mushrooms, would you?"

Well no, FuzzyWuzzy doesn't have any fungi at the moment but his nose knows how to find more and he is happy to carry Dooley on his back.

Dooley Paradise, a tortured lad who is rat-bit and bloody, a young lad deprived of light and shadow, food and conversation, does not find it odd that he has just become friends with a bear that he cannot see. The only odd sensation trilling his mind at the moment is that, he begins to realize, he is alive, indeed cognizant of his invisible surroundings. His body remembers the cold that rubs up against him and nips at his skin. He says, "My name is Dooley, pleased to meet you Mister Bear." FuzzyWuzzy shakes his booty in lieu of a hearty hand shake. He huffs the bear version of, "How-doo-dee-doo."

TumbleHouse

Eddie Plague is in a rage. He paces the third-floor, furiously kicking at anything in his path. The hole in the center of his face whistles like a teapot and bubbles like stew. He burns with antagonism and shudders with unsated revenge. At the phonograph, he sets the needle and cranks the crank. The speaker blows barrelhouse piano and harkens memories of great rowdy houses—Kansas City, San Francisco, Chicago. Eddie was the prettiest boy ever to inhabit these haunts. Fancy men and women were brought to tears of wanton lust by the suggestion of a smile, a wink, from Eddie Plague. And all the sissies and most of the women feared Eddie with the same intensity as their infatuated love. Eddie had come to BigCity to wallow in the pleasures afforded men of intelligence and cunning, men of great beauty. It would have been so easy, if only...if only.

There is a bookshelf of fiction in this room that once belonged to Dooley Paradise. Eddie recently perused *The Time Machine* by H.G. Wells. It will not leave him alone. Eddie needs a time machine to get back to the Backdoor Byway, to kill Bitch Bantam before she forever alters his face, to kill Slab Pettibone and his bear, to kill his imbecile partners Skunk Brewster and Charlie Debunk. Eddie needs to kill someone, anyone, and he needs it like a junkie needs a fix. He sweeps the phonograph crashing to the floor, walks to the bookshelf and tips it over, spilling and scattering a million words.

Eddie takes three calming breaths which do not calm him. He walks to the west wall where he has an eleven-year-old boy bound at the wrists and ankles, prone on the bed. Eddie

332

tells the boy, "I am going to kill you soon. I just can't decide whether I should rape you first or kill you first. Do you have a preference?" The boy cries silently and says nothing.

A loud rude knock at the door interrupts and enrages Eddie. He yells, "I am not to be bothered, away with you."

"It's me, Eddie, Girl. Something important. I gotta talk to you, now!"

"You will go away and leave me alone or you will not see tomorrow."

"I mean it, Eddie, this caint wait. You gotta open up. I gotta talk to you."

"I hear another word from you and it will be your last. Now, away with you."

"I caint go away, Eddie, not till I talk to…"

"Goddamn fucking cunt!" Eddie grabs his straight razor, storms across the room, unlocks and flings open the door.

Shag Draper has a gun in his hand. He shoots Eddie Plague in the neck. Eddie staggers backward. Shag shoots him in the gut. Eddie doubles and falls to the floor. Girl walks into the room trailing Shag's three goons. She watches impassively. Shag shoots Eddie in the chest, through the heart. He says to Girl, "This is yur mess now. I shall be leavin it for you to clean up. TumbleHouse is yurs to run. I shall be by as I feel like it. Yur to pay me the profits and I shall be payin you from the pot. And I shall be takin my favors in this room as I feel like it."

"I love you, Shag."

"Yeah, sure you do. Just make sure you never cross me."

Girl kisses Shag. Shag says goodnight and makes his exit. Girl takes a bottle of Doctor FixUp from her handbag and drinks of it. She takes Eddie's razor from his death grip then uses it to free the captive boy. She says to him, "Are you okay?" The boy is not okay but he is still alive so he nods yes. "Go on, get out of here." The boy goes out quickly. Girl closes and locks the door then goes to dead Eddie and kneels. She smells traces of patchouli oil through the gunsmoke. She uses his razor and slowly carves, into his once beautiful face, a chin to cheekbone scar to match her own.

The HuggerMugger

On the wall next to the printing press, Adelina Brown has tacked a photograph she took at the Wrinkle Ball. Warner Quackenbush departs his ostentatious coach holding hands with a seven-year-old girl who appears to be rabid. The girl's face is stuck somewhere in Adelina's brain, like an actor you can not quite name. She struggles to unravel the riddle—a connection or place.

Adelina cranks the letterpress and pulls front-page copies of tomorrow's HuggerMugger. ORPHANAGE REPLACED WITH PROSTITUTION - BAD DUCK RULES ROOST. The press clanks each impression with a metal slap that pains Adelina between her sleep-deprived eyes. Her fingers are black with ink. An hour from now, when her edition is run, she will scrub them pink with pumice soap then spend two hours staining them nicotine yellow in film developer. She will strain her eyes for three hours editing Guttersnipes. In the windowless back room, she will drain the ambient light and, in a swatch of illumination, project her sad story to the wall. She will absorb the moving images and recognize her own brilliance, then find bitter fault in every frame. She will marvel at her direction as the camera sweeps the eye to the action, pans in and out, composing and exposing like a virtuoso artist. She will despair over soft-focus, uneven development, jerky cuts, contrasty shadows, bad lighting. She will burn her fingers on the carbide-burning projector lamp.

Six hours from now, Adelina will tramp home and attempt to sleep, though sleep will not come. Instead whirlwinds of image and thought will spin and shake her into hyper-wakefulness.

The printing press is a foot taller than Adelina. Inked-type set right-to-left stamps left-to-right words, sentences, paragraphs, the proletariat news and opinion. Adelina needs to urinate. And to do this simple act of necessity, she must first shut down the press in the middle of a run, wash her hands, trudge out back to the sub-zero privy, sit on the cold hole, pee, clean, then walk back inside through the cold, re-ink and start up the press. Adelina holds it in and adopts the discomfort to commingle with her other discomforts. The letterpress chomps its plates together like fry pans.

Saddle Sore Productions

In the darkroom, Daddy Smithy can find his bottle of Doctor

FixUp with his eyes closed. He pulls the cork which sighs a sweet salute. He fills his cheeks, tilts back his head and gargles a tune:"

> "After the ball was over
> Nellie took out her glass eye
> Put her false teeth in water
> Corked up her bottle of dye."

He swallows, says, "Yum," and laughs out loud, then soft-shoes to the light switch to flip it on. He pushes up his sleeve and reaches into a pickle barrel filled with a solution of sinus-biting sodium thiosulfate, pulls up a t-rod holding six reels wound with thirty feet of film, transfers them to another barrel, this one over a drain, inserts a rubber hose and turns the tap high. After thirty seconds his patience runs thin so he reaches back in and takes out the top reel, unwinds a couple of feet, holds it up and checks the exposure and development, which is right on target. Daddy Smithy is ever aware of all the times he screwed up exposure, development, focus, loading, lighting, composition, life. Now, tonight, today, yesterday, last month and next year Daddy is on a roll. The terminal fuckup is some other guy, everything to this point was practice and practice makes perfect. The history of Daddy's future will be writ with fortune and fame which leads to a toast which raises the uncorked bottle of Doctor FixUp. Three cheers to the future past. Glug glug yum.

Filming of *The Rise & the Fall* is three-quarters finished, a few more studio scenes and some location shooting for establishing shots, street traffic, buildings. Then editing for a month or so. Then a premiere worthy of Phineas T. Barnum.

And then? And then money. And then more and better cameras, more and better actors, more and better crews, darkroom technicians, personal assistants, a studio in southern California. More and better movies, epics, comedies, action-adventure, sci-fi, horse operas, weepers, swashbucklers, G, R, NC17, XXX.

The Rise & the Fall looks great, the story works, the slapstick and melodrama work, the actors hit their marks and take direction, and Wilbur Szedvilas is a comic genius. Daddy has signed Wilbur to an exclusive contract and plans to make him a star. As for Wilbur Szedvilas's straight man, Wilbur Good, this will be his last photoplay with Daddy Smithy. Wilbur Good is unruly and scary and cannot act.

Because of Wilbur Szedvilas's talents, Daddy has rewritten his script almost daily to accommodate the actor's brilliant improvisations. *The Rise & Fall* has evolved into a soft-core sex opera with lots of T & A, and comedy. And while Daddy knows that *The Rise & Fall* is now a better movie he still has concerns that gurgles within. This is no longer the film his patron, Warner Quackenbush, expects. And tomorrow, well, technically today, as midnight has come and gone, Warner Quackenbush will be paying a visit to Saddle Sore productions. Hopefully, Warner Quackenbush will recognize the commercial possibilities of Daddy's improved product. And while this is what Daddy prefers to believe and expect, he is still jangled by the prospect of Warner's visit.

Daddy's communications with his patron have largely been via carrier pigeon Shag Draper, who has not a clue of the process or possibilities of moving pictures. Daddy is hoping to remove this middle-man after tomorrow, today, and deal in the future with Mister Quackenbush personally. And so, it is not simply the visit that has Daddy so on edge—it's a family thing.

Daddy regrets every day of his past and suffers guilt over his tenure as the world's worst dad. He has, as he likes to remind himself, done right with the youngest of the girls, Snooks. Snooks was always a notch removed from reality. She was scary from day one. As soon as she grew teeth she bit Daddy and anyone else who got too close. She was an unlikeable child and when Daddy cut his first deal with Warner Quackenbush, Snooks was part of the transaction. She would be a house servant in the Quackenbush estate, which would be a far better life than Daddy had provided. Shortly thereafter, Warner Quackenbush adopted Snooks Smithy as his own and now he's under specific instructions to meet and treat the child as a stranger. It all seems kind of weird to Daddy.

Back in June, Daddy had long days of exploding stress. His eyeballs shook to such a degree that all things seen were banged like a tuning fork. This was his last big screw-up, when he set the bear on fire and two people died. Girl was there with a boy Daddy now believes was there to kill him. Daddy doesn't blame Girl for hating her old man, if he were Girl he would hate him too. The boy had been killed by Wilbur Good, now Daddy's second-banana actor, who also attempted to whack Girl, but was foiled by Daddy himself. Wilbur has never made mention of the incident and Daddy has not the nerve to bring it up. Now all this stuff and the fact that Daddy is long overdue a screw-up, have put him on sharp edge. It just seems like all of these connections are adding up to something bad. Warner Quackenbush, Girl, Snooks, Shag Draper, Wilbur Good—they seem a mix that could prove explosive and it scares Daddy.

So Daddy does what he does, which is pick up his bottle

of Doctor FixUp and oil his motor. And just like that he says, "Ahhhhhhhhhhhh," laughs out loud and begins taking reels of film from the bath to hang up and dry. He looks at wet film frames and sees brilliance and it is so exciting he takes another drink. He sees vast seas of filled theater seats, every man, woman and child held rapt with glee, drama, adventure, titillation, awe. He sees flashbulb premieres, sparkling glamour, champagne, multiplying theaters like push-pins on a map crossing land, oceans, Academy Awards, multiplexes, video, DVD, pay-per-view. Daddy Smithy looks to the future and hopes he doesn't screw it all up.

NetherWorld

Dark coiled miles of cavernous intestine. Dooley Paradise sits leaning forward on FuzzyWuzzy's crew-cut back. FuzzyWuzzy pads ever forward, gingerly. He likes having a traveling companion. Both nature and Slab Pettibone have taught him to be leery of humankind, but he trusts Dooley and likes hearing the boy's voice. Dooley says, "I was thinking that this, me being here with you, is like the books I read by this guy named Slab Pettibone and he has these funny kind of fantasy adventures with his pet bear named FuzzyWuzzy and walking through the dark like this is sort of like something they would be doing. Maybe I should call you FuzzyWuzzy." The irony escapes FuzzyWuzzy but he nods his head and huffs little affirmations.

Chapter Fourteen

TumbleHouse

A foundling girl of fourteen lives on the streets with a small family of friends. At the thriving sexual swap-meet, on the borders of ScourgeTown, she hawks her young soul for the price of a dill pickle and a shot of spiderbite. She was once upon a time at TumbleHouse but now prefers bedding beneath a plank sidewalk to the terror inspired by Eddie Plague. Through a network of friends this girl is privy to marketplace gossip and certainty. This morning after learning Eddie Plague is dead and a girl named Girl has taken the helm, she walked to the HuggerMugger offices, in the Left Bank, where she passed this information to Adelina Brown. The girl and her family of street-arabs have become the center of focus for Adelina's film documentary, Guttersnipes. For the girl's trouble, Adelina gave her twenty-five cents.

Now, an hour later, Adelina enters through the TumbleHouse door. The first floor is quiet. Next to the door, an adult goon sits sleeping in a chair. This is the new Mook bouncer and it's obvious he is not up to the job. She walks quietly past him into the vast room. There are young girls and boys in their underclothes, like catalogue pages. Many of these kids recognize Adelina and are momentarily warmed with nostalgia, but as quickly shamed by their circumstances. They turn away from Adelina and hide their eyes. Adelina remembers every name. She goes to a girl her age, a girl with a puffy face, a good heart and low IQ. Adelina says, "Hi, Nelly. I've missed you. You were a good friend and you still are. Are you okay?"

"Uh huh, I guess so. Are you gonna live here agin?"

"I don't know, Nelly, that would be nice if I did and we could read stories again like we used to do."

"Uh huh, I remember."

"I have some business here, Nelly. Do you know where I'd find the girl named Girl?"

"I hate Girl but doan tell er I said so."

"It can be our secret, Nelly. Is she here now?"

"Up in Boss Dooley's room."

Adelina gives Nelly a hug then proceeds up the stairs to the third floor.

At the top landing Adelina stands looking at the door, picturing Dooley Paradise pulling it open from the other side, smiling, happy. She raps her knuckles three times on the frame.

Thirty seconds without a response and she raps her knuckles firm and loud on the door. Ten seconds later the door opens and Adelina looks at Girl and Girl looks at Adelina.

Adelina says, "I figured it was you but I was of hoping it wasn't."

"Please come in, Adelina. It's nice to see you."

Inside, Eddie Plague's remains have been removed, lain to rest in the sulphurous DreckRiver. To Adelina, Dooley's once tidy roost looks debased and befouled. Eddie Plague was an inapt housekeeper and Girl is worse. A fusty layer of grime is slicked over furniture like oily hair tonic. The room is steeped in decay. Five steps in and Adelina has lost her temper. To Girl she says, "What the fuck do you think you're doing here? I want you out of this room and this house and I want you out right this fucking instant!"

"If you're lookin for a fight, Adelina, I could twist you in half in about two seconds. But I like you, and I don't wanna fight with you. Come and sit and talk like friends. Maybe we can help each other."

Situated at the table, Adelina says, "Okay, Girl, how have you been? I see that scar on your face, and I am very sorry. You're still very pretty."

"Why are you here, Adelina? It's not like we're best friends, you're not here to hug me."

"I hope I don't have any reason to not like you. I hope you don't give me one. I'm here to find out what has become of TumbleHouse and what I can do to salvage it."

"TumbleHouse is just what you see, a whore house, and I'm the madam. We house thirty-seven pokes and they all make money. They're better off here than other places."

"Just about everybody is better off someplace else. That doesn't mean shit. You're a squatter here. By rights, I could insist you leave."

"Do you have a piece of paper somewhere that says that, because I know someone who does."

"Who?"

"Shag Draper."

"Shag Draper is vile and contemptible; someone should just kill the asshole."

Girl says, "If someone really could kill Shag, I'd leave here and be gone forever."

"If you're looking to kill Draper, or anybody else, then you shouldn't be looking at me. I think I can use the press and my new connections to get rid of Shag Draper. You'd be welcome to stay, but, except for vices, TumbleHouse goes back to the way it was before."

"But I'm here now, Adelina, and I like it here. I'm the boss here and that's not something I ever had before. The kids are getting fed and if they have to earn it selling pokes, so what? It's nothing I haven't done."

"So because you've lost your soul innocent kids should give theirs up as well?"

"It's not my place to worry about others, Adelina, and I'm here until Shag Draper is dead."

"I guess you probably still cannot read but you can look at pictures." Adelina takes a copy of the HuggerMugger from her coat pocket and tosses it face-up onto the table. "Take a look at this." She walks to the door and Girl says, "Goodbye, Adelina. I'm sorry we can't be friends. I would have liked that."

Adelina says, "Go fuck yourself sideways, Girl."

Girl picks up the HuggerMugger scans the headline, struggles through the big words.

WRINKLE BASH WELCOMES CAPITALIST SICKO

Next she sees the quarter-page photograph:

A doorman;

A bizarre little man, or boy, or biblical demon;

A little girl that looks much like Girl herself;

Snooks.

Girl breaks a sweat. Her guts boil. She goes for her bottle of Doctor FixUp.

Saddle Sore Productions

Wilbur Good wants to hurt someone, anyone. As a boolydog, Wilbur got to hurt people all the time, got paid for it. That was a good life. The life of an actor is dumb stupid, he hardly ever gets to hurt anybody and his buddy, Wilbur Szedvilas, has changed to such a degree that their friendship now limps along like a shot dog.

Wilbur Good is brooding like a method actor as Daddy Smithy rolls film and shouts direction. Wilbur is stripped down to his skivvies and wearing his police helmet, his police belt, on which hangs his nightstick, his handcuffs and his gun. Underneath a pillow of fat, he is dense with sinew and muscle. Daddy yells out, "Lick your lips, Wilbur, show us some lust." Wilbur licks his lips, though his lust looks more like anger.

Wilbur is sitting on the edge of an unmade bed while

actress co-star Sarah Heart does an oyster dance. Sarah wears demitasse-sized pasties up top and frilly bloomers below deck. She is stocky and solid. She has boulder hips, perky tits, and a bouncy caboose with dimple pits. She holds oyster-shell castanets while she shimmies the pearlescent globs into figure-eights around her boobs. She mugs salacious faces. Daddy Smithy yells, "That's great, Sarah, now stop suddenly and flip the oysters like we rehearsed and then put your hand to your ear. You hear someone coming up the steps."

Sarah finagles the oysters atop her mams and high-dives them, kersplat, onto Wilbur Good's face. Wilbur scowls, peels the snotty mollusks from his sour puss and slurps them down without ceremony. Sarah puts her hand to her ear, makes the international sign for I hear someone coming.

The setting, a three-walled room with a bed, a window to the phony outdoors, a door to a phony hallway, and a stairwell to nowhere. Off set, wardrobe and make-up whiz, Billie Époque does touch-up on Wilbur Szedvilas' nose. Annabelle Bilyeu sits close by. Wilbur Szedvilas leans to Annabelle and whispers, "Wilbur him not liking dancing fishshell guts tasty bad."

Annabelle wonders if there is anything Wilbur Good does not find tasty bad. She wonders how these two opposite-pole Wilburs ever came to be partnered. She glances over at Billie Époque who comments on Wilbur Good's thespian skills by the pinching of nostrils and rolling of eyes.

Daddy Smithy cranks film. "Okay now, Wilbur, walk to the door and peek out, yeah that's good, now close the door and say to Sarah, It's *your husband*. No, no, open your mouth more when you talk, look concerned." Now Daddy yells to Wilbur Szedvilas, already in character, "Get ready, Wilbur S., your cue is coming up. Okay, now, Sarah, that's good, hold your head and spin in a circle, that's it, you're in a panic, you don't know what to do. Now quickly pick up Wilbur G's clothes and shove them under the bed, great. Now, push Wilbur G. over beside the door. Okay, Wilbur S. enters the scene."

Wilbur Szedvilas is right on cue. He opens the door and bounds through the doorway, spins and slams into an invisible brick wall when he sees Sarah in her undies, he hubba-hubbas his eyebrows. Sarah responds accordingly, leans back onto the bed, bats her fake lashes. Wilbur Szedvilas beats his chest like Tarzan, ululates like a cur, begins quickly unbuttoning his uniform and drops his trousers. Meanwhile behind the open door...

"Okay now, Wilbur G., tiptoe up behind Wilbur S. and whack him a good one with your nightstick."

Finally, Wilbur Good gets to hurt somebody, and, at this time, there is no one Wilbur would rather hurt than his traitorous partner Wilbur Szedvilas, though no physical blow could ever hurt as bad as the emotional blow Wilbur Szedvilas has already delivered to Wilbur Good by switching his allegiance to a woman. Wilbur Szedvilas and Annabelle Bilyeu are goofy in love and Wilbur Good has nothing left to love except his ugly wife. Now, shillelagh in hand, Wilbur Good tiptoes up behind his once best friend and lambastes, with more power than the script calls for, the tippy-top of Wilbur Szedvilas's helmet.

Even though the blow is harder than anticipated, Wilbur Szedvilas does not lose character. With his pants down around his ankles his legs go rubber, up and down. His eyes cross then pinball around the edges. He wobbles, hops on one foot then the other, spins with a silly grin, doffs his hat to Sarah then stumbles fore and aft, walks backwards to the open window, topples over the ledge almost out, but then back into the room where he staggers forward and bangs his head into the edge of the open door, spins, mugs the camera, holds his head with both hands, again stumbles backward to the open window, falls headfirst through the window and out of the frame.

"CUT!"

Billie Époque and Annabelle Bilyeu applaud.

Wilbur Good grunts, walks off to a lonely corner to smoke a cheroot.

Sarah Heart gets up from the bed and dresses in a robe. She vanishes into a partitioned dressing room.

"Okay, everybody, take ten. And remember we have company any minute now, Mister Warner Quackenbush, and, as you all know, he's the man who writes the checks so we are all to be at our best."

Wilbur Szedvilas, on his back, two feet below the set window, remains prone a couple of minutes, digging the strokes that come with performance art. Wilbur has found his true calling. He hugs himself then climbs to his feet and goes in search of Annabelle, who he finds in a make-up chair, Billie Époque applying pancake and paint. Billie says, "Wilbur, you are the cat's meow."

"Just being like playtime silly dance. So much fun-time I should oughtr be paying Daddy Smithy."

Annabelle says, "Daddy Smithy is the one should be givin you a big pay raise, Wilbur me nutty lover. Yur gonna make the swine a rich man."

Billie says, "Speaking of rich pigs, look what the wind blew in."

Across the room, at the door, Warner Quackenbush and

entourage have arrived. Daddy Smithy welcomes one and all. Shag Draper is making introductions, his crutches are gone and he stays aloft with a gold-handled cane. His eyes are telling everyone to eat shit but nobody is paying attention.

Shag's ever-present goon squad shuffles around and blends into the scenery. No one notices them or Shag. All eyes are on Warner Quackenbush.

Billie Époque says, "What a freak."

Wilbur says, "Him looking like roundy-pully bug should oughtr be funny-book picture."

Annabelle says, "He sends creepies up the back of me neck."

Billie says, "Yipes, dig the kid. She looks like a biter."

Snooks holds Warner's right index finger and takes it all in. She still thinks she has died and gone to Hell, which, as it turns out, is a really great place to be. She is growing into a strapping young demon, claws sunk deeply into the riches of the world. Right now, she is feeling afloat in misty memory. She squints her eyes at Daddy Smithy and sees her eyes in him looking back at her. She burns a scowl into her face.

Daddy Smithy's bowels are thrumming like a blown woofer. His anus palpitates. He is trying not to look at the girl, his child. He is afraid she hates him. And, indeed, she does hate him, and remembers him now, although she recognizes these memories from a dream life, not the real one, like now. Snooks does not hate Daddy because he was a crappy daddy, she hates him because she hates everyone, except for Satan, her growth-retarded sugar-daddy.

Meanwhile Wilbur Good broods away in a lonely far corner and watches. If Wilbur Good could read Snooks's psychotic mind, he would probably give her a high-five, as Wilbur also hates everybody in this vast room. He walks to a window and looks out, but does not see the leafless trees in icy shrinkwrap. He sees instead the life he no longer has. He plots murder, makes a list and checks it twice: Shag Draper, the man who took away his job on the force. Billie Époque because Billie is a pervert. Daddy Smithy, just because. Annabelle Bilyeu because she has taken away his best ever buddy. And sadly, Wilbur Szedvilas because he has turned his back on his best friend for the love of a woman.

Across the room, Wilbur Szedvilas says to Annabelle and Billie, "I goink to me pal, Wilbur. Him looking droopy sad."

As he walks away, Annabelle says to Billie, "It hurts me, poor loveable Wilbur, his friend dassent act a friend no more."

And as Wilbur Szedvilas walks across the room, Daddy Smithy yells to him, "Wilbur, Wilbur buddy. I want you to come over here and meet somebody. I want Mister Quackenbush to meet the star of our photoplay."

Wilbur looks at his buddy's back, his lowered forlorn shoulders, shrugs and trudges over to the entourage at the front entrance. He smiles and holds his paw out to shake the famous man's hand.

Warner's tiny mitt disappears into Wilbur's huge shovel. Warner says, "I hear you are the man with all the talent."

Wilbur releases Warner and grins wide. "I hearing yuz all fame and fortune."

It is a good thing, Warner thinks, the film does not allow for sound. This guy could never transcend to talkies.

Daddy Smithy is so nervous he is burping hot-lunch remnants, and his kneecaps are vibrating. Did Mister

Quackenbush really just say that Wilbur was THE ONE with all the talent? Daddy is the talent! Without him, Warner wouldn't even know what film is and besides that... Jesus, Snooks is really creeping him out. She is looking up at him with a fixed stare like a cat obsessed with a bug on the wall. Daddy starts, lifts both feet off the floor and nearly loses bodily functions, when Snooks suddenly points at him and yells, "I want that, right now!"

Everyone looks at Daddy and to himself he says, *Calm calm calm calm calm calm calm,* then notices something in the twelve eyes fixed on him that makes him realize he is, in fact, saying, "Calm calm calm calm calm calm," out loud. Then all the eyes shift to his front jacket pocket, the actual bull's-eye of Snooks's aimed finger. It is not her blood father that has the attentions of Snooks, it is the bottle of Doctor FixUp peeking from his pocket. Snooks has a real good memory of Doctor FixUp. She is, after all, a former Smithy.

Warner says, "What have you there in your pocket, Smithy?"

"Ta-Tis just an ah medical remedy for my na-nerves."

When Snooks was born and her mother died, Daddy pretty much nursed her into toddlerhood with Doctor FixUp. She jumps up and down yelling, "Gimmie Gimmie Gimmie Gimmie Gimmie!"

"If she would like, I'd be happy to offer her a spoonful."

"Drugs? You would give my Snooks drugs?"

"Gimmie Gimmie Gimmie Gimmie Gimmie!"

"No na-no no no, of course not. I ah didn't mean ahh."

Warner casually grabs one of Snooks's curly golden locks and gives it a brutal yank.

Snooks yells, "Ouch," and gives Warner a couple on hard kicks in the shin, "Bad Baby Demon! Bad! Bad!"

Across the room, Billie Époque drops a pin, which everybody hears.

And who would we least suspect to put things back on track? Wilbur Szedvilas reaches into his trouser pocket and pulls out a platter-sized lollipop, says to Warner Q, "Mayhaps Girlie like licking sweetie-pops."

Warner nods approval to Wilbur, who hands the sucker to Snooks, who grabs it without a thank-you, and crunches it like chicken bones with her front teeth, all the while continuing surveillance on the bottle of Doctor FixUp in her former father's pocket.

And now all Daddy can think about is how much he wants to take the bottle from his pocket, grab it by the neck, strangle it down his dry gullet. He needs an excuse to duck all the prying eyes, take his medicine in private. "What say I get you all seated and I can show you the process of our moving-picture making. I believe everyone is just about ready."

With this, Daddy Smithy walks the gaggle to a couple of chairs set up next to the camera aimed at the bedroom set. He excuses himself, as his expertise is needed elsewhere. "You all just sit tight and we'll be a getting this show on the road, so to speak."

Wilbur Szedvilas goes to makeup for a powder. Warner Quackenbush sits in one of the chairs and Snooks sits in the other. The two bodyguards merge with the background. Shag Draper, the one guy in the place that needs to get off his feet, is left standing, straining his neck muscles with the exertion on holding himself erect on a cane and two mangled feet. Shag could well join the Snooks-and-Wilbur Good-Hate-Everybody-Club. He is brimming with loathing. Shag, however, can pinpoint his hate on a single subject. His scorn is aimed directly at the fecking insect, Warner Quacken-twatface-bush.

This morning Shag was on top of the world; he can still smell the gunpowder on his clothes. It smells like victory. Bang bang kapow, he dropped that Plague cocksucker like feckin Jessie James. These people do not seem to understand: Shag Draper is a mean lean gunslinger and an important political bigwig. These arseholes should be working for him, not the other way around. What the feck is wrong with these people? Can't they see?

In fact, Shag is looking rather dapper in a sharply-cut worsted three-piece suit, charcoal with stripes the color of ash. He is topped with a silk-banded beaver derby, red parrot feather leaning back with groovy attitude. He wears three beautiful guns, though only an unlucky few ever see them, in his boot, his waistband at the small of his back and under his left pit. The new cane is a beaut, highly polished ebonized-hickory, silver-eagle hood-ornament handle. Twist the eagle a click to the right and it unsheathes a two-foot stainless blade, reflecting evil-smile glints. He has been practicing at night in front of a tall looking-glass, balancing on his aching feet, samurai moves, whistling the air with the sword, making Zs. Shag figures he could kill every fecker in this place in under two minutes, though the two Wilburs could be a challenge—you would pretty much need to drop a building on them.

Shag has business to attend to, much more important than this shite. What he should do is tell Quacken-dickhead-bush, that he is outa there, see ya later freako, I dassent need yur shite. But Shag is not likely to say those things to Warner and the why of this is what irks him most. Shag doesn't really need Warner Quackenbush for anything. Business is good, the Mooks have their meathooks in all the vice and coruption they can handle. Shag controls police chief Dempsey Moon and his booleydogs. Shag also has a foxy lady, with a dirty mind, waiting on him at at TumbleHouse. He has much of what he wants.

So why does he spend his valuable time sucking up to Warner Buttholebush? Warner scares Shag. The fat wrinkled little-boy of a man has more power in his baby fist than anyone else, anywhere else. He can sit in his Cardinal Park castle with nothing more than a telephone and obliterate world capitals. Shag is drawn into servitude by centrifugal force. Warner Quackenbush is not a man, he is a force of nature. And how does one say no to a force of nature? Shag steps over to where Warner and the evil spawn sit waiting for the show to begin. He looks down at the vile tycoon and says, "Excuse me, sir, but I need ta be taking my leave. Thought I'd check in with you afore I took off."

"Did you just say words at me, Draper? I can't hear you down here. You need to come closer if you have something to say."

Shag knows well Warner heard every word yet still he bends at the knees, balances on his cane, bears the pain. "'Twas sayin I need to be off. I ave business needs attending to, you should understand havin ta take care a business."

"What did you say? I wasn't listening; I was looking at my Snooks."

And, indeed, the little monster is squirming on her seat. She ignores Shag and says to Warner, "I need to pee. Take me to go pee right now or I'm going to pee on your shoe."

"Snooks needs to urinate, Draper. Show her to the facilities."

"But I best be takin me leave, Mister Quackenbush, business, ya know."

"I know nothing of the kind. Take Snooks to the bathroom and bring her back, then you can take your leave."

Shag thinks about his guns, his new sword cane, closes his eyes for a moment, slices cold-cuts from the little twitch's face, and riddles QuackenSatan with connect-the-dots bullet holes. He opens his eyes and to Snooks he says, "Follow me, Miss, I shall show you to the privy."

Warner grins. "Hurry back."

Snooks follows Shag, purposely stepping on his heels. She passes by Daddy, loading film into a camera, and thinks, He is dead now too. Everybody is dead, everybody is in hell. She screams, suddenly, loud and shrill, imitating monkeys she saw making whoopie in the zoo. Shag nearly falls from his cane. Daddy Smithy does fall and cracks his butt-bone on the cement floor. Warner does not even bother to look and seems to be chuckling to himself. Daddy pulls himself up and, with nerves sparking, goes to Warner and says, "She is just about ready to go, sir, soon as my stars come out of makeup. What we're lookin at here is a sixth-floor hotel bedroom where much of the action takes place."

Warner says, "There should be a banner on the wall with a Signal Cigarette squaw and jingle."

"Oh, not to worry, sir, I've been putting your advertising banners to good use all through the filmed play. But for the scenes that take place in this room, well, a person wouldn't have an advertising banner in their bedroom. I think it's important that we have certain realism. All the better to capture the emotions of the stub-holder, don't you think?"

"No, I do not. Why would I think that? There should be a banner on the wall with a Signal Cigarette squaw and jingle."

"Tell you what; I know just what we can do. In this next scene I will have all our players smoking Signal Cigarettes instead of the placard. That way we don't lose story credibility. Kill two birds with one stone."

"I wholeheartedly agree, they should all be smoking. Also, there should be a banner on the wall with a Signal Cigarette squaw and jingle."

"I shall go get one from the box you so kindly sent over, sir. Should be no more than a minute or two."

And so Daddy Smithy goes to fetch product placement while Warner chuckles to himself and Shag paces in front of the bathroom door, and inside, Snooks pees, and at the back of the studio, Wilbur Good looks out the window and wonders if he will ever get his old job back, and in her makeshift dressing room, Sarah Heart snorts a couple of lines, and on his mark in the bedroom set, Wilbur Szedvilas gets into character using the Stanislavsky method, and in makeup, Billie Époque blots Annabelle Bilyeu's freshly painted lips with a puff of cotton.

NetherWorld

FuzzyWuzzy walks ever forward following his nose. Dooley's eyes are shut, the left forever, and the right for now. His cheek is at rest on FuzzyWuzzy's cool peach-fuzz back. Dooley wakes from a dreamless interlude and he feels cold sharp moisture against his cheeks and ears. He smells fresh air. It smells nice and it has been so long. He hugs FuzzyWuzzy, hoping this feeling never goes away. And, when it does not go away but rather increases in intensity, Dooley wakes up, sits up, and opens his eye. He sees ahead a hole in the blackness—moonlight, icy sparkles of refracted starlight. Dooley scratches FuzzyWuzzy behind the ears, says, "I think I'm going to cry, FuzzyWuzzy. Feel free to join in."

The DownStairs

Slab Pettibone navigates the down-stairs on scarecrow legs. Bitch Bantam holds to his upper arm and steadies him, as a beloved mother would assist a wobbly toddler. It is early afternoon and the DownStairs is quiet. Bitch and Slab take a foursquare table in the back. Bitch helps Slab pop his knee joints into place. Slab is thankful for Bitch Bantam's help. He has traveled beyond the notion of manly pride; he is gracious and Bitch/Missy, is a blessing.

Slab orders a sarsaparilla soda and a dill pickle. Bitch orders a coffee. Bitch says, "You're doin real good up on your legs, almost bettern me."

"Almost bettern you, huh? Mebby I should dance a jig."

"You better be kiddin. Are we early? What time is it?"

"We are right on time, Missy. I reckon your friend will be here real soon."

Indeed, Missy Bantam's friend Helen Beck will be

coming through the door real soon and Missy cannot hold still. Her best friend in the world, Slab Pettibone, will be meeting Helen Beck, her first and new true love. She stirs and stirs sugar into her coffee, clanging the side of the cup like a dinner triangle.

Slab says, "Those sugar cubes are probably all melted by now."

Missy says, "Oh," then drops in two more cubes, plunk plunk, and continues stirring.

In her life of servitude, Bitch's thoughts were often lost in fancies and as often simply sitting idle. Now, in her rebirth, she assimilates a spectrum of diverse thought. Who am I? Who will I be? How does Helen Beck feel about me? Will Slab like her? What is love? Am I in love? And, if so, what do I do next? Why is it, after lying dormant for eternity, that my sex parts hanker? Will Helen Beck bolt if I tell her I want to lie naked with her? Is Helen even aware of the nature of my nature?

Enter Helen Beck. Slab takes one look and says, "Yonder comes your sweetie and she looks like a real spitfire."

Helen approaches the table then nearly grinds into reverse when Slab rises to greet her. He towers and teeters on lumber legs. When Missy Bantam rises from her seat, Helen is frozen in motion. Missy once wished to dress like society dowagers, like Helen Beck, but, instead, she has found, along with identity, a style that is uniquely her own, fashioned by free lance design maven, Billie Époque. She wears a thin black leather shift cinched at the waist and fringed at the ankles and sleeves, a red rose appliqué on the bodice like Superman's S. She wears red silk leggings and short high-heeled boots. Her hair is short and otter-slick with pomade.

Helen smiles at Missy and gives her hand to Slab, who

takes it into both of his, seemingly for ballast. Missy says, "Slab Pettibone, I'd like you to meet Helen Beck and Helen Beck, I'd like you to meet Slab Pettibone."

Slab says, "The pleasure is all mine," and Helen and says, "Likewise." Everyone sits. Missy helps Slab with his legs. And then, because she cannot help herself, she leans to Helen and gives her a hug and a kiss on the cheek. For Helen, this is not a social hug but rather a public display of affection. It freaks her out, yet she wants more. Much more. She returns the affection and feels Missy Bantam's buff body crushed to her own. They return to their places and Helen flushes, Missy stirs her coffee and Slab says, "I've read accounts o your good deeds, Miss Beck. I've never been one for politics but I know good from bad. This city could use a good deed or two. Heck, I see things all about that just don't seem right or fair. Not that I'm a socialist or anything like that but I think things could be spread out a little more evenly. I'd be proud to volunteer to help out one o your crusades sometime. Do you plan to stay in BigCity for long?"

Bitch thinks with a quick pang—does she plan to stay long in BigCity? Would she leave? How could she leave?

Helen planned to leave in the spring and home is across the country. But could she leave? How can she know, without knowing what her future holds with Missy Bantam?

"Please call me Helen, Mister Pettibone. I do not know at this time," a glance at Missy, "how long I will remain here. It seems I have made a mess of my good deeds in BigCity. I hope to correct my mistake before seeking new causes. I understand that you're something of a celebrity yourself."

He says, "Please call me Slab, Helen. I write some. I play

myself in little fictional performances. It's not too highbrow but I enjoy it and make a livin. I guess the most impressive celebrity I know right now is our Missy Bantam here. I never have in my lifetime seen a blossom bloom as fast and full as her."

Now Missy is in the spotlight, which is where she does not want to be. Missy's celebrity is through the persona of Bitch, a woman both loved and hated by the fact that she can kill a man with her bare hands and she's got a hot bod.

"Mostly I'm just me, nobody famous. You two, you both know who you are; you got things that make you better than most." Missy is humble in the shadow of Slab and Helen Beck.

Helen is enchanted. "Oh, Missy, you are like the dawning of spring, the stars and the sky."

Slab grins. "See there, Missy, you inspire poetry."

Helen blushes.

How wonderful for Missy that here are two people with which she can share her innermost thoughts. Or maybe not, as her innermost thoughts are, at this moment, buck naked with Helen Beck in her arms. How does one share that around the table?

Helen had not meant to rhapsodize flowery, she is much too pragmatic for poetry. But Slab hit the nail on the head: Missy inspires poetry. For Helen, the bigger question is what does she inspire in Missy? Inspiration has long been Helen's sword. She is an inspiration guru, a drill sergeant. Aside from pure awe and attraction, and yes, even love, Helen sees in Missy Bantam a vehicle for her own causes and concerns. But, most of all, she wants whatever Missy wants for herself, and, most of all, she wants Missy to want her. Helen glances from Missy to Slab, who is looking at her. Funny, she hadn't noticed before, he has only half a moustache.

Funny, Slab had not noticed before, Helen wears a round black patch, like a beauty mark, on her cheek. He says, "How do you like this cold weather we been havin, Helen?"

"Sometimes invigorating and sometimes dull. I've found that many times the world wants to stop when the air becomes arctic. I try to maintain a constitution whatever the season."

Missy says, "I always felt like when it was cold I was kinda hidden away, but when it's warm everybody can see me."

Slab says, "I think you'd be hard not to see in just about any weather, Missy."

Helen says, "I could see you with my eyes closed."

Slab says, "See there, Missy, your girlfriend's gettin all poetical again," and as he says this he thinks, Oops.

Helen thinks, Girlfriend.

Missy thinks, Girlfriend.

Slab thinks, *Well heck-fire anyway, girlfriends are what they are, no reason to pussyfoot around it.* He soothes the atmosphere by paraphrasing, "Special friends, we're all special friends and I don't mean to embarrass anybody, but I can see plain as day you two ladies are what you might call special special friends."

And, of course, he has just embarrassed both women and even blushes a bit himself.

Missy says, to herself, to the others, "Special friend, special girlfriend." She reaches over and takes Helen's hand into her own and does not let go. Helen melts, yet a bugaboo invades her bliss. Two women, in public, in love, in lust. The eyes of her mores peering through the keyholes.

And now into the DownStairs comes Adelina Brown. When Helen sees Adelina heading toward the table, she takes her hand from Missy's embrace and stands. Introductions are made all around. Slab wobbles up on his saplings and smiles. Adelina shakes his hand. "It's an honor to meet you, sir. I've read all your books. I used to read them aloud to groups of small children. Children love your books."

"I am flattered, young lady. I guess kids like my books because I never really growed up. Please join us."

Adelina pulls up chair. Missy helps Slab back to a sitting position. Adelina says, "I grew up with a boy who was a great fan of yours. Your stories were his favorite journeys. I work for a paper and if it's possible, I'd like to interview you and take your picture sometime. You too, Miss Bantam. I hope I'm not rude, but I need to take a moment of Miss Beck's time with a matter we share."

No one thinks Adelina rude. She says, "That dick-faced pimp who has been running the TumbleHouse as a whore house, Eddie Plague, has been killed."

Missy says, "Eddie Plague."

Slab says, "Eddie Plague."

Helen says, "The man with the artificial nose, you know him?"

Bitch says, "I'm the one that bit off his nose."

Slab says, "Me too."

Bitch says, "Eddie Plague brought me here to BigCity, chained and naked. I'm happy Eddie Plague is dead."

Adelina says, "Wow."

Slab says to Adelina, "Who killed the scoundrel?"

"Shag Draper, but I can't prove it. Do you know who he is? Maybe you could bite his nose off too. Miss Beck broke both his feet with her hammer."

All around admiring eyes go to Helen. "If I were taller, I would have brained him. Please go on, Adelina."

"Shag Draper is running TumbleWhoreHouse but he doesn't have the backing of BigCity's muckamucks and the Mooks are just a band of idiot scofflaws. If he were publicly accosted and forced to account for his actions by someone as well known as you, Miss Beck, public opinion would force him out. We could retake TumbleHouse."

Helen says, "I'll make arrangements tonight."

Missy's in awe of her girlfriend's kick-ass way of taking charge. *I will make arrangements tonight.* Wow, just like that.

Slab is feeling lucky to know women such as these. He motions the waiter and orders another tall sarsaparilla.

Chapter Fifteen

The DownStairs

Slab Pettibone sits on a barstool strumming a ukulele and talking a tune.

> "Down in the wildwood sittin on a log
> My finger on the trigger and my eye on a hawg
> I pulled the trigger and the gun went blip
> Jumped on that hawg with all my grip
> Such a scrapie. Eatin hawg eyes. Love chitlins."

A passel of patrons tap their toes, clown around and dance doo-se-doos.

"Behind the henhouse tother night
Hit wuz awful dark and I had no light
I scrambled round got a holt of a goose
Rich folks thinks I let it a-lose
Jumped gullies. Rose bushes. Dodged bullets."

Slab can near forget his sadness in this caboodle, it is still in his heart but temporally free of his noodle. He has this joint in the thrall of his panache; he wears his sombrero and half a moustache.

"They put me in a jailhouse on my knees
All they gave me wuz a pan o peas
The peas wuz red and the meat wuz fat
I got stuck in the jailhouse just for that
Got sassy. Impudent. Wanted to fight."

Slab smiles even though his thigh-stumps are sore. He has only been up walking a day or a little more.

"Jailhouse warden puts me out n the yard
chains me up an spects me to be workin hard
This ain't no way a man to be livin his life
The warden is pickin flowers to take to my wife
Goin courtin. Hair slick. Predicatin vulture."

Slab feels pretty good when he counts up his friends but when he closes his eyes his trouble begins. He sees the love of his life, his soul mate, his amour, radiant and happy then dead on the floor. He sees flowery recollections of his bruin best friend and has never quit hoping he will see him again.

Memories. Fritter McTwoBit. FuzzyWuzzy.

The HuggerMugger

Two doors up from the Downstairs. Shrouded moonlight glistens with winter. A grimy hand slips from the shadows and raps a back alley-way door. On the other side, in the press room, Adelina Brown is inking a plate. She hears the rap at the door but then not really; the neighborhood is full of noise and tap-taps are easily dismissed. Again the tap-tap taps, this time more purposely. Adelina wears a canvas bib with Rorschach splats. Her hair is down, tied at the back. She walks cautiously to the door, says, "Yes? Who is there?" She puts an ear to the door and hears, "Adelina?"

Adelina slides the bolt, opens the door six inches. "Hello?"

No one is there though shadows can be seen breathing across the narrow way. From these shadows comes a voice familiar yet, yet...

"Adelina, it's me, Dooley."

"Dooley? Dooley! Is that you?" Adelina walks out into the alley.

"Wait! Not yet, I gotta tell you something first, stop, stop where you are, I gotta tell you something to lessen the shock before you see me."

"Please, Dooley I don't care, I don't care what you look like, please Dooley I need to see you."

"I have a bear with me."

"You what? You have a what, Dooley?"

"I have a bear with me and I don't wanna leave him alone."

"I don't really understand, Dooley. But that's okay, just please show yourself."

Dooley Paradise and FuzzyWuzzy amble forward from the shadows. Dooley is face forward on FuzzyWuzzy's back, his chin resting between FuzzyWuzzy's ears. FuzzyWuzzy has a yellow buzz cut. Dooley looks worse, his body tortured, begrimed and malnourished. His hair, long mud-man dreads. His beard is patchy. His left eye is gone, the socket is scabbed-over. Adelina wants to run to him, hold his head, kiss his broken face, but she is stymied by the bear, which is too surreal to comprehend. She hyperventilates. Dooley steers FuzzyWuzzy closer, slowly, as FuzzyWuzzy is also skittish. "It's alright, FuzzyWuzzy, it's alright, Adelina."

Adelina says, "Why don't we go inside where it's warm? You need a doctor, Dooley. It's okay, bring the bear inside." Her heart is jumping and she hiccups and she cries. She backs through the doorway into the room. Dooley and FuzzyWuzzy follow though FuzzyWuzzy hesitates, stops at the border. "Cmon, buddy, we can go inside, it'll be alright." FuzzyWuzzy is taking an unexpected stand. "Okay, he doesn't want to come in just yet, Adelina. We can just stay here for a few minutes. Adelina, you really are Adelina, you really are."

"Oh, Dooley," Adelina comes forward. FuzzyWuzzy sniffs her, lowers his head to her in hopes of a scratch between the ears. Adelina does scratch him, hesitantly, then brings her hands up to Dooley, who brings his arms forward. They touch each the other in tender bewilderment.

It is not that FuzzyWuzzy has concerns about going inside, but rather a vague scent in the air that has halted him, something good he tries to keep a hold of. His memory banks are searching his olfactory. He huffs and shakes his head.

"Dooley are you... I mean where... How did you find me? Where have you been? Oh, Dooley, I'm so happy you're alive."

"We were underground, Lina, and since we came back up top, we've been sneaking through the city trying to figure things out. I found a newspaper and looked at it to see what the date was. I thought it was, I don't know. Like in a Slab Pettibone book, I thought that, like years had gone by and everyone was gonna be old and...different. And then I saw the name, Adelle Liberty, like when we were kids, and I knew it was you. I didn't know where else to go. Adelina?"

"Yes, Dooley?"

"I didn't think I was ever...Oh, Adelina."

Dooley sobs and Adelina sobs and FuzzyWuzzy perks up his ears. Two buildings down, the open back door of the DownStairs blows smoke rectangles, laughter and good times, a ukulele tune, baritone rhymes. FuzzyWuzzy backs from the doorway. His snout radar has a definite blip. A single strand of aroma fills him with emotional nostalgia. He backs into the alley and points leftward. Dooley is alarmed. "Everything is okay, buddy. Here, how bout if I scratch your neck, you like that. I don't know why he's like this, Lina. This is not normal."

FuzzyWuzzy is spinning a circle, finding direction, huffing and bawling.

"Jump off, Dooley. Jump off, let him go!" But too late,

FuzzyWuzzy has launched himself and his passenger. Adelina brings her arms in close, holds herself, gropes for air and chases after Dooley.

35 Kerosene Row

Missy Bantam's living room is dressed in leather and dark wood. She has a bookcase with glass doors. She has books she is reading, has read and plans to read. She has primers, novels, text books on language and arithmetic, angry feminist tomes, a signed collection of Slab Pettibone Adventures. Helen Beck is browsing these spines. She takes out a copy of Bram Stoker's *Dracula*, thumbs the pages. "Have you read this, Missy?"

"Sorta, I'm workin on it. It's kinda hard to read and I doan really like it much. All the women are dumb and weak and the men are mostly mean or crazy."

"I've never read a book of this nature, never really ever understood the entertainment of fanciful fiction."

"Sometimes story books are like real people but more exciting and sometimes just being people is more exciting than storybooks. You wanna go upstairs and take off our clothes and get in my bed and kiss and touch and stuff?"

"Oh, ahhh…Missy ah. I…"

"Does that mean okay?"

"Yes, yes of course it's just, it's just. I don't know what, to do, you know, I have never…"

"Me neither, but I know what I like when I'm all by myself and I think we can figger out the rest."

"Oh, Missy. Oh, Missy. Oh, Missy."

Now silence as these two virgins, one tall, one small, hold hands, skim the stairs upward, nervous, unsure, to the bedroom, chenille and cotton, mahogany. They undress, each under the other's admiring and horny gaze. They go to the bed where they kiss and explore, spoken words no longer an option. And in the end, with their passion worn through, there is love and tears. Though sadly, in the end, they have not drilled deep enough to quite satiate the need. Good sex requires practice. And what has Helen done, if not entered a forbidden world, turned her back to conceived decency yet, is it not the wholesomeness of love that prevails, is this not a delicate, near melancholy, act of reverence, a cradle of affection?

And what has Missy done? Only what she deems natural, and yeah sure, all this love stuff is great and all this delicate maneuvering of soft fingers, lips, tongues, pink parts is the best, but Missy is not a delicate woman, she wants to pounce and be pounced upon, she wants to loosen the words from her head, that's good, Baby, oh yeah, rub that nub. She wants to hear Helen moan, yet they have remained mute, each afraid of the person they love the most. In the end Helen cries and Missy holds her. Love is a slow and difficult dawn in a transcendent forest.

The DownStairs

…Memories. Fritter McTwoBit. FuzzyWuzzy.

Slab Pettibone strums the final chord, adds three plinks, sets down his ukulele, picks up a bottle of sarsaparilla and slakes his thirst.

There are twenty-some café patrons at the tables and bar, working-class poets, drinking, celebrating irony. When FuzzyWuzzy and Dooley Paradise come charging in, from the back door everyone screams. FuzzyWuzzy is bawling like a lost cub. Slab Pettibone knows, immediately, tears erupt. He pushes himself from the barstool onto his new legs, opens wide his arms.

Dooley Paradise is charging through another non-reality. Only moments ago he had touched the base of his former life, Adelina Brown. Now he is back inside Bizarro World, confused and scared.

FuzzyWuzzy huffs and puffs and cries, he sees Slab now, and nothing else. Slab rises at a height unfamiliar to FuzzyWuzzy's memory which startles the bruin up on his back legs. Dooley holds to FuzzyWuzzy's scruff. Agile men and women are tripping over themselves. FuzzyWuzzy and Slab Pettibone collide. FuzzyWuzzy bear-hugs Slab and Slab hugs back, hollers, "Whoop whoop whoopey! Yaaa hoop hoop hoop yahooey! My bear ohh my big bear FuzzyWuzzy." FuzzyWuzzy expresses similar sentiments and rolls himself, Slab and Dooley to the ground. Adelina runs in from the alley, swoons and sits down hard in the nearest chair. Dooley is trying to squeeze sense into his head. FuzzyWuzzy really is FuzzyWuzzy. The Bear and Dooley has somehow landed in a Slab Pettibone adventure book. Slab is whooping and yahooing and sniffling and blubbering. A half-foot from his face is the face of a boy taken by hard times. Slab takes a deep breath, says, "Name is Slab Pettibone, son, you just take it easy and we'll be getting you all fixed up."

Municipal Row

A tall row of muscular buildings. The bunker-like Quackenbush Building crowned with a smoke-blowing billboard:

> *Little Squaw*
> *Sits All Alone*
> *She Calls A Wig-Wam*
> *Home Sweet Home*
> *Smoke Signals*
> *10 Cents*

The Stars and Stripes Saloon sits next to the three-story TigerCage brownstone, home to Shag Draper and the Mooks. Across the way, a man wearing City Jail striped pajamas picks up trash and puts it into a barrel handcuffed to his left ankle. Well-scrubbed men with fat bellies, side-whiskers, and top hats bluster about the stone steps climbing into the maw of City Hall. A large mean dumb-looking hulk in an itchy police uniform takes the steps two at a time, though he seems in no hurry.

Wilbur Good has come from the TigerCage where he was told Shag Draper is here, on the third floor in the mayor's office. Wilbur needs Shag to reinstate him in the Copper Squad. The acting gig is dumb stupid and he has been typecast as a buffoon. Wilbur is a cop and that's all he wants to be. If Shag Draper does not give him his job back, he's gonna kill the stupid dundershit. Wilbur's life has gone smelly bad and he feels a great need to kill anyone who touches his smelly bad life, but first Wilbur wants his badge back. It is best to wear a badge when you kill people.

Wilbur walks into the building and behind him a horse taxi pulls to the curb and unloads Adelina Brown, Slab Pettibone, Helen Beck and Missy Bantam. Helen looks around and says to all, "No one is here."

In fact, there are many people here but Helen's no-one is more specific. Last night she wrote seven letters which she put in the morning mail to politicos, press corps, Mayor Solly Gosterman, and Shag Draper. She had thought the usual interests would be aroused. She expected a crowd, but now here she stands in the face of a great snub. BigCity's dowagers and muckamucks have severed ties with the likes of Helen Beck and they own the press.

Adelina says, "I'm the press and fuck the rest of them."

Slab blushes, he's not accostomed to foul language from a girl.

Missy says, "Just us is all we need."

Helen is unsure.

Missy takes Helen by the hand. "You're an important person, Helen. You're the famous one and you're the leader. We need to follow you cause you're the one knows how to lead."

"Very well." Helen glances about and retrieves her hand from Missy's loving clutch. She digs out her hammer of justice and says a silent prayer then says, "Here we go," and steps forward leading the little war party up the steps into City Hall

Helen's stride is short but she walks quickly enough that Adelina has to run to keep up. Adelina is psyched. She has a note pad in her hand and three sharpened pencils in her hair. In her great side-pockets are ten sheets of eight-by-ten celluloid film in holders with dark-slides, a one-pound bag of magnesium flash powder, a dozen Lucifer matches and two flint lighters. Her rolling tripod with the eight-by-ten bellows camera and six-inch flash-pan seems built into her thin body. It takes about ten seconds for her to be set-up and cranking focus.

Adelina is lost to her thoughts. As the budding journalist, Adelle Liberty, she looks to be at the top of her game. Adelina Brown, however, is taking a risk with her identity. There is a warrant still out for her arrest, possibly posted on a wall here in City Hall. But, onward she goes, hiding the fugitive behind the camera and feeling protected by her own righteous indignation. Adelina pumps anger into her bloodstream and itches for action. At the stairway, Adelina doesn't hesitate and pushes the camera and tripod up one stair at a time. Without a word Bitch Bantam picks up Adelina's camera and takes the steps two at a time.

It seems to Slab that Helen and Missy and Adelina are walking just about as fast as people are allowed. Slab keeps up on his wobbly stork-legs like a man on a runaway horse. He approaches the twenty-three courthouse steps with his arms out wide, flapping wind. Nevertheless, he has a grin on his face. He is in a pretty good mood, though he would rather be home right now with FuzzyWuzzy. FuzzyWuzzy has gone through a hell that no bear should know. He is just a big puppy at heart and thus he needs love and assurance. Slab should be with him now. But Slab had promised the gals that he would come along to support them and here he is. And, thankfully, by sun-up, Dooley Paradise had walked to Slab's little bungalow, from Adelina's, to hang with FuzzyWuzzy. They were cradled together asleep when Slab left to join Helen and Bitch for the trek to City Hall. Now here he is, grinning and flailing his sticks up the stairs with no idea of how he will stop at the top or what awaits them.

Three floors above, a floor-to-ceiling window looks into Mayor Solly Gosterman's office where Shag Draper sits on the desk smoking a Signal and knocking the ashes to the floor. Mayor Gosterman paces between his desk and the window; a fat fly circles his head and threatens his easy nature. Shag says, "What ya need to tell the hens is ta go home and bake a feckin cake. TumbleHouse is mine and shall stay mine. These twitches ave no say. They ave not the papers. But I do and you do too so just do what I want you to do and everything is copacetic."

Solly Gosterman can't stand Shag Draper. Solly prays someone will kill Shag Draper. He says, "Why do you care about TumbleHouse? The public has heard enough about TumbleHouse. My gad, Draper, we are talking about a bunch of kids. Let them have the place."

Shag is mulling his retort when he notices Wilbur Good standing at the open double doors. Shag says, "Somethin yur needin can't wait? We're in a meeting ere, go away."

Wilbur says, "I good copper. I me needing badge"

"What's that? Hyme needing badge? You should learn how ta talk, ya dumb pook. You wants yur badge back, huh? The show biz not to yur liking? Where's yur partner? Thought you bums shared a single brain and did everything together." Shag laughs but Wilbur does not, nor does Solly Gosterman.

"Me pertner no more. I am wanting badge all just me, no more Wilbur and Wilbur. Just Wilbur me myself and me."

Shag smiles and winks at the mayor. "How does I know yur gonna be loyal and do what I tell ya to do?"

"I copper only. Yuz Shag Drapey being bossing."

"Oh yeh? How's about I tell ya to put a gun on the mayor here, mayhaps pull the trigger?"

Wilbur pulls his pistoler, aims at the mayor, says, "I does me duty."

Mayor Gosterman says, "This is not funny, Shag. I don't know what it is you're trying to accomplish here."

Shag is grinning, as is Wilbur, but the party is over when hammer-welding Helen Beck comes into the room followed by Slab Pettibone, Bitch Bantam and Adelle Liberty/Adelina Brown.

Shag looks at Helen Beck then Bitch Bantam then Adelle Liberty, who hides her face with photo gear, then up to Slab Pettibone who smiles and tips his sombrero. Shag looks again at Bitch Bantam and he wolf whistles. He says, "Yur back on the force Wilbur, don't put yur gun away." Helen bangs her hammer on the mayor's desk. The mayor hollers and falls backward into his chair. Helen says, "We have come for the deed to the TumbleHouse Orphanage. We do not expect to leave without it."

Shag casually clicks the handle of his cane, pulls out the long shiny blade and pretends to shave with it. "Feck yur rumpus, ya midget bitch." And to Missy Bantam he says, "Goes for you too, ya feckin skank." Bitch Bantam growls. The flash pan explodes and Adelle makes her first exposure: Bully Shag Draper swishing his sword above tiny Helen Beck, Bitch Bantam flexed and ready to spring, the mayor down below with his head in his hands.

Now Slab Pettibone steps forward. "I don't think we need introductions, sir. I know who you are and don't much care if you know me. I have come with these fine ladies here today to discuss a matter of importance. A grave matter concerning children. I do not believe that this meeting should be occasion to the kind of language you are using, nor is there call for insults. Furthermore, we are here to talk, we do not represent violence of any stripe. I would appreciate it if your policeman would please holster his weapon and that you, sir, would put away that silver toothpick."

Shag chops a triangle of air with his blade. "None of ya has any business here today or any other day. So, adios, cowboy, take yur feckin cows and go."

Mayor Gosterman steels himself and stands. "I'd just like to step in a minute and say a few things to everyone here, and first off I must say, Shag, er Mister Draper, I am not one to take sides in politics, but I hardly agree with the others. We are civilized here and City Hall is not a place for bearing weapons."

Along with a coil of rope Slab Pettibone uses for lasso tricks, he is wearing his prized Colt 45s in tooled tan-leather holsters with tassels and Slab's name writ in mother-of-pearl. Slab can twirl his six-shooters like flaming batons while shooting the fleas off a dog. He can draw, aim and fire faster than the drop of a hat. However, unless he is doing a sharp-shooter show, Slab keeps blank rounds in all twelve chambers. Slab is not a proponent of gun-control but rather believes ammunition should be limited. Wilbur Good, on the other hand, has plenty of bullets. His pistol is drawn and loaded. Wilbur has never been much of a marksman but he is thinking that maybe, if this meeting goes against Shag, he can get a clean shot at the dumberty puke and maybe get away with it. What he is hoping for is that the cowboy will blow Shag away and save him the trouble. Shag Draper is thinking that he might like to go one-on-one in a fast-draw with the wrangler. One need not be a cowboy to be good with a gun. Even with the sword in his right hand Shag could draw and fire with precision any one of three pistols on his person, at the drop of a dime. Shag is feeling an enormous desire to assert his authority, to put BigCity back in his pocket where it belongs. As such, he is not pleased with what the mayor has to say." As mayor of this fine city, I feel that this is a time for me to use the power BigCity has vested in me. The City is with you, Miss Beck, I think if Mister Draper here would be kind enough to sign over the deed to TumbleHouse, BigCity will happily stand behind your group and still, if need be, work with Mister Draper on the wheels of government."

Mayor Gosterman addresses the room paying special attention, even pacing his words, to the reporter, Adelle Liberty. She may be writing for a commie rag but it is his words she is putting into print, it is his picture she is exposing to film. Gosterman poses but Adelina is not quite ready to take the picture. She is waiting for Helen Beck to enter frame, maybe shake the mayor's hand. Adelina is scribbling all that occurs on her note pad. The camera's focus is fixed and Adelina has the rubber squeeze-bulb shutter-release looped around her wrist. Helen Beck walks into the frame and Adelina slides in a film holder and pulls the dark-slide. Like the mayor, Helen is familiar with playing to the press. Helen and the mayor smile and Adelina sparks the flash and squeezes the shutter.

After the radiation has dissipated, Helen Beck says, "I am so very happy, Mister Mayor, to see that your heart is with the people of your city. I am sure that you also, Mister Draper, want what is best for BigCity and will abide by the mayor's ruling."

Shag laughs. "The mayor has not the right to give away what belongs to me. Yur all here with no reason and mayhaps I need to remind the mayor and all the rest of youse who it is holds the weight around here."

Missy Bantam, who has thus far stood quiet, takes her turn. She says, "Scuse me, Mister Draper, but I get a feelin you're alookin to prove your self by bein rude. And I got a feelin you're lookin to mebby hurt somebody cause you think you can prove yourself that way. And I'm kinda hopin that you try somethin cause Ima bout ready to break your neck."

"Anytime ya wants to strip down and wrestle, chickie, jus let me know." Shag is having great fun. For him it is a foregone conclusion that someone in this room is going to die. Maybe, if Wilbur Good does his share, two or three people will die. Shag is figuring out who to shoot first, who to stab, who to shoot second. Now, he makes a discovery that makes him very happy. He smiles and leans toward Adelina who has come out from behind the camera. "Well well, good morning to youse, Miss Adelina Brown. Mister Mayor, ave ya been introduced to Miss Adelina Brown? Yur fine city holds a murder warrant for her arrest. Officer Wilbur, arrest this fugitive girlie and take er away."

Adelina's fierce moral conviction overpowers her fear. "My name is Adelle Liberty. I have identification to prove it." Wilbur has backed up to the open double doorway, giving himself a clean shot at pretty much everyone. His finger is on the trigger. His gun is cocked and aimed between Shag and Adelina. He wants to shoot Shag, though if he gets a chance he will shoot the girl. That the girl is even alive had cost him his job in the first place. Any second now Wilbur is going to shoot somebody.

Shag Draper is surrounded by the enemy but likes the challenge. The great thing is that Shag is the only one staying within the law. Shag is in the right and will happily kill someone to prove it. He says to Adelina, to everyone, "Yur to surrender yurself now this minute, ya little twat, or I swear I shall shoot ya where you stands."

The mayor says, "My god, Draper. Are you daft?'

"I'll shoot you too, you little speck a shite."

Helen says, "Please please, put down your weapons. This is not the place..." Bitch Bantam and Slab Pettibone have been in silent communication. Bitch is watching Shag Draper's hands, ready to attack if he twitches the wrong muscle. Slab is watching Wilbur Good. Slab is also ready to spring into action though it could prove difficult on stilts and with no bullets.

Shag says, "Time's up! Officer Wilbur, cuff her or shoot her now! The little twist is refusing..."

Wilbur is holding his gun steady, at the girl, at Shag, at the girl, at Shag. The trigger is pulled as far as it can go without detonation. Wilbur loves shooting his gun, he likes the noise and the smell and the destruction. Now, the fly that was previously pestering Mayor Gosterman lands on Wilbur's nose. Wilbur pulls the trigger.

Slab Pettibone has drawn both Colts and thrown them spinning at Wilbur Good. One gun knocks Wilbur's gun from his hand. The other gun thuds into Wilbur's left temple. It does not knock him out but sits him down.

Helen Beck is frozen.

Adelina turns to catch the action.

Mayor Solly Gosterman dives under his desk. While mid-flight he catches a badly aimed bullet in the posterior.

Shag Draper draws and his fires his pistol at Bitch Bantam while attempting to cut Adelina's throat with his sword. Bitch is a whir as she dodges bullets and drives into Shag. He is knocked off kilter but still manages to slash Adelina's left arm to the bone. She goes down to her knees from pain and shock though she still holds the squeezy bulb shutter release and attempts to make another exposure.

Wilbur is back on his feet and has retreved his gun and is shooting at everything that moves. Slab throws his lasso and ropes Wilbur like a bucking bronco, pulling Wilburs hands to his sides.

An errant bullet from Wilbur's gun travels through the flaps of Adelina's greatcoat, lighting the bindle of licifers and sparking the pound of magnesium flash powder. Adelina ignites like a supernova.

Everyone is blind and yet see-through like skeletons.

Slab's wooden legs are blown out from under him.

The mayor is rolled across the floor.

Helen goes into duck-and-cover.

And everyone blinks and blinks and blinks.

And everyone and everything is scorched.

And when vision is finally restored.

Wilbur's head hurts but it is no big deal.

Slab has climbed up onto a chair to assess the damage.

Mayor Gosterman has fainted.

Adelina Brown is dead.

Shag Draper is on the floor in front of the picture window. Above him, Bitch Bantam looms tall, poised like the end of the world. Shag still has his gun in his left hand and sword in his right but both arms are broken and he can't lift them from the floor.

Helen Beck stands and rubs her eyes until she sees the woman she loves, her violet eyes brimmed with anger, with murder.

Shag Draper looks up at Bitch Bantam; he is staying tough, refusing to buckle to this Sapphic giant. Even with his arms broken, he does not cry out. He smiles and says, "Suck me stem, ya feckin skank."

Bitch Bantam lifts Shag Draper by the shirt front and hurls him crashing through the window. Three floors below, he dies on impact.

PART THREE

SPRING

Chapter Sixteen

Orpheus Theater

Spring. A happy face sun, cartoon bluebirds, butterfly bouquets. On the great WhiteWay some guy is whistling the prelude to the "William Tell Overture." Below marquee lights a nervous man in a squished hat tilts a bottle of Doctor FixUp and squeezes out a double dose. Above the now partially-sedated man in the squished hat the marquee boasts:

THE ORPHEUS THEATER PRESENTS
A WORLD PREMIERE EXTRAVAGANZA
2 FULL-LENGTH MOTION PICTURES
THE RISE & THE FALL - GUTTERSNIPES
LIVE: SLAB PETTIBONE & FUZZYWUZZY THE BEAR

Press has been good. An hour before curtain and already a crowd has gathered. Never before has a BigCity crowd exhibited such diversity. Zeph Riley, the new owner of the Orpheus, is premiering a lowbrow sex comedy with a high-minded leftist documentary, a little something for everyone. Well, almost everyone. Right-wing prudes, the staid granddads of industry and Christian morals, remain at home harrumphing, beyond reproach. But the rest of the world is here, milling about below the marquee, edging the red carpet, eyes alert to celebrity sightings.

Daddy Smithy swirls through people and place like a dust-devil. No one recognizes Daddy—though if anyone has earned celebrity status, it is he. Daddy Smithy is the main man, the writer director producer of The Rise & The Fall, a history-making achievement. Daddy can see his future in CinemaScope. He invents cartoons and music videos. He gives advice to Thomas Edison and travels the globe in First Class. But, alas, Daddy's bipolar bean misfires and his major achievement suddenly becomes a major piece-of-shit. And now everyone does recognize him and they all point fingers at him, Daddy Smithy, the paradigm of failure in a mashed fedora. No, no, Daddy slaps himself back into positive, no one points to his failure. Everyone covets his success, Daddy Smithy a show-biz genius, a role-model for the youngsters. Daddy wags his head, looks at his watch, mumbles to himself, "Everyone is going to love it." Make it happen before it happens, then it is sure to happen.

Daddy stands to make big money on the success of *The Rise & the Fall*. But, even at his most optimistic, Daddy need more money to fully realize his prescient visions. For his next film he has adapted a book to screenplay, *Lost Time*, starring Slab Pettibone, along with comic genius Wilbur Szedvilas as the evil warlord, Commander Shenanigan; Annabelle Bilyeu as Princess Pancake Exotica. And, as *Lost Time* is a sci-fi adventure, a big budget is called for. It is this problem of funding that has Daddy Smithy again looking at his watch. Warner Quackenbush is due, and here he comes now, in a pumpkin coach, behind prancing white horses. Sound the trumpets.

A footman opens the coach door and bows. Warner Quackenbush departs the brougham like a fat penguin. At his side, Snooks Smithy Quackenbush is dressed, as usual, like a princess. She crashes about like a pinball. The crush of plain-folk stargazers vie to spy the little tycoon. Next, from the coach, emerges the scandalous teenage strumpet that finagled Warner Quackenbush's sick heart, Missus Warner Girl Smithy Quackenbush. Girl has become her sister Snooks's step-mother.

She is dressed in expensive ostentation. Her hat is crowned with fresh flowers, and laced with spun gold. She is tall and shapely and raw; the plastic glaze of a razor scar reflects her diamond earrings. She stands eight inches above Warner though he outweighs her by a hundred and fifty-five pounds.

How did this seamy connubial union and seemingly preposterous plot twist come about? When Shag Draper fell to the hereafter, Girl promptly cleared out of TumbleHouse, bringing with her a small fortune embezzled from both Shag Draper and Eddie Plague, along with the HuggerMugger photo of Warner Quackenbush with her sister, Snooks Smithy. She bought stylish clothes and took a room at The Paramount Hotel. She got her hair done and bought a big box of cosmetics. She took a coach to Warner's front door and lied her way inside.

She conked a guard with a sap, snuck around a maid to the elevator, and took a ride upstairs where she walked in on Warner and Snooks bare naked and throwing marshmallows at each other. She had two dainty but deadly derringers which she aimed at Warner.

Snooks looked up at Girl and went from an undisciplined spin to an abrupt stand-still. She screamed with glee until she threw up a sauce of marshmallow bile and fell to the ground laughing. Girl said, "Get up and come on over here, little sister. I want to see how you are, if you're okay."

Warner went to his knees, held his beloved Snooks around the waist, close. He told her, "You will go nowhere with that person. She is not even real. You stay right here with me."

But Warner's convictions were not fully committed to his words. Girl was a grown image of Snooks with an added dash of evil and intelligence. Could be Warner was looking at a soul mate. He said, "Egad!"

To date, Warner Q had spent little time around women and never desired their company or chatter. The enema-girls had served him well and now Snooks served his every kink even better. As a boy Warner had been so intimidating his own mother was afraid of him. No one had ever said NO to Warner Quackenbush. No one had ever slapped his hand from the cookie jar.

Girl saw it all: everything she desired and everything Warner Quackenbush desired. To the little tycoon and she said, "You're a horrible little shat. I'm gonna teach you how to take care of me and my sister." She dropped her guns and grabbed him by the collar and bitch-slapped him three times per cheek then spit into his face. Just like that, whack whack, whack whack,

whack whack, patooy. Warner Quackenbush was so suddenly in love, he nearly peed his pants, as Snooks had just done. Now, Warner and Girl are two months and two days married. And now, flanked by blank bodyguards, The Quackenbush Family stands on the red carpet for all to see.

Daddy Smithy hightails it to the curb, says, "Mister Quackenbush, er Warner, good to see you," and then to Girl he says, "Hello Girl, you look very nice today."

Girl takes Daddy in for a moment, which makes him edgy. "Hello Daddy, how are you?"

"Oh, well you know, busy busy busy," and as he says this, he noses downward to say, "And hello to you too, Snooks. Are you excited about seeing a moving picture?"

Snooks looks blankly at Daddy, scans the lively crowd, notices that all around, eyes are on them, she says, "Everything is for me."

"Yes, Daddy agrees, you're a very lucky little girl." And in this statement, Daddy attempts to wash away the guilt of his abandonment, his pimping, though he dares not, at this moment, meet Girl's accusing eyes.

Warner motions up to the marquee, says to Daddy Smithy, his father-in-law, "The marquee is supposed to say Signal Cigarettes. Why does it not?"

"What you need to know, Warner, sir, is that I felt this would be the best venue for *The Rise & the Fall*, which, as you can see by the enormous crowd, is quite true. I told the young man, Zeph Riley, the owner and promoter, that we required Signal Cigarettes on the marquee. It looks like there probably just wasn't enough room."

"There is not enough room on the marquee because, for

reasons I would like to understand, *The Rise & the Fall* is sharing the marquee with a rabble-rousing independent production of a political nature. Please explain to me why this is so."

Daddy is feeling a sudden jones for Doctor FixUp and is relieved when the attention is drawn away from him as Snooks has spotted the Tasmanian devil in the cage leftward of the ticket booth. She points and vociferates, "Looky looky looky looky."

Zeph Riley, ever the showman, has placed a ten-foot high barred cell in the shade of the entranceway. Inside, jumping up and down, whooping, spiting, growling, Orpheus employee Sow Madden is dressed in faux tiger skins and made-up with turkey quill fangs, tufts of steel-wool hair, silver claws like press-on nails. Sow is having the time of his life and getting paid for it. He rattles the bars and howls like a werewolf.

Snooks pulls Warner, by two pudgy digits, to the cage. She stands close to the bars and looks up at the feral human. Sow slobbers and screeches at the little girl who slobbers and screeches back. She points at the Tasmanian devil, says to Warner and Girl, "I want that."

Warner says to Daddy, "How much?"

"Huh?"

"The wild-man, how much? Who do I see about buying the wild-man?"

"I donno, he's just a guy works here at the theater. He isn't a real wild-man."

"I know he's not real, you dolt, I would like to rent his act for a playtime, for Snooks."

"Uh, I guess you'd talk to him about that."

"Why don't you take care of that for me, Daddy."

Warner has been without a proper lackey since Shag

Draper's demise, and so he orders about whoever happens to be at hand. For Daddy Smithy, an artist, a genius, and family for that matter, this attitude is not acceptable. "Yeah, sure, okay, but that's not what I really do, you know."

Snooks is feeling ignored, which is contrary to Snooks's needs. She whacks Warner's bulbous butt with her magic wand, says, "Bad Baby." Warner rubs his butt and glances to Girl who says, "Cut it out, Snooks. Try to settle down."

Girl has put the kibosh to her sister's participation in Warner's bent rituals. Snooks misses the games but Girl has locked herself into the demon's playroom in order to lock Snooks out. Still, even with Girl's nurture, Snooks maintains a slippery foothold on sanity. She would likely benefit from the effects of Prozac, Ritalin, Doctor FixUp. She picks her nose and eats the booger.

Girl halts this little family gathering in the aisle and, without a word, removes a golden flask from her handbag. Good news for Daddy, who has instilled a druggy family tradition in his offspring. Girl uncorks the flask, holds it and tilts a dose into her sister's mouth like a mama bird with a masticated worm. Warner despises drug use, though he would never contradict anything Girl does regarding Snooks. Daddy figures if the kids can say yes to drugs, then he should as well, so he quick-draws his Doctor FixUp and salivates with anticipation.

Girl says, "Here, try mine, Daddy. I had it made special."

Daddy says a thousand thank-yous, tries to hide his greedy nature with a phony nonchalance, takes the bottle and attempts to make three drinks look like one. The nectar goes down like sweet cider and spreads to his toes and earlobes. He closes his eyes while silk scarves caress his body, he settles in the rafters while the world below throws him kisses. He opens his eyes and says, "You think you could sell me a bottle of this, what's it called?"

"It's special made for me. I'll have some sent over to you."

And from Daddy, a thousand more thank yous.

From the stage funky piano music, a slow late-nite trumpet, syncopated percussion. The stage curtain says Ahhhhhh. The stage band, Mabel Scott, Pete and Repeat Kirby, riff and warm up. Orpheus employee Bug pulls curtain ropes and checks his cue list. Zeph Riley readies the stage, checks and rechecks, sees Daddy Smithy in the aisle, hollers, "How's it sound out there?" Daddy gives him thumbs up.

From behind the curtain, Orpheus employee Flopears walks down the steps into the aisle. He wears a canvas money bib, a tray of souvenirs; Slab Pettibone Round-Tuits and Signal Cigarettes Little Squaw playing cards. He walks a wide circle around the Quackenbushes, then out to the lobby through the front door, where he waves to Sow Madden in his cage, then, into the crowd, "Get jer souvenirs here." Business is good but the crowd is more interested in the arrival of Slab Pettibone and FuzzyWuzzy who have just stepped onto the red carpet. Slab signs autographs and shakes hands and hands out Round-Tuits. He no longer rides atop his bear, he walks. He has traded in his old pair of legs for a new more technologically sound and taller pair. He stands six-feet-two-inches and his sombrero tops at six-six. His handlebar moustache is full, waxed and curled into a smile. He stays close to FuzzyWuzzy and maintains physical contact. He says to some guy, "Hi how are you glad to meet you," then to FuzzyWuzzy, "Bear up, sweetie, we'll be away from all these people pretty soon, just another minute or so. Hi there how are you glad to meet you, been meaning to get A Round-Tuit."

FuzzyWuzzy doesn't like the crowd. He has taken to clacking his jaw and snapping his teeth to keep the human hands at bay. He has lost his patience with his celebrity status and he wants to run and hide.

Slab is aware of his bear's despair. The fire, wandering alone and lost, then surviving with Dooley Paradise: FuzzyWuzzy is a different animal from whom he was. Along with this new awareness of his bear's psychological makeup, Slab has acquired hindsight. FuzzyWuzzy had not liked show biz to begin with. Slab has unwittingly been an insensitive partner. Now Slab is too settled in his life and too old to fade back into the wilderness, which is where FuzzyWuzzy needs to be. He hopes it is not too late to make amends. He says to a young couple with a baby, "Hi how are you glad to meet you," then to FuzzyWuzzy, "Just a couple more minutes FuzzyWuzzy and we'll be a goin inside. We're just waitin for Missy to get here and I think this is her coach a comin up now. Hi there how are you glad to meet you, been meanin to get A Round-Tuit."

When Bitch Bantam steps from the coach, the crowd swells like a deep breath. Bitch is wearing fringed black leather trousers and a white tuxedo coat with tail-feather lapels. Her hair is a butch flat-top. Her violet eyes sparkle. She wears a brilliant aura like a blue Hindu Goddess.

Bitch greets FuzzyWuzzy by wrapping her arms around his neck and giving him a squeeze and a kiss. She greets Slab in the same manner, then steers them through the crowd. She says, "Comin through, scuse us, comin through." Slab says, "Hi there how are you glad to meet you, been meanin to get A Round-Tuit."

Through the bustle they go past a howling Sow Madden and into the theater just as a convertible horse-cab clip-clops to a stop and three new VIPs step down to the carpet. Wilbur Szedvilas and Annabelle Bilyeu and Billie Èpoque. Annabelle says, "Look at alla them people, Wilbur me sweet. They ave heard of yur moving-picture antics, yur a star you are."

"All together us made flickery picture. All together us being stars." Wilbur smiles, mugs and pratfalls for the entertainment of all. And on this happy day, Wilbur hides the dread of going inside and watching *The Rise & the Fall*. Not because he is self-critical of his performance, he loves watching himself on screen, he cracks himself up. Wilbur dreads watching the sad bad acting of his now dead partner, Wilbur Good.

On the very night of the day Shag Draper died Wilbur Good hurried home to have fun time humpy love with his ugly wife. It was a great night of fucky-yum and Wilbur cracked his wife's jaw in three places. Soon thereafter Wilbur went to sleep and his ugly wife took his pistol and put four bullets in his brain, two in his smelly-bad. No one bothered to report the crime and Wilbur Szedvilas buried his buddy along the DreckRiver.

Wilbur Szedvilas can remember when he and Wilbur Good were six years old. Playing in the mud, throwing rocks at each other, wrestling, punching, biting, laughing. Wilbur misses Wilbur, though he sometimes wonders why.

Meanwhile, Wilbur Szedvilas is in love with Annabelle Bilyeu and he is a movie star. He takes off his summer straw boater, spins it on a forefinger, flings it like a boomerang and it lands back on his head. Now into the Orpheus they go and head back stage to join the others.

Stage right, Mabel Scott and Pete and Repeat Kirby are rehearsing the melodramatic soundtrack for the docudrama, *Guttersnipes*. Working with Daddy Smithy, they have composed a musical score for both movies. Little known point of fact, Daddy Smithy made the final cut of Adelina Brown's movie, *Guttersnipes*. Shortly after putting Adelina in the ground, Helen Beck called on Zeph Riley and offered to finance the completion of *Guttersnipes* if Zeph could find a way to make it happen. Zeph and Mabel and Helen were in accord in respect to Adelina's work: it needed to be finished and it needed to be seen. Zeph went to Daddy Smithy.

In many ways the art of filmmaking has redeemed Daddy Smithy. His commitment goes beyond his aspirations. He readily offered his services to turn *Guttersnipes* into a classic for students through the generations. Daddy only asked that everyone in this assembled film crew swear on a stack of celluloid that he would remain anonymous. Warner Quackenbush would never know of Daddy's involvement in an outside independent production.

Daddy had been quick to understand Adelina's raw footage. He could see that, like him, she was inventing thought-provoking entertainment. Her camera had found a dramatic story in a family of three young street orphans. The camera dragged the viewer through the muck of crime and starvation and did so with a somber face. She tapped into emotions that Daddy had never felt and he, Daddy Smithy, without taking credit, would attempt to think just as she had thought and finish the same moving document she had striven for.

Today the public will see a film by Adelle Liberty that will stamp their brains with indelible images. No one will know of Daddy's selfless contribution: the happy ending where the guttersnipe kids, after so many hardships, are adopted by a funny rich guy (played by Wilbur Szedvilas) and his kind and beautiful wife (Annabelle Bilyeu) and taken to a deluxe apartment in the sky. Daddy believes he has done Adelina Brown proud and in the process created a template for the future of filmmaking.

Meanwhile, Wilbur Szedvilas and Annabelle Bilyeu have joined Slab Pettibone and FuzzyWuzzy. Slab straddles FuzzyWuzzy and sits lightly on his back, leaning forward to scratch behind his ears.

Annabelle says, "Wilbur and me ave just read *Lost Time*. Wilbur likes me to read out-loud so he can close his eyes and pretend himself in the story."

Wilbur says, "I play like evil Commander Shenanigan. Thinking like moving-flicker story."

Slab says, "I can see the scenes in my head when I write them. And it's not a stretch to imagine that I'm Slab Pettibone. But seeing it in moving-picture terms is something I have yet to experience. I'm excited about watching *The Rise & Fall* tonight. I've heard its real funny and I heard it might make me blush, though I am pretty easy in that area. You know, Wilbur, I guess this is as good a time as any to bring this up, I've been thinkin maybe my live performances would benefit if I worked the stage with a partner, someone naturally funny and physical. If that someone was you, we could do it between the films. It might be a lot o fun. You too, Miss Bilyeu, we could stage little productions. I spect you'll need some time to think on it and if you have better things to do, then you should do them. I just kind o wanted to throw it out there."

"I me love on-stage clowny fun. Cept how bout WuzzyFuzzy?"

"Well FuzzyWuzzy is the reason I been thinking about changing my act. I finally figured out that the reason you don't see more bears on the entertainment circuit is because bears are not really entertainers at heart."

"WuzzyFuzzy him likening outdoors open places."

"Exactly."

They all look at FuzzyWuzzy who yawns and huffs and cuddles with Slab. FuzzyWuzzy knows when people are talking about him and he has intuited a tender sadness welling inside Slab Pettibone. FuzzyWuzzy loves Slab and can feel that Slab has made a decision that will have great effect on them both.

To the right a couple of yards, Bitch Bantam and Billie Époque. Tomorrow night, in SodomHeights, at BigCity's brightest new spot, The BottomOutGrotto, Billie and Bitch are staging a fashion show. Billie has graduated from stage make-up and captured the spotlight in the emerging avant-garde with clothing and make-up designs for Bitch as well as some hot alternative-types, both men and women. Bitch has invested some of her savings in Billie's daring line of togs. She has also fallen in love with the gay camaraderie, the artistic, sensitive and subversive nature, the party lights. It was not so long ago Bitch dreamed of joining the refined bustle-bottomed women's club. But now, with new friends like Billie Époque, Bitch has found a common denominator and quickly joined their ranks.

Billie says, "I thought maybe Helen would be here tonight."

"No, I doan think so. I doan think she's even in town. She's busy with the Adelina Brown Foundation, startin up orphanages all over the place. Besides, she pretty much stays away from anyplace where she thinks I might be."

"It's too bad you can't be friends."

"Yeah, I know. But Helen's afraid of being with me or anybody else that doan hide what they are. She thinks there is somthin wrong with her for feelin how she feels and that means she thinks there is somthin wrong with me, an at the same time she doan really feel that way about me, just herself."

"What a shame."

"Yeah. But you know it was mostly me that broke us up. I just dint care about all her political stuff. I know it's all good but it's just not me, period. I doan wanna be around squares nomore, anymore, know what I mean? Besides, Helen wouldn't even hold my hand in public. I'm more political than her just by being me, jus like you, Billie, all a person gotta do is look at you to see politics that are more braver than carrying round a picket sign and a dumb hammer."

"Well I guess not everybody can be as progressive as you and me. I'm sorry it didn't work out."

"I'm not, not really, not anymore. One time I thought me and Helen was gonna live happy ever after but it doan, doesn't, bother me so much as I thought it would. And you know what else? What else is there's this girl I talked to a couple a times at the BottomOut. I was thinkin maybe I'd ask her over to the house sometime."

"Who? You've got to tell me. No, no, don't tell me, let me guess."

Zeph Riley walks out onto the stage. He goes center-stage and yells through his megaphone, "Listen up everyone, we're going to pull the curtains now. If you're not in the show then you should go ahead and take your seats. We're gonna open the doors for the public in a minute. Hey, Bug, close the curtain, would you, buddy, and go and get Flopears and make sure the ticket-takers are ready and check the colored entrance too."

Bug says, "Okey-doke," and goes about his duties as the others take the steps down to their assigned seats. As Bug makes his way down the aisle, he nods hello to the guy that used to be Boss Paradise, even though he is hardly recognizable as such. Dooley nods back and makes his way to the stage.

Dooley's clothes are without style or color, he wears a black derby pulled low, shadowing his eyes, one of which is hidden behind a leather patch. His hair is long and falls from the back of his hat to his shoulders. He wears a scraggly cactus beard. Over his shoulder, he carries a duffel and on his back he has tied a bedroll.

Leaving the stage for their seats, Warner and Girl and Snooks Quackenbush cross Dooley's path. Girl says to Warner, "You go ahead, get your seats, I'll be there in a minute." She stops and says to Dooley, "How are you, Dooley?"

"I'm doing okay, I guess."

"It's funny, but you and I have never really talked."

"Yeah, I guess not."

"I was sorry to hear about Adelina."

"Yeah, me too."

"You might not believe me, but I'm sorry about what happened to Gulper too."

"I believe you. I don't have any reason not to. I'm sorry too."

"Yeah, thanks."

"Well, I guess I'll see you around."

"Yeah, I guess so."

Dooley walks up the steps to the stage. He seems cloaked in melancholia, though, in truth, he is not all that depressed.

In some ways, the new Dooley is an improvement on the old. He no longer drinks spiderbite or snorts noseburn. True, he is no longer motivated by politics or ambition, but perhaps he had been in over his head from the beginning.

Dooley has not been back to TumbleHouse. He has remained at Adelina's little Left Bank apartment, with his small savings, a couple hundred dollars Helen Beck retrieved for him from his TumbleHouse hideaway safe. He spends most of his evenings at Slab Pettibone's house, hanging out with FuzzyWuzzy. Slab Pettibone has, as is his nature, taken Dooley under his wing. They have spent many hours talking together about the world and the past and the present and the future. And while it is not the future that we would have once supposed for Dooley Paradise, he does indeed have plans and a vision of what will come. The reason Dooley is here tonight is to finalize the beginning of his future. He walks up the steps to the stage and goes behind the curtain.

Bitch Bantam has remained backstage to spend a little time with Slab. Bitch has been busy with her new life and new friends and has not been hanging out much with her very best friend. She says, "Dooley Paradise just came in. Looks like he's all packed up and ready to go. You reckon FuzzyWuzzy knows what's goin on?"

Slab says, with a shiver of emotion, "Sure he does. Isn't that right, FuzzyWuzzy? You're all packed up and ready to go too."

FuzzyWuzzy looks at Slab, with puppy-dog eyes. Yes, he knows. Somewhere in the abstract corridors of his bruin brain he knows, absolutely, that tonight, after the show he will say goodbye to Slab Pettibone and leave with Dooley Paradise for the far reaches of less-populated places. FuzzyWuzzy stands on his back feet and hugs Slab the way a son hugs a father. He licks Slab's face with kisses.

Bitch says, "You gonna be alright?"

"I'll be fine, Missy. Isn't that right, FuzzyWuzzy, we're gonna be fine and it's all for the best?"

As Dooley joins them, it appears that Slab and FuzzyWuzzy are slow dancing to a bluesy tune. "Hi, Miss Bantam. Hey Slab, hey FuzzyWuzzy."

Bitch says, "Hi Dooley, looks like you're all ready to go. You got any places in your plans? Anywhere special you wanna go?"

"No, not really. But I have a couple of maps folded away and a compass. I'm going to head for places that stay warm all year round. I want us to spend time in the woods and forests where we can be alone. Sometimes I daydream about being a hermit or a lumberjack or a cowboy. Someday I want to write books about everything. I guess what I want is to I grow up to be like Slab."

Slab's face is red. He says, "Funny thing is I don't guess I ever really grew up so for a person to grow up to be like me, he would have to never grow up."

Now Zeph Riley yells from stage-right, "Just a couple a minutes, Mister Pettibone. We open with you center curtain."

FuzzyWuzzy rubs his wet nose on Slab's face, frizzing Slab's moustache. He huffs softly, like a lost cub.

Bitch gives FuzzyWuzzy a big hug, says, "I'm gonna miss you real bad, FuzzyWuzzy, but you're gonna be real happy, I just know you are." Now she hugs Slab, says, "I love you, Slab Pettibone."

Bitch and Dooley leave Slab and FuzzyWuzzy and walk

out to the peanut gallery. The theater has filled with a happy mass of stub-holders. People all about strain their necks to see Bitch Bantam as she takes a seat.

Bitch Bantam hardly notices all the fawning eyes recording her history. The drama of Slab and FuzzyWuzzy has filled her with questions of love and loss. Bitch has had so little to love in her life that she is still confused over the elements. How is it she loves Slab Pettibone in a way that could never be altered, yet she had loved Helen Beck passionately and now she does not? There are so many kinds of love and so many kinds of loss. There are so many complexities in life that Bitch sometimes feels she is back at the beginning, chained and naked. But more often Bitch Bantam feels that life is a good thing and everybody is still at the beginning all the time anyway. And tomorrow FuzzyWuzzy will be gone and Slab will be sad and so will she, but still it will be a good day and it will go forward like every other day.

Next to Bitch, Dooley Paradise is lost to his visions of tomorrow. His new life. He says to Bitch, or maybe just to himself, "It's funny the way things turn out."

Behind the curtain, Zeph Riley says, "Okay, Slab, curtain in fifteen seconds and counting down." Slab and FuzzyWuzzy walk to their marks. Slab blows his nose and wipes a tear from his eye. He says, "Well, sweetie-pie, I guess this is gonna be your last curtain call. I don't think it's likely but just in case I forget to tell you later, I love you, buddy. Always have and always will."

And though he is unable to voice it, FuzzyWuzzy will always love and remember Slab Pettibone. And even now, at this moment, FuzzyWuzzy's love for Slab goes beyond his distaste for show business. In a few moments, FuzzyWuzzy will hit his marks and take his cues like a true professional. For one last time, FuzzyWuzzy and his famous companion will be the legendary stars of adventure and romance. For one last time.

Now the music has come up, Mabel Scott rumbles the ivories, Pete Kirby blows a king's entrance, Repeat Kirby drum-rolls Zeph Riley onto the stage. Zeph comes out singing,

> *"Me name is Zeph Riley*
> *I yam here to present the show*
> *Comedy drama extravaganza*
> *And now it's time to roll."*

In the audience, Wilbur Szedvilas claps his hands, says, "Huzzah huzzah!"

Snooks Quackenbush wiggles in her seat and makes barnyard sounds. Warner Quackenbush gives Snooks a covert pinch and Girl a sidelong glance. Girl Quackenbush ignores them and takes her flask of designer feel-good from her handbag. She takes a drink then hands it to her right. Daddy Smithy takes the flask, says, "Thank you," and fills his cheeks. In his head he says, Everyone is going to love my movie Everyone is going to love my movie Everyone is going to hate my movie Everyone is going to love my movie.

Zeph Riley backs from the stage and yells through his megaphone, "Ladies and gents, Slab Pettibone and FuzzyWuzzy the Bear!"

Slab Pettibone and FuzzyWuzzy take the stage. FuzzyWuzzy roars and stands up tall on his back legs. Slab twirls his six-shooters and fires smokey rounds. He yells, "Yaaa hoop hoop hoop yahooey!"

THE END

ABOUT SCOT SOTHERN

Writer/photographer Scot Sothern bounced from job to job for 40 years. His first solo exhibit, *Lowlife*, was held at the notorious Drkrm Gallery in Los Angeles in 2010. His first book, *Lowlife*, was published in the U.K. by Stanley Barker in 2011. The British Journal of Photography called *Lowlife*, "The year's most controversial photobook." Scot's work has since been in gallery shows in Los Angeles, New York, Miami, London, and Paris. In 2013 Scot took a two-year stint writing biweekly columns, Nocturnal Submissions and Sothern Exposure, for VICE Magazine. In 2013, *Curb Service: A Memoir*, was published by Soft Skull Press. *Streetwalkers*, stories and photographs was published by powerHouse Books in February 2016. Writer, Jerry Stahl, called it "An absolutely amazing and essential book." *BigCity* is Sothern's first novel. Discover more at:

www.scotsothern.com